PRAISE FOR GINA ROBINSON'S
SIZZLING ROMANTIC SPY THRILLERS

SPY CANDY

"Sassy and delightfully entertaining."
—Beverly Barton, *New York Times* bestselling author

"Gina Robinson . . . will leave you craving more."
—Gerri Russell, author of *To Tempt a Knight*

"4 stars! Robinson delivers with this excursion to spy camp! With the perfect amount of suspense and humor, this story will stay with readers long after the book is over." —*Romantic Times BOOKReviews*

"Gina Robinson's debut novel has everything you'd want in a terrific story: intrigue, action, great characters, and realistic dialogue." —ParanormalRomance.org

"A really fun book . . . from a great new author . . . delicious in so many ways . . . I can't wait to see what Gina comes up with next." —CraveMoreRomance.com

"Robinson's first romance is a hilarious thrill ride filled with plenty of spy references and spoofs that will keep the reader delightfully entertained and looking forward to her next book." —*Booklist*

"Lots of action . . . plenty of hot, sexy, yummy guys . . . The next time I am in the mood for something filling that I can sink my teeth into, I am going to read a Gina Robinson book. Gina Robinson is on fire."

—ManicReaders.com

SPY GAMES

"Fast, snappy, and cute."

—Susan Andersen,
New York Times bestselling author

"4 stars! Robinson delivers an entertaining story of stalking, spying, secret identities, and hidden agendas."

—*Romantic Times BOOKreviews*

"Gina Robinson will take you on a journey that will excite you and keep you on the edge of your seat."

—TheBigThrill.org

THE SPY WHO LEFT ME

GINA ROBINSON

St. Martin's Paperbacks

R

This is a work of fiction. All of the characters, organizations, and events portrayed in this novel are either products of the author's imagination or are used fictitiously.

THE SPY WHO LEFT ME

For information address St. Martin's Press, 175 Fifth Avenue, New York, NY 10010.

ISBN: 978-0-312-54239-9

Printed in the United States of America

St. Martin's Paperbacks edition / November 2011

St. Martin's Paperbacks are published by St. Martin's Press, 175 Fifth Avenue, New York, NY 10010.

10 9 8 7 6 5 4 3 2 1

For Jeff—you're always my hero

12/11

ACKNOWLEDGMENTS

I'm blessed to have an extremely supportive, creative, and talented husband. He travels frequently and widely for business. On one trip to China, he was an honored guest at an outdoor group Chinese wedding. He sat in the front of the crowd at a special table for VIPs as the twenty-eight couples, dressed in Western wedding attire, were married. Jeff's experience provided the inspiration for the Chinese wedding scene in this book.

I'd like to thank Liu Jiang for translating Chinese phrases for me and sharing information about Chinese culture.

My agent, Kim Lionetti, was terrific, as always. She came up with the idea of branding the series of proposals I sent her as the Agent Ex series. She and fellow agent Jessica Faust brainstormed and conceived the fun titles for the series.

I have a wonderful editor, Holly Blanck. Her revision suggestions have made the book so much better than my original version. Thanks to Holly and all the staff at St. Martin's Press for the editorial direction, the cover I love so much, the marketing, sales, and everything you do.

And thank you to my readers. I truly appreciate all of you for reading my stories!

CHAPTER ONE

There are two things a girl would really rather not experience on her Hawaiian vacation—the monthly curse and a run-in with her soon-to-be ex. For the first time since puberty, Treflee Miller had managed to dodge the first. She was staring at all six-foot-two, well-muscled, lying, spying, ran-out-on-her inches of the second as he hefted her cousin Carrie's bags up the steps of the Big Auau Sugar Plantation's lanai.

He'd bleached his brown hair to a sun-streaked blond and grown a goatee, but it was him. The corner of his mouth curled into that sexy half grin of his and his eyes danced with flirtation as he stared at Carrie, not seeing Treflee.

Treflee flushed, feeling an unexpected jolt of jealousy. Whether she wanted him or not, he was still her man. Her mouth fell open into what was surely an unflattering gape. What was *he* doing here on her vacation? Shouldn't he be playing spy boy, not bellhop, on something other than U.S. soil?

Damn! She didn't have the divorce papers on her. Technically, he wasn't legally her ex-husband. *Yet*. He'd run off on another top-secret mission without signing the final paperwork. If only she had them with her, she'd make short work of her still-married status.

She snapped her mouth shut and gave him her hard-core "I'm so angry I could kill you" glare. He should have known it well by now. She'd aimed it at him with regularity this past year. When he was around, that is. But he clearly hadn't noticed her yet as he flirted with Carrie.

In the distance, past the stately trees of the plantation and waving fields of sugarcane, the Pacific Ocean sparkled behind him. The scent of plumeria and ginger wafted toward Treflee, tinged with a hint of his all too familiar, and totally hot, cologne. The man knew how to scent himself, that's for sure. It was commitment and the thought of family life he had trouble with.

As his gaze lifted from Carrie to Treflee, his eyes went from dancing to clinically cold.

"T—"

He cut her off. "*Aloha!* Ty Smith. General-purpose vacation instructor and island guide." He sounded deceptively friendly and charming.

Yeah, he could really put it on. But as he extended his hand and leaned toward her, he flashed her a hard-edged "you blow my cover and there will be hell to pay, nearly ex-wife or not" look. His threatening look was much more convincing than hers.

She backed off, but not before she mouthed the word "bastard" for his eyes only.

"Treflee Miller," she said, voice dripping with artificial sweetness. "Vacationer." And hacked-off wife, she could have added, but it wasn't totally necessary. She thought he pretty much knew how she felt.

"*E komo mai!* Welcome to Hawaii. And your week of fun and adventure." Ty's voice gave away nothing of his displeasure and discomfort at seeing her. His ability to hide his emotions made him a fantastic spy. And a miserable husband.

Treflee didn't want an adventure. She loathed adventure. She longed for peace and quiet, sunbathing and solitary beach walks at sunrise and sunset. Maybe the occasional tropical drink featuring a heavy dose of pineapple juice and rum.

It had been Carrie's sadistic idea to drag her beleaguered bridal party to Maui after she dumped her fiancé, Kane, a week before the wedding for cheating on her. Carrie had planned a Hawaiian wedding and honeymoon and she was going to get them. Well, a Hawaiian vacation anyway, with her bridesmaids in tow. Why would the girls complain? They'd already paid for their nonrefundable airfare. She was simply making sure Treflee and company got to benefit from it.

Carrie was not your typical weepy, depressed ex-bride. A lady cop, she had a take-no-prisoners personality. If she wanted to go to Hawaii with her nearest and dearest, they were going with her. End of story.

So she had salvaged what she could of her wedding budget, sweet-talked the hotel she'd reserved for her wedding into letting her bridal party stay sans wedding, and booked a vacation package for all of them. And here they were, dancing supportive attendance to her as if she were still the happy bride and they were still the dutiful bridesmaids.

Beside Treflee, Carrie's curvy, amply endowed best friend, Laci, whispered in her ear, "He's hot. This is going to be fun."

Yeah, it's going to be fun all right. If Treflee could keep from murdering Ty. She shrugged noncommittally.

"You don't like?" Laci asked, nodding toward him, obviously incredulous.

"Not my type." Treflee could lie pretty well, too, when she wanted to.

There were six in their party, with enough baggage for a dozen. And Treflee wasn't thinking strictly of luggage. If Ty was planning on carrying it all in for them, they were in for a wait.

Treflee grabbed her bag, not out of any charity toward him, but because she was wilting in the afternoon sun.

The plantation door opened and a heavy, middle-aged Hawaiian woman dressed in a muumuu stepped out, followed by a broad-shouldered blond guy. The woman spread her arms in an all-encompassing gesture of welcome. *"Aloha auina la!"* She nodded toward the blond guy and he started grabbing bags.

"Meet Greg, my fellow instructor, and Tita," Ty said. "She's the big *wahine* around here."

Tita's rich laugh shook her body and brought a smile to Treflee's face. "Who you calling big, skinny boy?"

"I meant that in the most honorable way, as in you're the boss lady." He gave her a deferential nod of his head, but his grin said he was half teasing.

"You mean *kahuna, haole*. I'm the big *kahuna* and don't you forget it."

"Yes, *wahine*."

With a smile and a flip of her hand, she dismissed his lack of respect. "Come, let's get you all settled in and refreshed before your night on the town."

Ty handed Carrie's bag to the blond guy and grabbed Treflee's. "We need to talk," he whispered in her ear.

"There's nothing to talk about," she said. "I'll have my lawyer e-mail or fax you the papers here. We'll never have to talk again."

He gave her the look again. "No e-mailing. No faxing. We'll talk." He turned to Tita, and nodded toward Treflee. "Which room?"

"Makai one."

"Excellent." He hauled Treflee's bag into the building, up the beautiful, coiling wooden stairs, and down a hallway with her trailing after him, trying to take in the sights so she didn't explode with anger. She only maintained control out of a sense of patriotism. What if blowing Ty's cover meant vital U.S. secrets got out, security was breached, and we had another Pearl Harbor on our hands? It sounded melodramatic. But you never knew with Ty. You never knew anything.

He walked so fast, they lost the rest of the girls.

Finally, he came to an abrupt stop in front of a red door in the middle of the mellow, sea-foam-green hall. He pulled a universal key from his pocket, let them into the room, and pulled the door closed behind them.

Being led into a bedroom by Ty used to be a totally exhilarating experience. She'd be lying if she didn't admit to feeling a thrill of the old excitement. She brushed it off, relegating it to a somatic response.

The bedroom was truly spectacular. Just what she would have picked for herself. Large comfy bed covered with tasseled pillows and a linen comforter. Bamboo floors with deep cream throw rugs. A ceiling fan floated lazily above it all. At the far end, a door stood open onto a balcony that faced the ocean. The white curtains surrounding it fluttered in the ocean breeze. Paradise.

Ty broke the spell by speaking. "What are you doing here?"

Ty was his real first name. He hadn't been terribly creative in his choice of cover. Maybe he was tired of answering to so many different names.

"Why the surprise?" She snorted. "Any spy worth their salt would have looked at the guest log and seen my name."

"Tita keeps the guest list. I barely glanced at it." He paused, frowning, looking as if he couldn't have missed something as obvious as her name, even at a glance. Suddenly, he cursed beneath his breath. "Wait a minute— *you're* Betty Miller?"

"What? Betty! Are you crazy?" She hated that nickname and he knew it. Her given name was Elizabeth. Everyone called her Treflee, a childhood mutation of trying to call herself Bethy and being unable to make the "th" sound. Beffly had somehow morphed into Treflee and stuck. Her mother had wanted to call her Betty. *No way.*

"You're Betty according to the list." Ty shook his head, looking at her suspiciously. As if she'd tried to pull one over on *him*.

"That Carrie and her warped sense of humor. I'm going to strangle her." Only the family and Ty ever called her Betty, and only when they wanted to pull her chain.

Treflee had another beef with him. "Speaking of my cousin Carrie, you were flirting with her!"

"Flirting with the ladies is part of my cover—" He stopped short as if registering what she'd just said. "Your cousin?"

"Yeah, duh. You'd know that if you were ever around long enough to attend a family function or two." Spite was not an easy thing to keep out of her voice.

He cocked a brow. "She wasn't at our wedding."

The man had a photographic memory. "She was serving in Iraq."

"You never showed her a wedding picture? She didn't seem to recognize me."

Treflee shrugged. "I'm sure she saw one a long time ago. I haven't been in the mood to flash one around lately." Did she sound put out? She didn't think she sounded sweet. "You're obviously incognito now. I doubt she'll make the connection. The bleached-blond look is good on you."

He ignored her jibe. "I don't recognize the others."

"I just met the others. They're all Carrie's friends, fellow cops and former military. Except for Carla. She's a nurse. You'd better watch yourself." Treflee couldn't help smiling. "Cops have a habit of sniffing out the truth."

Carrie and Treflee lived states apart. They weren't actually that close. Mostly it was blood and the devoted relationship between their mothers that bound them. Carrie had been under duress to make her part of the bridal party. When the whole thing fell through, she couldn't very well exclude her from the vacation, even though Treflee had tried to wiggle out of it.

She put her hands on her hips as they stared each other down. "I checked the weather every day for the past six months."

When he was away on a mission, they communicated by posting seemingly innocuous comments on their hometown's local weather blog. Their comments were actually coded messages to each other.

"You always check the weather," he said.

He was probably being deliberately obtuse just to frustrate her. "You know what I mean."

"What would I have said, Tref? Graupel?"

Graupel? That one wasn't in their lexicon. Graupel was hail snow. *Hail snow?* Then it hit her—*hell no!*

"Very funny, Ty. Hail hath no fury."

"That's obvious."

She crossed her arms. "You could have been dead for all I knew."

"And lying in a ditch," he added. "If I was dead, Emmett would have shown up at your door with a folded American flag and your widow's benefits."

Okay, he has me there. As chief spy, Emmett Nelson was the Agency's harbinger of death.

Ty ran his hand through his hair and sighed. "How can I get you to go home?"

"Sign the divorce papers."

"You don't have them on you."

"I can get them. If you insist on the no e-mailing, no faxing rule, I'll call my lawyer and have him overnight them."

He snorted in disbelief. "E-mailing, faxing, overnighting, texting, posting them to a Web site, skywriting, or carrier pigeoning, I can't take the chance. I'm on an important mission. I can't have anything around anywhere with my real identity, anything that will blow my cover."

She lifted her chin. "You have me."

He shook his head and crossed his arms. "Do you have a picture of me in your wallet?"

"Egocentric bastard," she said. "I shredded every last picture I had of you months ago."

"On your cell phone?" He grabbed her purse from the bed where she'd dropped it. Before she could stop him, he had the phone and her camera out. He dropped them in his pocket.

Shoot! There might be a picture or two of him still on the phone. Call her a sentimental fool.

"I'll return these when I've checked them out." He pulled her wallet out and leafed through as she stood watching him, fury making her almost speechless. Only a few sputters managed to escape her lips.

Finally, he dropped the wallet back into the purse and the purse back on the bed. "Clear. Now, go home before anyone gets hurt." His eyes twinkled wickedly. He was deadly serious.

"I can't. Ex-bridezilla out there will hunt me down and kill me." She explained about Carrie. Besides, she wasn't leaving without her divorce. When she finished her story, she shrugged. "So, sorry, but I'm staying. Want to fill me in on the mission?"

"If I told you that—"

She waved her hand at him. "Yeah, yeah, yeah, you'd

have to kill me. That's what all the spies say. You really should come up with something more original. You know it's all this secrecy that killed our relationship?"

He smiled. Her heart thawed just a tiny bit. She'd always loved his smile and the way he got her sense of humor.

"You won't tell me?"

"What do you think?"

What she really thought was that it was a crying shame they hadn't worked out. She always liked sparring with him. Instead, she said, "As long as I'm here, I may as well enjoy myself. I've never seen you at work before. This could be fun. Take-your-nearly-ex-wife-to-work day. I like it."

He gave her a warning look. "Don't say a word. Nothing slips, got it?"

She held up her hands to show him she was no threat, no threat at all. "Hey, silence is my middle name."

He arched a brow and patted his pocket. "I'll return these later." He turned and walked to the door, pausing before he left to speak over his shoulder. "I'll be watching you."

"Just like old times," she said and winked, trying to get his goat.

He shook his head and left.

Treflee plunked down on the bed and put her head in her hands, taking a deep breath. She'd never imagined seeing Ty in his element would shake her up so much or that witnessing him flirt with other women could still make her jealous. But he'd definitely thrown her equilibrium off. Hadn't he always? Hadn't that been part of the excitement *and* the problem?

When she finally calmed down, she got up, opened her suitcase, and pulled her travel jewelry pouch out. She reached into it and pulled out the dangly charm bracelet Ty had given her when they were dating. He brought her back a charm from every mission. When he originally gave the bracelet to her, it had a single charm on it—a tiny silver heart locket. Now it was loaded with charms.

As she opened the locket and stared at the miniscule picture of Ty, her eyes watered and she couldn't help sniffing. What type of a charm would Ty have brought her back from this Hawaiian mission? A silver palm tree? A gold Maui sandal? A hibiscus flower? Or a white pearl?

Deep down Ty was a romantic and had a wicked sense of humor. The pearl was her birthstone, and a white one represents honesty and faith. Yeah, he would have gotten a big kick out of the dual meaning. As if *he* were ever honest.

She told herself *she* only brought the bracelet with her so she could see how well the big, honking *black* pearl she planned to buy for herself would look on it. But in all honesty, sentimental fool that she was, she never left home without it.

You aren't as smart as you think, spy boy, she thought. She had a bit of leverage after all.

Ty strolled back to his room, feeling almost schizophrenic as he forced himself to stay in character—calm, lazy, nonchalant, not a care in the world besides catching the next wave or downing a mai tai. On Hawaiian time. Inside, he seethed. He rarely felt this convoluted, even when facing the wrong side of a gun barrel unarmed. Which had happened a time or two.

Damn Treflee for showing up like this.

He hadn't even checked the guest list properly before she'd arrived. He'd stupidly assumed NCS had cleared everyone on it.

Tref's presence posed a bigger danger to his safety and mission than a long-range ballistic missile. If he'd been less distracted by his thoughts of Tref, he might have avoided having to fraternize with a drooling guest just then. Laci lay in wait for him outside his bedroom door. He walked headlong into her long, perfectly manicured tentacles almost before he registered her standing there.

How had Treflee thrown him off kilter and out of his game so easily? What if Laci had been an enemy agent rather than a sex-starved redhead? It was as if his wife were the enemy's secret weapon, an agent annihilator who operated by turning his brain to mush. *Women.*

"Ty!" Laci's face lit up with a predatory smile as she took his arm. "Going somewhere?"

He forced himself to smile lazily down at her. Ty, the tour guide, would play up to the female guests, hoping to earn a big tip, or a repeat customer. Ty, the real him, liked to be the pursuer, not the pursued, in both business and pleasure. And he was strictly a one-woman man. Though his wife frequently told him to tell that to *Ripley's Believe It or Not* and see if *they* believed him. She sure as hell didn't.

"Gotta hit the shower and pretty up before the big cruise tonight." He forced himself to keep a low, slow, sexy tone.

"You look pretty damn good to me already." Laci squeezed his arm as if testing to see if he were a piece of ripe fruit.

Well, he wasn't. Not for her.

He shook his head. "Tita wouldn't agree."

Laci arched a brow. "Really?" Her tone teased.

"Tita has high standards for going out in public. And a dress code." He gestured to indicate his outfit. "A T-shirt and cargo shorts don't cut it. She'd tell you a well-dressed guide is good for business." He winked at her.

In return, Laci smiled as if she wanted to eat him up. She ran her hands over his chest. "I could help you slip into something . . . *fun.*"

Which he took to mean her.

As a spy, he had all kinds of moves. None of which he was interested in using on her. He casually reached into his front pocket for his key. Treflee's camera and phone slowed down his smooth escape. He had to rummage around in his pocket until he found what he was looking for.

"Maybe some other time. When we have *more* time." Did he sound suggestive enough? As if he were a man who liked things slow and hard? "Right now, Tita will have my ass if I'm late."

He pried Laci off him. With a quick, fluid move, he slid the key in the door and escaped into his room, flipping the dead bolt behind him. So this is how women feel when they elude the arms of an octopus.

He paused and listened until he heard Laci's disappointed footsteps padding down the hall. Yeah, he knew how to read the sound of footfalls. Anger was easy. Disappointment and what-the-hell-just-happened-here confusion had a stop-and-start pattern. His self-satisfied grin was short-lived, as common spy sense overcame him.

Ty didn't believe in coincidence. He had learned that lesson on the job. Of all the honeymoon spots in the world Treflee's cousin could have chosen, she showed up at Big Auau with Treflee in tow? At his little corner of the tropical world? Nope, too much to swallow.

Treflee was many things, including an energetic, playful blond nymph in bed, but she wasn't actress enough to fool him. Her surprise was genuine. Although he was sure she'd been trying, she hadn't succeeded in intentionally tracking him down. All the evidence pointed to her being an innocent pawn.

If she'd found him on her own, she'd have the divorce papers on her and a pen ready to thrust into his hand the second she spotted him. Good to know the Agency hadn't screwed up there and left a trail for just anyone to follow to him.

That left only one viable option—the Agency, and his boss, National Clandestine Service Chief Emmett Nelson. Listing Treflee as Betty on the guest list was exactly Emmett's style.

Ty cursed beneath his breath. Emmett liked his spies to remain single. As often as possible, he recruited them when they were young and unattached. He expected them to remain that way. Emmett violated his own policy when he recruited Ty.

Ty was already engaged to Tref and refused to give her up. Emmett conceded. He needed a young man with Ty's intelligence, lack of fear, and acting abilities.

Ty breached Agency policy when he told Tref he was being recruited and asked her advice on whether he should take the job or not. He figured if he was going to drag her into a life of secrecy and danger, she had the right to know what she was getting into. She took it well. In fact, she took it with a surprising amount of enthusiasm.

"Take the job? Why would you turn it down!" she said, reminding him they were young and ready for life to show them some fun. Life practically owed it to them. "Besides, think how sexy it will be to have a spy in my bed!"

Tref herself was not adventure material. She was steady, calm, responsible, too cautious to be a daredevil, and solidly independent. She liked everything quiet but lovemaking—soft music, solitary strolls, and thoughtful time to herself. But she loved a good vicarious thrill; someone else's scary story. The perfect balance to him. He could hardly sit still. He lived on action and adrenaline.

They decided he'd go out and bring back his thrill. His scary tale.

His spy life bought them the perfect marriage. No ordinary, dull routines to fall into. No drone of a day-to-day worker's life to live. No "Hi, honey" followed by a peck on the cheek when he came home from work. More like grab him by the collar, drag him to the bedroom, and wrap herself around him.

Their sex life sizzled, fueled by absence that made their hearts grow fonder, or at least lustier, and the romance of their double lives. The mundane front they presented to the world amused them. The lies they told their friends, family, and neighbors entertained them. The secrets they kept from the world made them inseparable.

She wanted a career, not a family. Or so she told him. She wanted a loyal lover, not a ball-and-chain type of husband. She had her freedom and he had his.

He thought they'd had a rock-solid, happy marriage. He went off on adventures and came home to report them to her. Names, locations, and classified details removed or changed to protect his career and both their lives, of course.

Then something happened. He still hadn't exactly figured out what. It was like a switch had flipped inside her. She started complaining. He had all the fun. She did all the work. She wanted to start a family. She wanted a baby. A baby needed a father. A father who was around.

He shook his head. *A baby!*

When he hesitated, they fought. Small arguments at first, but larger ones followed. Suddenly she wanted a divorce.

If there was one thing Emmett Nelson hated more than married spies, it was divorced agents. And not because of any sentimental morality on his part. Agents' exes were a liability, a national security breach waiting to happen. Messy business.

He gave Ty orders to fix his marriage and fix it fast.

"Make the woman happy, damn it!" had been Emmett's exact words to him.

Hell, Emmett hadn't needed to order Ty to fix things. He *loved* Tref. He *still* loved Tref. He'd always love her. He had no intention of letting her go.

He would have fixed his marriage then and there. If he'd known how. Short of that, he did the only sensible thing— took evasive action and hid out, hoping to buy time. Hoping Tref would miss him, come to her senses, and realize they were meant to be together. Hoping he'd figure out *how* to win her back.

He'd checked the weather, too. There hadn't been any messages from spylover23, Tref's screen name. So truf-flesguy, him, had remained stonily silent as well. Certainly neither one of them had any intention of mentioning sunny weather, their code for "I love you."

Ty knew Emmett's game. The threat of this "coincidence" was implicit—make up with your wife. *Now.* Or your entire career is on the line.

Fantastic. No problem. Nothing like asking the impossible.

All Ty had to do was avenge George Hsu, a fellow agent and friend who'd been murdered on assignment here in Hawaii. Follow Shen Lin, the little prick of a Fuk Ching Chinese crime gang member suspected of killing George on orders from the Revolutionary International Organization of Terrorists, or RIOT as they were commonly known in the espionage world. Hope Lin would provide him a way into Sugar Love Plantation, RIOT's Hawaiian lair. Keep an eye on Hal Rogers, a Hawaiian-born CIA analyst and traitor who was planning to sell the top secret Pinpoint Project to RIOT. Complete George's mission to stop RIOT from starting a war between China and the United States. *And win back my angry wife's love.*

And the *pièce de résistance*? He had less than a week to do it.

Ty pulled Treflee's camera and phone from his pocket, feeling an almost overwhelming urge to smash them, or his fist, against the wall.

Instead, he took a deep breath and turned the camera on.

CHAPTER TWO

Treflee had given Ty a bad time about not recognizing her name on the guest list, but she hadn't recognized his real identity, either. Before embarking on this grand adventure, she had taken a peek at the vacation package brochure online, complete with tour guide bios, no photos. Of course, she had a good excuse for not recognizing her husband—different last name and a totally fabricated bio.

Their vacation week would begin with a shopping trip to Lahaina and a sunset cruise with three free drinks included in the package. And shopping? Hey, she could do that. Maybe she'd even look for that black pearl she wanted. If she had time after spying on Ty.

She wondered if he secretly loved being a "tour guide," living the high life like movie spies do. Treflee figured no real spies lived this way—shopping, cruising, surfing, taking scenic waterfall drives. Not unless they were on vacation themselves. At least according to the stories Ty used to tell her.

Not that she could tell if Ty had lied to her. He openly admitted having to change certain details of his missions. If he'd been living this kind of cushy life, and lying about it, while she held down the fort at home and went into the office day after day to handle employee complaints, she was really going to kill him. Slowly. With lots of torture involved.

She hid out in her room until it was time to meet. She joined up with the bridal party—Carrie, Laci, Brandy, Carla, and Faye—in the parlor. There was no formal lobby. The old sugar plantation house was more of a bed-and-breakfast than a hotel. Carrie's group had the entire place to themselves for the week.

Auau was an elegant, high-end, intimate, romantic setting with a fantastic ocean view. Most of the year, the owners rented it out for weddings, a cog in the Hawaiian wedding industry along with the neighboring plantation.

As Treflee joined the group, she gave Carrie a hug. "Very funny registering me for this little vacation as Betty."

Carrie frowned at her. "What are you talking about? Why would I hack you off? You hate that name."

It was Treflee's turn to frown. "You didn't?"

"You're Elizabeth to the airlines and Big Auau." Carrie shrugged. "I figured I couldn't go wrong using your legal name."

Treflee smiled, trying to cover her confusion. Who was lying and why? "Sorry. My mistake. How are you holding up?"

Carrie gave her a look that said she was crazy for asking. Carrie was a tough cookie, not a heartbroken whiner. "Fantastic. We're going to have the time of our lives on the cruise tonight."

The girls were dressed in strapless evening dresses of varying lengths and tightness, and spiky heels, all of them going for sexy and sultry. If Treflee had her guess, she'd say they were the outfits they'd been planning to wear to the now defunct bachelorette party.

Treflee had dressed in a simple empire-waist sundress with a subtle Hawaiian print and flat, strappy sandals. She carried a large woven tote edged with pink trim. Personally, she thought they were overdressed. This was Hawaii, after all.

Ty strolled in smiling, dressed in a white linen shirt, tan slacks, and canvas boat shoes. Conversation came to a screeching halt. Carrie's bridesmaids ogled him as if he were the stripper they'd reluctantly canceled for Carrie's party. Someone even whispered, "Take it all off."

Treflee did a possessive mental growl, trying not to let anything show on her face. She knew the body beneath the clothes nearly as well as she knew her own. It was indeed droolworthy.

She made a fist, trying *not* to remember how it felt to run her hands over his broad shoulders and naked chest. Trying to forget how he used to make a muscle just for her to squeeze and admire. And how she used to trail kisses all the way from his bicep to his lips.

She wondered if he was enjoying playing stud muffin?

Greg came in behind Ty, looking like an explosion of color gone very wrong in his garish Hawaiian print shirt. Fortunately for him, and anyone who cared about style, standing next to Ty, he may as well have been invisible.

"Ladies!" Ty flashed his most charming smile. "Tonight we party. But first, the ladies shop till they drop in Lahaina."

The girls jockeyed for the key position next to him. Treflee was used to his effect on women, and mostly immune to it now. It used to bug the heck out of her. Maybe it still did. A little. She really didn't like being an eyewitness to it.

Sometimes she wondered why Ty didn't just sign the divorce papers and get on with the lady killing. She could be as self-serving and vain as the next person, but realistically, she wasn't even in the same league as some of the attractive and appealing babes who threw themselves at him. He could have had a good stash of eye candy to his credit. In her weaker moments, she wondered what he ever saw in her. In her strongest moments, she wondered what she saw in him.

Ty diplomatically offered one arm to the woman paying the bills, Carrie, and the other to her best friend, Laci. Tall, thin Faye, the amply hipped, dark-haired Brandy, and the nurse, Carla, crowded around them.

Treflee held back and filed in line next to Greg. A few hours alone in her room had given her time to think up a plan. She was going to find out what Ty was up to here in Maui. Two could play the game. And once she had enough on him, she'd blackmail him into signing the divorce papers.

The CIA has a motto engraved in stone just inside the door at Langley, "And ye shall know the truth and the truth shall make you free."

Treflee was taking the Agency's motto to heart. She couldn't go on living with this ache, wondering where Ty was, who he was with, or whether he'd come home alive. She couldn't keep hoping he'd suddenly decide to settle down and become the family man she wanted him to be. And she absolutely couldn't hold on to the pain of her secret and keep blaming him. As agonizing as pulling away from Ty was, she had to put him behind her. If the truth of what he was up to in Maui brought her freedom and peace, then she had to find it.

Step one of the plan meant befriending Greg to see what he knew. Step two—follow Ty around Lahaina while she was supposed to be shopping. Step three—search Ty's room as soon as she got the chance. She hadn't gotten as far as deciding what step four should be yet. She prayed it wouldn't be necessary.

She smiled at Greg and took the arm he offered her. He looked pleased that someone had noticed him. In front of the plantation house, they piled into a chauffeured party bus. Treflee had to clamp her mouth shut to keep her jaw from dropping as she stepped inside. The bus was more Austin Powers than Bond—magenta carpeting, tan leather couches, flat-screen TV, and fully stocked bar.

Ty took his place by the bar, cranked on the surround sound system, and flipped on the pulsating, multicolored lighting. Treflee was in a nightmare—a garish nightclub. She could feel a migraine in the making already. Strobe lights and pounding music brought them on, which was why she preferred softly lit piano bars and jazz.

Greg shot her a concerned look. She must have looked a little green. Or maybe it was just the strobe. She was definitely angry with Ty. He was showing off his pouring skills and biceps at the bar while Carrie and her friends paired up and did hip-bumping, cleavage-shaking dances for his entertainment.

Treflee turned to Greg. "How long is the ride to La-haina?"

"Fifteen minutes," he shouted over the bump-and-grind tunes playing. "If we were going straight there. But we're taking the scenic route so we can take advantage of the party bus. Brace yourself for a long ride."

Greg was evidently not a party animal, either. Or maybe he was just a nice guy. He took her elbow and guided her to a seat on the perimeter of the bus as far away from the action as was humanly possible. Which unfortunately wasn't far.

"Can I get you something?" he asked, looking like he had to be polite, but didn't relish breaking into the group of ladies crowding the bar and ogling Ty. He probably feared he'd come into contact with a bump from Brandy's ample hips and end up in the hospital. She was really getting into the dancing.

Treflee leaned into him to speak directly into his ear,

hoping he'd hear her. "No, thanks. I'm not cruel enough to send you into that." She nodded toward her cousin's group.

He gave her a thankful smile.

Treflee returned his smile, hoping to look sympathetic. "Have you worked with Ty long?" He'd been MIA for six months and she was dying to know what he'd been up to.

"Not long. A couple of months."

Bastard, she thought, eyeing Ty at the bar. Had he been partying it up all this time? Watching him, she was beginning to wonder if spies really did live the good life and he'd simply been lying to her about that, too. "Have you been an island guide long?"

"Three years."

Ty turned the music up.

She nodded and leaned closer to Greg so he could hear her. "Must be hard working with a guy like Ty."

Greg gave a little appreciative snort and shrugged. "He's what the ladies expect when they come to the island, part of the fantasy and escape from reality," he shouted in her ear. He paused. "You seem immune."

"I'm going through a bad divorce." She couldn't help frowning at Ty. "Men aren't high on my list right now, present company excluded."

"I'm nonthreatening is what you mean." He looked resigned.

"There's nothing wrong with a safe man," she retorted, wondering how to find out more about Ty without seeming obsessed by him. "So he's just a pretty face?"

"No. He's good at his job. Excellent, in fact."

"The flawless man," she said with more than a touch of irony. "Good at what he does as well as good-looking. He must have some irritating habits."

He nodded toward the group of ladies, just as Ty wrenched

the music up another notch and did something that made the colored lights spin faster. "Mostly that."

Treflee felt herself flushing with anger and a surprising amount of jealousy. She had to know. She simply had to know. Besides, proof of infidelity might win her some sympathy points with a judge if Ty still refused to sign, and some more dollars from Ty in a renegotiated settlement. "That's just part of his job. Is he that lucky with the ladies in real life? Is he seeing anyone?"

"What?" Greg cocked his ear to her. "I can't hear you."

"Is Ty seeing anyone?" she repeated at the top of her lungs just as the music shut off and the bus went quiet. Her question echoed off the bus walls, seemingly reverberating forever in the sudden silence.

Her eyes went wide.

Someone just throw a bucket of water on me so I can elegantly melt away and die like the Wicked Witch.

Ex-bridezilla and her ladies-in-waiting stared at Treflee. Ty gave her a deadpan stare that said he had her number.

She fumed in her seat. She couldn't see his eyes in the dim light, but she'd bet her life they were dancing with malicious amusement. He'd shut the music off on purpose, the rat. As promised, he was keeping an eye on her.

Her question wasn't what it sounded like, she wanted to shout. It really wasn't. But there was no point. And shouting an explanation would have blown his cover. So she slumped in her seat and prayed they'd reach Lahaina before she died of embarrassment or killed someone, namely Ty.

Somehow Treflee survived the rest of the trip to Lahaina, but she'd never been so happy to get off a bus, even as a kid after a long day at school.

"I thought you said he wasn't your type?" Laci teased, obviously amused that a girl like Treflee thought she could attract a guy like Ty.

If only she knew. Treflee's tongue nearly bled from biting it so hard to keep quiet.

Ty got out first and offered the ladies a hand down from the bus. When it was Treflee's turn, she blinked in the bright sunlight, thankful for fresh air as she snubbed the hand he offered. He grabbed her anyway and tugged with more force than was strictly necessary.

She tumbled into his rock-hard chest. The man still had it. And if the unsteady patter of her heart was any indication, she still had it for him.

But the tug was all a convenient ruse so he could whisper sweet threats in her ear. "No more stunts. I told you not to blow my cover. Shutting off the music in the bus was purely intentional. Caught you in the act, didn't I? Stay out of my business, Tref. I'll be watching you."

"Stalking me now? Lovely," she shot back.

"Watch yourself," he said, and let her go, before turning to dazzle the other girls.

The bus dropped them off on Front Street facing the Lahaina Center. Greg made his escape immediately. Ty said his good-byes and hurried off to "run some errands" before joining everyone on the cruise later.

Treflee watched him walk down the street with panic making a mockery of her normally calm heartbeat. She couldn't let him get away. She had to follow him.

"Are you coming?" Carrie said, snapping her out of her panicked stupor. "I thought you were immune to his charms. I thought you hated men?"

"I do. Except for Greg. He's nice."

"Uh-huh," she said.

Treflee looked at Carrie's bridesmaids. "They're staring, too."

"But they're not pretending to be uninterested." Carrie waved to the girls. "Let's get a move on. We don't have much time before the cruise."

They moved as a herd toward the entrance. Treflee had to lose them while not losing Ty. He was already halfway down the street.

Carrie grabbed her arm and tugged her along with the gang. "There's a good reason I didn't pick you for maid of honor," she muttered.

Fortunately, fate intervened. As the rest paused to coo over a display of designer handbags in a specialty shop window, Treflee spotted a corner art gallery across the way. She loved art galleries. Carrie hated them.

"Look!"

They followed her pointer finger and frowned in unison.

"A Salvador Dalí copy. Melting watches. I love that one. I'm going in," Treflee said.

"Then you're going alone," Carrie retorted, with a frustrated look that clearly said her mother was going to owe her big-time for foisting Treflee off on her.

Treflee ignored her. "I can spend hours ogling art." Which Carrie knew to be true from the time Treflee dragged her to the National Gallery of Art in Washington, D.C. "You girls go on ahead. I'll meet you at the cruise dock."

Not surprisingly, no one argued. They dropped into the handbag store as Treflee meandered into the art gallery. The minute they were out of sight, she dashed back out of the gallery and down the street just in time to see Ty turn the corner.

You'd think flat sandals would be good for running. Better than heels on any account. But they had no arch support. Treflee had shin splints by the time she reached the corner and saw Ty duck into Woo Ming's Chinese Emporium. *The old "stop by for an afternoon egg roll" trick,* she thought and smiled to herself at her snappy Max Smart humor.

Chinese restaurant? The U.S. and China weren't necessarily the best of friends. Being married to a spy made her suspicious of the simplest things, like the sudden urge for a cup of green tea and a fortune cookie. But if he was having tea, Treflee was watching him drink it. And if he tried the old briefcase switch drop, she was going to catch him at it. Just not on her camera. He still had that.

Note to self—buy a new camera, she thought. Unfortunately, no time for that now.

She took a second to catch her breath as she wondered how to sneak in behind him without him seeing her. In the hierarchy of spies, Treflee was more on the level of Max Smart than James Bond. She considered hoping there'd be a bead curtain she could hide behind in there. Or maybe a potted palm. Short of that, she was probably out of luck.

Fortunately, there was a tacky tourist shop next door with a rack of Hawaiian shirts and a table of floppy straw hats displayed on the sidewalk. No cameras, though. She bought a hat and positioned herself, hat shading her face, on a bench across the street where she could watch the door.

A couple of tourists went in for the early bird special. A few tourists came out. Ty stayed in. Ten minutes passed. Then twenty. She was bored out of her mind. If this was spying, Ty could have it.

Finally, she made up her mind. She was going in, baby, no matter the consequences. If Ty was sitting there calmly eating Peking Duck, so be it. She adjusted her hat and was off.

Inside the restaurant, it was cool and quiet. Someone had left the front desk unattended. A couple of people sat at red booths sipping ice water and eating fried rice, but no Ty.

Treflee frowned as she wondered if he'd given her the slip. Not willing to give up, she wandered down the hallway toward the ladies' room. He shouldn't be in there. Which left her with two options: the men's room and a door marked office/employees only. She wasn't going into the men's room. Not as her first choice.

The office door was closed. She put an ear to it, but couldn't hear anything. There was no reason to storm in like Iron Man. Maybe she'd just try to get a peek inside first.

Afraid of someone hearing the latch turn, she gave it the gentlest push imaginable on the off chance she'd get lucky. And she did. Someone hadn't closed it all the way. It cracked open just enough for her to see inside, and she put an eye to the door. That's when she realized how curiosity killed the cat. She nearly had a heart attack.

A young Chinese man lay splayed on the floor with his neck slit open, a pool of bright blood forming around him. His glassy eyes stared sightlessly at the ceiling as a pair of vulturelike flies buzzed around him.

Oh my gosh, oh my gosh, oh my gosh!

Ty stood over him with his shirt and hands covered in blood.

CHAPTER THREE

Fear does strange things to people. In Treflee's case, it brought up the flight response. She ran. Just ran. Down the hall. Past the startled Chinese waiter. Out the door. Into the street. Around the corner. Her hands shook, and beyond, "Run, Tref, run," she couldn't think a coherent thought to save her life.

Finally, she spotted a little ice cream shop. Dad always bought her an ice cream when she was upset. She guessed this qualified. Her nearly ex-husband was a killer! Or so it appeared if she were the kind of girl to leap to conclusions. Which she was. And she couldn't do a thing about the killing. Not a thing.

Yeah, she *could* call the cops. If she could borrow a phone. Ty still had her cell. But she might be blowing an important U.S. intelligence operation. Maybe thousands of lives depended on it. For all she knew, Ty had just taken out a terrorist or someone who was selling nuclear secrets or psychotic drugs. She couldn't, she could not, call the cops. Ty and his agents would have to take care of it.

So she did the only thing she could. She bought a cup of ice cream. Cold, creamy coconut ice cream.

When the teenager behind the counter asked how she could help her, Treflee had to point to it because she still couldn't form words. Then her hands shook so badly she was barely able to get her wallet out and pay.

She took her ice cream outside and sat at a table beneath a big, bright blue umbrella. She stuck her tiny plastic spoon in the ice cream and watched it melt as the "Oh my gosh" mantra repeated itself in an endless loop in her head.

She didn't know how long she sat there. It could have been five minutes or an hour. She wondered vaguely if she was missing the cruise. She should find a taxi to take her back to the plantation. She had no desire to party.

How was she ever going to face Ty?

Never, never ask the universe a rhetorical question like that. Odds are it will answer you and you won't like what it says. No sooner had the question popped into her mind than Ty called her name. Treflee started so badly, she knocked the ice cream cup over.

She looked up to see him standing before her, appearing out of nowhere as if he'd been transported there. That was the thing about him. He could creep up on anybody. He'd been trained in the art of sneaking.

"Tref?" He righted the ice cream cup and dropped a napkin on the spill to mop it up. His gaze flicked between the ice cream and her. "You okay?"

He knew her too well. She wasn't a girl to waste ice cream, especially not coconut.

Treflee stared at his pristine white shirt, taking it in with the same calm as if she'd seen a ghostly apparition. As cold as she felt, she was sure the blood had drained from her face.

Her gaze trailed to his surgically clean hands. As far as she could tell he didn't have a cell's worth of blood on them, not even under his fingernails. His hair was dry and he was giving her a look of concern that didn't show a jot of trauma in it, or give any hint he'd just killed a man. At that moment Treflee wished she had a black light she could shine on him to reveal blood residue.

How in the world had he made the transformation? Where had he gotten an identical set of clothes? Spies-R-Us?

"I've had a hell of a day," she said in a voice that was shakier than she liked. "Running into you again hasn't been easy." Which was the understatement of the century, and completely true on both encounter counts, especially the last bloody one.

He looked at her ice cream again. "I can see that. Let me get you another one—"

"No!" She grabbed his hand to stop him and immediately released it as if his touch scorched.

He arched a brow.

It was thoughtful of him to offer. Had her stomach not been in such turmoil, she might have taken him up on it. She could certainly use the comfort. That was another thing about Ty. He could be sweet when he wanted to be.

"Look," he said, pulling up a metal chair. "Let's put this divorce unpleasantness behind us while you're here. This is Hawaii. Enjoy yourself."

Then stop killing people, she wanted to scream. Instead, she thanked her good luck. If the divorce was the tack he wanted to take, she was all over it. It was better than admitting to the scene she witnessed earlier. "Not easy to do, Ty, when I have to watch you act like some kind of gigolo with my cousin and her friends."

"It's just part of the job, Tref." His voice was touchingly tender and sincere.

Treflee thought maybe he was getting the wrong impression from her degree of upset. She tried to work up a little indignant anger to show him she wasn't pining away for him.

"That was always the problem, wasn't it?" she said,

feeling the old defensiveness and hurt again. "You get to flirt, and who knows what else, as part of the job . . ."

She really hated imagining the what-else. "If I flirted here, there, and everywhere on the job like you do, the office would be buzzing with gossip and innuendo. Someone would have to report me to my supervisor. I'd be fired and never allowed to work in human resources again." She gave him a challenging look.

To her surprise, his returning expression was sympathetic. "I was never unfaithful, Tref. Never."

She hated when he sounded like that. She wanted to believe him so badly. "What's being unfaithful? Doing the full-blown deed? Stopping just short? Sticking your tongue down another woman's throat?"

Ty grabbed her hand and put it on his heart. "It's straying from the heart. Feeling something for another woman that I've always felt only for you."

Her eyes misted over. Ty could be so touchingly dramatic. He'd always been like that. That's part of why she fell in love with him. She pulled her hand away and tucked it in her lap.

"Give me another chance, Tref."

Feeling on the verge of tears, she shook her head. On top of everything else, after what she'd just seen him do, how could she ever consider staying with him?

"We've been over this before, Ty," she said softly. "We aren't good for each other. I need someone who's around, physically present, there for me."

He frowned and pressed his lips together. He wasn't the kind of man to beg. She knew that.

He sighed and glanced at his watch. "We have a cruise to catch." He pushed back in his chair, stood, and extended his hand to her.

"Sign the papers and I can be out of your hair instantly," she said, lamely.

"When I get back home."

Is he ever really coming home?

"Promise?"

"You have my word."

How do you trust the word of a man who will say anything and has the poker face of a master?

The harbor was just a few blocks away. They walked to the dock in silence. What was there to say? Treflee was terrified that if she talked too much she'd give away what she'd seen. And, although seemingly calm, she knew he was angry at her for not jumping to give him another chance. She felt perfectly horrible.

Greg and the girls were waiting for them aboard the *Lahaina Dream,* a gleaming white sixty-five-foot glass-bottomed yacht with deep sky-blue trim. Treflee liked blue. She wasn't big on boats.

Laci leaned over the rail, spilling her cleavage out for all, particularly Ty, to see, and waved at them with the tiny umbrellaed cocktail in her hand from the upper deck. "Up here. Grab a drink and join us. The view's to die for!"

Uneasy with that visual, Treflee shot a look at Ty.

"Jumpy?" he said, and smiled.

"I need one of those tiny umbrellas," she said as they boarded.

They joined the others at their reserved table for eight on the upper viewing deck. Treflee downed half her mai tai on the way up from the main deck. Two kinds of rum and orange curacao, gotta love it.

Laci, that redheaded floozy, patted a chair next to her and smiled at Ty. "I saved you a seat."

He sat and she settled herself uncomfortably close to him, her bare arm brushing his. She shot Treflee a triumphant look with a diamond-clear message—Treflee may have snagged Ty for a walk in Lahaina, but she meant to shag him.

"Tref," Carrie said, sounding obviously put out. "We went back to the gallery to find you, but you gave us the slip."

"I went for ice cream," she said.

Carrie rolled her eyes. "You could answer your cell, you know."

Treflee shot Ty the evil eye. He looked totally unfazed.

"I must not have had service," she muttered, peeved that she couldn't explain. She gulped down the rest of her mai tai and flagged the waiter for another. "Where are Brandy and Faye?"

Carrie pointed across the deck to where the two had cornered a pair of handsome men.

Judging by the men's expressions, they'd just been ambushed. The girls could use a lesson or two in seduction techniques to augment their brusque war room skills. She glanced at Ty and scowled.

Fortunately, Treflee's rum kicked in about then. A pleasant calm settled over her jangled senses as she looked across the crowd. There were probably a hundred and twenty people aboard the boat. And not a child or family unit in sight. Suspicious, Treflee glanced around at left hands. There was a shocking lack of wedding rings.

If not for the calming effect of rum and curacao, she could have killed that Carrie! She'd booked them on a meat market cruise and not even bothered to warn her.

Worse yet, or maybe better yet, depending on your point of view, a tall, dark man ogled her from across the deck. If Treflee hadn't just seen a dead man and had actually *been* single, she might have been flattered and taken up the invitation in his eyes. He had honey-colored skin and looked like an exotic mix between Hawaiian and mainlander. Not exactly handsome, but he had a face that would be hard to forget. Hoping to discourage him from making contact, she turned away.

Treflee's gaze flitted to the door just as the engine roared to life and they pulled away from the dock. *Too late to jump ship.*

Dinner passed in a blur of grilled mahimahi and pineapple salsa. Treflee was sorely tempted to get her last free drink, a third mai tai. But two was her limit. Alcohol loosened her tongue, and she needed her wits.

She stared at the magnificent deep-hued Hawaiian sunset, feeling melancholy with Ty, the man she'd loved, now the evidence of her failed marriage, sitting at her table. No romance in sight. Just broken pieces before her eyes.

She paid little attention to the conversation until Faye and Brandy returned unexpectedly before dessert.

"They ditched us." Brandy scowled, referring to their two prisoners of love.

Treflee wondered how that was possible aboard a confined boat.

"The nerve," Carrie said with more venom than one would expect. "Bastards."

"Yeah," Faye added.

And she's the erudite one, Treflee thought.

"Men! Don't you just hate them?" Carrie said. "They're all lying, scheming, cheating jerks."

Obviously sensitive to the dangerous turn the conversation had taken, Greg suddenly excused himself. Ty looked like he wanted to bolt, too, but Laci had him by the arm in a death grip. He wasn't going anywhere.

The alcohol and the creeping dusk messed with Treflee's senses and made her sentimental. She sniffled. Just a little. "Amen," she muttered, feeling totally drained.

Carrie set her wine glass down and shot her a surprisingly sympathetic look before turning to Ty. "Excuse her," she said. "She's going through a bad divorce. Asshole of a husband left her without signing the divorce papers. Just abandoned her."

"Maybe he didn't want a divorce," Ty said. "Maybe he still loved her."

Right, Treflee thought, fighting a lump in her throat and refusing to look at him.

Carrie rolled her eyes. "Funny way of showing it. He took the coward's way out. He didn't stay around to fight for her, did he?" She shook her head. "Look at her. She's like a lost kitten. I had to drag her on this vacation. We'd be two of a kind. Thank goodness I came to my senses and ditched the jerk just before the wedding. At least I'm free."

There was just the slightest hint of pain in Carrie's voice. You had to know her well to hear it, and Treflee had known her since birth. They were born three weeks apart.

"Oh, honey," Carla said, using what Treflee supposed was her nurse's bedside-manner voice. "I didn't know."

Treflee had just met them all on the flight over from the mainland. They weren't in the confide-in-you stage yet.

Carla gave Carrie a look that said she understood now why Treflee wasn't into partying. "He just abandoned you? Why did you want the divorce? What did the bastard do? Let it all out. You're among friends."

You know, sometimes life just hands you a gift. Treflee's gaze flicked to Ty. Laci tightened her grip possessively. Treflee sighed heavily, as if she didn't really want to talk, but in reality, she was dying to lash out.

"Oh, it was just, it was just *everything.*" Treflee threw her hands up and shook her head. "He traveled all the time for his job, like eighty percent of the time. Or more. He missed our anniversary, holidays, my birthday. He was gone so much, he never even *met* Carrie, my closest cousin, almost a sister to me." Treflee sniffed, faking sentimentality. *Okay, I'm laying it on a little thick. Who can blame me?*

"I was the little red hen. I had to do everything myself—manage the house, pay the bills, get the car fixed. A few sympathetic calls, texts, and e-mails did *not* make up for not being around to help out. I felt like I was single. With none of the fringe benefits. Online dating would have offered more companionship and support."

"There must have been *some* benefits," Ty said, and looked down at the dessert plate the waiter set before him.

"You mean the trinkets he brought home and the secrecy?" Treflee crossed her arms and ignored the coconut cream pie before her, wondering what had possessed her to think she could attack him without him firing back.

"Hey, give him a break. A guy gets home from a business trip, the last thing he wants to do is *talk*." Ty winked at the girls, who nodded and smiled.

Damn his charming soul!

Treflee balled her fist in her lap. "Yeah? Well, I had a pretty good idea he wasn't talking for other reasons. Code of the road, you know. The occasional trip to the titty bar . . . and more."

"Titty bar! Men! Adolescents who never grow up." Laci's knuckles turned white as she dug bright pink fingernails into Ty's arm, indignant with anger.

He winced. Served him right. For just a vengeful instant, Treflee hoped she drew blood.

She'd hit the right button with Carrie's friends. Women who served their country side by side with their male counterparts evidently found strip clubs demeaning.

The other girls joined in, swearing and calling Ty, actually to his face though they thought it was behind his back, all kinds of names. Treflee had to give them credit. They'd picked up some colorful expletives in the army.

She was suddenly enjoying herself. Retribution is oh so fun when you have the upper hand.

She glanced at Ty to see just how good of a spy face he'd put on. Was he squirming? Seething? He looked calm. But inside, Treflee hoped he was roiling.

"Yes, *Ty*," she said, emphasizing his name, "was full of secrets. He never talked to me."

The girls all looked at Ty.

Carrie turned to him and apologized. "Her almost ex is ironically also named Ty." She sighed and shrugged. "Sorry. No offense intended."

Oh yes there was!

He smiled like, no problem, I understand. Okay, so he was doing a pretty good acting job.

"I wanted a baby," Treflee said truthfully, letting her heart and disappointment sink into her tone. "And he didn't. I loved Ty. I wanted to make a *family* with him. What's so wrong with that? That's what people who love each other do." *And I needed a baby to fill the void left by the one I'd lost.*

Ty looked down at the table, frowning.

Carla patted Treflee's hand.

Faye's eyes grew hard. "How long were you married?"

"Seven years."

"Seven years! The honeymoon phase is long over by then," Brandy said. "Why didn't you just feed your pills to the plant?"

"Oh, I did. I even told him I was on the patch, and then I used a fake one. But he was careful," Treflee said. "He always insisted on using protection."

"Controlling SOB!" Faye shook her head.

Treflee nodded, keeping tabs on Ty with her peripheral

vision. He was showing no signs of cracking. So she went in for the kill just as he lifted his mai tai to his lips. "Oh, it wasn't *all* his fault." She sounded so magnanimous. "So much traveling wore him out. He was just so tired. You know, he couldn't always . . ." She trailed off delicately.

The girls' eyes went wide. They leaned in toward her.

"He couldn't always get it up," Treflee said just loudly enough for them all, and the people at the table next to them, to hear. What a blatant liar she was. If there was anything Ty was good at, the sack was it. He never had any trouble keeping things up. Keeping them down, more like.

Ty sputtered. All the ladies looked at him as he choked on his drink.

"Sorry!" Carrie laughed. "Something about talking about impotence, even another guy's, upsets men."

So do lies about his own performance, Treflee thought.

Treflee shook her head sadly. "Yeah, yeah. And all the tiredness and being off schedule affected his staying power, too."

Ty reached for his water, talking as he coughed. "Swallowed down the wrong pipe."

Treflee smiled to herself. *That was low, but he deserved that shot below the belt. He really did.*

Fortunately for Ty, the sun had slipped below the horizon and the stars were beginning to twinkle. With the sun gone, it was time for the below-deck entertainment to begin.

An announcement blared from the loudspeakers. "Passengers, please report to the glass-bottom viewing deck for our fantastic Polynesian dancing show!"

Ty zipped out of his chair and toward the stairs with Laci almost running to keep up with him as she hung like a barnacle on his arm. The rest of the group followed.

On the lower deck, they took seats on benches around

the glass deck viewing area. An array of exotic, curvy hula girls and several ripped, dark, and handsome Polynesian men danced onto the glass in a rustle of grass skirts. Treflee was pushed to the edge of the crowd with about five women between Ty and her and Greg on her right. Probably just as well. She didn't think Ty was thinking kind thoughts about her at that minute.

"Hula, hula!" Carrie said in a hubba-hubba tone as she spotted the men. "I want one of those."

Beside Treflee, Carla's gaze was glued to the male dancers.

"Careful," Ty said. "You're in danger of being as bad as Treflee's husband."

Was Treflee the only one who caught the irony?

Carrie waved aside his concern. "We're single. We're allowed."

"All right, how reflective is that glass?" Carla said, leaning forward for a closer view. "I'd like to see some wildlife and I don't mean tropical fish."

"Oh, for a stiff breeze right now." Faye sighed.

"In the hull?" Treflee asked.

"A big fan would do," she retorted.

"I doubt they're commando under those skirts," Treflee said, trying to maintain her rain-cloud status in the group. "They've gotta have on a Speedo."

"Nooo!" Faye said. "That would kill the fun."

"I vote for commando." Brandy was leaning forward with her elbows on her lap and her head in her hands, mesmerized.

Tiki torches blazed around the perimeter of the hull, reflecting in the glass of the viewing area. A band of Hawaiian musicians started strumming ukuleles and pounding drums. The dancers began undulating and swishing, their hands telling a story Treflee wasn't interested enough to follow.

The last time she'd seen a hula, she'd been with Ty in Waikiki. She didn't feel like remembering that right now. Being on the edge of the show, and emotionally and physically exhausted, she quickly lost interest and zoned out, staring almost sightlessly at the dark pane of viewing glass nearest her.

This vacation was turning into a bigger disaster than she had even imagined. Was there any way she could blackmail Ty with the dead guy, get her divorce, and come out of the whole thing without being charged with treason or something?

She was lost in her thoughts when a thump startled her. It wasn't the beat of a drum or the patter of feet. The dancers were deft and moved across the glass quietly. Treflee frowned, thinking at first that a fish must have bumped into the viewing glass. But when she looked, there was nothing there.

Her frown deepened. Why couldn't she just enjoy the show?

She was still frowning and staring when a face appeared from the water and pressed against the ocean's side of the glass. The face of a man she recognized—the dead guy from Woo Ming's.

She screamed.

CHAPTER FOUR

The dancers froze. The drumbeat stopped. A hundred-plus pairs of eyes stared at Treflee as she pointed toward the face in the water and gesticulated, muttered, played a bad game of charades, and did everything but speak coherently about the dead guy with the tiny fish nibbling at his face.

Greg understood first and cursed beneath his breath as he put his arm around her and whispered for her to cover her eyes. "Stop the boat! We've hooked a floater."

Ty jumped into action, taking a look for himself before grabbing Greg, yelling to the crew for a wet suit and gear, and heading to the main deck as Treflee disobeyed Greg and stared pale-faced into the dead zone along with everyone else.

A few minutes later, a pair of divers appeared behind the glass as everyone watched. They grabbed the body and pulled it away.

Someone called the coast guard. Carla jumped up and, screaming that she was a nurse, headed to the main deck to provide medical assistance. As if that would help the Woo Ming guy. He was lucky his head was still attached to his body, and Treflee was willing to bet he had no blood left. No, that guy had been dead for hours. He was way beyond help. And Treflee needed that third mai tai. *Badly*.

Sometimes the show does not go on. Sometimes it's just disrespectful to watch a gig full of eye candy and undulating hips when some poor fool's just turned up dead and swimming with the angelfish.

They kept everyone in the hull as the boat immediately headed back to Lahaina Harbor. The crew offered people coffee and tea, nothing stronger. They were met at the dock by the coast guard and the cops. Although Treflee had discovered the body, neither showed much interest in little old her. If only they knew!

Treflee guessed simply seeing a body through a glass window didn't hold much vital information for them. They asked her just the one cursory question—where'd you see the body?—and then escorted her from the hull to the main deck.

Greg and Ty were on the main deck, standing in a pool of water over the tarp-covered body with a crowd of cops around them. As Treflee came up the stairs, she watched Ty's profile in the overhead lights. A chill rippled down her back. He looked completely calm.

He turned to look at her so suddenly she didn't have time to wipe the guilty, knowing expression from her face. He saw it. She knew it by his subtle reaction to her. He knew she knew something.

The man knows me too well.

A courteous crewman escorted her to the waiting party bus for the ride back to the plantation. This ride was the polar opposite of the ride to town—no drinking, no flirting, no wild lights or music. Just hushed conversation, questions, and surmises about what had happened to the guy.

Since Treflee had gotten the best look at the dead guy

because he appeared in the glass pane nearest her, she bore the brunt of the questioning.

"I can't tell you much," she said, and shuddered. "His eyes looked dead and glassy. His hair swished back and forth in the water. His skin was pale and ghostly. And fish were nibbling at his face." Treflee choked up on the last sentence.

The fish-eating mental image pretty much shut them up. For a while.

"Did you see any wounds?" Faye asked Treflee, shifting her skinny butt in her seat and leaning toward her.

Treflee paused, frowning in thought. She knew what and who killed him. But what had she actually seen in the glass window? It was better to play it safe. She shook her head. "It was all so shocking and gross. I don't remember anything but the face. It looked like it came straight out of a nightmare."

Back at the plantation, Tita greeted them with the equivalent of a Hawaiian hot toddy—warm coconut milk spiked with rum. The other girls gathered in Carrie's room to gossip more about the evening's events and dissect the police procedure and response from a military, cop-type-girl point of view.

Treflee didn't particularly want to be alone, but she couldn't stand another question. So she begged off and headed to her room where she changed into her pajamas—a cotton cami and shorts—and a knee-length robe. She lay down on the fluffy bed, staring wide-eyed at the ceiling. Trying to sleep was futility at its finest. Especially after she realized that neither Ty nor Greg were around.

Now that the police had a body, would they trace the murder back to Ty? Would Emmett Nelson, head of the National Clandestine Service and Ty's boss at the CIA, be able to cover for him?

Treflee was worried. On all counts. And curious about Ty's mission. Did it involve the dead Chinese guy? She needed to get a look at Ty's room. She doubted he'd left any incriminating evidence around, but at the very least, she could retrieve her camera and phone.

Treflee had no idea how she was going to get into his room. But however she was going to do it, she wasn't leaving any fingerprints behind. She grabbed the pair of manicure gloves she'd brought with her. What could she say? She liked soft skin. Every few days she slathered her hands with lotion and slept with gloves on.

She checked the hall. All clear.

She knew which room was Ty's. Earlier, she'd seen him come out of it. She was no good at picking locks, though heaven knows she'd tried. And she knew Ty—he was careful about locking up. But just on the off chance she'd get lucky twice in one day, she went to his room.

She put on her gloves and gently tried the door. It fell open in front of her. That was almost too easy. She wondered for a second if this was a trap. Ty knew her as well as she knew him. He'd expect her to try to get her stuff back and spy on him.

She hesitated, wondering if he'd booby-trapped the room. She scanned the floor at her feet, looking for the old match-in-the-door trick. When she didn't see one, she shrugged. *What the heck.*

Treflee slipped into the room and closed the door behind her, pulling the security latch to slow Ty down if he came home before she could get out.

He'd left his patio deck door open, which seemed a bit odd. She stiffened, on alert.

The white curtains floated in the evening breeze. She relaxed. It would take a stronger man than Ty to resist that fresh ocean breeze and the moonlight slanting in to light the room with shafts of silver. For all his bravado, he had a romantic streak in him.

Speaking of romantic, her gaze flitted to his bed. Her chest tightened with longing she'd been trying to get rid of, and a lump formed in her throat. There was a time he would have been waiting for her in that bed, wearing nothing but a come-here-and-let's-get-it-on look.

She walked to the bed and ran her fingers over the comforter. It was useless and silly, totally futile remembering. Not to mention it fueled the frustrated yearning.

She missed him. She missed so much about him—the way he made her laugh. The way he made her feel safe and protected. The way he could tell a story to make even the most mundane thing sound fun. How he pushed her out of her comfort zone into adventures and experiences she'd never have had without him. Although, to be honest, she could have done without this one.

Treflee did her best to push the memories of better times away. *Get back to the mission, Tref,* she admonished herself.

There was a lamp on the dresser and one on the nightstand. She debated turning one on, then decided against it, afraid it would give her away and shatter the beauty of the setting. She could live with moonlight.

As her eyes adjusted to the dark, she scanned the room and frowned. The man hadn't changed. He was still frustratingly messy. Piled clothes filled the upholstered chair by the curtains and spilled onto the floor. Towels, rumpled shirts, and shoes littered the floor.

She tried to think like Ty. Where would he stow her camera and phone? If she was lucky, he'd simply tossed them in a drawer, though he was usually more creative than that.

Yeah, she had a lot of experience spying on him. Though

she couldn't say she ever really caught him at anything or discovered any clue about what his missions were, she worked hard at it. The man was good at what he did. Her skills as a spy basically sucked.

Ty was smart enough to realize she was always trying to find out what he was up to. He used to call her his own little Cato. She kept him on his toes like Cato did for Clouseau. Only when she pounced on him, she did it with sex appeal, and he never minded taking her.

Fortunately, Ty didn't have as many options for hiding things here as he had at home. Treflee was hoping that would work to her advantage.

She walked over and opened a dresser drawer.

Great. Typical Ty. When she did the laundry, she folded his briefs in thirds and then in half. And she bundled his socks into nice, tidy balls. His socks were unmatched and his underwear not even folded.

She sighed. Ty used to hide love notes for her to discover in odd places, including his drawers, when she was snooping on him.

She leaned over the drawer to get a closer look, half curious to see if he'd left her a note this time. If he had, it was likely to say, "Fooled you. They aren't here. Mind your own business," not "I love you."

She frowned. Something was off. She glanced at the chair piled with clothes and back to the drawer. This wasn't ordinary Ty messiness. This was much worse. Someone had rifled through Ty's things!

A chill rippled up her spine. The breeze brought the goose bumps on her arms to new heights. The silver glow of the room shifted to gray. She had to get out of here.

Too late, she heard the weight of a footstep behind her.

Before she could spin around, someone threw a plastic lei around her neck from behind and wrenched it tight, stifling her scream in her throat.

* * *

It's been a hell of a day, Ty thought as he parked in front of the plantation house and jumped out of the car. In no mood for company or conversation, he kicked off his shoes and headed to the beach behind Big Auau for a cool, moonlit walk to clear his head. The soft, dependable pounding of the surf soothed his nerves and provided the perfect white noise to drown out the doubts, the horrors he'd witnessed, and the dark turn of his thoughts.

Could the day get any worse? First his hacked-off wife showed up out of the blue from the mainland, hounding him about that damn divorce. Then moments before he arrived at Woo Ming's, persons unknown slit Shen Lin's throat, effectively eliminating Ty's planned way into the tightly guarded Sugar Love Plantation, the neighbor plantation to Big Auau.

He flicked a glance down the beach in Sugar Love's direction and scowled at the fortress pretending to be a wedding plantation.

Damn it, I need to get in there and find out what RIOT is up to and when the sale of the Pinpoint Project is supposed to go down. I'll have to find another way. And quickly.

The thought of Shen Lin getting the jump on George and strangling him before George could react sent a shiver down Ty's back. George had been the best wushu expert the Agency had had in thirty years. A regular Bruce Lee with the mild manners and soft-spoken nature of George Smiley.

George had saved Ty's ass in what they later laughingly referred to as the great Beijing Pearl Market Caper. Ty had taken on six monkey knife fighters each armed with a kris when George appeared out of the shadows to take down four of them, leaving Ty with a measly two to handle.

Ty ran his hand through his hair. Now someone even

more deadly and skilled had gotten the jump on Lin. Of course, Lin's killer got away clean. And Ty had had the misfortune of arriving while there was still a spark of pleading life left in Lin's eyes.

Lin had been cocky, always ready with a story of his sexual exploits told in his Chinese New York accent. But he'd been a hell of a waiter. If Lin hadn't murdered George, and been aiding the world's most dangerous terrorist organization, Ty wouldn't have minded shooting the breeze with him when he dined at Woo Ming's.

Ty couldn't just stand by and watch Lin die without at least making an attempt at saving him and pumping what info he could out of him. Which turned out to be exactly nothing. Hard to talk with a slit throat. Talking is also not the first thing on your mind as your lifeblood is spurting out of you before your eyes.

In the end, all Ty accomplished for his humanitarian effort was contaminating the crime scene, incriminating himself in Lin's murder—being covered in the victim's blood will tend to do that—and nearly blowing both his cover and the mission.

And for all his trouble, he had had to duck out of Woo Ming's without getting his favorite Kahlúa-barbecued pork eggroll. All that foiled lifesaving left him with too little time before the sunset cruise to clean the bloody mess up himself.

Turned out calling Derek and his informal hazmat team to dispose of the body hadn't been the best move, either. Next time he'd have to remind Derek to dump in deeper, shark-infested waters. There'd better be a good story behind why Lin's body only made it as far as the harbor.

Which led to Ty's favorite event of the day, the complete hat trick. Lin's body ends up as a floater wedged against the bottom of the glass-bottomed boat *for Treflee to find and freak out over.*

She was supposed to have been getting pelvis-pounding, lust-inducing ideas from watching bare chests, undulating hips, and the swish of grass skirts. To remember the time he'd taken her to Waikiki five years ago and humored her by taking a hula lesson with her. The grass skirts they'd bought. How they'd laughed and danced a seductive hula all the way to bed. How much he loved her then . . . and now.

So that when he professed his undying love after the cruise, gave her the eighteen-inch princess-length string of perfect white pearls he'd bought for her months ago, and made his move, she'd be hyped up and receptive. But, no. He was the one who had ended up all wet tonight. A complete failure on all missions.

He took a deep breath and stared at the moonlit-tipped waves as they crashed in. The sand felt cool and refreshing beneath his feet. He dug his toes in and wished he could stand there forever with nothing more important on his agenda than simply breathing.

But he never shirked duty. Back at the plantation house, a whole host of problems awaited him. In unison with the thought, he turned to look over his shoulder. A flutter of curtains by a balcony door on the second floor of Big Auau caught his attention.

What the—

That's my room! He frowned, staring intently at the scene. *I didn't leave the door open. Which means—*

He caught a movement so faint it might have been a hallucination. He focused in on it. The silhouette of a woman being strangled emerged. Her long, silvery hair fluttered as she struggled against a hooded figure tightening a garrote around her neck.

Treflee! His heart pounded into overdrive.

Hang on, baby! He took off at a run up the sand hills toward the house, praying he'd arrive in time, willing her to fight right, fight smart. Hoping she'd remember what he'd taught her. *Fight the attacker, not the hold, Tref!*

Instinctively, Treflee clawed at the lei around her throat. Her gloves got in the way.

Get loose! Get air!

A plastic flower broke off in her hand. She tossed it away without thinking, pulled off her gloves and dropped them, and felt the strain of the exertion immediately.

Crap! Every molecule of oxygen counted now. *Every single one.*

She tensed her neck and struggled to get her fingers between her throat and the cord. Her attacker reacted by wrenching harder. The plastic cord gave, stretching just slightly before he could wrench again and correct it. Enough for her to get half a breath. If she were very lucky, the cord would snap completely. But somehow getting the strangler to keep twisting and tightening in the hopes the cord snapped before she did seemed like a flawed strategy.

She couldn't breathe. Couldn't think. Couldn't smell. Couldn't cry out.

She stumbled, fighting to stay on her feet.

Behind her, the man with the plastic lei breathed evenly and calmly in her ear, so close she could feel his body heat and sense his excitement.

She bet he had a hard-on as he killed on little cat feet while she panicked and struggled futilely as her cousin and friends dished about their evening in the surrounding rooms. Without strain or a single grunt to give him away and bring them running. Extinguishing her life as easily as he sipped rum on the beach. *Damn him!*

Her eyes stung. Her throat burned. Her body felt like a lead weight pulling her down.

Memories. Her life flitting before her eyes? Ty's voice echoed in her head.

Fight the attacker, not the hold, Tref!

Through the haze of her quickly fogging brain, she remembered now what he'd shared with her from his training.

She dropped her chin against her chest, which bought her a quick, shallow breath. Enough to give her a burst of strength.

Act quickly! Mean it! You'll only get one chance.

Adrenaline driving her, she threw her arm out in a forty-five-degree angle, made an elbow, and slammed it behind her directly into her attacker's stomach.

He let out an *oomph* and doubled forward, loosening his grip enough for her to take a breath.

Before he could recover, she pounded a fist downward into his groin, just like Ty had taught her.

He groaned and bent farther forward, dropping the lei to clutch his crotch. She caught a deeper breath and pulled the lei off, noticing a Chinese character tattooed on her attacker's neck as she did.

Her animal instincts called for blood. *Finish him, finish him, finish him!*

She was too weak in body and too gentle in spirit to give in to the bloodlust. She bent over, hands on knees, hair falling forward over her face, and took a breath that ached all the way down her throat into her chest. Nothing had ever hurt that good before.

Run! her mind screamed. *Escape!*

She would have. If she could only make her feet of clay move. She should have. Behind her, the happy strangler had stopped groaning and started softly cursing. Or so she assumed. She didn't exactly understand the language he spoke. Which meant nothing good on all fronts.

She had at her disposal, just a wall or two away, several lady cops, a large *wahine*, and a nurse. She only had to call them. She opened her mouth to yell and did a pitch-perfect impression of the silent scream.

She heard something rustle just outside the balcony door and looked up, brushing the hair from her face.

Ty swung onto the balcony from the jungle of a garden below as nimbly as Tarzan, landing lightly and gracefully on his feet, a regular Baryshnikov.

In the dim room, the moonlight highlighted the take-no-prisoners look in his eyes as he charged past her. She pushed to stand and turned to watch him go after the bad, bad man who'd tried to kill her.

The lei-strangler, however, was apparently no coward. Even though he was a good four inches shorter than Ty and a lot more slightly built, he ran toward Ty in full frontal attack mode. Just before the two collided, Strangler did an aerial leap over Ty and bounded off the balcony into the night.

Ty stared after him. Treflee could tell he was wondering whether he should follow. Finally he muttered something beneath his breath and came over to put his arm around her.

"Now who would want to kill you?" he asked in a tone so full of irony that despite her weakened, recently oxygen-deprived condition, she felt like slugging him.

"This . . . your—"

He put a finger to her lips and gave them a gentle stroke. "Shhh. Rest your voice."

She brushed his lecherous finger off and made a gesture indicating his room, frustrated with the annoying skip and deep, raspy tone her voice had developed since nearly being choked to death.

"Ah," he said, nodding. "My room. You think they were after me?" he whispered, his voice surprisingly tender.

He bent down and picked up the plastic lei. He held it out by a finger. "And they thought they could do it with this tacky, highly lethal thing? Or is it yours?"

Under other circumstances, she might have given him

a piece of her mind. But her throat ached. She was dead tired. And frustrated on too many levels to count. Instead, she gave him a gentle shove for insinuating she had poor taste. Which she did. In men.

He flipped on a lamp on the dresser. "Let me take a look at you. Make sure you're okay." He caught her in his arms and pulled her close so suddenly she couldn't protest.

As he brushed her hair out of her face with the strong square hand she used to love to hold and squeeze, she realized her sense of smell had returned. At a totally inopportune and weak moment. Not good.

He smelled like cologne, adrenaline, and pheromones. Not that you could consciously smell pheromones. But they must have been there or her body wouldn't be reacting as if pulling him onto the bed and breaking her vow of no sex with the nearly ex was a good idea. He gently tilted her head back and ran his hand down her throat.

Her pulse leaped in her neck as he leaned in to inspect her throat.

He clicked his tongue. "Tardieu spots." His warm breath brushed against her skin, reminding her of the Latin lover imitation he used to do to to amuse her. Throw her back over his arm, trail kisses down her neck . . .

Come to think of it, that move almost always ended in bed.

Tardieu spots. Concentrate on Tardieu spots, Treflee told herself as her traitorous body ached for his touch and goose bumps of delight rose on her arms. He was probably making that up, spewing something he'd once heard his mom, who was a pediatrician, say. He had a photographic memory, but he misapplied it when it suited his purposes.

He tilted her head farther back still, exposing the length of her neck, leaning in to her throat so closely she wondered if he was going to kiss her like he used to—from lips to everywhere.

In that insane, stunned moment she knew why vampires were such sexy and horrifying creatures. The neck, vulnerable and exposed, was a lover's dream, the ultimate triumph of trust. A whisper-soft kiss on it was erotic. A suck, a lick, love bite, brought shivers.

He continued his examination, moving his hand all the way down the length of her neck, over her collarbone, to the top of her trying-not-to-heave, or at least not obviously, breasts.

When he skimmed the tops of her breasts lightly with his fingertips and they budded up for him like spring roses, she came to her senses and pushed him away.

"Uuu . . . uuu . . . uuuu!" With no voice, she could only sputter her disapproval using soft vowel sounds.

Somehow he got the point anyway.

"You, you! Cad? Beast? Maniac?" He laughed softly, looking totally nonplussed and unapologetic. "No? Not the word you had in mind? Come on. I'm not good at guessing games. You have to help me out here."

She glared at him.

Smiling wickedly, he took her hand and pulled her toward the bathroom. "Nasty sputter. You need water."

In the bathroom, he ran her a glass of water and handed it to her. "Drink it. Slowly."

As she drank, he turned her toward the mirror and pointed out the deep purple-blue specks forming in a line across her neck. "Tardieu spots. We'll need a cover story."

"Wha . . . !" Those spots would not look good with a bikini! And since turtlenecks were pretty much out of fashion all year long in Hawaii . . .

Her eyes stung. This was all just too much.

"Ah, come on. Buck up, Tref." He put his arm around her. "Those tiny bruises don't look nearly as bad or as incriminating as that time we were naked in the hot tub in Palm Springs. You remember?"

Unfortunately, she did. With high-definition, oh-I-can-feel-it-do-it-again clarity.

He leaned in to whisper in her ear in a low, sultry voice, "I sucked on your lips." He stared at them in the mirror.

Caught in the memory, she licked them without thinking.

The hot water in the hot tub had made their skin ripe and flush; everywhere they kissed and sucked each other had left a hickey. She'd never had so many hickeys in so many delightful, and obvious, places.

"I sucked on your toes."

Her toes tingled at the thought as she tried not to wiggle them and definitely *not* to remember any more. Heaven knows he knew how to work her toes.

He stroked her cheek. "Your cheek." He nibbled her ear. She caught herself leaning into that nibble, almost hoping he'd thrust his tongue right in, too. As she arched her neck, it ached again, bringing her to her senses.

Damn that man! How did he have such sensual power over her?

She pulled away and pointed a finger at him in a stern movement that meant "Stop it!"

He looked totally nonplussed.

Back to business. She sniffed, waving her hands around wildly, hoping he caught her meaning—enough monkey business! And what do we do now?

She strode out of the room with him following and pointed to the phone.

"We can't call the cops, Tref. You know that."

Yeah, I do.

She gestured to the rooms next door, playing charades and trying to convey her concern for the others.

"They're safe enough. I'll get someone on it and make sure. But I got a good enough glimpse of your attacker to be ninety-nine percent certain he belongs to the guys I'm after. I doubt he'll hurt the others."

Her next question was tricky. She looked around for pen and paper. Not seeing any, she went to the bed and pulled the covers up, pointing at them.

He was quick on the uptake. "You're worried about my cover?"

She nodded.

"You think it's blown?" He shook his head. "Could be, but I doubt it. I've been hanging around some shady dudes, the kind who like to know who they're dealing with. They probably sent someone over to see if I was who I pretend to be. Suspicious bastards." He laughed. "It won't take me much to find out for sure what they were up to. In the meantime, my cover's been staged pretty thoroughly. There's nothing here to give me away." He paused. "Except you."

She flinched, mouthed the words "What about me?" and pointed to herself. Fortunately, he knew her well and got her meaning.

"What about you?" He shrugged. "Oh, that. They operate under the same principle as the Agency—leave no witnesses. I doubt he meant to kill you. Probably just wanted to choke you unconscious before you got a look at him."

Was that supposed to be reassuring? Somehow that "just" rankled her. That and the apparent fact that attempts on someone's life were an everyday occurrence for him.

He pointed to her neck again. "We either have to cover that up or explain it." He tilted his head and watched her with obvious caution in his eyes. "I vote for explaining. It's easier. But first I'm taking you to the emergency room to get checked out. We'll think of a story on the way."

No! She shook her head. She wasn't spending her one vacation this year in the emergency room. No way! She was fine. Unfortunately, she had no voice to tell him with.

"Yes, Tref. No arguing."

As if she could.

"Laryngeal fracture, hypoxia, edema to the neck, all

potential complications from strangling. We can't take a chance."

Nice to know he's so well informed on strangling, she thought.

He grabbed her hand and pulled her off his bed. "Now to get you out of here without anyone noticing. How do you feel about jumping off a balcony?"

CHAPTER FIVE

One balcony drop, two hours, and three X-rays later, they arrived back at the plantation. The emergency room doctor had given Treflee her diagnosis—she'd live—and prescribed rest.

Rest? No problem. Treflee was so exhausted Ty had to carry her from the car to the house like a groom on his honeymoon. Up the plantation steps, through the door, and to her room, where he gently deposited her on her bed and refused to leave. In true spylike fashion, he'd spirited them about as if they'd disappeared with the wave of a wand or maybe never even existed in the first place. Not a single soul had seen them either leave or enter. The man was good at his job. *Too good*.

Seeing the way he operated, Treflee realized he could have sneaked a dozen women in under her nose in her own home and she'd never have known. Not that she was the jealous type, but thoughts like these did cross her mind. James Bond had not given the spying profession a reputation for loving fidelity. And since Bond was a male fantasy, why shouldn't real spies, like her sexy husband, seize on the stereotype and grab that perk of the job?

Ty fluffed her pillow for her and plunked down next to her.

"Tref, no protests," he said when she signaled for him to get out.

She should have sensed something was up and staked out her territory before it was too late. He'd set her down squarely on the left side of the bed. *Her side*. When she had slept with him.

For the last six months, she'd taken up residence in the middle. And why not? There was no need to be stingy with the space of their queen-sized bed back home. Or this one here. It was her vacation. Her cousin was paying for this. She wanted all the space Carrie had bought her.

She glared at Ty, sorry she didn't know sign language. She didn't suppose mock sign language would do. Unfortunately, the only clear finger gesture she knew she was afraid he'd take as an invitation to avail himself of his marital rights.

As she opened her mouth to squawk, he shook his head. "Save your voice. You know I can't leave you alone until I know for sure what's going on. Maybe not even then. You got a glimpse of the guy. He may not be happy with that." He pulled off his shirt, revealing his very tanned, very buff abs and arms.

She told herself she wasn't attracted to very tanned men. No, not at all. They were skin cancer risks. Widowmakers.

He pulled off his shoes and slid off his slacks, revealing the pair of skintight boxers she'd bought him for their last anniversary. They'd always enjoyed a good romp on their anniversary, a celebration of the wedding night.

She did not look at the package those boxers wrapped. She refused to look, refused to check whether any interest had arisen in him.

He smiled and slid between the sheets.

She was still dressed in her cami and shorts. She'd been forced to wear them to the emergency room where

Ty had made up some ridiculous story about her running into a clothesline. Out for a moonlit exercise walk along the lawn next to the beach, and busy admiring the view, she'd walked straight into the temporary clothesline Mrs. Ho at Sugar Love Plantation next door hung up at night to air the spare linen.

Mrs. Ho was always forgetting to take it down when she brought the linens in. And since it was practically invisible in the dark, it posed a definite strangling hazard. Tita had complained more than once that sooner or later a guest was bound to stroll into it.

Just why did Treflee have to be that guest?

Of course Ty would make her look like the clumsy one. And she couldn't even refute him.

If there was any justice in the world, you'd have thought the emergency doc would have been the tiniest bit suspicious of that piece of malarkey. Maybe accused Ty of spousal abuse and given her a good laugh and a ha-ha moment.

No, of course not. Because Ty was a world-class liar. Everyone believed him! Even in the face of the contradictory, blatant truth.

No, he kept his cool and stayed in character, pretending to be the concerned tour guide who found her, collapsed and nearly unconscious from the force of hitting the line at power-walk speed, nearly hanging herself.

He'd convinced the doc of the story, adding all kinds of delicious details. Even saying he'd speak to the neighbor about the dangers of low-hanging, unmarked clotheslines.

"Morning?" Treflee managed to whisper, meaning how were they going to explain his presence in her room in the morning?

He caught her drift without her having to elaborate.

"No worries. I'll be out of here before anyone notices. I *am* a master at sneaking around."

She rolled her eyes. But he was right. No one would catch him unless he wanted them to. She slid under the sheet, pounded her pillow, and turned her back to him.

Apparently unfazed by her cold shoulder, he leaned over, brushed the hair away from her face, and kissed her cheek. "'Night, sweetheart."

Oh, brother!

"And, Tref?"

She cocked her head to indicate *"What now?"*

"Don't go rifling through my room again. It's futile. You'll only find what I want you to. And you never know who you'll run into."

"Point taken," she mouthed. Who knew, maybe he could read lips. Just in case he could, she added, "Stay on your side!"

He grinned and settled in beside her. She drifted off to sleep almost before her eyes closed. Later, she'd blame it on the sedatives the emergency room doc had given her.

Sometimes when you first wake up in the morning everything is dream-hazy perfect. Life is as it should be—soft sunlight filtering in, the rustle of palm trees against the window, a hint of orchid and plumeria perfuming the air, your husband's arm nestled gently around you—

Ty's home, Treflee thought as she smiled, feeling that wonderful sense of comfort and security his warm body next to hers gave her.

Then she remembered—

This wasn't then. And it certainly wasn't home.

Her eyes popped open. He woke up as she threw his arm off her.

She glanced at the clock on the nightstand. "Seven! You've got to go!" Hallelujah! She had a voice again.

Ty yawned and stretched, looking very much like the cuddly, sexy, she-could-just-run-her-hands-all-over-him-again-and-again husband she had once loved.

"Wow, love the new vocal tone. Sexy! Very Lauren Bacall. You ought to keep it." He pushed up on one elbow and ran a hand across her throat before she could react and stop him. "How do you feel this morning, my pet?"

Yeah, until he spoke.

"Out! And don't let anyone see you."

He gave her a look and rolled to a sit. "Judging by your warm, fuzzy attitude, you're feeling better, I can tell." He gave her a totally patronizing chuck under her chin. "Remember the clothesline tale."

"Sure," she whispered. "But I'm only spewing that bunch of baloney if someone asks."

"They will. Be prepared with details." He grabbed his pants, shirt, and shoes and headed for the door without putting them on.

She scowled at him.

"Just saying." He reached for the doorknob. "Today we hit the surf. Put on some board shorts, the shorter the better, and do you still have that black string bikini top?"

"Out!" She spoke in the tone she'd use on a bad dog. And he was, after all, wasn't he?

He laughed and turned the knob.

"Hey! Aren't you going to put those on?" She pointed to his clothes like a mother scolding a child.

"Hell, no! The ladies want a look."

He ducked out the door before the pillow she tossed reached him.

She clenched her hands into fists. *Curses, foiled again!* Nothing got to that man.

She sighed. Afraid you're going to be killed is no way

to live. She had to find out what Ty was up to, get her divorce, and get out of here. He could tell her not to have the divorce papers sent, but that didn't mean *she had to listen and obey*. Hadn't they nixed that obey bit from their wedding vows? And for good reason.

She still had six full days in Hawaii. She was going call her lawyer and ask him to send the papers. She fell back onto her pillow. She couldn't have the papers sent here to Big Auau. Plus she wanted everything unquestionably legal and done by the book. Her lawyer had contacts everywhere. Surely he had a lawyer pal in Lahaina he could send them to who'd make sure everything was in order. She'd simply have to find a way to pick them up.

First, though, she had to find a phone she could use without being detected. Ty still had hers.

She glanced at the door. Carrie had an unlimited-minutes plan. If she borrowed her phone to make a quick call, Carrie wouldn't mind.

A quick shower, an unauthorized entry into Carrie's room, and a hundred-and-fifty-dollar billable call to her lawyer later, Treflee came down to breakfast feeling slightly peevish about inadvertently obeying half of Ty's absurd command. She *was* wearing ridiculously Daisy Duke–short pink and black floral board shorts. She wouldn't have been wearing the shorts if she'd had anything less revealing and waterworthy on her. Or time to run to the local surf shop.

At least she wasn't wearing that black bikini top he liked. And yes, it was in her suitcase. Instead, she wore a skintight, short-sleeved, pink rash guard she'd bought for Hawaii back when she thought she'd need the sun protection. And that maybe attracting an appreciative male look or two might perk up her spirits while she waited for her divorce. Unfortunately, the rashie, being nearly as formfitting as a wet T-shirt, left less to the imagination than her string bikini top.

She heard Carrie and company laughing and talking as she came down the staircase and crossed the koa wood floors toward the dining room. What a gorgeous view of lawn, beach, ocean, and the hills of Lanai in the distance. So tranquil. So peaceful. Who could imagine someone had tried to kill her here last night? In the sparkling morning light, the whole thing seemed like a bad dream.

Surprisingly, her stomach growled. Fighting off death was hard exercise. Ah, a delicious breakfast of Belgian waffles soaked in coconut syrup was just the thing. No one ever had to call her twice where anything coconut was involved. But, wait a minute—was that hamburgers she smelled?

"Hey, sleepyhead! About time you're up," Carrie called to her as she lifted a forkful of gravy-laden something to her mouth. Carrie, of course, lived on military time. She'd probably done more before breakfast than most people do in a day. "Come have your loco moco, the breakfast of surfers, dude!"

She laughed at her own surfer imitation. "Seriously. This is awesome. Plenty of great protein to keep you on your feet and in the curl." She went back to shoveling it in.

Laci sat next to Carrie. "Whoa!" she said when Treflee got close enough for her to see her bruised neck. "What happened to you? You look like you've been in combat."

Before she could answer, Ty came in behind her. "Tre-flee, good to see you up and about." For the benefit of the table of women looking on, he appeared to give her shoulder a sympathetic squeeze, but she felt the warning in the way he pinched her unnecessarily hard. *Stick to the cover story.*

"Feeling any better?" He sounded completely concerned, the concern of an impartial and courteous stranger whose job it was to look after her. He gave her a quick shoulder rub and released her.

How in the world did he do that, affect that casual tone?

"Fine," she managed to croak in her newly found deep voice.

Carla put down her fork, put on her nurse's demeanor, pushed back from the table, and came over to Treflee for a closer look. "My gosh! It looks like someone tried to strangle you! Is that a flower-shaped bruise right there?"

Carla leaned in, breathing down Treflee's neck.

Ty leaned in, too. "That does look like a flower. Weird." He gave her shoulder another squeeze. "She had a run-in with a clothesline last night," Ty helpfully supplied for her. "Over on Sugar Love Plantation."

Tita ambled around the corner just then, carrying a plate of the suspicious-looking loco moco. "What! What am I hearing? Who was hurt?"

Ty repeated what he'd just told the group.

Tita upbraided him with a look. "And no one told me?"

"Why should I disturb your beauty sleep, *wahine*? I had it under control." Though Ty was behind her, Treflee could just picture him grinning and shrugging.

Tita set the plate down at an empty place at the table and indicated Treflee should sit, pulling out the chair for her. Carla returned to her seat. Ty let Treflee go. Tita patted her shoulder as she sat and shook her head at Ty, obviously forgiving him like a patient mother amused at his antics.

She made a grunt of disgust and put her hands on her hips, mumbling something in Hawaiian. "That Mrs. Ho and her clothesline! She does not embrace the spirit of *aloha*—compassion, love, and care for all."

Mrs. Ho isn't the only one with a lack of aloha *spirit.*

Tita shook her head. "She only thinks of herself. Always trying to one-up and outshine everyone else. She is not *ohana*."

"Family," Ty translated.

Tita made an elegant, graceful gesture reminiscent of the way a hula dancer describes a wave. "She thinks the ocean breeze is best there at the edge of our properties. She hangs the clothesline for her own linens and those of her special guests. She does not care for the safety and enjoyment of anyone else. I think she forgets to take down the line when the clothes are dry *on purpose*. She wants to hurt my guests."

Ty laughed. "Don't be a conspiracy theorist, boss."

Tita snorted. "She's very private and secretive. She doesn't believe in sharing." Her tone clearly indicated this was an affront to her personal belief system.

Tita inspected Treflee. "How are you feeling, *ipo*?"

Carla cut in using her no-nonsense tone. "Treflee needs to see a doctor."

Ty shot her a lazy look and winked. "Took her last night. Spent two hours in emergency."

"What! Where were we? Why didn't we know about your late-night run to the doctor?" Carrie's expression said she expected nothing less than disaster from Treflee.

Beside her, Laci looked decidedly unhappy with the bit of intel about Ty taking Treflee to the emergency room and spending so much time alone with her. You could almost see the wheels turning—how minor an injury could she withstand so Ty would have to play knight in shining armor to her damsel in distress?

Treflee knew of a strangler who might be available to accommodate her.

"It was late. I couldn't sleep and went out for a walk. You all were in your rooms. Ty came to my rescue and insisted I get checked out. There was no reason to wake any of you. The doc says I'll be fine." Treflee picked up her fork and picked at the loco this-can't-be-breakfast moco. Rice topped with a hamburger patty, covered with brown gravy, topped with a runny egg, sunny side up, and sprinkled with green onions, which floated unattractively on the yellow ooze.

Raw eggs? Not for her. Salmonella poisoning? No, thank you. Because of raw eggs, she never even ate raw cookie dough or cake batter and you knew those had to be delicious. She picked around as unobtrusively as she could and took a bite of rice as Tita watched.

Seeing her struggle, Tita took pity on her. "Your throat! Of course. Let me get you something softer from the kitchen. What would you like?"

"Scrambled eggs?"

"Coming up."

The doorbell rang. Tita frowned, then hefted her girth toward the door, mumbling about the presumption of early-morning guests. A young Chinese man stood on the lanai, carrying a large woven basket filled with an assortment of Hawaiian goodies generously sprinkled with plumeria flowers. Treflee had to crane her neck to see him.

"You have guest here by name of Tleflee Miller?" he asked in a thick accent.

"In the dining room," Tita said. "What do you want with her?"

Without answering, the young man sidestepped past her to the dining room. "Miss Tleflee Miller?"

Treflee raised her hand.

"From Mrs. Ho." The young man held the basket out to her. "She very sorry to hear of your accident and hope these gifts may help you as you heal."

The hair on the back of Treflee's neck stood up. *How did Mrs. Ho hear of my "accident"?*

Carrie shook her head. "News certainly travels fast."

"Mrs. Ho always knows what goes on on her property," Tita said. "She never misses a trick."

Ty seemed unconcerned and unsurprised by the arrival.

Which made Treflee wonder what he had to do with this sudden care-package delivery.

When Treflee didn't reach for the basket, Ty jumped up and took it for her. "Mrs. Miller doesn't have much of a voice this morning, but she thanks Mrs. Ho for her thoughtfulness."

The Chinese man nodded and departed before anyone could reply or question him further.

Tita shut the door behind him and came up to stand next to Ty, inspecting the goods. "Coconut oil, coconut soap, guava coconut lip balm, and Mrs. Ho's prize candied pineapple. She's very proud of that candied pineapple." She snorted. "Her cook makes it for her."

Treflee studied Ty. Boy, he was good! She was now *convinced* he was involved with the arrival of the basket. She should have been so proud of her husband. Somehow, in the middle of the night while waiting for her in emergency, he'd managed to convince Mrs. Ho the "accident" had occurred, in the first place, and was her fault, in the second. And had gotten her to send a gift basket as verification of the story. Or sent one himself.

Though the basket sounded like coconut heaven to Treflee, it brought up a tsunami of guilt. Unless Mrs. Ho had sent the strangler, she wasn't responsible for Treflee's injury and had spent a pretty penny for nothing.

Ty was staring at her, trying hard to telepath her cover story to her. His eyes pleaded with her to say something, for heaven's sake!

Oh, yeah, she should probably play along. "How thoughtful."

Tita waved a hand. "Thoughtful?" She shook her head. "No, Mrs. Ho thinks only of harmony and avoiding a lawsuit. You got hurt on her property. Her harmony is out of balance. For her own sake, she owes you something to make you whole. She should have come herself to make sure you're okay, not sent a boy with a basket."

"Speaking of the basket, I'll just take this upstairs for you." Ty turned.

"Wait! I'd like a look." Treflee tried to stop him.

"It'll be in your room."

This was the problem with being married to a spy. They were suspicious of everything. He was probably going to paw through it looking for bugs or who knows what. And she'd just bet he'd take the good stuff for himself.

Treflee let him go. She'd find out what he was up to later. She smiled at Tita. "Even so, I'd better write a thank-you."

"First, you eat. Or you'll never make it through your surfing lesson today."

CHAPTER SIX

B ack in Treflee's room, Ty ran his handheld bug detector over and around the basket and its contents. NCS
had been watching Mrs. Ho since before George's death.
The marriage-mart matron was the head of RIOT's
Hawaiian operations.

Unfortunately, the dragon lady Mrs. Ho's happy wedding establishment had so far proven to be impenetrable.
NCS hadn't been able to get as much as a delivery boy
in. The Agency was sure she was buying the Pinpoint
Project software from their rogue analyst Hal Rogers byte
by byte and sending it to the Chinese branch of RIOT
from Sugar Love. But NCS hadn't been able to intercept
it. Or get an invitation to tea.

The best NCS had been able to do was feed Hal bad
code and data. NCS had been trailing Hal for nearly a
year now. The guy was a low-level geopolitical analyst for
Langley. Flags went up when his bank accounts suddenly
unaccountably grew.

Hal worked on the Pinpoint Project, an analysis tool
that used both open-source and intelligence data to pinpoint the location of enemy fleets, satellites, and missiles,
and predict possible outbreaks of terrorism, violence, and

even war. Since RIOT's mission was to cause war between nations, in their hands, the tool would be a nightmare.

Last night, Ty had sent Greg, his fellow "tour guide" and NCS agent, over to stage an accident with the clothesline and complain to Mrs. Ho about Treflee being injured. Despite Greg's best efforts, she wouldn't let him any farther in than the entryway. He'd gotten few particulars about the layout of the place. The lobby looked pretty much like Big Auau's, a great place to hold a wedding reception.

As a result of Greg's encounter, Ty was staring at a basketful of Hawaiian body care products.

His bug detector lit up.

Bingo! An enemy bug was stuffed beneath the wood excelsior shred that filled the bottom of the basket. He swore to himself, removed the bug, and disabled it.

It was Chinese, of course.

There was no way to determine if it was from the MSS, the Ministry of State Security, China's intelligence agency. The U.S. and China had been "cooperating" to bring down RIOT. But neither side trusted the other. China wanted the Pinpoint Project, too, and was certainly working on their own version. But it was always easier to steal the Americans' technology. And nice to know your adversary's technology and capabilities.

The U.S., of course, had no intention of letting China get its hands on Pinpoint. It was part of Ty and Greg's mission to make sure China kept its hands off.

For their part, the Chinese were working with the U.S. to place an agent inside Sugar Love. Greg and Ty were awaiting a signal that they'd been successful.

Or the bug could have been courtesy of Mrs. Ho and RIOT.

RIOT, an association of terrorists, criminals, and crime syndicates, was headed by Archibald Random, a rogue

American with a hatred for the United States government and a genius IQ.

The Agency believed Random's ultimate goal was to rule the world. It sounded crackpot, but that didn't make Random any less dangerous. He was surprisingly cunning in his quest to control the world's financial markets, obtain weapons of mass destruction, foment unrest, disrupt the flow of oil, cause distrust between allied nations, and even greater distrust among foes.

RIOT had operatives in nearly every country. They mimicked foreign intelligence operations, pretending to be Chinese, Russian, American, Korean, Middle Eastern, Indian, South American, whoever suited their purpose at the time in order to best disrupt diplomatic relationships. Random would love nothing more than to start World War III and see the United States fall. He pictured a world where *he* was the superpower.

The bug also could have come from the Fuk Ching, the New York street gang with Mafia-like protection rackets that had recently been filtering into Hawaii. RIOT's mode of operation was to hire local crime organizations like Fuk Ching to do their dirty work.

Although George had certainly died at Shen Lin's hand, Ty's mission was to find out who was ultimately responsible for George's death—the Fuk Ching gang or RIOT.

Despite Ty's confident words to Treflee, it was possible RIOT had discovered his true identity and mission. Not probable, but possible.

Ty's cell phone beeped, indicating he had a top secret text. He logged in with his thumbprint to retrieve the message.

NCS confirmed that Treflee's Lahaina Lei Strangler was definitely Fuk Ching. Just as Ty had suspected. He'd seen the Hawaiian Fuk Ching gang's symbol tattooed on the attacker's neck. NCS believed the gang was checking Ty out, wanting to make sure he was who he said he was, and the operative they'd sent to do so encountered Tref unexpectedly in his room.

Good news. Sort of. Was Fuk Ching checking up on him on their own? Or were they doing so on behalf of RIOT?

Now Ty had a new problem—what did the Fuk Ching think of finding a woman searching through his room? Who did they think Treflee was? A jealous lover? A PI? A spy?

Damn that woman! He knew she'd go looking for her things. Which was why he'd hidden them and the strand of pearls he had bought for her. He just hadn't considered she'd cause this much trouble doing so.

They took a van to Lahaina. You'd think after the disastrous dinner cruise the night before, the mood would have been subdued. But, evidently after you've been to war, worked in an emergency room, or policed the mean streets of a city, a single dead body turning up is not enough to put you off your fun. Even if fish were eating his face.

Carrie and company laughed and joked as Treflee remained mostly mute and smiled along, plotting how to get to the Lahaina lawyer's office after ten to pick up the divorce papers her attorney had sent over. All she had to do was sign them in front of a witness at the office and then convince Ty to sign them sometime before she went home to the mainland.

Could a divorce be revoked or denied because one of the parties coerced the other into signing? Treflee really didn't care. What was Ty going to do, blow his cover?

Cheered by the thought, she smiled as they pulled up in front of the Don't Drop-in Surf Shop on Breakwall Beach oceanside of Lahaina Harbor.

"The Don't Drop-in? Not very spontaneous, are they? I hope we have reservations," Treflee observed.

Greg sat next to her, dressed in loud board shorts. He smiled and slid the van door open, hopping out to help the ladies disembark. " 'Dropping-in' is a surfing term."

"And it's bad form?" Treflee guessed.

"Impolite," Greg said in his sparse way of speaking. "Might lead to a fistfight."

Treflee nodded as he handed her out onto the warm beach grass. The time of year was the fall equinox, and it was only nine in the morning, but the sun still had power. Carrie had planned her wedding for September twenty-sixth, the first Saturday after the equinox. She had some weird notion about perfect balance and a feeling that being married on a day near the equinox would lead to a harmonious married life. Shows what she knew. She hadn't even made it to the altar.

That didn't necessarily jinx the twenty-sixth. Maybe it had just been doing its job restoring a balance to Carrie's life that the marriage would have messed up.

Ty piled out of the driver's seat and opened the back of the van, grabbing the ladies' beach bags. The lesson was supposed to last two hours and would be followed by lunch and more surfing or shopping. That's when Treflee planned to make her break for the lawyer's office.

"Looks like we have a perfect day today—sunny weather!" Ty said to the group, but he was staring at Treflee.

Though her heart raced at his words, she figured he was just pulling her chain, that he really was referring to the weather. In their code-speak, sunny weather meant "I love you." She ignored him.

There was a light breeze. The surf crashed in gently. Off in the distance, inside the surf break, a couple of middle-aged women stood on what looked like surf boards and paddled lazily with long paddles. It looked like heaven to Treflee, much more fun than possibly drowning in a wave.

She pointed. "That looks like fun! Can we try that?"

Seven pairs of eyes stared blankly back at her.

Ty shot her a half-cocked grin, handed her her oversized beach bag, and grabbed her arm, pulling her toward the surf shack. "Come on, Cousteau." The way he caressed the famed oceanographer's name reminded her of the inside joke they had about Inspector Clouseau and Cato. Purely intentional, she was sure. "You're going to love this."

"Last time someone told me that, I ended up seeing tiny fish eating a dead man."

Ty didn't even flinch.

Inside the surf shack, they signed a bunch of papers, the kind that say if you're maimed or killed, you won't bear any ill will toward Don't Drop-In or, more importantly, sue them out of business. The thought of dying in the surf, however improbable, was not pleasing to Treflee in the least. She still loved the idea of stand-up paddling.

After signing the papers, they headed to the beach where their boards awaited them, neatly arranged in a line in the sand. There were six girls, four Don't Drop-In surf instructors, and Greg and Ty, both of whom were also certified to give lessons.

Treflee hadn't even known her husband could surf, let alone teach. But she should have suspected it. He had brought several pairs of board shorts home from a mission one time, and there was the telltale hint of coconut oil on his clothes. Why had she imagined he'd merely lain passively around a boring chain hotel pool somewhere?

This was not the kind of mystery that kept a relationship fresh. This was the kind of mystery best kept mysterious because it gave Treflee another beef with Ty. Was he off surfing "on a mission" while she was back home taking the garbage out? That hardly seemed fair, whether she'd prefer to stand-up-paddle or not.

The instructors, whose names Treflee promptly forgot, but who would all answer to "dude," were an all-sorts mix of eye candy in various shades of tan, sun-bleached hair, six-pack abs, and relaxed flattery. Any one of them would have made a normal woman swoon. So why did Laci have to remain fixated on Ty?

Ty was, after all, a married man. Married to Treflee. And his explanation that he wanted to work with Treflee to keep an eye on her after her unfortunate dance with the clothesline should have sufficed. But, no. Laci had to give Treflee the evil eye.

For her part, Treflee would have traded instructors in a heartbeat if she thought she could have gotten away with it. But Ty was building up to something, some new chapter in his cover story, something that would give him closer access to Treflee. She was as convinced of this as she was that the ocean waves meant her ill will. She wasn't a good swimmer, after all.

She'd once almost drowned in six feet of water in the wave pool of a water park. To be fair, it was the fault of those darn floaty rafts. One knocked her under an on-coming wave and when she resurfaced another got her with a sucker shot. She took in a lungful of water and panicked, sinking into the water, unable to find a raft-free area to surface in. If Ty hadn't grabbed her and held her above the waves until the wave cycle stopped and the pool went calm, he'd be free to make a move on Laci right now.

Treflee stuffed that lovely bit of nostalgia back beneath the surface. She didn't like remembering she owed him her life.

After some general instructions on safety and basics, they found themselves facedown on their boards in the sand, digging for China. Using her hands as sand shovels didn't do her manicure any favors.

"Hey, toss me a real shovel and watch me make a sand-castle!" she called to Ty in her husky voice.

"Shut up and swim."

She cocked a brow. "Swim? Really? That's what you call this?"

The beach quickly filled with tourists and locals and other surf school participants. By the time they lashed themselves to their boards with a leash and got to practice paddling and mounting their boards in shallow water, Tre-flee was getting that crowded-wave-pool panic.

And Ty was getting a little too familiar with the way he was grabbing her butt and brushing her breasts as he instructed her and helped her back onto her board when she fell off.

"Act like you like this flirtation," he whispered in her ear. "We need an excuse to be together. We want the others to believe we're falling for each other."

"Are you crazy?" she hissed back.

He laughed for the others' benefit as if she'd just said something extremely amusing. "Don't blow all my hard work by scowling. Give me a little flirty smile. I know you know how to do it."

She glared.

"Fake it." He stood in the water beside her, leaning over her and putting his arms around her as he showed her the proper position to lie on her board.

"I never fake it."

He laughed again. "You never had to."

Now she laughed for real. "Cocky bastard." He was such an arrogant scoundrel.

"Okay, good." He brushed her breast and slid his hand down her leg to check her leash. "You're hot. You're wet. I think you're ready to mount."

The innuendo in his voice reminded her of sitting naked on him, breasts bouncing, hips undulating, her hair falling over her face and his as she bent to kiss him . . .

Shake it off, Tref! Remember this man is no good for you. Someone tried to kill you because of him!

She shook her head.

"Now remember. You ride goofy."

"Yeah, thanks for that shove in the back so we could find out," she said. They'd all stood in the sand and their instructors had given them a push in the back to see which foot they stepped out with to catch themselves. Left foot first is normal. Right foot first is goofy. Riding goofy foot means your right foot is forward in your stance on the board. Of course she was goofy. Clumsy and now goofy. She'd never live it all down.

"My pleasure, my goofy girl." He grinned. "Right foot forward when you get onto the board into the crouch. On the count of three . . . one . . . two . . . three!"

She hoisted herself up and on, screaming with glee as she rocked and fought to keep her balance. She did it! She did it!

Ty smiled up at her, and for just an instant, the ice between them thawed.

Laci's scream next to them broke the spell. Treflee turned just in time to see Laci topple into the water, creating a larger splash than a slender girl should make. Should Treflee really feel so happy about it?

Laci came up sputtering, her tiny string bikini top wet and plastered against her, barely covering her budded nipples.

Laci, fair skinned and lightly freckled as she was, should have been wearing a rashie. Treflee hoped she had some first-class sunblock on. If not, she was going to be a tomato by lesson's end. Ah, the price of trying to attract men with a skin show.

Laci refused to get back on her board. Instead, she swept her wet hair back in a weak imitation of a shampoo commercial and arched her back, showing off her ample breasts. She ignored her yummy, bronzed, sun-flavored instructor and appealed to Ty with a lame attempt at playing helpless. "Ty, could you?" She indicated her board.

Ty sighed and flashed Treflee an apologetic look. "I'll be right back. In the meantime, practice paddling out to the wave."

Treflee sat on her board, and turned to face the surf, practicing her paddling. The waves rolling toward her were small and gentle, baby waves perfect for baby surfers, no taller than three to four feet at their crest. So why did the theme from *Hawaii Five-O* play in her head along with the accompanying shot of that huge, deep blue curling wave?

You have nothing to fear but fear itself. Only she really didn't believe that and wished, for the first time all vacation, that Ty would come back. And hurry.

A man's voice interrupted her growing panic. "Looks like you're ready to tackle the big one."

She turned and stared into the exotic almond-shaped hazel eyes of the man from that ill-fated dinner cruise. The man who'd been staring at her then and was staring at her now as if she were a cup of fluffy cotton-candy-pink Hawaiian shaved ice.

"Oh," she said, wondering how he'd sneaked up on her. "I . . . where did you come from?"

He had a deep, rich laugh. He wasn't as handsome or buff as Ty or any of the other instructors, but he wasn't bad-looking, and seemed to have a larger vocabulary than "dude" and "awesome." Something about him drew the eye.

"You mean you didn't notice me paddling madly through the crowd toward you? I've wanted to meet you since last night on the cruise. And now fate has tossed me another chance."

"Oh," she said again, flattered. "That cruise is something I think we'd all rather forget. What a tragedy."

"Yeah, very disturbing." He nodded toward the small, meek waves rolling in. "Ready to try?"

"I'm only just learning," she stammered. "I've never actually been up before. They guarantee that here, to get you up on your board and surfing in your first lesson."

She glanced down at her board. She wasn't exactly flustered. She wondered, though, if she should seize this opportunity to show Ty she was moving on and considering other men. Maybe then he'd get the message that she was over him.

"I've been surfing since I was a kid." He nodded toward Ty who was trying, along with one of the dudes, to get Laci on her feet on her board. "Looks like he'll be tied up for a while."

He did a head tilt toward the surf. "The waves are perfect for a beginner right now and not too crowded. Wait much longer and it'll be harder to get up. You'll be fighting the crowds and only get a couple of rides in." He smiled at her. "Come on. I'll help you. I'm a great coach."

She bit her lip and glanced at Ty again, not liking the easy way he ignored her and flirted with Laci. She felt a sudden stab of jealousy and defiance.

Carrie paddled up beside her and gave the new guy a once-over. She flashed Treflee a conspiratorial look and said, "Who's your friend?"

Treflee looked at him helplessly and broke into a grin. "I don't actually know your name." She glanced at Carrie. "We just met."

"Oh." Carrie shot Treflee a look that said she didn't mean to interrupt.

"Halulu." He grinned. "Means to roar or make a racket. My mother's Hawaiian. She said I was born screaming. What else could she call me? My dad's a *haole*. He and all my friends call me Hal."

Treflee found his name story charming. "I'm Treflee. This is my cousin Carrie."

Carrie's instructor came up beside them at just that moment. "*Wahines,* time to stop posing and catch a wave. The surf is pure sex today!"

Treflee forced herself not to glance at Ty. Sometimes word association was a terrible thing. Instead she looked at the waves. They didn't look pure sex to her. He was probably trying to psyche them up. She eyed him cautiously. "Can you take both of us out at the same time?"

"Dude!" He winked at her.

"Well." Treflee shrugged. "How can I resist the pleas of two handsome men? Why not! Here goes nothing."

"Schweet!" Carrie's coach said.

Ty was using his hypnotic you'll-do-what-I-say voice on Laci to calm her down. A famous Hollywood hypnotist to the stars had taught this technique to him one afternoon in Vegas. Unfortunately, it had never worked on his wife.

Laci was clinging to him, nearly choking him, as she pretended fear of the water. If that woman had a fear of anything it was ending up in bed alone at the end of this day.

He glanced up to see Treflee paddling out to sea with one of the instructors, Carrie, and—

His heart stopped and he felt himself losing his legendary unflappable cool. She was paddling out with Hal Rogers, the Langley geopolitical analyst and suspected traitor Ty had been watching. The man who was selling top secret software to RIOT. A man who in all likelihood had aligned himself with the Fuk Ching gang, and besides selling his country out, was somehow implicated in George Hsu's murder.

Treflee knew how to pick them. This was both perfect and perfectly disastrous. Treflee could be his in to Hal, his unsuspecting mole. The man looked like he wanted to eat her up, which made Ty want to punch him out. How was Ty going to win Tref back while encouraging her to encourage Hal? How was he going to keep Hal out of her pants? And keep her safe at the same time? All without blowing his cover?

Damn it all!

CHAPTER SEVEN

Carrie's instructor paddled with the three of them out to where the surfable waves broke. The technique was simple. You sat on your board facing the waves until you reached the right spot. As a wave came toward you, you spun around to face the shore down on your board. When you felt the current of the wave catch you, you pushed up to a crouch—and you were surfing!

"Here comes da kine," Dude said above the roar of the surf. "Dudettes, spin!"

Treflee spun her board toward shore, heart pounding, surfer music going through her mind, trying *not* to think about wiping out. She lay down on the board.

"Wait for it," Dude called above the roar of the surf. "Wait until you feel it."

"*How* will I know?" Treflee yelled back.

"It's like love, dudette. You know it when you feel it. It sweeps you away."

Totally unhelpful analogy. What did she know about love? She was on the brink of a failed marriage. Her heart pounded. She felt sick with excitement and dread. And then she felt the wave swell, felt the crescendo, and the motion swept her up.

The trill of excitement. The pulse-pounding thrill. The

giddiness. This was it! She pushed to a stand, teetered, caught herself just before losing her balance and going over. She bent into her goofy-foot crouch. She was riding a wave!

Dude was right! It *was* like love. Like intimate love-making with your soul mate. She laughed and whooped. She was surfing! Surfing!

That whoop almost cost her her balance. She wobbled and corrected, vowing to concentrate. *Stay on your board, baby! Ride this thing for all it's worth!*

She caught a glimpse of Carrie on her board beside her. Out of the corner of her eye, she saw Dude and Hal give her a thumbs-up. She focused on her reference spot on the shore.

Unfortunately, in the foreground of her beautiful focal palm tree, Laci was throwing herself at Ty as he tried to get her up on her board.

Curses! Treflee wobbled, corrected, and bobbled, pointing her board directly at them. *Wouldn't it be awesome to wipe them out?*

She laughed. *Wicked woman!*

Adrenaline and evil thoughts kept her on her board all the way to shallow water near shore. Fortunately for them, Laci and Ty moved out of her way long before she reached them. Concentrating like crazy, Treflee dropped to one knee, held on to the rails, then stepped off into the water, laughing.

Hal pulled up beside her with an idiot grin on his face. "Dude!" he said, imitating the instructors. "You're a pro!"

"Finally! Something I'm good at."

"I bet you're good at riding lots of things." Hal winked at her.

The way he said it should have made her blush.

Carrie dropped off her board beside them.

Carrie's instructor dude paddled up. "Juicy, huh! Again?"

"Oh, yeah!" Treflee said in unison with Hal and Carrie.

The four of them turned to paddle back out. After several more successful rides, instructor dude left to watch them from a distance. Hal stuck with Treflee, who couldn't get enough of riding the surf.

All too soon, the instructor signaled them from shore and yelled, "Last wave, dudettes! Then lesson's over."

"Hey." Hal cleared his throat as they paddled out for their last ride. "Have lunch with me?"

The question took Treflee by surprise. She'd been having so much fun, she hadn't really even been thinking of him. She'd just met him. A refusal danced on the tip of her tongue. He was attractive and fun, but . . .

Lunch should be safe enough and just the ticket she needed to get into Lahaina to see her lawyer. Lunch, lawyer appointment, grab her papers, and rejoin the group in time to catch the van back to the plantation.

"Sounds perfect. I'd love to."

With that, they paddled out.

Laci and Ty paddled up beside them. If Laci didn't get up on her board this time, the Don't Drop-In was going to have to refund her money.

They paddled into the surf, waiting for da kine. Treflee saw one she wanted. She was on the inside and had the right of way. She spun her board and Laci, poser fakey extraordinaire, snaked in and cut her off. Treflee had to drop out and wait for the next wave as she watched Laci take to her feet like an expert and cruise toward shore with Ty surfing beside her.

The little bitch! Treflee shouldn't have been so jealous.

She spun her board around without paying much attention to what was going on around her and caught the next wave, picking out her reference-point palm tree onshore.

A Chinese man stepped from behind it and trained a pair of binoculars on her. She froze, feeling the hairs stand up on her neck as the ocean spray misted around her. He could have been bird-watching, or thought she was particularly juicy, but . . .

His height, his posture, there was something sinisterly familiar about him—

Wham! Something slammed into her board from behind. Treflee lost her footing and went flying face forward into the foam as the wave kicked her butt. Her board flipped, still attached to her ankle by her leash. As she hit the water, it koshed her on the back of the head. She saw stars and fought to hang on to consciousness. Above her, sunlight filtered through the crystal-blue water, illuminating the sharklike silhouettes of surfboards cluttering the water above.

Afraid of being hit again, she panicked and sucked in a breath full of water. *This is it! I'm going to die. Be sucked into the bottomless depths of the ocean never to be found again.*

A second later, a strong pair of arms grabbed her and pulled her to the surface. She gasped for air and came face-to-face with Ty, mesmerized by his eyes, which sparkled with confidence, encouragement, and possession.

Déjà vu! Her world tilted off kilter, just like it had the first time she'd ever seen him. Just like it had the last time he'd saved her from a wave pool.

Another wave hit them, nearly knocking them over.

She gulped in a mouthful of water. Ty shoved her board into her arms, pulled her into his arms and held her over his head into the open air as the wave crashed over them.

She took a deep breath, shaken by her own emotional response to him. Hero worship. Gratitude. That's all it had to be. That's all she felt for Ty.

As the wave rolled by, Treflee realized Ty was *standing* in just over five feet of water with her in his arms and her board still lashed to her ankle in hers.

He pulled her close and started walking toward shore. "I can't take you anywhere."

She trembled. "I'm bad with waves." She started to sputter.

"Hang on. Take a breath, baby. Here comes another one." He took a deep breath and lifted her up above the water, her Herculean hero, toward the sun as if making an offering of her.

For her part, she was happy to worship the sun, feel it on her skin, and breathe in the fresh marine air as the wave crashed beneath her around Ty. It was good to be alive. Good to be in Ty's safe, strong arms above the danger.

When it ebbed, he brought her down, clutching her to his chest, and started walking again.

"How come you didn't get out of the way when that girl lost control and barreled right into the back of you? These waters are full of beginners. Didn't we warn you to keep a sharp eye? I waved at you and pointed for you to watch out. Didn't you see me?"

She stared at him. "I didn't see a thing."

He frowned. "You have to pay attention, Tref. These are dangerous times. You can't be oblivious."

She knew he didn't just mean the surf around them. "I *was* paying attention, until Laci snaked in and cut me off." After that, she'd been preoccupied with trying to catch the next wave and then . . .

She shivered. Another wave rolled past them, but by now they were in shallow enough water that her head stayed above water as she cuddled into his chest.

"The Lei Strangler was watching me from the shore," she whispered into his chest and pointed.

Ty glanced in the direction of her finger. There was no one there.

She frowned. "He's gone now."

"That's a long way off. Are you sure it was him? You

barely got a moonlit glimpse of him last night." She could tell he was trying to be reassuring. "It was probably just some guy admiring the view, thinking what a juicy dudette you are."

Why did her heart still flutter when he complimented her? Why did it beat with the same high she felt riding a wave? She peered into his eyes, wishing . . . for what? For things to be different? For him to be a different kind of man? The kind who preferred a nine-to-five office job and quiet evenings at home to playing James Bond?

She shook her head. "It was *him*. The man from last night."

"You barely got a glimpse of him," he reiterated. It was almost a command. A Jedi mind trick—this is not the Chinese man you're looking for.

"It *was* him, Ty. I'm telling you. I remember the tattoo."

His arms tightened around her. "What tattoo?"

"A large Chinese character on a background that looked like a jagged red lightning bolt. It covered most of his neck."

They reached knee-deep water. Hal, Carrie, Carla, and the instructors ran out to meet them, cutting off further conversation. One of the instructors carried a first-aid kit. He unleashed her board and took it from her. The others waited on shore with anxious expressions, crowding around Greg for reassurance.

"Give her some air," Ty said as the group clustered around them.

Carla directed Ty to put Treflee on a beach towel someone had laid out for her. He put her down as gently as the concerned, loving husband he used to be. She hadn't even realized she'd been clinging so tightly to him until he pried her loose. She let go then, embarrassed and confused as he squatted in the sand beside her.

Carla crowded in, hovering above Treflee. As she stared

into Treflee's eyes, she mumbled something about how this was supposed to be a vacation, but with Treflee around there was no danger of her nursing skills getting rusty.

A reed-thin Chinese girl burst through the crowd to hover next to Ty. She waved at Treflee hysterically, pointing and saying something in Chinese.

Seeing her, Treflee realized she must have been the person who'd knocked her off her board. She started to tremble uncontrollably.

"She's upsetting my patient," Carla said in the impatient, imperious tone of an emergency room doctor. "Get her out of here."

Ty stood and took the Chinese girl's arm, whispering something in her ear that seemed to calm her. He handed her off to Greg, who had been standing with the others. He returned to Treflee's side as Greg led the girl away toward the surf shack.

"Her eyes aren't dilated." Carla took Treflee's pulse. Why do nurses always do that? It was pretty obvious Treflee was alive. "Do you hurt anywhere? Did you hit, bump, or pull anything when you crashed?"

Treflee pointed at the back of her head. "My board hit here."

Carla felt her head like a phrenologist reading Treflee's future, only all she found was pain.

"Ouch!" Treflee rubbed her head where Carla had probed.

"You've got a big goose egg."

No duh!

When Carla finished her examination, she pulled a bag of instant ice out of the kit and opened it, squishing it between her fingers to activate it. She handed the bag to Treflee. "Ten minutes ice on. Ten ice off. Repeat. You're lucky you weren't really hurt. You should be fine."

"Dude, you ate some good foam!" Carrie's instructor

dude said from the sidelines, as if trying to encourage her. "No worries. Every surfer eats foam." He nodded. "It's like part of the experience."

Carla closed up the kit and shooed Ty away from Treflee. "Give her some air. She'll be fine."

Laci sidled up and clutched Ty's arm, whispering in his ear as she pulled him away after Carla dislodged him from Treflee's side. Teaming up on Treflee—no fair!

Ty could have resisted. He was her husband. He had a right to be by Treflee's side. Instead, he glanced down at Laci and gave her a flirty smile. It hurt watching him jump back into character so quickly after her near-death experience.

Yeah, she knew it was his job.

As the others moved off, Hal plunked to a sit next to her in the sand. He looked embarrassed. "Sorry I didn't get there first." He glanced at Ty.

Treflee shot Ty a quick glance as a swell of jealousy overcame her. "You're here now." She smiled at Hal, trying to quell her surge of anger at Ty for deserting her for the job. "Don't feel bad. It's his job to look after me. Us. He's one of our tour guides while we're here on vacation this week. I'm sure there are liability issues."

"Ah," Hal said, sounding amused and somewhat reassured he hadn't lost her interest. "I suppose you'll want to take a rain check on lunch?"

She glanced at Ty and his beach barnacle Laci, and the others who had started gathering up the equipment from the beach. "I'm feeling better."

"What you need is a little one-on-one attention." Hal turned around.

"Hey, tour guide," Hal called out to Ty. "Mind if I take this one off your hands for a while and feed her lunch? I promise to watch her closely." He reached over and squeezed Treflee's hand. "At the first sign of head trauma

or concussion, I'll rush her to emergency. Scout's honor."
He laughed.

Ty studied Hal and shrugged. "Whatever our guest
wants. The van leaves for the plantation from King Street
at one sharp." He turned back to Laci as if he hadn't a care
in the world about what Treflee did or who she saw.

Treflee stared after him, her heart in her stomach,
fighting back against her hurt feelings.

"Well?" Hal asked, hope and anticipation dancing in
his eyes.

Damn Ty! She thought they'd been reconnecting. She'd
thought . . .

Well, she was a stupid little fool for considering putting off the divorce for one second. What could she say?
She needed an excuse to get to that lawyer's office.

She smiled at Hal. "I'd love to. Where do you have in
mind?"

Ty watched the spark fade from Treflee's eyes as he gave
Hal the okay to take her to lunch. The moment was over.
He'd killed it. He cursed his job and its conflicting missions. He'd blown it. For now. He'd make it up to Tref
later, rekindle the moment. Find some way to explain.

She wasn't over him. He'd seen her eyes light up when
he'd mentioned sunny weather. It had just been a quick
spark. There and gone. But he'd caught it and it gave him
hope. She still wanted him, no matter how much she protested. She hated the spy lifestyle as much as he loved
it, but she was as trapped in it as he was.

He'd get the mood back. But right now, he needed Treflee to play spy for him.

He caught up with Greg in the surf shop's men's changing room, the only place totally safe from Laci. He hoped.
He wouldn't put it past Laci to "accidentally" wander in
for an eyeful.

Greg, his spying NCS cohort in crime, was just stepping into the communal shower.

Ty got out of his wet trunks. He stepped up to the showerhead next to Greg and lathered up. Despite the pretense, surfing wasn't Ty's favorite thing. He liked riding the waves, but hated the sticky feeling of dried saltwater and sand on his skin, which itched and stung.

With the white noise of running water for cover, he filled Greg in. "Tail Treflee. I'd do it myself, but I can't take the chance of either Hal or her spotting me."

Greg shook his head as he soaped up. "Dude, I can't believe you sent your wife off to have lunch with that traitor. I thought I was supposed to be her nonthreatening escort while she's here?"

Ty shrugged and rinsed his hair. "It was the opportunity of a mission."

"You're a stronger man than I am." Greg turned his shower off and reached for a towel.

"Just don't let her out of your sight, Mr. Master of Disguise."

"Whatever you say, boss."

Later at the van as Greg helped him load up the gear, Ty dropped a bug and tracking device into Treflee's beach bag.

If that slimebag Hal tried to take any liberties at all, Ty would be on him before he knew what hit him.

Hal drove a red Porsche Boxster convertible, accelerating away from the clunky plantation van as they pulled away from the surf shop. *If the car makes the man, we're off to an excellent start,* Treflee thought, trying to console herself and move on from Ty.

Hal drove the short distance into the heart of town with the roof down and pulled to a smooth stop in front of a cheeseburger joint on the waterfront.

He came around and opened her door for her, offering her a hand out of the ground-hugging car. "They make the best grilled pineapple cheeseburger on the island and serve their famous tropical salsa as fry sauce." He leaned in and whispered into her windswept hair, "You'll love it!"

Treflee smiled back at him and ran her fingers through her hair. After icing her bump, she'd showered and changed into a tank, shorts, and rhinestone-studded flip-flops at the surf shop.

Hal was almost too good to be true. He'd picked the perfect restaurant for the way she felt and was dressed. "I'm starving. A burger sounds like heaven."

He took her hand and pulled her toward the entrance. "In that case, welcome to the Pearly Gates."

She liked his sense of humor and couldn't help smiling. Funny how smiling can make you feel better all by itself.

Inside, the hostess led them through the kitschy bamboo-walled interior to the back terrace overlooking the ocean. She seated them in the shade of an awning where the pop music that blared inside provided a pleasant background ambience and allowed them to talk without shouting.

Hal held Treflee's chair out for her, an endearing, chivalrous move in such a low-key establishment. One thing Treflee was definitely looking for in husband number two was a man who took care of her.

"Wow! Look at the view. So crystal clear today. You can see Lanai as if it were right next door." She sat and stared at the view a second longer, trying to get a grip on her emotions and forget about Ty. "I like this place already. Do you eat here often?"

"Whenever I can." Hal went around the table and took a seat.

The hostess handed them each a large, laminated menu complete with cartoon drawings, and disappeared.

Treflee smiled at him as sexily as she knew how, testing her rusty flirting skills—anything to reassure herself she was still attractive and desirable, even if Ty had pawned her off on another guy.

She gazed at Hal with what she hoped was a totally enthralled look, imagining the way she used to look at Ty before things went sour. "You know, I know *absolutely* nothing about you. Other than you look great in board shorts and can surf a four-foot wave like a pro."

He laughed, obviously flattered. "Hey, I have skills. I can ride *way* bigger waves than that. I can even create a few." His tone nearly made her blush. She had the feeling he wasn't speaking strictly of ocean waves.

"Oh, I bet you can," she said, still staring at him as if he were pure beefcake. "Are you here on vacation? Or are you a local?"

"Neither and both. I was born and raised here on Maui," he said, studying her in the intense way of a man who's interested and admiring. "I live on the mainland now. Virginia. I'm here on business. Seeing an important client."

"Important client, huh?" Treflee picked up her menu and pretended to study it. "Is she young and beautiful?"

"Would you be jealous if she was?"

She lowered her menu just enough to peek over the very top of it at him. "Maybe."

He grinned, looking pleased. "Old. Definitely not blond and *gorgeous* like you."

She liked the way calling her "gorgeous" rolled off his tongue. Treflee looked down at her menu and smiled as the waitress brought them water and took their drink order. Hal ordered them each a Maui mai tai and asked for hers in a pineapple mug.

When Treflee shot him a quizzical look, he answered, "You look like you could use a souvenir, a reminder of your surfing victory." He winked. "The glass comes with the drink. The mai tai will clear your head and mellow you out."

A clear head sounded like a terrific idea, but alcohol usually had the opposite effect on her. Worse, even as she smiled at Hal, her initial ire and jealousy of Laci were starting to wear off. Never a good thing when you're a married woman out on a revenge date with an attractive, interested guy. Too easy for guilt to creep in. Like she was the cheater, here.

Maybe that ice pack had really worked. As she studied the menu, she began to think more clearly. She was suddenly suspicious—why had Ty been so eager for her to go to lunch with Hal in the first place? How was he so sure no lei strangler would get hold of her? Or that Hal wasn't some modern-day Ted Bundy or an enemy agent out to kill her?

Could it be Ty wanted her out of the way while he was off playing spy games?

Palming her off on a date, who'd gladly play guard unawares, probably seemed like a good way to keep her occupied, out of trouble, and out of his hair.

It also wouldn't surprise her if Ty had planted a tracking device or a bug or both on her somewhere. She knew good and well that after the attack last night he wouldn't leave her totally unprotected. And she'd lived with him long enough to suspect him of any spy trick.

In case Ty *was* listening, she'd have to be careful not to mention anything that would give away her plan to pick up the divorce papers.

"Have you decided?" Hal asked her.

She looked up.

He laughed. "You look perplexed. Too many choices?"

She smiled. She'd have to be more careful about letting her thoughts bleed onto her face. "Everything looks good."

She set the menu down. "I think I'll have to go with that pineapple cheeseburger you mentioned."

"Good plan."

She put her napkin in her lap and smiled into Hal's eyes as she brushed a strand of breeze-blown hair out of her face. "Now that that's settled, I want to know everything about you, Surfer Dude."

"Everything?" He arched a brow. "You sure? That's a tall order."

She shrugged and teased back. "Well then, just start with the icebreaking essentials. Tell me about your job. What are you doing for this client of yours?"

"Oh, that's top secret." His tone was joking and flirtatious.

He'd probably fallen prey to that old adage about a bit of mystery being good for a relationship. How could he know how much she hated top secret business?

"Seriously!" she said. "What business are you in?"

"I work for the government."

"Ah." She nodded. Government workers weren't high on her list right now, especially the kind with high-level clearances and a license to kill.

He picked up on her lack of enthusiasm. "But I run a small consulting firm on the side. I'm a geopolitical analyst."

As she stared at him, the hairs on the back of her neck stood up. A government geopolitical analyst from Virginia, as in right down the street from CIA headquarters at Langley? Too much coincidence. Seriously, what were the odds?

Her smile felt frozen in place. All the enjoyment of flirting and having Hal drool over her faded away.

Ty had set her up and prostituted her out to spy for him. Who was Hal really—a traitor, a mole, an enemy agent, a terrorist?

She tried to cover the shock she'd let slip on her face by playing dumb. "A geopolitical analyst?" She frowned, trying to look confused. "What is that—like a red state, blue state determination kind of thing?"

Hal laughed. His eyes lit up with excitement. "Hardly. Think global."

What she really thought was that she could kill Ty with her bare hands. No way was she doing his spying for him. Bastard! At the first opportunity, she was out of here. *Date over.*

Hal kept talking, trying to impress her. "Geopolitics covers a wide scope—everything from determining where war is most likely to break out to how to use cultural norms and politics to penetrate a new market opportunity."

She said the first reasonable thing that popped into her head that she thought would shut him down from telling her anything more about what he did. "You must travel a lot."

Now she was certain Ty was listening in. Maybe even watching her from behind a palm somewhere. If he'd managed to ditch Laci. She'd have to be very careful about picking up the divorce papers now.

Just what did Ty want to know from this guy? Whatever it was, she was determined *not* to find out.

Hal smiled, oblivious to her new lack of enthusiasm, or maybe trying to rekindle it. "I've been to Hong Kong and Taiwan. Earlier this year I spent several months in Beijing."

China? A cold shiver crept up her back. Way, way, way too much coincidence. Think dead Chinese waiter.

"How interesting." Her tone was flat.

"It was. Fascinating culture." He paused, probably sensing her waning interest. "Are you interested in the Orient?"

She shrugged. "I've always been more of a Western enthusiast."

He studied her, confusion creeping into his face about what he'd done and where he'd gone wrong. She could see he was beginning to worry he was losing that loving feeling.

She had a moment of doubt. What if he was just an ordinary guy? And if he wasn't? Just what kind of a dastardly fiend was she dealing with? She'd have to be careful. She couldn't upset him or tip him off to her connection to Langley. She channeled her limited high school drama skills and changed tack, putting a smile in her voice. "Tell me about this client of yours—not part of your government work, is she?"

His smile brightened. He looked relieved he'd piqued her interest again. "No, no! She's one of my private sector clients. I've been consulting with her, giving her the advantage of my analysis skills. I've developed a special software tool for her.

"In fact, I'm delivering it on Saturday. Getting a big payoff and then I'm partying." He reached for her hand. "How about joining me?"

Ty sat in a Lahaina surfer bar that should have been featured on *Diners, Drive-ins, and Dives* in the dives category. The food was cheap, plentiful, and tasty. The bar was crowded with tattooed, well-built surfers, both male and female, eye candy as far as the eye could see, all hitting on each other. The guys were mostly shirtless. The girls wore skimpy bikini tops. The place smelled of beer, sweat, and coconut oil. The perfect spot to take Carrie and company for lunch to continue the surfer fantasy–themed day after their lesson.

Greg begged off to tail Treflee, which left Ty in charge of the henhouse, most of whom he hoped would be diverted by the surfer dudes around him and leave him alone to do his job. Zulu Fong, Fuk Ching gang leader, extortionist, suspected arms dealer, and rumored to have been Lin's boss, just happened to frequent this particular dive. In fact, he currently sat in a corner booth, shirtless, displaying an elaborate flying red dragon tattoo that covered his chest and curled around to his back as he held court. The Hawaiian Fuk Ching gang symbol was tattooed on his forearm.

Zulu was young, no more than thirty, taller than your average Chinese man, and taut with stringy muscles and sharp eyes. He was also arrogant.

Before leaving the surf shop, Ty had received a message from Langley. Their informants said Zulu ordered the hit on Shen Lin at Woo Ming's. He'd wanted it bloody and served up midday. He was sending a message. But just what that message was eluded Ty and NCS. Why had Zulu put a hit out on his own man? Just how had Shen Lin screwed up? Like RIOT, the Fuk Ching didn't tolerate failure. Failure to do the job resulted in death.

Laci sat next to Ty at the round table. Carrie sat on his left. The other girls circulated. Laci made a lame attempt to get him to take off his rashie and blend in.

"Ah, come on," Laci coaxed. "This place is really more of a 'no shoes, no shirt, plenty of service' type of place. Don't be so stuffy! Maybe our waitress would actually bring out our order if you flashed a little skin." She pouted. "I'm starving."

"A shirt's considered stuffy now?" He only listened to Laci with one ear. He tried not to frown as he listened to his wife flirt with that scumbag Hal through the earpiece in his other ear.

Carrie took a swig of her beer. "Leave him alone, Lace. Personally, I like a modest man. Anyway, he deserves his peace after saving my cousin from certain drowning." She smiled at him, a wan, tired smile that stopped just short of her eyes.

He noticed she didn't smile a whole lot.

"You saved my ass," she said to Ty. "Mom would kill me if I didn't bring her favorite niece home in one piece."

Hal's attempts at hitting on his wife floated through the earbud. Ty was used to this split personality, "living two lives at once," kind of existence. He still felt like taking a slug at the guy. It took all his acting skills not to let his anger show in his face.

If he'd had any sympathy, he would have told Laci to take a hike. Her cause was lost. And old Hal needed a few pointers in seduction. The guy should know upfront that intrigue did not turn Tref on. And when it came to the intrinsic sexiness of top secret work, Ty had the idiot beat hands down.

Instead, he joined Carrie and took a long pull of his beer, shifting in his chair to face her when he was finished. "Your mom's favorite niece, huh? Is that why you brought Treflee along?"

Carrie arched a brow and shook her head. "What are you saying, big guy?"

He chuckled as he moved his foot out of a sticky patch of spilled beer on the concrete floor. "You two don't seem that close. I'm just wondering why you chose her to be one of your bridesmaids and invited her here. Family obligation?"

Laci snorted and scooted her chair back. "I'm going to the ladies' room while you two discuss Carrie's wack-job of a family. Please be done with this conversation by the time I get back." She stood and strode off.

Carrie sighed. "Forgive Laci. She hasn't had much luck with men lately. She's becoming bitter."

"Maybe because she comes on a little strong?" Ty added.

Carrie smiled and this time it reached her eyes. For the first time he saw a family resemblance to Treflee in her.

Carrie would be an attractive woman if she smiled more. "Yeah, maybe that's it. She's trying to live up to her red hair."

Carrie paused and studied Ty. "I saw the way you looked at Tref out there when you rescued her."

Ty's heart stopped. *Shit! Was I that obvious?*

"I like you," Carrie continued. "You seem like a nice guy, so let me clue you in. Pending divorce aside, Treflee loves her husband."

Not what it sounded like from the lunch date she was having. He gulped, trying to remain cool and uninterested.

"Yeah, she may deny it." Carrie set her beer down and ran her finger around the rim. "But I'm a cop. Give me five minutes in the interrogation room with her and I'd have the truth out of her.

"Tref's a romantic, a dreamer, a girlie girl, and stubborn. She was crazy about Ty. Happy. Almost glowing." Carrie threw up her hands.

"Then for no reason, she snapped. Went all reclusive for a while. No one knows why. She wouldn't say. Claimed she was fine. But I bet there's a story behind it. There always is."

Carrie had his full attention now. He'd noticed the change in Tref, too. He'd thought he was the only one who had, that she was like that just around him. That she'd gone pissy over him being gone so much.

"She started ranting about how tired she was of all his traveling. Though she'd been supportive before. She got this idea it was time to pop out a kid or two. For him to stay home and be a father." Carrie shook her head. "Though his sense of adventure was obviously what drew her to Ty in the first place.

"Call our whole clan hopeless romantics, but no one in the family gets why she's throwing away the love of her life because he's not ready for a baby yet." She shrugged again. "Hell, maybe he never will be." Carrie looked him directly in the eye. "I've never met him. But my mom and aunt, Treflee's mom, tell me it's obvious he loves her and doesn't want this divorce. Whether he ran out like a coward or not.

"I'll tell you this. I'd rather have a man who loves me by my side for life than a dozen kids." She paused. "If I had to choose one or the other."

Ty swallowed hard. He felt sorry for Carrie. The woman obviously hid a tender side beneath her tough-girl exterior. He wondered for just a second why she'd dumped her fiancé. It wasn't his business to ask.

Carrie stared at him again. "To answer your original questions—I asked Tref to be in my wedding as a favor to my mom and aunt, and because she's my closest family member. I dragged her along to Hawaii for her own damn good.

"She wanted to stay home and read." She shook her head. "Tref needed an escape. Needed to get her mind off things. I figured if she experienced the fun of travel and adventure, she'd see things through Ty's eyes and reconsider."

Whoa! A hidden ally, Ty thought, wondering how he could make use of her.

Carrie sighed. "I'm hoping she'll get a big dose of the single scene." Her voice dropped. "And see it's no picnic, either. Having a loyal man around one week out of four is better than no man at all."

He knew he should say something to comfort Carrie. But he had no idea what. And besides, the voice in his ear was saying the delivery was going to go down on Saturday.

Whoa! Way to go, Tref! My wife would make an ace spy.

Over at Zulu's booth, it looked like court might be over and they'd be moving out.

Fortunately, Carrie bucked up without help. "The whole family's angry with Tref for pursuing this divorce. We're secretly rooting for Ty. My mom and hers are sisters. They both adore Ty. I want to see them and her happy.

"Despite Treflee and me sometimes seeming like oil and vinegar, we're family. I'd give my life for my cousin. Do anything to protect her." She paused again, giving him a look that reminded him of a protective father at the trigger end of a shotgun.

"Back to my point—I saw the way you looked at Treflee. It wasn't lust I saw. You thought there was some connection, something more going on."

Carrie tilted her head and frowned as if in thought as she studied him. "I've only seen a few photos of her Ty. You bear a passing resemblance to him."

Ty's mouth went dry as he fought to stay in character, hoping Carrie didn't make the connection that he *was* Tref's Ty.

"Which probably explains part of the reason she's attracted to you," Carrie continued.

He tried not to let his relief show. "You're saying she doesn't just like me for me?"

"I'm just telling you, if she wants to have a fling with you while she's here, if that's what she needs to realize how foolish she is, that's fine by me."

Carrie pointed her finger at him. "Just don't hurt her or you'll answer to me."

He held up his hands and protested. "Hey, no worries—"

"Can it," Carrie said. "I know what I see. And while you're at it, I wouldn't lose out to that Hal character. I don't like him."

Just then there was a commotion at Zulu's table and he rose to leave. Fortunately, the door to the ladies' room was down the hall just beyond where Zulu sat.

Carrie followed Ty's gaze and laughed. Damn, that

woman was good. He'd have to be careful around her and remember she had the instincts of both a warrior and a cop.

"You're itching to escape before Laci gets back." She didn't pose it as a question. She waved her hand at him. "Go! Make your escape. I'll get the girls back to the bus on time."

He smiled back at her. Tref had always complained about her cousin, but Ty liked her. Maybe someday he'd tell Tref what a gem she had in Carrie. "You sure? It doesn't take much for these bruddahs to go aggro."

She rolled her eyes and gave him an "oh, please" look. "Go, surfer boy. You may have brawn, but I can take grown men down and cuff them before they know what hits them. I can handle things here."

He believed her. He pointed at her and smiled. "I owe you." He turned to leave and make his escape.

"Damn right!" she called to his retreating back. "I'll make your excuses."

Outside the bar, he waited in the shadows to follow Zulu.

CHAPTER EIGHT

Treflee ate only half her pineapple cheeseburger. Ty's shenanigans and having to fend off Hal while not totally offending him had killed her appetite, though nothing seemed to dull Hal's ardor. Not even revealing that she was going through a messy divorce and was an emotional wreck right now. He evidently liked a good chase. Or maybe he was relishing some hot sex as the rebound guy.

She glanced at her watch. Just half an hour until the van left. If she wasn't on it, Ty would come looking for her. She didn't have much time.

Hal smiled at her. "Time flies!"

She nodded, trying to sound mildly disappointed. "It's almost time to catch the bus."

"Don't worry about that. I'll drive you home."

No way was she going anywhere alone with this guy. Not even to his car.

She smiled coyly at Hal. "That's sweet of you. But I *have* to be on that van. If I'm not, my cousin Carrie will kill me." She pretended to pout. "She's paying for this vacation and expects us all to do exactly what she wants, when she wants." She'd told him about Carrie while they ate.

Just then Hal's cell phone rang. He glanced at the

number and then looked at her apologetically. "I have to take this."

He excused himself and walked to the end of the terrace to take the call.

Treflee seized the opportunity and flagged the waitress. She showed her the address she had for the lawyer's office. "Do you know where this is?"

"Sure. It's just a few blocks up the street off the waterfront." She gave Treflee quick directions.

Luckily it's close by.

Hal returned to the table.

Treflee stood before he could sit. She pulled a twenty from her purse and tossed it on the table. "It's been fun, but I've got to go. Hell hath no fury like my cousin."

As she turned to leave, he grabbed her arm. "Wait! Don't forget this." He handed her the pineapple mug and pressed her crumpled bill into her hand, running his hand over her bare arm. "I had a great time today. Lunch is on me."

His touch gave her the creeps. She shuddered and dropped the bill and the mug into her bag, eager to break away from him.

Hal misread her shudder as a sign of sexual interest, goose bumps of delight. "When can I see you again?"

"Carrie has a full schedule planned." She tried to sound helpless, like not being able to see him was beyond her control, a gentle brush-off. She didn't want to ever see him again, but she didn't want him trying to strangle her for dissing him, either.

"We can work around that." He gave her arm a squeeze and released her. "I'll call."

She smiled, relieved he didn't have her number. "Thanks for lunch." She turned and started walking.

"Hey! What's your number?" he called after her a second too late.

She acted as if she didn't hear and kept walking, trying hard not to break into a run.

Treflee raced up the street. By the time she reached the Ailaini Building, she'd broken into a nervous sweat. Fortunately, Hal hadn't followed her. Espionage was the pits! She was so going to give Ty a piece of her mind when she saw him.

Speaking of Ty, she had another problem. If he had a tracking device on her, he'd know exactly where she was. And if he'd planted a bug on her, he'd hear her ask for her divorce papers. The thought gave her almost as much anxiety as having lunch with Hal, the probable bad guy.

Unfortunately, she had no debugging equipment on her and would have had no idea how to use it if she had. Her best bet was to think up a good cover story—quickly. She spotted a souvenir shop and dashed in to buy a few postcards. She could always claim that's what she'd been up to.

Back on the street, she decided the most likely place to plant a bug was in her bag. Just outside the store, she dumped the contents of the bag onto a bench and quickly riffled through her stuff. No obvious bits of tracking electronics stood out to her.

She dumped her stuff back in her bag. She'd just have to keep her fingers crossed.

She hurried to the law office. What exactly was she going to say when she got there that wouldn't give her away if Ty was listening in?

A middle-aged woman sat at the receptionist desk. Treflee introduced herself, still wondering what to say.

"Treflee Miller, you say?" The woman smiled and pulled a sheaf of papers covered in the traditional blue lawyer's folder from her out-box. "I suppose you want these?" She opened the papers and handed Treflee a pen. "I'll be your witness."

The receptionist pointed to indicate where to sign. When Treflee was finished, the receptionist took out her notary seal and made her official mark. "His needs to be notarized, too."

Treflee nodded, hoping that if Ty was listening in, he hadn't heard the words "his" and "notarized." If he had, he'd be sure to figure out what she was up to.

The receptionist scooped the papers up and handed them to her.

Treflee thanked her. "What do I owe you?"

"It's taken care of."

"Great!" She stuffed the sheaf into her beach bag next to the pineapple mug and slid the bag over her shoulder.

In her hurry to get back to the van, she wasn't paying attention to where she was going. As she burst out of the law office into the hall, she bumped into a tourist wearing a straw hat. Or maybe he bumped into her. Hard to tell.

He steadied her with a hand on her shoulder. "Excuse me!"

"Sorry! My fault," she said.

He nodded and they moved on.

One of the straps of her beach bag had slid off her shoulder. She pushed it back up as she headed out to catch the van.

Well, that went amazingly smoothly! She smiled to herself. *Order me not to send for them—right! As if Ty could stop me. He isn't quite as smart a spy boy as he thought.*

When *was* the best time to spring these babies on her imperious, spying husband? Probably just before she disappeared through airport security. She smiled to herself.

The others were already loaded up and waiting as Treflee approached.

Ty shot her a grim look and jumped out of the driver's seat to hold the door open for her.

Gee, what a gentleman.

"What happened to your date?"

She shot him a deadpan look. The last thing she needed was him taunting her right now. But it was so like him to poke at her when she couldn't retaliate. "As if you don't know. I'll deal with you later."

"I hope so," he said.

Treflee climbed in the van and Ty slammed the door closed behind her. Safely buckled in her seat, she patted her beach bag next to her.

Mission accomplished.

As the van pulled up to Big Auau, they were greeted by a Chinese explosion—suitcases, trunks, purses, boxes, and bags, and milling people covered the lanai and the lawn halfway to the beach. Tita stood on the lanai trying to shoo the Chinese away as if they were gulls who'd come begging for bread.

Ty and Greg jumped out to investigate. Treflee and the girls followed them.

"What's the problem, Tita?" Ty yelled.

"*Haole!* Thank goodness!" She waved over the crowd as she used her girth to block the door. "They won't go away. I can't make them understand there's been a mistake. We're booked."

She waved some papers at him. "They keep shoving these at me and pointing. But they're all written in Chinese." She threw up her hands.

Ty ran up, took the papers from her, and scanned them.

Treflee frowned at him. *Of course he can read Chinese! But will he give himself away?*

He pointed at a line on one of them. "Here's the problem. Someone typed the wrong address."

Tita squinted where he pointed and nodded, looking relieved.

Oh, good cover, Treflee thought, impressed. Her husband was a pro for sure. He'd found the one bit of English on the page. She was certain he could read every Chinese word.

"I'm guessing they belong with Mrs. Ho. Why don't you go give her a call?"

"You block the door," Tita commanded. "Don't let them in. They're pushy and rude. I'll never get rid of them." She frowned as she relinquished her position and waddled off to phone Mrs. Ho.

Then for some unknown reason, call it post-traumatic shock, at the sight of all those Chinese people, Treflee began to shake uncontrollably. First a hooded Chinese man had tried to strangle her, then a Chinese teenager nearly drowned her, then her lunch date had a Chinese connection. What if this crowd of innocent-looking Chinese tourists hid another killer?

Greg appeared at her elbow. "You look pale. Are you feeling okay? Is your head bothering you?" He took her arm. "You look like you could use a lie-down. Let me take you to your room."

Ten minutes later, Mrs. Ho arrived, shouting, "这是怎么回事儿" *[zhe shi zen me hui shier?]*

Ty understood quite clearly. *What's the problem here?*

He'd also read the travel documents and seen the coded message he'd been looking for—there was a Chinese agent among the newly arrived tourists.

He listened in on Mrs. Ho's conversations with the tourists, playing as if he couldn't understand, as he and Greg unloaded the women's gear from the van. Unfortunately, the woman didn't let anything slip.

Fifteen minutes later, Mrs. Ho had rounded up her guests and whisked them off to Sugar Love.

Five minutes after that, Ty rendezvoused with Greg on the beach. "The Chinese agent is in place at Sugar Love. We're to await word from her." He told Greg the code words to expect.

"Excellent," Greg said, but he didn't sound as enthusiastic as he should have.

"What's up?" Ty asked.

"I just got a message from Emmett. Langley just discovered that Hal somehow managed to get good code and data last time."

"What!" Ty scowled. *Another complication. Just what I need.*

Greg nodded, sympathetic. "We have new orders. On the volcano tomorrow expect a drop from one of our guys from AMOS. He's bringing you a data card with bad data. We're supposed to swap it with Hal's."

They discussed the orders and formulated a new plan before returning to the recent Chinese invasion of Big Auau.

"We're going to have to sweep the grounds," Ty said. "Make sure none of the Chinese planted a bug."

Damn, I hate these mundane bug sweepings.

"Already called the exterminator." Greg glanced at his watch. "He'll be here soon."

Ty nodded again and took a deep breath of fresh salt air. "What about Treflee?"

"What about her?" Greg grinned.

"Come on, man," Ty said.

"Insecure bastard!" Greg's grin deepened. "She had lunch, then ditched the guy to buy some postcards in a dive of a shop not far away."

"Postcards?" Ty cocked a brow. "For whom? Dear old mom?" He frowned. "I don't think so. Hal mentioned Virginia and government work and she turned to ice. She's on to me. I think she's up to something." He was impressed. He'd underestimated Tref. He hadn't thought she'd catch on to his game so quickly, if at all.

Greg frowned. "I wouldn't let my wife near that piece of shit Hal."

"I didn't ask for commentary." Ty paused. He'd been distracted by his conversation with Carrie and hadn't caught everything. "Did she kiss Hal good-bye?"

Greg shrugged. "Ask her yourself." He turned and walked off. A few paces away he paused and looked back over his shoulder. "All the commotion when we arrived upset her. She looked pale. I took her to her room. You better check on her."

Treflee had recovered enough to get control of her senses again. No wonder she didn't like intrigue. She couldn't believe she'd developed a phobia of Chinese people. Ridiculous! She was certainly no racist and she refused to be. She'd fight this phobia with everything she had. First, though, she had business to attend to.

She let the curtains fall back into place in front of the window where she'd been watching Ty and Greg from her room. They were out on the beach talking.

They looked way too chummy. Which made her doubly suspicious of Greg. He probably *was* an NCS agent. She wondered if Tita was, too. Next time she got a chance, she was going to ask Ty. Not that he'd tell her if he didn't want to.

Back to the task at hand. With Ty occupied, now was the time to hide the papers.

She glanced around the room, looking for the ideal spot.

Under the mattress with her locket? Too obvious? Maybe. But then again, he didn't even know she had the papers. Why would he be looking for them?

She grabbed her beach bag from the chair where she'd tossed it and opened it up, smiling with the thrill of success and power as she peered in.

What? Her mouth went dry. *Where are they?*

Her hands were ice, shaking as she rifled futilely through the bag, fighting off the trembles.

Noooo! My pretty blue legal file is gone! Disappeared.

She dumped the contents of the bag on the bed and pawed through them as if dumping the bag would make them reappear. Pineapple mug, lipstick, sunblock . . .

No divorce papers! They were gone, gone, gone! All gone!

Oh, no, this can't be. She was in big, big trouble now. If those papers fell into the wrong hands . . .

Thirty minutes later, Treflee had searched her room, the lobby, and the grounds—no papers. She stood in the shade of a magnolia tree next to the plantation van and hit the electronic key to unlock the dang thing. This was her second reconnoiter of the van. The first time the thing had been locked tight.

She'd already peered through every window, trying every angle and contortion she knew to try to get a look under the seat or down the crack between the seats. At least the papers weren't flaunting themselves openly in plain view. Finally, she'd had to go to Tita with a lame story about leaving her pineapple mug in the van. Could she have the key so she could retrieve it?

Fortunately, Tita had been distracted and mumbling something about having to send Mrs. Ho a gift to make up for ill-treating her guests. And she'd have to deliver it personally because that's what you did, not send over some errand boy. She hadn't asked a single question, just handed over her car keys and asked Treflee to bring them right back.

As Treflee slid the passenger door open, her beach bag slid off her shoulder. In it was the trusty mug. She pushed the strap back up. Every good spy needed to keep up the cover and avoid suspicion. If Tita asked about her success, Treflee would produce the mug. A glow of happiness wouldn't be out of place.

Treflee hoped Ty hadn't cleaned out the van.

If Ty found them first . . .

Better not to think about that.

She scoured the van—the seat she'd sat in, the surrounding seats, everywhere. Nothing!

She took a deep breath and tried to reassure herself.

So what if they were lost? What damage could those papers do? Seriously. They were simply papers that, when properly signed and notarized, voided the marriage of Elizabeth and Ty Miller. Floating around loose in the world, how could such innocent-looking papers possibly blow Ty's cover?

The more she thought about it, the more she came to the conclusion that Ty had overreacted about her sending for them. That really, unless someone actually saw her stuffing them under his nose, or saw him signing them, or compared his signature on them to one of him playing Ty Smith, what harm could they do?

Ty had always been able to pull one over on her and make even the most outlandish story convincing. That's the way he was, why he was successful as a spy.

But it sure seemed like he didn't want a divorce. What other reason did he have for not signing the papers and making her a free woman? Maybe he really did still love her?

The thought sent her heart racing out of control. Sometimes hope and optimism were abysmal companions.

Even if he loved her, Ty was still Ty. He didn't want a baby. And she couldn't tell him why it was so important to her to have one. Why she *needed* one. Right or wrong, she'd kept that secret too long. Telling him now would only hurt both of them and make things worse.

And even *if* he loved her, he didn't love her enough to put her above the job. So it was all futile and pointless.

Seriously, if you loved a woman, did you throw her unsuspecting into the arms of an enemy spy, mole, or all-around bad guy and listen in?

Yes, she was still peeved at him. And better off without him, even if her heart protested, she reminded herself.

She weighed her options. Embarrassment and cost aside, she could simply ask for another set of papers. Which would have been a perfectly reasonable thing to do *if* she thought she could get away with picking them up again without getting caught. But more importantly, as she scoured the van, getting more desperate by the second, she became convinced that she hadn't dropped the papers and they hadn't fallen out of her bag. She'd been so careful, had clutched her bag so tightly.

She sat on the van floor and went back over every move she'd made since picking them up. She had put the papers in the bag at the lawyer's office. Hooked the bag over her shoulder. Not so much as even one strap had left her shoulder until she'd looked in the bag in her room and the papers were gone.

Except for when that stranger bumped into her and one strap slid off . . .

She felt a sudden chill that wasn't due to the cool shadow of the shade or the ocean breeze coming in through the open van door.

Why would someone pickpocket my divorce papers?

Treflee wasn't in her room. Ty went looking for her. He spied her searching the lobby and grounds for something. He tailed her when she asked Tita for the van keys.

Concealed in the trees, he watched Treflee toss the van. Time to shake things up.

Treflee stepped out of the van and slid the door closed, heart pounding. She'd been carrying her wallet full of cash and credit cards in the bag. The thief had ignored it in favor of a bunch of legal papers?

No, she'd stepped into something deep and sinister. And she wasn't sure what it was or what to do. Her mind elsewhere, she spun around and started. "Ty!"

He stood not five feet away from her in the shadow of the magnolia, eyes dark and searching as he dropped his cloaking device and spoke. "Looking for something?"

She hoped he didn't know about the divorce papers already. But she wouldn't put it past him to have had her followed and ordered the theft himself.

He stepped toward her. She kept her chin up and tried not to give her fear away.

She still wasn't used to the goatee and shaggy blond hair. He always came home from his missions clean shaven and with his hair his natural color. So normal seeming and routine. The new look gave him a dangerous, sexy edge, as if he were a man she didn't know, but reacted to all the same.

She flushed. "Found it."

She pulled the plastic pineapple mug from her bag and waved it at him. She felt like flaunting it in this handsome husband-stranger's face. How dare he send her out on a dangerous date and still think he had the right to spy on her? "A little souvenir from lunch. *From my date.*"

Before she could react, he grabbed the mug from her and slammed it into the trunk of the tree. It hit with a thunk that made her jump and tumbled to the base of the tree, where it rolled to a stop.

"Hey!" she protested, and lunged forward to retrieve it. "That's mine."

He caught her arm and stopped her. "Cheap. And probably bugged." He spoke evenly and calmly, with that tone he used to charm people. "That should give whoever's listening in a headache."

Because she knew him so well, she saw the almost imperceptible tick in his jaw and the slight thinning of his lips. He was angry. Or jealous. *And he doesn't know about the papers. If he did, he would have accused me as soon as he smashed the mug.*

Relief only reminded her of why she was mad at him.

"Ass!" She shook his hand off and glared at him. "Don't send me off to do your spying again. I could have been hurt or kidnapped."

"Don't be so dramatic. I taught you how to take care of yourself."

She frowned at him. "You didn't give me a weapon. Or a warning." She took a breath to calm herself. "Just who is Hal?"

He shrugged. He didn't have the good grace to look contrite or even make a lame attempt at denial.

When he didn't reply to her question, she grew madder still. "And don't flirt with that redheaded ditz my cousin calls a best friend in front of me again, either. I thought the cover story was supposed to be you and me"—she pointed between them—"having a flirtation. What happened to that plan?"

Wrong thing to say. His eyes lit up and he took a step into her, pressing her up against the van door. Heat radiated off him, giving life to his cologne and the smell of sand and sun on his skin, igniting feelings in her that she was trying to forget.

He smelled like Ty. He felt like Ty. *Her* Ty. Her heart skipped a beat.

He lowered his voice. "You want flirtation . . ."

He lifted her long hair off her neck and ran his fingers tenderly through it.

A breeze cooled and kissed her neck. She quivered, remembering a hundred other times he'd stroked her hair in a way that made her feel like the sexiest woman alive. He hadn't lost the knack.

"Poor, bruised baby. Don't be angry. I had you covered." With one hand, he softly stroked the ringed bruise the lei had made. "When I catch who did this, he's going to pay." He caressed the words, making the threat sound like a declaration of his undying love for her.

He lowered his lips to her neck and softly trailed kisses up toward her ear while a breeze cooled her neck.

She shivered, mesmerized. He knew what she liked. It had been so long since he'd kissed her neck like this. Kissed her *anywhere* like this. She must be crazy. Yes, she was crazy, but she didn't push him away. She leaned into him.

And then, out of the corner of her eye, she caught a glimpse of red hair and fair sunburned skin as Laci stepped out onto the lanai. Laci's head turned, and she froze. Yes, Laci definitely saw them. All Treflee's possessive instincts kicked in.

When Ty let her hair drop to run his hand along her thigh, she relaxed into him. She sighed as he kissed her jawline and turned her head into his kiss until his lips found hers. She wrapped her arms around his neck, welcomed his tongue to dance in her mouth, and pulled him into her.

This was her Ty, and just as he knew how to kiss her, she knew how to kiss him. She ran her fingers through his tousled hair, traced the soft, delicate rims of his ears with her fingertips, ran a fingernail lightly down the back of his neck until he shivered beneath her touch, and pressed her breasts against his rock-hard chest.

This was her Ty, but new and exciting. She'd never kissed a man with a mustache. Never kissed *him* with a mustache. Deep down, she realized that's what made its tickle erotic, the scrub of his beard tantalizing.

He cupped her butt and pressed his pelvis against hers until she felt his hardness. She tilted her head, opened her mouth more fully to him and kissed him back, deeply, with all the hunger she'd felt since coming to Hawaii.

He let go of her bottom and put one hand behind her head, tantalizing her with his tongue as he took the offensive, holding her as if he'd never let her go.

She looped her arms around his neck and moaned softly, losing all track of time, all track of everything but Ty.

"Uh-hum." A man cleared his throat.

Thanks to Ty's skill with his hands, lips, and tongue, she hadn't even heard the man approach.

Ty dropped his hand from her neck. She pulled back from him guiltily and looked at the ground.

"We should probably get a room," Ty whispered in her ear. "Your bed. Tonight. Don't lose the mood." He took her hand and squeezed it.

Then he dropped her hand and turned to greet the man with an exterminator logo on his shirt who'd just walked up. "Hey, dude. What'd you find? Are we being overrun with roaches?"

Saved from my own folly by the exterminator.

Heart pounding wildly, Treflee turned and walked away, toward the plantation house. She was so confused by her reaction to Ty, she barely registered that Laci had disappeared from the lanai. Why should she be so disappointed by the appearance of the exterminator and having to cut their act short? Ty had just been running with the cover story, hadn't he? He was joking about bed. He had to be. But she was shaking.

Halfway to the house, Faye and Brandy ran out to greet her. They flanked her, joining her in lockstep. She acknowledged them with a nod of her head.

"Going back to the house?" Faye asked.

Ignoring the warning look Treflee shot them to leave her alone, Brandy caught her arm. "I wouldn't go in there just now. Laci is hacked off at you."

"At me?" *So she had seen.* Treflee slowed down. "Why? What have I done to her?"

From her other side, Faye cleared her throat. "She thinks you're poaching."

Poaching? Poaching! Treflee wanted to scream. Poaching her own husband, stupid pigheaded man. She was trying her best to get rid of him. Sort of.

She opened her mouth to give them a piece of her mind, and shut it again just as fast. Call her patriotic or simply foolish, but even as upset and confused as she was, she couldn't out one of the U.S.'s top spies. She refused to be involved in a Valerie Plame–type affair.

"I didn't know she was so into Hal," Treflee said evenly instead. "All we did was have lunch."

Brandy applied enough pressure on Treflee's arm to draw her to a halt. "She saw you kissing Ty."

Treflee took a deep breath. "*He* kissed me." She shrugged and shook her arm free from Brandy's grasp. "He's a player. Half his job around here is to flirt with us."

"It's a big deal to Laci," Faye said. "Look, we aren't the enemy. We're just trying to help you out and keep the peace around here. Laci's great on so many levels. Really a good, loyal friend. But she's possessive about guys. You don't cross her. Things get ugly."

Brandy nodded along as Faye talked. "Why don't you

take a nice stroll on the beach until the storm clears? Give us a little time to talk her down."

Treflee's gaze bounced between the two of them. She didn't care two nickels if Laci was hacked off. "I'm going to my room."

She strode off toward the house. The other two girls hung back.

Just inside the door, Laci confronted her. "I saw you kissing Ty." She blocked the way to the stairs and rooms above.

"Yeah?" Treflee tried to push past her.

Laci was a brick house, totally unmovable. Her green eyes flashed wildly with fury. And her sunburned face turned an even darker shade of red. She should have worn sunscreen. She was going to pay for her folly with a fresh batch of freckles.

Treflee held her ground, getting angrier by the second that some other woman had designs on *her* husband. For as long as Ty refused to sign those papers, he was still hers, which gave her the right to kiss him if she damn well felt like it.

She glared at Laci. "It was just a kiss."

She meant it. Contrary to what Laci thought, it *was* just a kiss. Treflee would be a fool to think it was more.

Without warning, Laci shoved Treflee. Caught off guard, Treflee tumbled back against the wall, rattling the house and knocking a hanging glass vase full of plumeria off its hook in the process.

The vase crashed to the floor and shattered on the hardwood just as Tita waddled into the room from the kitchen, carrying a large gift basket filled to overflowing with home-baked goodies, fruit, and macadamia nuts. "What's this!"

Laci backed off and away from Treflee. Treflee shook herself, a prize fighter loosening up after a blow.

Tita set the basket down on a sofa table and surveyed the damage. "What happened?"

Laci shrugged. "Sorry." She pointed to the mess. "Put this on my bill." She glared at Treflee and stalked off, leaving her to explain.

Treflee squatted to pick up the pieces of glass and avoid Tita's intense gaze. "Vacation jitters." She tried to laugh it off, make light of it. "She got too much sun today. She got burned. Badly. She could use some aloe from your garden."

"I'll cut some for her and bring it up to her." Tita put a hand on Treflee's arm. "Leave it. You'll cut yourself. I'll call the maid to clean up." She reached beneath Treflee's arm and tugged to pull her up.

When Treflee stood, she found Tita studying her. "This is about Ty?"

The woman was perceptive. Treflee nodded.

Tita shook her head and let out a deep sigh, mumbling beneath her breath in Hawaiian. "Fighting over a man is bad business. When will you learn, my little *ipos*?" She shook her head again. "It will only get you into trouble."

CHAPTER NINE

Treflee begged off the afternoon and evening activities to rest. But there was no rest for the weary.

Carla popped in to check on her when she got back from snorkeling. "You shouldn't have crossed Laci. The girls warned you." She checked Treflee again for late-breaking signs of a concussion from her smack-down by the surfboard. "She's making life miserable for all of us! You don't know how she can pout and rant."

Treflee had a fair idea.

Carla pronounced her concussion-free and sat on the edge of the bed next to her, pleading with her. "Look, I know you're going through a bad divorce. Hot guys falling all over you has to be a big boost to the old ego." She paused, looking like she was trying to properly frame her words. "But what's a vacation romance to you, in the long run? It's not like it's going to last."

She has no idea. Still, Carla's words stung.

"You have the handsome Hawaiian-looking guy," Carla continued. "Can't you just let Lace have Ty to herself? Let her sink or swim on her own without competing with you?"

As if she were a femme fatale, a siren who could turn men on or off with a glance! Carla's faith in her should have been flattering, but uncontrollable jealousy aside, Treflee faced a dilemma. Wanting to oblige and stay as far away from Ty as possible on the one hand, and forced to stick to a cover story that Ty might decide to renege on again at any second on the other. All weighed against her own safety. Face it, she needed his protection. Which meant staying close to him no matter what.

Treflee bit her lip. "I wish it was that simple." *Too true.* "But I can't give him up just now."

At dinner served family-style in the plantation dining room, Ty was absent. Greg presided and happily announced, "Get to bed early tonight. The van rolls out of here for the volcano at four A.M. sharp! We don't want to miss the sunrise at the House of the Sun."

"Four A.M.!" Treflee stared at him. "You're kidding?"

"Nope. Sunrise is at six-fifteen. Two-hour trip. Do the math." He grinned. "Dress in layers for cool-weather bike riding. It'll be thirty degrees colder at the crater than down here. Bring your overnight bag, rain gear, and camping clothes. We'll be tent camping near Hana tomorrow night. Weather looks great. Nothing but sunshine in the forecast, but things can change quickly up on the mountain and on the windward, tropical side of the island."

"Bike riding! Camping!" Treflee turned to glare at her conniving cousin. "You never said anything about bike riding and tent camping."

"Last-minute change of schedule just before we left. It looked like fun." Carrie shrugged. "Be glad we're driving to the top of Haleakala and riding down, not the other way around."

"I didn't bring bike-riding gear."

"Don't worry." Carrie winked. "They provide mountain bikes, helmets, pads, and rain gear." Her smile widened. "I brought an extra pair of bike shorts you can borrow."

Yeah, great consolation. Carrie was two sizes larger than Treflee. A new suspicion dawned. "Just how long is this bike ride?"

"Twenty-eight miles." Laci spoke from across the table to her for the first time all meal, radiating enjoyment over Treflee's dismay. "What's the matter? Not in shape for a downhill cruise?"

Treflee wanted to smack her, or even merely tap her lightly on those red, burned shoulders of hers.

Carrie interceded. "Anyone under ninety who's ridden a bike in the last twenty years can make this trip." She smiled at Treflee. "You'll do fine."

Maybe. But not at four A.M.! That was strictly Carrie's territory.

And how in the world was Ty planning to protect her in a tent?

She had visions of sharing a sleeping bag. *Oh, boy! Best not to think about that.*

At ten P.M., Treflee lay in bed, staring up at the ceiling fan lazily turning. She'd showered and set the alarm for three-thirty. Five and a half hours—way too little sleep for an eight-hour girl like her.

Dead tired, bruised, and sore, she couldn't sleep. Living a spy's life was too complicated. She'd bungled everything, including her relationship with Laci. The last thing she needed was Laci as her enemy. She had enough of those already.

And more than her share of bruises. The ones on her neck had gone from red to deep purple. And now she had bruises on her head, arms, hips, thighs, even her butt, from her surfing adventure.

Her skin was dry from the salt water. She'd slathered herself in the coconut oil from Mrs. Ho. And put the guava lip balm on her lips to avoid sun chapping. She wore her cami and shorts. Trying to feel somewhat sexy and less like a disaster site, she'd spritzed on her favorite perfume, with the result that she smelled like a well-perfumed and somewhat exotic fruit salad. Try as she might, she wouldn't be able to sleep until Ty rattled the door and tried to break into her room.

Oh, yes, she knew he'd give it the old spy try. He'd promised and he *always* kept his promises.

She looked through the dark toward the door and the dresser she'd slid up against it. She wasn't exactly trying to thwart Ty. She was trying to put aside temptation. *Hers.*

After this afternoon, she didn't trust herself to resist him. Her heart raced just at the thought of him in her bed. Which was very bad indeed. If she slept with him, she'd lose her resolve and her heart. She'd take him back and be right back living the lonely, frightening life of a spy's wife. Always worried he wouldn't come home. Always yearning to make a family with him.

She sighed, wishing she had those divorce papers so she could get him to sign them before she changed her mind. What, exactly, was she supposed to do about them? How could she possibly recover them? And why, oh why, would anyone besides her or Ty want them?

She thought about telling Ty. She had no doubt he could deal with whoever took them much better than she could. But she hated the thought of his reaction. No, it was probably better to conceal their very existence from him. It was just one more secret to keep.

Thinking of Ty—where was he? He'd disappeared after the exterminator left, not to be seen again, the coward.

Why hadn't he tried to break into her room yet? Sorry, but old wifely habits die hard. She wouldn't be able to sleep until she knew he was back safely and completely unable to penetrate her room.

*   *   *

All quiet on the western front, Ty thought as he crept down the hall from his room to Treflee's just before eleven. He'd heard there'd been a little catfight between Laci and Tref over him earlier. Whoa, he was flattered. And wished he had been there to see it.

Laci, yeah, he could see her taking a swing at someone over a guy. Now Tref was another matter. He hadn't known the wife had it in her to come to blows over anything, especially him.

He grinned. *She still loves me.* Every sign pointed to it. Winning her back didn't look so hopeless, after all.

Earlier, Tita had caught him on her way to deliver a basket of apology to Mrs. Ho for inconveniencing her guests. Mrs. Ho would expect it, she'd said. Only she was going to deliver hers in person, with a personal apology.

He warned Tita. "Hold on there. Think this over a minute, will you, *wahine*? Give her that basket and you'll be starting a gift war."

Tita frowned at him. "It's the right thing to do."

He shook his head. "Mrs. Ho will feel obligated to give a gift for a gift." Ty didn't relish the expense and hassle of having to call the exterminator again and again with every gift delivery. "Then you'll grumble and have to outdo Mrs. Ho by giving another, nicer gift. This war could bankrupt you. For the good of Big Auau, reconsider?"

In Ty's experience, once a gift war started, it wouldn't end until the non-Chinese person gave up and suffered the dishonor of not giving the last gift.

Tita shrugged and ignored his warning. "I'll take the chance."

As he watched her stroll away, he decided he'd have to use the coming war to his benefit. Poor Tita. She had no idea what she was in the middle of, or that he and Greg were secret agents.

He watched her go and then went into town. He spent

the afternoon and evening doing his real job—keeping tabs on Hal and Zulu, setting up the details for the drop on the volcano in the morning. So much less personal drama in town than at Auau, it was almost relaxing. Give him political intrigue and murder any day over women's bickering and fighting with the wife.

He'd taken Tita's cue and was bringing Tref a little reconciliation gift—the pearls. He usually gave her a charm for her bracelet when he came home from a mission. He'd bought her the string of pearls months ago, way before she'd shown up in Hawaii, the highest grade and quality he could afford. Because he missed her and couldn't stop thinking about her. Because he wanted something bigger and better to prove it.

She always laughed when he told her she was constantly on his mind when he was away. She could never believe that she was anywhere near his thoughts while he was off chasing adventure. She didn't get how much he loved her. Every mission was for her, so her world would be safe.

A dozen, hell, a hundred times over the last six months, he'd been tempted to break his silence and post a comment on the weather blog apologizing, saying he'd consider having a baby if it was what she wanted. It wasn't that he didn't want to have a child with her, or didn't want to be a father. It was more his concern about his future child's safety that had made him hesitate in the first place. As he knew better than anyone, the world was a dangerous place in which to live.

But he knew Tref. It was better to try to win her back in person. And even then, he wasn't sure she'd believe he was sincere. He wanted to prove now that kissing her earlier wasn't just part of his cover.

He smiled, picturing the way Tref would respond when he came in late and slid into bed ready for sex.

Strip naked. Crawl in behind her. Get hard as she sleepily curled her bottom into him. Press against her.

Then he'd slide his hands under her cami. Stroke her breasts until they budded up and listen to her breathing quicken to a soft, sexy, dreamy sigh. He got hard just thinking about those sighs, how happy the pearls would make her, and how terrific they'd look above her naked breasts.

He put the key in the lock. It unlocked easily enough. But when he pushed the door to open it, it wouldn't budge. Something blocked his entrance.

Frustrated, he rested his head against the door and took a deep breath. He resisted the urge to pound on the wall and yell at her to let him in. The pearls would have to wait for another day.

Damn that woman! She'd barricaded the door. If she thought she could keep him out . . .

Treflee smiled as she heard the door rattle.

Ah, there he is! Nice try, Ty!

No way he could break through. The door to her balcony was equally secure. She only wished the room had been less sparsely furnished. More barricading furniture could only have been a good thing.

Now that he was home safely and she was securely blockaded in her room, she could rest easy. She snuggled into her pillow and turned over to sleep.

Ty studied the situation from the lawn below Treflee's room. He'd bet she'd barricaded the balcony door, too. And booby-trapped the window? Probably.

He frowned and made a mental calculation. No way she had enough furniture or strength to go floor to ceiling with her barrier to entry. Looked like he needed his glass-cutting tools and rappelling gear for this mission. Man, she was testing his determination to win her back. Good thing he never gave up.

The bed sagged next to her and she felt a cool breeze ripple over her. Treflee woke with a start. As she opened her mouth to scream, a hand clamped over it.

"Shhh. It's just me."

Ty!

"Nice try, baby."

He sat next to her, radiating heat and power. She should have known.

"Next time use more furniture."

She wrenched his hand free as he laughed softly. "Is that supposed to be helpful? I didn't have more furniture."

She felt the bed move as he shrugged. "Too bad. Did you really think you could keep me out?"

He slid down next to her and rested his head on his elbow as he studied her. She couldn't see his eyes, just his stationary silhouette. "If I can get in, the bad guys can, believe me. Breaking and entering isn't my strong suit. Mmmm . . . is that coconut oil and Dolce and Gabbana perfume I smell?"

"How *did* you get in here?" She squinted toward the source of the breeze, the window, as her eyes adjusted to the dark. "You broke a window?"

"Cut. I cut a window. Less messy that way," he said in a matter-of-fact tone. "I'll replace it in the morning."

She shook her head, not sure how to proceed with him. Part of her wished she could have gotten him to play handyman around the house so easily. "And what if the bad guys want in tonight?"

"Ah, it just saves them one step. They'd break it anyway." He ran his hand over her bare arm. "You're beautiful in the moonlight."

He sounded so sincere, her heart caught, for the instant

before she remembered he was a professional liar. At least the bruises she was so self-conscious about blended right in with the dark. "How about you fix the window and leave now?"

"Oh, come on, babe. Let's drop the BS about you wanting me to go." He ran his hand over her hips and squeezed her thigh. "I heard you defended my honor today and got thrown into a wall for your trouble."

"Laci started it." Treflee flopped over on her back and fanned her hair out on her pillow. "And I wasn't defending your honor. I was peeved at being called an adulterous slut for kissing my husband. I hate all this lying and subterfuge. I don't know how you do it."

He pulled his shirt off and slid between the sheets next to her. "You get used to it."

Wrong answer. She gave him a little shove.

"Wow, let a woman get a taste of violence and she goes wild." His tone was jovial.

"Shut up. I don't like this . . . this charade."

"I know, babe. Just give up and admit you love me and can't live without me." He caressed her cheek with the back of his fingers. "Drop the divorce bullshit. Have a fling with me here."

He lowered his voice into the dangerous sexy range. "Have a fling with your tour guide. Me under cover, under your covers." He kicked off the sheet, flipped over, and balanced on his arms above her.

Her body reacted to the sight of him perched over her, silhouetted by moonlight, muscles bulging, heart on his sleeve, by tingling all the way to her toes. She bit her lip.

"Help me on my mission, babe. Work with me. Don't make me have to trick you into it."

At last, an admission of guilt.

He leaned down and kissed her neck. "Be my own little Bond girl."

"Bond girls don't always make it to the end of the movie alive." She tried hard to suppress the sigh that rose naturally at the feel of his warm, probing lips on her skin. "Sometimes they drown in vats of oil or are found dead covered in gold paint."

"The main girl always lives to make Bond a very happy man at the end of the show." His kisses moved upward until he was gently biting her jawline, and finally, upward until his lips met hers. "You have always been my main girl."

She'd been right to barricade him out. She couldn't resist him. She opened her mouth to him, and her legs. As he slid his tongue in her mouth and settled his body between her legs, she wrapped her arms around him and ran her fingertips over it until he shuddered.

He's aroused and ready. Just the way I like him.

She shouldn't be doing this, but she couldn't stop herself. She curled her legs around his back and rocked into him as she kissed him back with a hunger she couldn't restrain. They both still wore their shorts—hers, thin, soft, barely perceptible Egyptian cotton, his, cargo shorts with stiff pockets.

Oh, she loved the hard feel of him against her.

She rocked and rocked against him as he pounded back. Clothed from the waist down, she felt giddy, like a teenager again, enjoying the build, sensations, and teasing.

"Tref," he whispered as he slid his hands beneath her cami and whisked it off.

Such a simple action. Such a rush as her bare breasts met his chest. She closed her eyes and sighed. *I've missed him.* Missed the feel of him, the smell, the closeness when they made love. Maybe one little last good-bye roll in the hay wouldn't hurt . . .

He kissed her breast and slid his hand over her stomach

and to the waistband of her shorts, pulling at the string to untie them.

She rocked against him again, unable to get enough of the hard feel of him, feeling on the very edge. Willing him to get her pants off and get inside where he belonged.

And then his pants buzzed. Her eyes flew open.

His pants vibrated again. Considering the heightened state she was in, it wasn't as if she didn't like the sensation, but . . .

Someone is calling him? Now?

He ignored it. But it buzzed again and again, to the point of distraction.

"Is that a phone buzzing in your pocket or are you just happy to see me?" she whispered in his ear. "I don't think this is what the phone company meant when they said to reach out and touch someone."

He nuzzled her neck. "It's these damn, new experimental vibrator shorts Q's developed," he whispered back. "The ladies are supposed to love them."

"Get rid of them," she whispered back. "You don't need them."

As he pulled his shorts off, the phone slid out of his pocket onto the bed next to her, the screen glowing brightly.

"Damn!" he said.

She recognized that tone. "What? Who is it?"

"Babe." The inflection of that one word could convey so many meanings. This one was apologetic and meant, *"A mission calls. I have to run."*

"No!" she said. "You can't go now!"

He was already sitting up on the edge of the bed, leaning over to search the floor for the shirt he'd tossed away. He found it and pulled it on.

"I'm sorry. It's urgent."

And my need isn't?

Her eyes had adjusted to the dark, but she couldn't see his face. He sat with his back to her.

"You can't spare two more minutes?" she asked, not meaning to sound so sexually frustrated.

He turned and stroked her cheek. "Two minutes? Give me some credit. I plan on taking way longer than two." He shook his phone. "This can't wait." He leaned over and bent to kiss her.

"And I can?" She turned her face away.

He ended up kissing her cheek. "We'll continue this when I get back."

She pulled the covers up around her chin. "Don't bother coming back."

"Don't be like that, Tref."

She didn't reply. She felt his weight leave the bed as he stood.

"What about the open window?" she asked him. "You're just going to leave me vulnerable?"

And believe her, she felt extremely vulnerable and ready to shatter completely.

"I never leave you unprotected," he said, without turning around.

She watched as he walked to the window, picked up a rope and hook, and crawled out the window, swinging to the balcony and flying into the night like Batman.

Then he was gone. Just like always, the job came first. It came before pleasure. It came before her. It came before *everything*. Hard not to feel jealous and spiteful about it.

As always, he left her having to deal with the shattered pieces. Just like he left her every time. Fortunately, this time she only had to cope with sexual frustration, disappointment in him, disillusionment with love, and an open window, a clear invitation to anyone hanging around with a lei ready to strangle her.

At least this time he hadn't left her alone, scared, and miscarrying the baby he never knew about into a toilet.

She sat up, slipped her cami over her head, pulled her knees to her chest, rested her head on them, and cried. As she did every time she thought about the empty ache inside her and the little thrill-seeking child that would never be.

CHAPTER TEN

The alarm played "Aloha Oe." Mmmm . . . happy sigh. The weight of Ty's arm felt comforting and warm around Treflee. So nice to have him home. Good thing he was the one who always got up first. But why had he chosen a corny oldies station to get up to? She snuggled in.

"Tref! Tref, babe. Time to get up and meet a volcano."

"You're not making any sense." She lazily opened one eye. Three-thirty. "Go back to sleep." She pulled the coconut-scented sheet up to her chin. *Coconut?*

Her eyes flew open! This wasn't home. And it wasn't happy days, either. She tossed Ty's arm off her. How had he sneaked back in without waking her? At least he hadn't tried to resume where they'd left off. He'd been smart enough to leave her alone when she was angry and hurt.

"What are you doing back?" Thankfully her voice was back to normal.

"Good morning to you, too, sunshine."

It was pitch-black in the room, but she was sure he was grinning.

"Out!"

"No way," he said. "I still have another fifteen minutes to sleep."

"Don't you have a window to fix?" She rolled to a sit.

Fifteen minutes to get ready. Men were just plain ridiculous with how little time it took them to get handsome.

"A guy'll be here at sunrise to take care of it." He rolled over.

She grumbled and went to the bathroom to get dressed. When she came out, the lights were on, the bed was made, and Ty was dressed in a pair of skintight black bike shorts and a moisture-wicking white T-shirt. The thing about bike shorts—they show every bulge. *Every bulge.* And the man had a nice one.

She averted her eyes.

She, on the other hand, was dressed in a loose T-shirt and Carrie's extra pair of neon-orange bike shorts. Good visibility, Carrie had told her when she'd balked at them. Cars can see you coming for miles. *Yeah, no duh.* Hers were also two sizes too large. Even made with a healthy dose of spandex, they bulged at the hips and made her look like she was wearing a pair of cutoff jodhpurs.

His gaze roved over her.

"Don't say anything," she said. She tugged at the extra material around her hips. "These are Carrie's."

"Way to come prepared."

"Oh, shut up! No one told me we'd be bicycling down a volcano."

"Look on the bright side—it's better than being sacrificed to it." He grinned.

She rolled her eyes.

He turned and grabbed something off the nightstand. As he did, the reflective strips on the sides of his shorts caught the light. Yeah, reflective strips did the trick. Let's see, reflective strips or orange the color of safety vests? She could just picture her cousin—yeah, orange worked for her.

Ty turned back and held her phone out to her. "Liar! You had a picture or two of me still on it."

She shrugged. "Simple oversight on my part. I imagine you scrubbed them off?"

"Oh, yeah. But if you can't live without one, I'd be happy to pose for another in either my surfer dude or bicycling disguises." He strutted, making a muscle to show off. "Hell, I might even put on my Speedo if you ask me nicely."

She shook her head at his peacock antics, trying not to let her admiration for his body show, and grabbed the phone from him. "I'll pass."

"Your loss." His turn to shrug. "Your boyfriend called. And texted. Several times. Tell him that's overkill. It looks desperate. Chicks don't dig desperation."

She looked at her phone and suppressed a shudder. One missed call. Three new texts. All from Hal. "How did he get my number?"

"You didn't give it to him?"

She shook her head. "No! Like I'd give out my number to someone you set me up to spy on." She tried to sound exactly as exasperated as she felt. "But I bet I know who did."

"Laci?" he guessed.

"You got it. The bitch. She wants me diverted so she can have you all to herself."

He chuckled.

"It's not funny!" She gave him a gentle shove in the shoulder, warning him to knock it off. "But keep it up and I can make it funny. I'll just bow out gracefully and turn you over to her, carte blanche. You can be her new boy toy. Won't I have fun watching you try to escape from her clutches?" *Not really.* But she wasn't going to tell *him* that.

Treflee stared at him, trying to pin him with a look. "Who exactly *is* Hal? Tinker, tailor, soldier, spy?"

Ty rubbed his shoulder.

As if I really hurt him!

"Let's just call him a person of interest," he said.

She silently read Hal's first text. "He wants to see me again. Fat chance." As she reached for the delete key, Ty grabbed her wrist and stopped her.

He stared into her eyes, looking like he was working up to saying something.

She got a bad feeling. Ty was never at a loss for words. Lies and glib comments rolled off his lips with surprising ease. "What?"

"Don't take this the wrong way, but I need you to go out with him again."

"No!" She shook her wrist free of his grip and took a step back away from him, shaking her head. "No way! I don't go out with bad dudes."

"He won't hurt you."

"Uh-uh." She shook her head more vehemently. *As if that could dissuade Ty when he wants something badly enough. I know better.* "I'm not the spy here."

"Babe."

Not that word again! Not spoken in that sexy, silken key.

"Don't call me that!" she said. "And don't use that tone on me. It won't work."

"Okay, my little coconut, do it for love of country."

Still clutching the phone, she put her hands on her baggy jodhpur-bike-short-clad hips. "What's at stake?"

"Life as we know it."

She rolled her eyes. "Seriously."

"Seriously. The free world. National defense."

She blew out a breath. "Really?"

"Would I lie?"

"Is that a rhetorical question? You're a professional liar and you know it." Still, she was fully awake now. She couldn't believe he'd even given her something that vague rather than his standard I-can't-say-anything line. This must be serious.

"Text him back. Tell him you're busy today and tomorrow morning. That you're off on an overnight trip to Hana with the girls. But you'll be back tomorrow afternoon and would love to see him."

She stared at him as if he were crazy.

"Please."

Sometimes you can't fight fate. Even though Treflee hated spying with the core of her being, and she was a world-class coward and scared spitless, she caved. "If I do, do you promise you'll sign the divorce papers as soon as this mission is over?"

He shrugged, seemingly casual and unconcerned, but his eyes were hard. "Yeah, sure. Anything you want."

She didn't fully trust him, but she didn't have many options. "Okay, then. Tell me what you want me to say."

"Tell him you're hot for his bod and can hardly wait to see him."

She gave him her deadpan stare. "Very funny. Now give me something I can work with. Nothing too eager or sexual."

He shrugged. "You're no fun."

She texted Hal exactly what he dictated.

"Thanks," he said when she finished. "Time to get to the van. We don't want to miss the sunrise." He took her arm to lead her out.

She dug in her heels. "Wait a minute. There are a few things I need to know first. How much backup do we have? Is Greg an NCS agent?"

He stared at her, looking as if he was weighing how much to say. Finally, he shrugged. "Yeah."

"Tita?" she asked.

He shook his head no. "Come on. Let's get going."

"Wait! One last thing—what's our cover today? Are we into each other? Or will you be taking me up on my offer and putting the moves on Laci?" She put a tease in her voice, but her heart hammered as she asked the question—traitorous thing.

"Jealous?" He perked up and his eyes twinkled.

It was probably just her imagination, but he looked hopeful.

"Just trying to get the cover story straight. I don't have as much practice as some people." She looked him in the eye, hoping he caught the accusation in her tone. "I need to know how to play things. Consistency makes not get ting caught in a lie easier."

He didn't flinch. He grinned and whispered in her ear, "Today you're hot for me. Can barely keep your hands off me."

"Really." She arched a brow, trying to conceal how near he was to her true feelings. Last night had been too close. If not for that phone call . . .

"And you?" she asked.

"Crazy about you. Like I've been since the first time I saw you." His tone was dangerously low and sexy. Convincingly sincere.

He was probably just being glib. But tell that to her heart. And why in the world did she feel almost breathless?

He squeezed her arm and leaned in closer. "And hoping to get lucky. *Very* lucky."

Her pulse raced and she felt flushed. Of all the great guys in the world, why did she have to have do-it-on-a-lab-bench chemistry with Ty? The one guy who broke her heart.

She swallowed hard. "Good. If I'm going to be acting, it's nice to have my motivation." She took a deep breath, trying to cover how flustered he'd made her. "Let's go ride a volcano, Joe."

Four lousy hours of sleep. Ty'd gotten by with a whole lot less. There was the time in Afghanistan when he'd gone forty-eight straight without sleeping. But since playing beach bum and abandoning nine-to-five for picking up odd jobs here and there these past months, he'd grown lazy and used to sleeping in.

Yeah, he could have dozed in the van like the ladies who surrounded him. But he had a mission to plan.

Much as it galled him, Treflee had attracted just the right man's attention at just the right time, succeeding where some of NCS's top femme fatales had failed. Maybe the Agency had overestimated Hal's ego and shot a little high with some of their attempts to get close to him. Or maybe they'd underestimated Hal's analytical skills and knowledge of NCS's MO and ability to spot a setup. Having hung around Langley, he was smart enough to be suspicious of beautiful women who suddenly showed too much interest, no matter how coy they tried to play it.

Treflee was anything but fawning over Hal. Maybe he found that a turn-on. The best thing she could have done was walk out on Hal after lunch. With that one move, she'd solidified both of Ty's missions. Hal wanted her. Ty could use that.

Ty wanted her, too. Wanted her back. He had renewed hope he could make her see how much he loved her, and make both himself and his boss happy.

Somehow even after suffering what should have been a crushing rejection, Hal had decided that Treflee *was* in his league. Damn him! The thought galled Ty to no end.

Tref was beautiful, sexy, hot, and when she wasn't on the warpath with those damned divorce papers, as sweet, sensitive, and understanding as they came. She was The One. *His One.*

But something had changed the last time he'd come home. It was like something had snapped in her. He'd been off on a mission. When he left, everything was great.

A few months later, when he came back he was suddenly pretty much the biggest ass on the face of the planet, in her opinion.

It couldn't have been anything he'd done. He hadn't been around to mess up. He asked what was wrong, but she wouldn't talk about it. Her mother, her friends, no one knew anything or had any ideas what had happened. Suddenly Treflee wanted a baby. *Now.* He wanted time to think it over, make sure he was ready. That made him a first class jerk.

A baby was a liability for a spy. Another person to love that the enemy could use against you. Or hurt.

If Ty hadn't known better, he would have suspected she'd been trying to get pregnant without telling him. But that was crazy. They'd always been honest with each other about their relationship. They didn't keep secrets like that from each other. She would have told him.

He dismissed the very idea. It was more likely watching her friends and coworkers having babies that had sparked her sudden maternal urges.

She filed for divorce. And he left. If only he could find out what had happened, he could make it right. Fix it. That's what he did, fix things. Save the world. So why couldn't he save his own marriage?

In the meantime, he had an opportunity to show her what she was missing and giving up. Sometimes what he thought he really needed was a geomarital analyst to tell him where they'd gone wrong.

Women were too complex. Ty preferred the straightforward nature of his other mission—stopping Hal from delivering the real Pinpoint Project to RIOT.

Part of the intel for the Pinpoint models came from the Air Force Maui Operations Observatory, or AMOS, located at the crest of Haleakala. With practically no light pollution, Haleakala was the perfect spot for an observatory, and it housed the Department of Defense's largest telescope.

Hal had been assigned to go to AMOS and collect the data, see how operations ran, and assess how to use this data in the new tool. Not only did Pinpoint predict enemy actions, but if it fell into enemy hands, it could be used to predict the location of American submarines, battleships, satellites, even drones, with pinpoint precision.

Unfortunately, Hal did more than his job while in Maui. He was busily selling the Pinpoint Project off a piece at a time to RIOT, using the Fuk Ching as an intermediary.

The State Department wanted the whole ring caught red-handed. Time was running out. Saturday was fast approaching. And now Hal had real data to pass on.

Ty was supposed to expect a drop—a nonvolatile secure digital extended-capacity memory card, SDXC card, with altered data and falsified code—from an air force officer during the crowded sunrise viewing at Haleakala's summit. Somehow Ty had to switch it for the drive Hal planned to sell.

That's where Tref came into the plan. Ty was going to use her to get to Hal. But she wasn't going to like playing Bond girl.

Greg pulled the Auau van into a parking lot at the base of the volcano and turned the engine off. A van and trailer from the bicycle touring company waited to take them to the top of the mountain. From here, Greg would drive around to the campsite near Hana and set up. Ty would stay with the women, meet his contact, and escort the women on their ride down the switchback roads of Haleakala to Baldwin Beach Park in Paia. At the park, he'd pick up a rental van and drive the women to Hana.

In a secluded pool beneath a waterfall near Hana, he planned to seduce his wife.

* * *

Treflee woke when they made the transfer to the Exciting Maui Bicycle Adventures van. Groggily, she decided she didn't want an adventure. She wanted a sunrise stroll on the beach. She could have gotten up nearly three hours later and just walked across the lawn to the beach for it.

It was still dark. Settled into her new seat, she wanted to go back to sleep, but the twisting switchbacks and narrow road made her too nervous and carsick. She stared straight ahead instead.

Half an hour later, they wound up Haleakala Crater Road and came to a stop at the second visitors' center, the one at nearly ten thousand feet. The parking lot was filling quickly.

Keoni, their beefy Exciting Adventure guide, looked more like a football center than a cyclist. He opened the van door and ushered them out. "*Aloha*. Welcome to Haleakala!"

Carrie scanned the thickening crowd. "It's getting busy already."

Keoni looked around and shrugged. "Eh, no more than usual. Don't worry. There isn't a bad seat in the house. The horizon's a large stage."

Carrie didn't seem reassured. Without waiting for Treflee to get out, she, Carla, Faye, Brandy, and Laci headed toward the viewing spot.

Treflee was last out of the van. Ty gave her a hand out and hung on too long. "Still remember how to flirt?" he whispered.

"Barely." She wanted to goad him.

"Give it the old college try." He leaned in and kissed her neck.

"Stop it." Ignoring the tingles running down her spine, she pushed him away. "The others will see."

Moot really. Carrie and company were already elbowing

their way to the front of the crowd, vying for a spot on the edge of the crater.

"Come on." He took her hand. Without pushing or shoving, he led her through the crowd to a spot by the visitors' center right in front of the railing that kept visitors from the crater and stood behind her.

Ty was good. He knew how to invade enemy territory and personal space while looking oh so innocent. As the crowd grew and pressed in behind him, he pressed up against her. Despite the chill in the air, and being bundled in a sweatshirt and baggy bike shorts, she was aware of his body heat and the familiar posture of his body protecting hers. Ty always made her feel safe.

As the sky turned from gray to light blue, Ty's arms were suddenly around her.

On the far horizon, the edges against earth turned slowly pink, then deep red. To the Hawaiians this was sacred. The crowd of hundreds grew silent. A park ranger began performing the *mele oli,* a melodic, ceremonial chant to welcome the sun and the day, as the sky above grew bluer and the sky below turned orange then golden.

"Here comes the sun," Ty whispered in her ear just as the tip of the golden sun peeked above the mountain.

It lit the clouds above orange, pink, and gold. As it warmed the earth, ground fog rushed down the sides of the crater and into the bowl. The sun shone through the fog, throwing shafts of sunlight vertically through it.

It was hard not to get caught up in nature's spectacle. Hard not to feel that something large, profound, and eternal was happening. Hard not to feel all alone in the crowd. Treflee's eyes stung with the emotion of it all.

She'd never seen a sunrise so beautiful or pristine before. Sunrise on the top of a volcano.

As the sun rose fully to the point where it sat in the

bowl of Haleakala, Treflee couldn't take the feeling of insignificance and loneliness. She leaned back into Ty.

He lifted her hair from her neck and kissed it.

This was peace and heaven.

"Awesome," she whispered.

"Oh, babe," he cooed into her ear.

The sun climbed higher, lighting everything on fire. With Ty holding her, Treflee felt the fire, too. Everything felt right. Maybe it was right. Maybe she'd been wrong. Maybe Ty did care. Maybe they *were* soul mates. Maybe what he gave her was enough.

She turned in his arms to face him, looked up at him, deep into his eyes, to see if he felt it, too. His eyes sparkled. He tilted his head and leaned down to kiss her.

Her breath caught. She lifted her face to him. His insistent lips came down on hers. She wrapped her arms around his neck, closed her eyes, and opened her mouth to him.

Never in her life had she experienced anything like the thrill of kissing Ty on this volcano, in this communal place where heaven met earth, backlit by sunrise. Where her soul seemed to collide with his and she felt the full meaning of her wedding vows—she was one with him.

She wrapped a lock of his hair that fell down the back of his neck around her finger. Her tongue danced with his. He kissed her greedily. She couldn't get enough of him.

She was lost in his kisses, so oblivious to the world around them that she was startled when someone jostled into them. Treflee's eyes flew open in time to see a man clap Ty on the shoulder before moving on.

From her vantage point, she only got a fleeting look at the stranger as he blended with the crowd and disappeared.

Ty put one hand in his jacket pocket.

And then it hit her. He was checking for something. This was all a setup, a drop he'd carefully planned. Kissing her at the spiritual moment of sunrise was probably the signal all was clear to proceed. The guy, a fellow spy, had bumped into him and placed something in his pocket.

Even here, in this pristine, sacred place, Ty was working. And working her. She pulled away from his kiss.

Now that the sun was up, people began dispersing. Her awareness of her surroundings came back. The park ranger was telling people to come back and see the sunset or return to watch the stars. The park was open twenty-four hours. Very little light pollution up here. Lots of observatories. The Air Force Maui Observatory was even here. Very important air force spot. Largest telescope the air force owns. No, you can't take a tour. Top secret stuff there.

Air force installation? What a coincidence.

Treflee stared at Ty and whispered, "That was a drop, wasn't it?"

When he didn't answer, she shoved him away from her. "You're always working. Always. Whenever I need you, even if it's just to reach out and touch you so I know I'm not alone in the universe, you're working. Was kissing me a signal?"

"Tref—"

"Can it."

He put a hand on her shoulder. "I know you're pissed, but stay undercover or the deal's off."

Her heart raced. She wanted to slap him. Hard. Hurt him like he kept hurting her. She wanted that divorce. She *needed* that divorce so she could move on.

"That wasn't the deal." She hated the way her voice shook.

He reached out and stroked her cheek. "Look, I'm sorry. Is it so wrong to mix business and pleasure? Can't a guy do both at once—save the free world and get the girl?"

He looked and sounded sincere and truly puzzled by her reaction.

She swallowed hard and took a deep breath.

He reached for her, stroked her chin, put his hand behind her head. "Kiss and make up?"

She stared at him.

"Don't fight. People are watching," he whispered as he leaned down and rested his forehead against hers.

"Fine." She could pretend it didn't matter. She could act as well as he could. She reached up and stroked his chin, then very gently kissed him on the lips as lightly as a butterfly landing on a flower.

Keoni yelled at them and waved them over. "Come and get it. Breakfast's ready!"

She pulled away. "Great. I'm starving."

CHAPTER ELEVEN

Keoni had set up a continental breakfast with tea and coffee in the back of the van. It was nearly six-thirty. The sun continued to put on a show, lighting up this cloud and that, changing the color scheme as it rose higher and higher toward daytime. From her volcano vantage point, Treflee felt almost as if she were free-falling above the clouds obscuring the body of the island. Her emotions were certainly on a downward slide.

Damn Ty for using her. She blinked back tears, trying to pretend they were the result of the emotional power of the sunrise. Soon the clouds would burn off, leading to another beautiful day in paradise. If only she could find a way to put Ty out of her mind and enjoy it.

Treflee had been so wrapped up in her thoughts, it wasn't until she got close to the van that she noticed the group of Chinese people at the bicycle tour van next to theirs. The Chinese group lounged and breakfasted on bowls of runny porridge, dunking strange fried crullers in it as they talked and laughed. Their breakfast looked like something you might see in a bad Chinese remake of a Dickens movie. More gruel, sir, please!

But the Chinese gang ate with gusto, appearing content and excited. Maybe it was only her imagination, but

THE SPY WHO LEFT ME

they seemed poised on the brink of an adventure and happy about it.

This particular Chinese group was all handsome people between twenty and thirty-five or so, an even pairing of men and women. They wore identical black spandex bike pants, lightweight bright yellow windbreakers emblazoned with Chinese characters and a logo of a red dragon surrounded by a red swoosh that looked as if it had just been dashed off by an artist's brushstroke, and matching yellow T-shirts. Just below the dragon logo were the English words "Chinese Adventures, Tailor-Made Experiences."

Treflee recognized them at once as the Chinese wedding party from Mrs. Ho's. Plus the words "sponsored by Sugar Love Plantation" printed on the backs of their jackets were a dead giveaway.

The whole group was a walking billboard.

It's funny how initial perceptions taint observations. When she'd first seen the Chinese group milling and crowding around at Big Auau, she'd assumed they were bride and bridegroom, together with their bridal party. But now as she watched them, she was struck by how they each seemed paired off as couples, obvious couples. In love.

What a stark contrast to Carrie's ex-bridal party. While some of Carrie's girls may have been looking forward to a one-night stand with one of the groomsmen, they were all decidedly unattached.

Treflee frowned, perplexed, playing a game of "guess who's the bride" to divert her thoughts from Ty and occupy herself as she helped herself to a Styrofoam cup of coffee and a coconut-cream-filled pastry.

Next to her, Ty put his hand in his pocket while he sipped his own cup of black coffee. The pocket into which she'd seen him drop whatever he'd received earlier.

Curious. True, whatever Ty was investigating involved

the Chinese. But she'd never known him to be unnecessarily wary or cautious. Which meant—this particular set of people was somehow tied to his mission.

She stared at them, momentarily stunned and horrified by the realization. Her coward instinct kicked in. She pictured the dead Chinese waiter and inhaled deeply; remembered the feeling of suffocation as someone garroted her with a lei.

Running blindly through a Halloween house of horrors was nothing compared to the knee-buckling fear and panic coursing through her now. She leaned against the van to steady herself and took another deep breath.

"You're oozing," Ty said. He pointed to her pastry.

She'd pinched it so tightly that coconut cream was seeping out the bottom.

She barely acknowledged him and didn't even taste the coconut cream as she automatically licked it off.

She had to get out of here. Get home. As soon as possible. Whatever was in Ty's pocket suddenly seemed like the key to her freedom.

With it, she'd have leverage over him. Unfortunately, she was a terrible pickpocket. But not such a terrible flirt. Not if she put her mind to it. If she could make him believe she was no longer hurt or angry, if she could get her hand in that pocket . . .

She'd have to be careful or Ty would figure out what she was up to.

She'd been so busy plotting her escape, she hadn't realized she was still staring at the Chinese wedding party until she felt a tug on her sleeve.

"You no like our breakfast?"

She turned to find a pretty, young Chinese woman standing beside her.

"Congee and yu za kuei, deep-fried devils, very good."

"Oh! Sorry for staring." *And thank you for the cover*

story. Thank goodness the Chinese woman didn't know what Treflee had really been thinking. "You speak English! Yesterday at the plantation, I didn't think anyone could."

The woman shrugged and smiled shyly. "I shy. Not confident with English. Do better one to one than in crowd."

Treflee nodded. "I didn't mean to insult your breakfast." She held up her cup of coffee and pastry and forced herself to smile. "I'm sure ours looks equally unappealing to you."

The woman made a comical face. "You right."

Treflee laughed, juggled the coffee and pastry into one hand, and extended her other. "I'm Treflee."

"Abi." She took Treflee's hand and smiled. Handshake complete, Abi pointed toward the lone single man in her crowd. He was watching them. Treflee couldn't decide if he looked happy that Abi was talking to her or not.

"My husband soon," Abi said in her thickly accented English. "Feng. Feng mean wind. Abi mean bird. He wind under my wing." She made a flapping motion with her arm and laughed at her own humor.

"You're the bride! I was wondering," Treflee said. She hadn't guessed Abi.

Abi waved her hand over her group. "All brides. And men marry us. Twelve couples."

I frowned. "Bridal couples? All of you?"

Abi's smile deepened as she nodded vigorously. "Yes. All. We get married Saturday. Twenty-sixth. Double happiness day. Good day for wedding."

"All on the same day?" Treflee shook her head. "What a scheduling nightmare!"

Abi shook her head, no. "No nightmare. Get married all at once. Same . . . how say?"

"Ceremony?"

Abi nodded.

"What! All at once, really?" Treflee had never considered a group wedding. In her opinion, every girl deserved her unique, special day. That was the American way. She couldn't stop herself from saying so.

"No. It good thing. Group wedding in China done all time. Sometime even employer do for promotion.

"This wedding dream made true. No pay for big American wedding at home. This way, free. We enter contest with *Chinese Bride Magazine,* Chinese Adventure Travel Agency, and Sugar Love Plantation." She said the name so clearly it was almost comical.

"Get whole thing no cost. American white dress. Trip. Flowers. Cake. Food. Three-day honeymoon stay. Wedding video by Mrs. Ho. All free.

"Mrs. Ho do very best videos and wedding pictures, very impressive. *Everyone* want."

"You're very lucky then," Treflee said, sensing she should act impressed.

Abi nodded. *"Chinese Bride Magazine* do feature story on Mrs. Ho. Say she tell romantic story that make her videos special. Tech guy analyze her video files. Say very large. Hi def. Big bit technology. Use only .gif and .wav files. No lossy technology for Mrs. Ho. Excellent quality."

Treflee had to smile at the cute way Abi parroted things like "lossy technology," whatever that was, from a magazine article. She was certainly a smitten bride. "But you're away from family and friends. Too bad they couldn't see you get married in person."

Abi smiled deeply. "No problem. Mrs. Ho have video room in basement of Sugar Love. Stream our wedding with live feed to family and friends and *Chinese Bride Magazine* readers in China. For family, just like they here! Big deal for everyone."

"How nice," Treflee said.

"Yes. Nice. We get have wedding picture in travel brochure, too. *Chinese Bride Magazine*. Ad for travel agency. Five minutes of fame." Abi winked.

"Can't afford in China. Feng want impress me. Convince me he the one. Love me much. Girls scarce in China." She smiled her lovely smile again and giggled. "Must win me or I choose someone else. He be alone. Not get girl as good as me. Not get any girl maybe."

Though from her tone it sounded like there was fat chance of Feng not getting her. The light in Abi's eyes as she talked about Feng made Treflee sentimental. She remembered her own wedding day and how things used to be with Ty, who was still standing very quietly next to her.

"Feng enter contest. So many forms to fill out. So much, how you say, tape? He almost get discouraged and give up. But he do it. For me. Write big letter why he want wedding. He very good writer. Win. I marry him."

"On double happiness day," Treflee added, feeling her eyes mist.

Abi was so thin and petite, her voice so melodic, she made Treflee feel like a big, pale horse by comparison. Abi would be a beautiful bride.

Abi looked at Treflee's group and pointed. "You stay at wedding house. Your friends with you? Who marry?" She leaned in and whispered as she slyly pointed at Ty. "You marry him?"

Treflee's heart skipped a beat. For a second, she thought she'd been found out.

"No!" Treflee shook her head and explained about Carrie's canceled wedding. "So no happiness at all for my cousin on double happiness day." The thought made Treflee terribly sad.

She wasn't sure Abi understood the whole story, but apparently she got enough.

"You come my wedding!" Abi's eyes lit up. She nodded hopefully.

"Well . . ." Treflee wasn't keen on spending any more quality time with potential bad guys or enemy agents. And judging by Ty's reaction to them, one of Abi's party must have been just that.

"Must come! Blond American at wedding good luck! Be honored guest. Take picture to show family in China. Very good thing."

Treflee couldn't see any way to refuse. "Sure. I'd be delighted."

Abi nodded toward Ty. "Bring guest if you like."

Feng waved at Abi. "Have to go now. Nice to meet you. See you later!"

Next to Treflee, Ty grinned widely. "You make friends fast. Don't wait too long to invite me along as your date. My calendar fills up fast and I need time to press my slacks."

"Who says I'm inviting you, eavesdropper?" She gave him a flirty little smile and took a big bite of pastry, actually tasting it for the first time.

"A little bird indicated I should be your first choice."

Since he seemed so interested in Abi and her party, Treflee had the feeling the real reason Ty wanted to go to the wedding had more to do with business than pleasure. If that was the case, and someone in their party was the enemy, she'd be safer with him beside her than not. In the unlikely event she actually went to the wedding. She shrugged. "It's a date, then."

Message received, Ty thought as Abi walked away. "Wind under my wing" was the code phrase that meant a friendly message. Very clever the way she'd delivered it, talking apparently innocently to Tref while delivering the message to him.

Abi was MSS. Ty hadn't recognized her at first or at Big Auau. She was good with a disguise, playing the shy, young bride-to-be. But now he remembered her clearly. She was one of George's former MSS contacts. George had been hot for her, had had a real thing for her. Damn, he missed George. Too bad George and Abi had never worked out.

NCS had been trying for the last six months to discover how Mrs. Ho was smuggling the data Hal sold her out of the country and into their Chinese contingent. They suspected she used steganography, stego as it was called in the business, to hide messages in innocent-looking pictures or music files. Unfortunately, stego messages were hard to detect and often encrypted when found.

The CIA had analysts using stego-detecting software on every picture and piece of music Mrs. Ho posted anywhere on the Web. Nothing.

Abi had just handed them the golden ticket. Stego images on live feed video. Ingenious. Family and friends of twelve couples viewing it simultaneously along with multitudes of magazine subscribers. Just try to find the RIOT agent who was reading the file for the algorithm and data Hal was selling.

A video lab in a basement at Sugar Love. That was new, too. Very few basements in Hawaii, especially so close to the beach. There wasn't one in the plans the CIA had for Sugar Love.

Ty wondered if Mrs. Ho might have found a useful series of uncharted underground caves or lava tunnels. That was about the only kind of basement that made sense there. Either that or she had one hell of a sump pump.

Ty hurried off to contact Emmett with the good news and get the guys at Langley hustling.

Twenty minutes later, breakfast completed and cleared, Keoni herded them into the van for the ride down to the sixty-five-hundred-foot level just outside the park. That was where the downhill bicycling ride would begin. Despite Keoni's reassurances—twenty-one switchbacks but only two hundred yards of pedaling—Treflee felt like a bag of nerves. Her idea of an ideal bike ride was a pleasant cruise along a nice flat, dedicated bicycling trail. No cars allowed.

She didn't like downhills, particularly steep downhills. Too easy to get going too fast. Carrie called her a menace with a brake.

The last time she'd been on a ride with Carrie they'd been seventeen. Carrie sped along, leaving Treflee in the figurative dust to get lost in Carrie's sprawling suburban neighborhood. Nearly an hour later, Uncle Al showed up in the truck, finding Treflee resting in the shade with her bike propped against a tree. Without comment, he loaded the bike in the truck bed and took her home. At least Carrie had sent help.

When Treflee voiced her fears about being left behind, Keoni reassured her. "Not to worry. I'll be following with the van."

Yeah, and probably honking for her to get a move on.

"Can't I just ride in the van?" Treflee asked.

"No, you cannot!" Carrie scowled at her. "You big chicken. You're over five feet tall, older than twelve, not pregnant, weigh less than two hundred and fifty pounds, and have no health problems. You're completely qualified and fit for this. And you signed the form!" Carrie used her brook-no-opposition cop voice, sounding completely calm.

"You're not missing out on the view and adventure by cowering in the stuffy van. You're going to ride down the mountain with the rest of us if it kills you." Then she turned back and resumed her conversation with Laci and Faye.

The part about not being pregnant stung.

For the moment, Laci seemed to have decided to ignore Treflee and the close-quarters way she curled next to Ty on the van seat.

Well, all's fair in love and spy play. Two could dabble in seduction and deceit. A wife scorned had every reason, no, make that right, to use everything in her arsenal to gain the tactical advantage in a divorce war. Treflee was only planning to seize hers in the form of that top secret drop. She smiled at Ty. *Which means getting close to you,* she thought, hoping her heart could handle it.

Ty put his hand on her knee, his very strong, hot hand. He squeezed and slyly slid his fingers around the side of her leg to stroke the inside of her thigh with his thumb.

Good thing she was wearing loose bike shorts. Too bad they were so thin that they barely dulled his touch.

Damn that man and his knowledge of her erogenous zones! Stroke the inside of her thigh and she'd follow him anywhere. She went weak and tingly in all the wrongly right places.

He knew exactly the pressure and movement to use to turn her on as he pretended to flirt and leaned in to whisper, "You'll do fine. Piece of cake."

She retaliated by pressing her legs together and trapping his hand as she rested hers on his athletic-pants-clad knee, then gliding it up his thigh over his pocket.

Empty! Where had he stashed the drop he'd gotten?

He smiled innocently at her, but she got the feeling he knew what she was up to.

Keoni stopped the van in a pull-out area just outside the park boundary. Ty helped him unload the bikes. The Chinese bicycle tour van pulled up next to them.

Keoni issued everyone helmets, bikes, and lightweight windbreakers. He gave them a set of safety instructions. "If you get going too fast, brake with your right hand. It controls the rear wheel. Brake too hard and too fast with your left, which controls the front wheel, and you'll go flying over the handlebars.

"Ignore honkers. Don't let them rattle you. Most people in cars are polite, but a few are impatient jerks. Give them wide berth.

"I'll be behind you in the van. Pull over at the third scenic viewpoint for a photo op. We'll have a few of them. We'll be stopping for lunch at a protea flower farm. I think you ladies will like that."

Carrie and crew adjusted their seats like pros, all looking as if they were riders in the Tour de France, dressed in stylish, tight-fitting black spandex bike shorts with reflective stripes, the bike tour jackets, curve-accentuating, moisture-wicking bike shirts, and bike cleats. In her borrowed baggy traffic-cone orange shorts and yellow jacket, all Treflee needed to pose as a piece of candy corn was a white helmet. No such luck. Hers was black.

Treflee wasn't playing dumb as she fiddled with her seat. She was simply inept. However, her ineptness provided another body-search opportunity as Ty came over to help.

She let him put his arms around her as he showed her how to lower the seat. She pressed up against him, hoping to get a feel of that drop in a front shirt pocket. Or maybe he'd strung it around his neck. Hopefully he hadn't passed it off to someone else already. He had to have it on him.

He seized the opportunity for an "accidental" breast brush and whispered in her ear in a breathy way that made her shiver with pleasure as he issued instructions.

Anyone watching them might have told them to get a room. Or so Treflee imagined from the sidelong daggers Laci sent her. Treflee desperately *wished* they could get a room—so she could search his clothes and body for her ticket to move on with her life.

The low clouds from the top of the mountain had settled into a patchy fog at 6,500 feet. Keoni warned them about visibility issues. "Just take it slow. The clouds will break another thousand feet down or so. Then you'll have trouble keeping your eyes off the view and on the road."

Despite being a larger group, the Chinese wedding party got on their bikes and moved out first. They were already out of sight in the fog past the first switchback bend before Treflee's group took off single file down the road.

Treflee didn't have to insist on bringing up the rear. She settled in naturally and took a perverse pleasure from imagining how hard poor Keoni was working to keep that van going so slow. Is there a gear below first?

Ty rode directly in front of her. Even in the on-again, off-again fog, the view was nothing short of spectacular. Ty had a very nice butt and well-muscled calves that mesmerized her as he pumped. Treflee was way too nervous to dare to peek out at anything other than the road and the view directly before her. The last thing she wanted was to go missing in the mist over the edge of a switchback.

Three successful switchback negotiations later, she began to relax and sneak a look or two out over the gray horizon. A handful of cars respectfully and cautiously passed the group without incident. A couple honked their irritation, but gave the cyclists wide berth.

Despite Keoni's admonition to stick together, their group had spread out. Well, that's to say Carrie, Laci, Carla, Faye, Brandy, and even Ty had pulled significantly ahead of Treflee. She could no longer see them through the fog. Only poor Keoni, who was being paid to do so, stayed with her, headlights on, illuminating her billowing orange shorts and making her butt look big, she was sure. She just hoped he didn't fall asleep at the wheel from traveling at such a drowsy pace. She rode with the right handbrake squeezed tight.

You know, there really wasn't so much to this adventure

stuff after all. You just had to have a little confidence and take things easy. Wait until she got home and told everyone at the office about her experiences. They'd never believe she'd actually surfed *and* biked down a volcano.

Treflee was concentrating on the road and busy plotting exactly how she was going to get Ty out of his clothes so she could search them for the drop. It took her a second to recognize the distinctive whir and whiz of bike spokes and speed approaching behind her. She moved farther to the right, expecting the newcomer to call out, "On your left!," and buzz past her.

She didn't bother to look into her mirror until it was almost too late. A lone biker, medium height and slender, dressed head to toe in black gear and wearing mirrored shades that obscured the face, pulled up next to her. She waved him on, urging him to go around her.

He closed in on her, crowding her toward the guardrail.

Idiot! Maniac!

She gestured more frantically and screamed at him. "Go around!"

That's when she spotted the gun in the newcomer's hand.

Her mouth went dry. Ty had never taught her what to do in a situation like this. Her pulse leaped past target-exercise speed right into the dangerous panicked range in a single beat.

The guy bent over, leaned down, and extended the gun toward her front spokes.

What the—

Instinctively, Treflee veered away from him and released her pressure on the right handbrake. Her bike wobbled. She nearly overcorrected and lost her balance as she surged forward in front of the bastard. She shifted into high gear.

Where the heck was Keoni? Why wasn't he slamming this maniac into the mountainside with two thousand pounds of touring van? He could hardly mistake the two of them. She was the one in the flapping orange pumpkin shorts!

Treflee looked under her arm at the cyclist. He was gaining on her already. Her pursuer hunched over his handlebars, pumping as he flew toward her. And the bastard had muscled thighs with the power to crack a walnut.

Pumping! The guy was certifiable!

He obviously outweighed and outmuscled her. He'd be on her in a flash. If he got close enough to pull the trigger . . .

She stared at the road ahead, furiously ticking off her options: forced off the road over the guardrail, shot, or missed a hairpin turn and crashed into oblivion? *Pick your poison, girl.*

The fog had thickened. She had no idea how fast the next hairpin turn was coming up. The only indication of the road at all was a pair of headlights aiming at her on the uphill side of the road.

The Mad Biker pulled up beside her and extended the gun again.

She veered in front of the oncoming headlights. A horn blared. The car swerved just in time, allowing her enough room on the narrow uphill shoulder to squeeze by and emerge unscathed. Behind her she heard the squeal of brakes and Keoni laying on his horn.

She peeked behind her. Mad, Bad Biker was still on her tail.

She refused to be forced off the road and over the guardrail into central Maui and certain death, a sacrifice to Pele, the volcano goddess.

The fog cleared just enough for Treflee to see the hairpin turn approaching. She leaned into the corner and began pumping with all her might as she hunched forward, trying to make herself aerodynamic. The only drag on her was her silly, wide, baggy-hipped bike shorts that blew and puffed in the wind like panniers.

Her bike computer speedometer registered thirty miles an hour. Then forty. Her heart pounded as though she were going sixty. One tiny rock in the road, one bump, and she was history.

Down the straightaway, the bad dude cyclist nearly caught her.

Treflee prayed for bad aim. She glanced at the gun. A long, scary needle stuck out from it. She frowned.

That's no gun. That was a bike tire pump!

The bastard meant to stick it in her spokes, strip them from the hub, and send her tumbling headfirst to her death. Death by bicycle pump—no, thank you!

She put on a burst of speed and broke out of the fog and into the sunshine.

Below her, the girls took the next corner with Ty following them. She was gaining on them. And gaining way too much speed to control.

She considered throwing on the brakes and letting her assailant sail by. But she was afraid at the speed she was going she'd lock up and be thrown headfirst over the handlebars. She didn't have enough faith in either her tour-company-issued windbreaker or brain bucket for that maneuver. Instead, she leaned into the corner again and prayed.

She lost sight of Keoni. She wished for the first time that Ty was behind the wheel.

Ty would force that bastard off the road without causing a scratch to her. But she had no faith in Keoni. She'd signed a waiver holding the tour company blameless in the unlikely event of an accident. But waivers weren't ironclad legal vehicles. Wanting to avoid a lawsuit and any blame, especially if she died, were probably enough to keep Keoni in check and well back out of the action.

The bicycle-tire-pump-wielding bad dude was flying up beside her with pump in hand, looking like he'd club her with it if it came to that. In just a matter of seconds he'd pull even and stab it through her spokes.

At that moment, the hairpin turn closed in too fast. She reacted too late, missing the turn and sailing off the road through a gap in the guardrail.

CHAPTER TWELVE

Ty heard honking and squealing tires for the second time in minutes. He looked back up the mountain just in time to see Treflee pop out of the fog and down the straightaway above him toward the switchback turn. You couldn't miss her in those orange shorts.

The woman was flying down the mountain. *Totally unlike her.* He frowned. Something was wrong.

An instant later, his heart plummeted into his stomach as another cyclist appeared from the mist, hot on her tail, obviously in pursuit.

Was that a bicycle pump the other guy was wielding?

Oh, shit! The guy has to be either RIOT or Fuk Ching!

Ty applied his brakes and spun his bike around to face back up the mountain. He shifted into hill-climbing gear, stood on the pedals and pounded forward. Balancing the bike with one hand, he pulled a camera from his pocket and snapped a picture of the guy. He replaced the phone and pulled out a small, accurate pistol, ready to take action.

He watched Tref with growing horror. No way he'd get to her in time. She was going too fast. The one time in her life she'd turned speed demon on him.

It didn't take Lance Armstrong to realize she'd never make the corner. Yelling a warning at her was futile. Ty didn't waste the energy. He had to draw the attacker away from her. From here.

He pulled the bike over next to the guardrail, ducked behind the cycle, holding it up and using it as a shield. To the casual observer, he could have been just another biker worried about a tire or a loose chain as he squatted in the dirt. He rested his arm on the bike frame, steadied himself, and took careful aim, waiting for his moment.

The pump-wielding bad dude was just behind Tref. One or two good pedal turns and he'd pull even. No way Tref could outpedal him. She had beautiful, shapely thighs, thighs he thoroughly loved to caress. But strength and speedwise, she'd never be hell on bicycle wheels.

Ty expected her attacker to pull even with her and jam the pump through her front spokes. That would cause the spokes to shear from the hub, and would be for all intents and purposes like riding a bike without a front wheel. The front of the bike would sag and send Tref flying headfirst over the handlebars. At the speed she was cruising, she'd be lucky not to snap her neck and end up dead.

As the guy's front tire pulled even with her back tire, he leaned down, reaching to stick the pump in her spokes.

Not as effective, but that would work, too. Acting on instinct, Ty fired.

The guy flinched and pulled his arm back just as Tref took the turn too wide and sailed through a gap in the guardrail, airborne like a prize dirt biker at a BMX event.

The attacker was obviously a more experienced biker. Even favoring his right arm, he managed to pull inside and negotiate the switchback turn. He cruised down the road toward Ty, looking around for the source of the shot, going too fast for Ty to chance another. Ty had just grazed his arm. He could see the trickle of blood staining the guy's sleeve.

Ty waited for the guy to return fire. Nothing. He had to be unarmed.

Ty's gaze bounced between the assailant and where Tref had disappeared out of sight over the hill. He had a choice—go after the lady or the tiger?

Tref could be lying on the hill dead or dying. He felt sick.

On the other hand, he needed to bring this bastard in, especially if he'd killed her. And the guy might still go after her to make sure he'd finished the job.

Lady. No contest. If there's even the ghost of a chance that I can save her. His heart pounded. *I can't lose her.*

Dressed in the bright yellow windbreaker, Ty looked like a rubber ducky and practically had a target on his back. He pulled it off and tossed it over the bike to create a blind as he escaped and went to Tref.

A car engine revved to life at a scenic pullout just up from him. *A getaway van.*

He'd been so focused on Tref, he hadn't paid it any particular attention. Every scenic spot was full of cars of tourists snapping pictures.

He swore beneath his breath. No way he could turn his back on that. Could be full of assassins and guys who'd just as soon shoot you in the back as look at you.

He leaned the bike against the guardrail and jumped the rail. A bike wasn't a great shield. A bike and a guardrail combined were only marginally better. Peeking past his coat, he positioned himself to take a shot at the van as it drove past him.

Tref was always messing with his concentration.

Tref's attacker rode toward the getaway van. He caught sight of Ty's position and pointed and gestured toward him to someone in the van. A van window rolled down. A pistol barrel appeared and pointed itself in Ty's direction. A pistol with a high-powered sight.

* * *

For one fantastic, exhilarating second, Treflee was airborne. The next, the bike hit solid ground in a cloud of dust. Hard. The shock jolted through her, rattling everything from her teeth to her toes.

Hooray for mountain bike shocks!

She almost lost her balance and toppled off. Only her white-knuckled death grip on the brakes kept her in place.

Fighting gravity and the bike, she leaned to the left to keep from toppling over. She overcorrected to the right. She fell over, bike on top of her, and went into a slide for life down the slope. It would have been a pretty neat trick if she'd meant to do it. Or had any control.

She clawed at the ground, kicking and screaming, trying to get a hold of something or get the bike off. But her windbreaker had caught in the gears and the two were now one.

They kept sliding, heading directly for a patch of bushes. She closed her eyes and covered them with her hands, preparing for impact.

A hundred twiggy hands clawed and scratched her. Finally, the bike snagged on something. The windbreaker ripped loose. She slid several more feet before coming to a full and complete stop.

She was breathing hard. Stinging everywhere. But that was a good sign, right? Meant she was alive and not paralyzed or something.

She froze. Afraid. What if the bad guy was still coming after her?

See no evil, but she had to look. When she opened her eyes, she was covered in dust, branches and leaves, scrapes and scratches. And completely surrounded and concealed by bushes like a rabbit hiding in a warren.

A shot zinged off the guardrail next to Ty. All that stood between him and a hole in his head was a thin piece of lightweight yellow fabric, a few bits of metal, and a whole lot of air.

He took aim uphill at the van window just as Keoni finally popped out of the fog in the Exciting Maui Adventures van.

Unfortunately, also at that moment, another tour of single-file sightseeing cyclists passed Keoni and came around the corner. The lead sightseer zipped into the scenic pullout, interfering with Ty's shot. The bad dude fell in with the rest of the group, keeping them between him and Ty until he reached the van.

Ty cursed as Tref's assailant tossed his bike in the back of the van and jumped in. The van peeled out, scattering the rest of the group of riders, somehow managing to avoid hitting any of them.

The van would have to come past Ty. He hoped to take a shot at it and disable it. But, as bike tours go, some riders are fast and some slow. The line spreads out. And some are hotheads who want revenge for nearly being blown off the road. The lead two newcomers took off beside the van as it passed them and crossed in front of Ty.

Those two idiots biked between Ty and the van, obscuring his shot. He took a deep breath and cursed again as the van driver hit the accelerator and blew past him and the cyclists.

Ty watched the van careen down the hill, waiting to see if it would come back for another shot at him or Tref. It wasn't stopping.

Farther down the mountain, now tiny specks of yellow, Tref's cousin and her friends continued on their merry way. Oblivious until the van bore down on them and they scattered to the shoulder like pepper in water, escaping unscathed. Unaware even then of what had happened to Tref. Maybe that was for the best.

Ty turned around and scanned the volcano for her.

Oh, baby. Where are you?

All he saw was barren mountain. The woman had disappeared into thin air.

Up the mountain, Keoni was slowly driving downhill, caught behind this latest wave of cyclists. Ty jumped the rail again and flagged him down.

Treflee cowered undercover in her bush. Any idiot villain worth his evil reputation should spot the bike and bright yellow arrow of a windbreaker nearby and have a look around for her.

Unfortunately, this bush was covered in flowers. And flowers attract bees. Bees scared Treflee almost as much as bike-pump-wielding maniacs. She was allergic, though not in the anaphylactic way. Just major swelling around the sting and a case of blood poisoning the last time a wasp got her. Arm the size of a tree trunk. Bright red streaks up it. The doc said she just barely got treatment in time. Another few hours and she might have lost the arm. Or her life.

She'd just escaped death at the hands of a mad, villainous biker and a too-steep switchback turn. It would have been downright embarrassing, to say the least, to be taken out by a mere bee now.

She lay very still, not wanting to madden the increasing number of bees in the bush, and frankly too scared to move, as she weighed her options.

"Tref! Treflee, baby!"

Ty! Thank goodness.

She scrambled out of the bush on her hands and knees and popped to her feet, waving. "Here! Over here!"

He spotted her and waved to someone behind him. "Found her!"

Unfortunately, springing out of the bush upset a bee. It buzzed her. She screamed. Ty swung around, drew his gun, and looked for a villain.

Despite the trauma, she almost laughed. What he really needed was a fly swatter.

He relaxed as he spotted the bee. He ran to her and smacked the bee down with his bare hands.

Relieved, Treflee threw herself into Ty's arms and snuggled against his chest as he wrapped his arms around her. Why did he have to feel so safe?

"Baby," he said. "Baby, thank God you're all right." He kissed the top of her head and squeezed her tight.

"Did you get him?" She couldn't believe the venom in her voice as she spoke into his chest.

"He won't be flying home to the hive."

"Not the bee!" She teetered on the ragged edge of hysteria. "Did you get the bastard who tried to kill me?"

She had no doubt Ty'd gone after him. She wrapped her arms around her husband, sticking her hands into his back pants pockets. Just like she used to do all the time. But she was looking for something more than reassurance this time. She wanted that drop. She hated the regular Mata Hari she was becoming. But, damn it! She was scared.

She wriggled her hands deeper into his pockets and cupped his butt. The man had a tight, grabable ass. But except for a nice, new condom in its wrapper, his pockets were empty!

Did he really think he was going to get lucky with her out here on the mountainside? Or was he planning on using his French tickler on somebody else?

She didn't know which thought upset her more. He shouldn't be carrying a condom around like an optimistic frat guy at a party.

Ty kissed her head again. "No. The bastard got away."

She removed her hands from his pockets, struggling in the process. She shook her head, dismayed. This wasn't like Ty. "I can't believe the bad guy gave you the slip. No one *ever* gives you the slip."

He slid his arms around her waist and pulled her roughly to him again. "I was rattled."

Rattled? Ty? Over me?

She waited for him to say more. Admit something deeper.

Instead, he rested his chin on her head. "Don't worry. I snapped a picture of him and texted it to HQ. They'll make an ID and put out an APB. We'll get him."

She tried to pull away, but Ty held firm. "He was in disguise, all in black. There's no way—"

Just then Keoni came puffing up, out of breath from his uphill run to them. "What's going on?"

He bent over, his hands on his knees, looking up at them in their clench as he caught his breath. "How is she?"

You'd think a cycle tour guide would be in better shape. It was pretty clear now why Keoni drove the van.

"I'm fine," Treflee said into Ty's chest. "Except some guy tried to—"

Ty squeezed her. Hard. Tight enough to silence her and remind her of their cover.

"Dude!" he said, falling back into that cover character she hated. He spoke to Keoni. "She got going too fast. Lost it. Some guy cut her off. She flew off the road at the corner." He gave her a playful chuck under her chin. "She's tough. She'll live."

Treflee squirmed around to get a look at Keoni. He stared at them, obviously wondering about their intimate stance.

"Hysterical," Ty said before Keoni asked the question. "Trying to calm her down."

Which was almost the truth.

Keoni nodded, but he was still frowning. Probably not sure this was the kind of calming down she needed.

"You going to be okay?" Ty said to Treflee.

"Sure." She wiggled in his arms. "You can let go now. I won't freak out. Thanks."

Ty released her and ran his hand through his bleached hair as he studied her. "Looks like we dodged the bullet."

It may have only been Treflee's imagination, but she thought he was being tongue-in-cheek. It would have been just like him. Dodged the bullet, indeed!

Ty smiled that vacant, beach-bum smile at Keoni. "She's got a few scratches and bruises." He shrugged. "Don't know what I would have told Tita if I'd lost a guest. She'd kill me."

Keoni nodded his agreement, looking just as relieved to see Treflee on her feet and talking. She imagined visions of lawsuits were fading.

"Yeah," Keoni said. "We haven't lost a guest yet, either. This is the first, uh, off-road"—he cleared his throat—"incident we've had." He paused and looked worriedly at Treflee. "Not our fault, you understand. We're not liable for other bikers' reckless behavior. Now, if we could find him—"

"I'm not going to sue," she said straight-out.

Keoni nodded automatically, but didn't seem to be listening. "We could go after him."

Ty shrugged. "Dude dressed all in black. Wearing sunglasses."

"We'll call it in," Keoni said, continuing to brighten up as he pinned the blame firmly elsewhere.

"No!" Treflee said. "No calling it in."

Ty shot her a grateful look. For obvious reasons, he didn't want the authorities involved. And neither did she.

Keoni gave her a questioning look. "But—"

"No calling it in. I'm fine. I'm not spending a precious minute of my vacation filling out forms in a police station."

Keoni chewed on the corner of his mouth. "Maybe we should get you to a doctor, just in case—"

"No!" she said again, shaking her head. "Carla, one of our girls, is a nurse. She can look me over. But really, I'm fine."

Keoni looked at once relieved and doubtful. But who was he to argue with a paying guest?

"Let's get out of here and catch up with the others." Ty nodded toward the brush. "The bike and the windbreaker are over there on the other side of those bushes."

Keoni went after the bike and jacket. They waited as he stuffed the torn jacket under his arm and rolled the bike over to them.

"You're not going to charge me for damage to those." Treflee addressed Keoni.

"No, no, of course not," Keoni hurried to reassure her.

"Good." Treflee felt suddenly exhausted.

She stumbled as they started back toward the van.

Ty shot her a concerned look. He swung her up into his arms.

This time she didn't struggle. She put her arms around his neck and rested her head on his shoulder. Whether she liked to admit it to herself or not, she wanted to rest in his arms for a while. Just until the shaky fear in her subsided.

At the van, Treflee dusted herself off and picked the leaves out of her hair. Ty doused her with antiseptic from the first-aid kit and bandaged the worst of her wounds. Keoni threw the bikes in the trailer. Each absorbed in their own thoughts, no one spoke. After a few minutes, Keoni jumped in the driver's seat and they were off.

Used to following slowpoke cyclists and living on Hawaiian time, Keoni wasn't exactly a speed demon behind the wheel, but he knew the roads and drove smoothly. Slow and steady, no surprises, no sudden stops, was just fine with Treflee.

She closed her eyes and sprawled across the seat,

leaning her head against the window, glad to be alive. Just how many more surviving-the-spy-life days was she going to have to endure until she was safely home on the mainland and alone, spyless, in her own queen-sized bed? And how bruised, scratched, bitten, battered, and sore would she be by then?

Sleeping alone used to scare her. She used to worry about being jumped by an enemy agent looking for Ty. No more. No one, not even the neighbor's annoyingly neurotic three-legged dog, had had the temerity to attack her on her own property.

What did scare her was the fact that the mad biker had come after her. Her! There was no mistake about it. But why? What had she done? Who did they think she was?

In the seat behind her, Ty was playing with his cell phone. Putting out the spy equivalent of an APB, no doubt. How long would it take NCS to bring that nefarious biker in?

The three of them made good time and caught up with the others at the protea farm lunch stop with plenty of time left to eat and still stick to the schedule. The girls' bicycles were parked outside the general store and conscientiously locked in place just as Keoni had instructed at the top of the mountain.

"I need a beer," Keoni said, as he jumped out of the van.

Ty nodded and slapped Keoni on the back. "I hear you, bro. The first one's on me."

Treflee scanned the area for dangerous pump-wielding assassins. Shouldn't that have been Ty's job? Then she stared at her two macho-men protectors—nearly ex-husband, beach bum, spy, and big former football-playing half Samoan, half Hawaiian bicycle guy. "Hold it right there, *bros*. One of you two is going to be driving to the beach park after lunch."

And the other one is supposed to be fully alert so he can fend off killers, she might have added.

Keoni shrugged. "I weigh three hundred pounds naked. Before breakfast. One beer isn't even going to register on a Breathalyzer."

Ty nodded his agreement as she tried to pin him with a look and convey he was on spy duty. "What?" he said in a tone that was way too innocent. "I'm not driving."

With that reassuring confrontation under her belt, they entered the crowded store. Tourists and lunching bicycle-tour-takers lay every way Treflee looked. Most of them were clad in black of some kind. Black shorts seemed particularly chic among this crowd. Not what she needed to see. She wasn't particularly fond of cyclists right now. She felt jumpy and skittish.

"Relax!" Ty whispered in her ear. "No way our guy just stopped by for a bite of Hawaiian barbecue on his way out. If we haven't picked him up by now, he's trying like hell to get off the island."

How very reassuring.

The Chinese tour group occupied half a dozen tables in the corner. Terror and apprehension every way she looked. How could she be sure it wasn't one of these guys who'd tried to rip her spokes out?

Three times is a charm, as they say. Twice already, she'd been attacked by someone of Chinese descent. She couldn't be sure about the biker in black. But judging by his build, she wouldn't be surprised if he was Chinese. That made three. Maybe now that she'd survived her third she was safe?

No, much as she'd like to, she didn't believe that.

The Chinese group hardly noticed her. They laughed and spoke in their singsong tones as they ate with disposable chopsticks they'd brought with them, gesturing at each other with them as they spoke. Abi caught her eye and smiled.

Treflee forced herself to smile back.

"Don't worry about them, either," Ty whispered. "What you need is some food to perk you up."

They found the girls huddled at a table near the lunch counter. Even as her eyes adjusted to the dim interior light, it was clear to Treflee that there was trouble in paradise with the Carrie clan. Ty and Keoni seemed aware of it, as well.

Ty turned to her. "I'll order you something from the lunch counter. What do you want?"

His tone and stance telegraphed he wasn't going near those girls with a ten-foot surf paddle. *Coward!*

"Coconut ice cream," Treflee answered without hesitating. Boy, did she need ice cream. In spades.

His gaze darted between Treflee and Carrie and company. "You need protein."

"Ice cream is protein."

Ty rolled his eyes. "Yeah, real well balanced. How about some carbs and fruit and veggies?"

"Ask for a cookie with it. Coconut counts as fruit."

He shook his head in a way that left it clear he wondered why he bothered. "I'll pick something," he whispered.

Then chivalry disappeared. The two men hightailed it to the counter, bypassing the ladies. For her part, Treflee wondered what all the excitement was about as she walked up to Carrie's table. Maybe they'd heard about her accident and were indignant on her part. Maybe there'd been a horrible crash. Something along the lines of a speeding van full of bad guys bursting into flame on the road to Haleakala would have been nice. One could hope! And pyrotechnics always made for a good story.

Laci looked up at her, eyes snapping with jealousy. "Look what the boys finally dragged in."

Faye was a little more observant and astute. "Whoa! What happened to you?"

Treflee shrugged. "Some dude cut me off at the corner. I took a tumble down the hill."

Carla sighed. She reached over and pulled a leaf off Treflee's bike jersey as Treflee sat down. "You missed one." Her expert gaze flicked over the bandaging job Ty had done. "Cleaned those good and used plenty of antibiotic ointment, I hope?"

"Oh, yeah."

Carla looked skeptical. "Want me to take a look?"

"Later," Treflee said, shuddering at the thought of Carla ripping off her bandages. "What's going on here?" She scooted up to the table.

"Kane." Faye looked horrified just speaking the name.

Carrie stared at the table. She looked worried, too. And scared. Treflee couldn't remember ever seeing Carrie scared.

"Kane?" Treflee repeated. At least this had nothing to do with her. The pressure was off.

Carrie's ex-fiancé, Kane, was a big bear of a guy, but solid muscle. The kind of guy who'd probably been a chunky kid. No one messed with the burly cop now. And it was no use verbally sparring with him, either. He wasn't the kind of guy who ever had a word to spare.

"What about Kane?" Treflee asked, fearing the worst.

"He wants Carrie back." Brandy sounded as if she were issuing a death sentence.

Now? Just days before the wedding Carrie had called off?

Good thing Treflee was already sitting because her legs went weak as her anger rose. Though maybe the weak legs were the aftereffect of actually having had to pedal down the mountain for more than her allotted two hundred yards.

"What? How do you know? When did this happen?" Treflee took a deep breath as she tried to digest the news.

"He texted her as we were coming down the mountain." Brandy flicked a glance in Carrie's direction. "Texted her!" She sounded amazed at Kane's audacity.

"He's coming to Maui." Faye's eyes were round.

Brandy ignored Faye's interjection. "Upset her so much she just took off down the mountain. We had a hard time keeping up with her."

At least Kane's text explained why they'd all taken off and left Treflee to the mercy of a man in black spandex.

Carrie mutely stared at the table as if she weren't the center of the conversation.

"When will he be here?" It seemed like a logical question.

Brandy nearly bit her head off for asking. "He didn't say."

Out of the corner of her eye, Treflee saw Ty approaching with her ice cream and a plated lunch.

Treflee reached across the table and squeezed her cousin's hand. "Do you want to see him?"

Carrie shook her head, pulled her hand away, and burst into tears.

Treflee started so badly she nearly jumped out of her chair. She hadn't seen Carrie cry since they were kids. The sight tugged at her heart. She shot her cousin a sympathetic look, feeling genuinely sorry for her, wanting to comfort her somehow, but having no idea how. "Don't cry, Carrie. We're here for you."

Ty slid the plate in front of her—two mounds of rice, a scoop of macaroni salad, and chicken katsu. Then he turned right back around and darted off, taking her ice cream with him.

Judging by the way men reacted to tears, Treflee wondered if the most effective weapon on the battlefield wouldn't be a great big female cry-fest.

She ignored the yummy-looking macaroni salad in front of her and addressed the group. "We'll just have to protect Carrie and keep Kane away from her, then, won't we?"

CHAPTER THIRTEEN

After lunch, Ty helped Keoni load the bikes into the trailer for the drive to Paia. Just as he loaded the last one in, his phone made the distinctive ping of an incoming encrypted text message from headquarters.

"Hey, dude, I'll be right back. I gotta respond to this."

"A la-dy?" Keoni strung the last word out suggestively.

Ty glanced at Tref.

"Ah, a one-woman man, huh?"

Ty grinned and shook his phone. "This is just business." And he was off to go use his top-secret decoder ring to read his text. Playing spy was like the best boyhood game there was.

Ty walked away from the group and logged on to his secure phone. Emmett wanted him to call.

Ty made sure he couldn't be overheard and dialed. "Hey, boss," he said when Emmett picked up.

Emmett launched straight into business. "Got your message about the video feed and basement. We're on it.

"The guy who attacked Treflee has no record. He's an astronomy professor at the University of Hawaii. Regularly does research at the Haleakala Observatory as part of a grant. From time to time he works on the university's joint ventures with the air force on Haleakala at AMOS."

Ty sighed. So that's where he came from—an observatory. Just like Ty's contact. A shiver ran down his back.

"Our guy's a Chinese immigrant. Married. Lives on the Big Island with a wife and two kids. Wife and he were naturalized ten years ago."

"Who does he work for?" Ty tried to keep his end of the conversation cryptic, just in case.

"RIOT. The getaway driver was his wife."

Good. We've rooted out two terrorists.

"We have them in custody."

Heart pounding, Ty asked a question he knew Emmett would understand. "And me?"

Damn Tref again! If my cover is blown and I'm kicked off the mission . . . or worse, out of the Agency . . .

He owed it to George and his country to complete the mission. He had to stop RIOT from obtaining the Pinpoint Project. And he had to win Tref back. He couldn't imagine life without her.

"You're good. In the clear," Emmett said. "We picked the mad biker and his getaway driver up at the bottom of the mountain before they could communicate with anyone. We checked their equipment. We're confident they didn't get any messages off."

Excellent. Ty had really been sweating that one.

"We'll interrogate them," Emmett said. "But I doubt we'll get much. They're low-level operatives."

Ty had a terrible thought. "Why did they go after Tref?"

"RIOT and their associates, the Fuk Ching, are under the misapprehension that your wife is our master spy."

"What!" Ty cursed beneath his breath. "How in the hell did they get that idea?"

Emmett laughed. "Seems Treflee's always where the action is. They were particularly suspicious when a woman staying next door to Sugar Love Plantation showed up at lunch with Hal."

Ty cursed some more. He'd put Tref in even more danger.

"One more thing," Emmett said. "Word on the street is some dumb, blond beach bum has been fawning all over Treflee. That would be you?"

Ty pictured Emmett swilling a whiskey and having a good laugh over that one with the boys at Langley. Ty scowled. "Yes."

"Always working hard," Emmett said. "Humint proof you're making progress on Mission Reconciliation?"

"Absolutely," Ty said. He refused to admit failure yet. He'd get there in the end.

Emmett gave him instructions. "Let them continue to think Treflee is the spy. The less they suspect you and Greg, the better."

Ty argued with him. "Damn it, Emmett! No. This is too dangerous."

"She'll be fine. You've taught her how to handle herself in a pinch. And you'll be there to bail her out. You'll be her hero. Missions accomplished."

Yeah, right. Ty pictured Emmett having a good laugh over that one, too. Somehow Ty couldn't imagine Tref with hand to forehead, whispering, "My hero," before falling into a grateful faint in his arms.

"Keep up the good work." If Emmett had been there in person, he would have slapped Ty on the back.

Good thing Emmett couldn't see him gritting his teeth.

"Hey, bro!" Keoni called to him. "Time to head out."

"Duty calls," Ty said.

"Go to it," Emmett said.

Ty broke the secure connection and jogged to the van.

Treflee was just stepping up into the van when Ty caught her arm and pulled her aside.

"What was up inside?" he asked in a whisper.

"Man troubles," Treflee replied. "Carrie's ex wants her back." She shot Ty a pointed look. "He's coming to get her."

"Coming to the island?" He sounded surprised.

She nodded. "You got it. And she's scared." Treflee sighed.

"Is he a danger?"

Treflee shrugged. "I honestly don't know. I had to swear we'll protect her."

Ty gave her a look that clearly left the impression he thought she wasn't up to the task. "Good thing she has her other bridesmaids, the cop/soldier girls, with her."

"What!" she hissed back at him. "I think I can take care of this. Who's survived three attacks in three days, huh, master spy?"

He smiled at her, all flirt and beach bum, looking devilishly sexy in his suntanned skin, making it hard for her to stay mad at him and hang on to her hurt feelings. He leaned in and whispered in her ear, "And who's saved your delectable, beautiful hide each time?"

She frowned. "Okay, I'll give you the lei guy, and the surfing incident. But I handled the biker on my own."

He raised a brow.

"Okay, fine, you swatted the bee and pulled me out of the bushes, but I was already safe by then." She lifted her chin.

"You didn't happen to notice how he suddenly flinched and backed off right as he was about to stick that pump in your rear spokes? Why was that, I wonder?"

She stared at him. A horrible thought dawned on her. "You didn't?"

He nodded.

"You shot at him?" She went cold. "You could have hit me!"

"But I didn't, did I?" He looked too smug. "I need to

get back to the range. My aim's off. I just grazed his arm. I meant to take him out."

She was certain he was trying to rattle her.

He took her arm. "Cheer up. I have some good news."

Up close he smelled like yummy, yummy coconut oil, the kind that reminded her of a summer beach romance . . . and sex. Yes, sex on the beach was not just a drink to them.

Treflee stared deep into his eyes. She hoped he meant what she thought he did.

"We got them. Picked them up at the bottom of the mountain."

She threw herself into his arms and hugged him. "I love you!"

Spontaneous hugging of the nearly ex is not the best move in a ditch-him-and-get-on-with-life plan. Even if you *are* eternally grateful to him. She realized a second too late what she'd just said and done.

She cleared her throat and pulled away. Well, at least she now knew why Bond got the girls. Relief is a powerful inhibition inhibitor. Or so it appeared.

Ty was staring deep into her eyes with his mesmerizing truth-serum stare.

Keep him guessing. A little mystery was good for a nearly defunct marriage.

She smiled up at him under her lashes. You know what? She could see herself enjoying flirting with him. He deserved to be tormented. Yeah, the old "flirt with him and leave him wondering if you meant it" trick. Just her style.

Laci stepped between them and up into the van.

Ty grinned at Treflee and leaned in to whisper, "Time to drop back into our cover characters." He held out his arm for her to get on.

She took the only vacant seat. Ty plopped in beside her. Right beside her. So close the heat from his thigh next to hers made her flush. She turned sideways in the seat and leaned back against the window, savoring the moment. The bad guys were off the mean streets of Hawaii! It was a real *Hawaii Five-O* moment!

Keoni closed the doors, fired up the engine, and they were off, hopefully *not* on another adventure. The other girls were tired. They settled in and fell asleep just a few minutes out of the parking lot.

Treflee was too wound up. She studied Ty, trying to figure out how she could be so conflicted. Loving him, hating him. Wanting him. Wanting to hit him. Angry at him. Grateful to him. All in the space of a few minutes. It had all been so simple and wonderful in the beginning.

The first time she met Ty, she accidently shot him in the leg with her pink Pepperstriker 2000. Of course, you're not supposed to shoot someone in the leg with pepper spray, even she knew that. The guy who sold it to her demonstrated specifically how to go for the face. He said the striker's ergonomic grip was *supposed* to help her aim. And it might have, if Ty hadn't sneaked up on her from out of nowhere.

She was in college, working late all alone on a project at a building on the edge of campus just after midnight. She should have called for an escort home. But she worked on projects late two or three nights a week and calling for an escort was a hassle. So she bought the pepper spray, determined to be independent.

She'd paused at the building exit, set her backpack on the floor and kneeled beside it to dig out the spray before heading out into the dark night. She had it in her hand, with her finger on the trigger, when a pair of legs clad in jeans and topped off with a pair of Vans appeared before her simply out of nowhere. She swore she hadn't heard anyone approach.

"Hey," a deep, sexy voice said to her.

She was startled, panicked, and pulled the trigger,

shooting spray right into his shin. Which was when they both found out that yes, pepper spray *can* penetrate denim.

She started coughing from the residual fumes. Her eyes watered. Her heart raced. She looked up into the coughing, tear-streaked face of the most handsome guy she'd ever seen, and her breath caught. Even with red, watery eyes he was gorgeous. And he was laughing as he tried not to wince from the pain in his leg.

"I'm so sorry. I'm so sorry." She automatically reached out to brush his pants off with her hand.

"Don't touch my leg!" He leaned down and grabbed her wrist with a strong, warm hand, stopping her just in time. "It's practically lethal right now. Nice to meet you, too. I'm Ty." He gave her a hand up. "Never had a girl make me so hot in just a few seconds."

She blushed. He was joking, referring to the pepper spray, of course, but somehow he made her feel beautiful all the same.

"I'm Treflee."

"Pretty name." He coughed again. "Got any baby shampoo on you, Treflee?"

She stared at him and blinked, trying to see past the tears streaming down her face. Her mascara was probably running. Looking at this hot guy, she was suddenly worried about how she looked, which was probably a wreck. "Baby shampoo? Is that a non sequitur to keep me off balance? Or do you have a point?"

"Baby shampoo helps wash the pepper spray away and stop the burn." He covered his mouth with his arm and coughed into it.

"Sorry!" She couldn't stop apologizing. She felt really bad. He was being so stoic and understanding. "I don't have any on me."

She looked at his jeans again and wiped her eyes with

the back of her hands. "My roommate might have some back at the apartment." Which was the truth. Her roommate used it because she thought it was gentle on her hair.

He arched a brow. She felt mortified. She hadn't meant to seem brazen, as though she were inviting him home after she'd just met and attacked him. She was simply trying to help.

"We could cut the pants leg off? If we had scissors." She winced and looked apologetic. She didn't have scissors, either. "Rip it off with brute strength?"

He clicked his tongue and shook his head. "Trying to rip my pants off already?" Beneath the watery tears, his eyes danced with amusement. He grinned.

She blushed. "What's the alternative? Take your jeans off and walk around campus in your boxers?"

"So you think I'm a boxers guy?"

"I was too polite to say tighty-whities."

He laughed and broke out coughing again. When he gained control he said, "Why don't I just wait forty-five to fifty minutes for the effects to wear off and the burning sensation to start to fade." He nodded toward her backpack. "Get your stuff. I'll walk you home."

She hesitated.

"Don't worry. I'm not going to attack you. If I was, I would have taken you up on the offer to remove my pants. Plus I know you have a pepper gun on you."

"It only had one shot."

He laughed. "Probably shouldn't have told me that."

"Yeah." She smiled. "Are you going to be okay?"

"Want to sit with me and have a coffee while we wait an hour and find out? I know a great all-night diner."

"Yeah," she said, feeling unaccountably giddy for having just shot a very handsome someone.

He picked up her backpack, tossed it over his shoulder, winced, held his pants leg away from his skin, and opened the door for her with his shoulder.

Then they went to have coffee and talked until three in the morning. He kissed her when he dropped her off at her campus apartment. Ty was the first person who'd made her smile, really smile, since her dad had died from cancer the month before.

The next time she saw Ty, he gave her the new, improved Pepperstriker 3000, which came equipped with a safety lock, and promised her lessons on how to use it.

To this day, he still didn't trust her with a firearm. Looking back, she realized she'd loved him since that first time she met him. No one else had ever made her feel so safe, or so happy and loved.

How had things gone so wrong?

Ty raised a brow and wiped his chin with his shoulder. "Do I have something on my face?"

His question brought her back to the present. "Just looking at you." She sounded too breathless and infatuated for Treflee the wife. But just right for a woman supposedly infatuated and wanting a fling with a hot tour guide. "You're incredibly easy on the eyes."

Ty had always told her the easiest and most believable lies began with the truth. She smiled and looked down. "I bet all the girls tell you that."

By which she meant—in code-speak—were there more girls?

He seemed to realize her intention. He tipped her chin up and stared into her eyes. "There's only one girl's opinion that's ever mattered."

Her heart fluttered. She sighed, wishing it were true. Or maybe it was true, just not true enough. "When this . . . fling . . . is over, we . . . I . . . have to go back to real life."

She pulled her feet up on the seat and curled up, wrapping her arms around her knees.

"What's wrong with your real life?"

She tilted her head, staying in character. "Surfer *and* psychologist?"

"Being out in the surf gives you perspective, you know?"

She didn't, but she didn't call him on it, either.

"You didn't answer my question." He reached over and disentangled one of her legs, pulling her foot to rest on his thigh.

He untied her shoe. Took it and her sock off and tossed them on the floor.

She wiggled her toes and sighed. It felt so good to be barefoot. Ty knew she hated wearing shoes.

He squeezed her foot, just like he had a hundred times before after she'd had a long day at work, just in the way that made her go weak in the knees and released every ounce of tension in her body. He squeezed it hard and stroked the inside of her arch with his thumb.

That was too much, too intimate. From the way he was looking at her, he knew it, too. She tried to pull away. "Someone could wake up and see us," she whispered.

He mouthed the word "so?" as he held on tight.

It was just like Ty not to care. And no doubt he was fully aware and on alert to the state of the others—asleep, or awake and watching and listening.

He settled her foot into the heart of his lap, right into his warm, quickly hardening family jewels. He stared her directly in the eye as he ran his hand over her calf in a way that made every pleasurable nerve in her body jump to attention and her breath catch.

He stroked her leg again, kneading her calf, then cupping both hands around it and squeezing as he ran them up to her knee. "You're tense. Loosen up. Talk to me."

Talk to him? With him touching her like that, with her foot tantalizingly near him?

But she gave him points for guts. One little slip of her foot and his voice would jump two octaves higher. Not that that's what she had in mind.

She nestled her foot deeper into his lap, wriggling her toes and feeling him grow harder still. Remembering where this kind of play used to lead.

He didn't give anything away and neither did she.

"You really want to know?" she asked at last.

"Yeah. I do." He remained stoic as she snuggled her foot against him.

She took a deep breath. "In real life, I'm all alone." Her voice broke unexpectedly. It was all so clear to her, she *was* all alone. Empty.

His hands stilled. His Adam's apple bobbed. He stared at her but didn't say anything.

She swallowed hard and studied him. He looked like his thoughts weren't pleasant. "What about you? What's *your* real life like?"

He stared out the window past her, his eyes unfocused. His brow furrowed. "I'm following a dream. Doing what I was born to do. I can't imagine ever giving this up. Ever doing anything else."

He focused on her again. "As long as the surf lasts and the adrenaline's high, this is the life." He rubbed her knee with the palm of his hand, then cupped it tightly in his hand.

She bit her lip and nodded. *Irreconcilable differences.*

"But at the end of the day"—he bent down and kissed her knee—"life's a beach when there's no one to share your triumphs with." He looked up at her.

Did she imagine it or was he pleading with her to understand?

Her breath caught. She fought a nearly irresistible urge

to run her fingers through his hair. She clenched her hands.

"Ever thought of giving up the nine-to-five office drag and just hanging out in a place like this?" he asked out of the blue.

She frowned at him. "What do you mean?"

"You know what I mean. Live in the moment. Be spontaneous."

She sighed. "Chase adventure? Like you?"

"Yeah, why not?"

She stared at him. For the moment, he was so in character, so much like an actual beach bum, she practically didn't know him. And yet she did. "What about a home?"

"Home is where the heart is."

She shook her head and laughed. "Now you're just spouting clichés."

"I'm serious. What is home?"

"Don't go existential on me." She paused. "I need stability."

"Really? Why?"

"Because." She paused, trying to frame her thoughts. "Because in the long run, jumping here and there in search of adventure is no way to raise a family."

"And you want a family?" His voice was tender, the question sounded sincere.

They should have discussed this before they married. But the thought of children had never come up. Until her accidental pregnancy she'd never thought she wanted children. And he didn't want them even now.

"Yes." She didn't mean to sound so emotional. But since the miscarriage, just the mention of a baby brought tears to her eyes.

He was quiet for moment. "Even if kids are part of the game, why not?" He looked and sounded totally serious.

Did that mean he wanted children? That he'd relented?

"If you're there with the person you love, why can't you raise a family anywhere?"

She studied him, startled to realize he was serious. They'd been over this ground before. Many times. He wanted her to follow him on some of his longer missions. Be part of his cover life. Be with him.

It struck her for the first time that maybe she hadn't always been there for him. She hadn't thought he'd needed her support.

"Some people need more security." She sighed. "We have conflicting lives. You and I would never work, beach boy. It's a good thing we just have these few days and then it's over." And she meant it.

He squeezed her knee and stared intently at her. "Give us a fighting chance, Tref."

CHAPTER FOURTEEN

The rest of the trip into Paia passed quietly. Treflee slept snuggled into Ty, resting her head on his shoulder. The experts say you can't sleep unless you feel secure. Just how well would she sleep if she knew even part of what he knew?

He watched her doze, wondering about her suddenly flirtatious nature. Either she was having way too much fun staying in character or she was up to something. In any case, her plan was going to backfire on her. You can only play with sexual heat so long before you get burned. And he meant to scorch.

His only concern was whether he'd have the staying power he wanted once he actually touched her, or whether he'd lose himself all too quickly. He hadn't had sex in the six months since he'd left her. Just her breast brushing against his arm as the van jiggled along aroused him.

Fast and furious wasn't what he had in mind. He had to make her see how much he loved her. In those close, intimate moments after lovemaking, he had to coax her into telling him what he'd done that was so heinous she was tossing him out of her life. He had no intention of being her boy toy. He wanted to be her husband again. That was the mission, his personal mission now that had nothing to do with Emmett's orders. He wanted her love and nothing short of it.

Keoni pulled the van to a stop in Baldwin Beach Park. Treflee stirred and sighed. In the instant before she was fully awake, she looked up at him and smiled in the loving way she used to when she first woke in the morning, looking almost like she was about to kiss him. Then she woke enough to come to her senses and pulled away.

Too bad. He could have shown her how good a wake-up kiss could be.

The second Big Auau van waited for them, just as planned.

"Wake up, sleepyhead. We're here."

Tref rubbed her eyes. "Where's here?"

"Historic Paia."

Keoni jumped out of the driver's seat and ran around to open the van door.

The other bridesmaids and the ex-bride stirred and woke up. Carrie popped to attention like the soldier she'd been and prairie-dogged out the window.

Ty nudged Tref. "What's she doing?"

"Looking for Kane."

"Why would he be here? How would he know where she is?"

Tref stretched and sighed. "Kane's a cop, an expert tracker. That's his specialty. Always gets his man and all that."

"I see." Ty shook his head, feeling skeptical. "And she thinks—"

"Yep."

Carrie had stepped to the van door. She looked around cautiously before slowly getting out.

"Oh, boy." Ty couldn't help sounding frustrated. The last thing he needed was a jumpy client and a cop tracking them.

"Yeah." Tref nodded her agreement. But when it was her turn to file out, she paused at the door, too.

"Worried about Kane?" he teased her.

She frowned at him. "You know who I'm worried about."

He leaned in and whispered in her ear, close enough to do a little heavy breathing just to rattle her. "Stay close to me and in character and you'll be fine."

She shook her head and got out of the bicycle tour van.

Oh, yeah, Treflee planned on sticking to Ty like Super Glue or something even stronger. Well, maybe not Super Glue, that stuff *never* let go. She was dissolving this "two shall become one" union in favor of the separate halves soon. Maybe she'd just stick to him like that high-strength poster tape—hangs on for as long as you need, releases when you want it to, and leaves no scars behind.

The coast, literally the coast, seemed clear and sparkled prettily in the just past high noon sun. Oh, to be on the beach, wading in the surf, a blanket on the sand, half a dozen beach reads at her fingertips, and a cooler stocked with diet cola. Now that was the life.

Damn Ty and his constant intrigue. When this was all over and done with, she was going to take a real vacation. One where she didn't run into any nearly ex-husbands. Fortunately, there was only the one. And she was smart enough to check with Emmett about where that one would be before she booked her next getaway.

Laci and the girls formed a protective barrier around Carrie. Treflee had never known her cousin to be such a coward. Treflee was convinced Kane was no danger to Carrie physically. He was a cheater, not an abuser. That left only her heart at stake. Which confused Treflee— wasn't Carrie the one who'd called things off? Couldn't she just tell Kane to take a flying leap and go home?

Treflee caught herself. Wasn't she in the same situation as Carrie? Well, similar. But as she knew, it wasn't all that easy to just let go of someone. She knew that all too well and felt a sudden pang of sympathy for Carrie.

Ty asked the girls if they wanted a few minutes to stretch and enjoy the beach. They declined, strangely eager for a three-hour car trip along a winding, slow road almost guaranteed to make one carsick. Ah, well, the fickleness of adventurers.

Ty held the Big Auau van door open for the ladies to climb in. When Treflee tried to board, he caught her arm. "Ride up front with me. I could use the company."

What was he up to? It really didn't matter. She was grabbing that front seat. With her tendency toward motion sickness, she wasn't taking any chances.

Laci overheard and horned in. "What? You mean one of us can ride up front with you?" She smiled sweetly at Ty. "I'm more fun and I can read a map." She winked at him.

Yeah, reading a map was code for putting her hands all over Ty as he drove. On Ty's leg, up his thigh, squeezing, teasing until she found something she liked and got what she wanted.

Ty gave Laci his slow, sexy smile. Which irrationally irritated Treflee. He let his gaze rake over Laci as if he were enjoying every inch of the view, and then sighed as if it were a pity he'd already asked Treflee to join him.

"He doesn't need a map. He has GPS." Treflee took his arm. "Besides, I get carsick easily."

Carrie chimed in. "Yes, she does. Let her ride up front, Lace, or we'll all be sorry."

The truth was, Treflee hadn't actually gotten carsick since she was eleven years old. Woozy, yes. But actually losing the cookies, no. She reserved that for vicious roller coasters and roiling seas.

Laci's smile remained in place, but her eyes grew hard as she glanced at Treflee. "Sure."

Seats settled, they all piled in. Ty fired up the van. They backtracked a few miles into Paia proper where they stopped at a local restaurant full of touristy flavor to pick up their catering.

Carrie eyed the bar and grocery store that flanked it on either side. "I need a drink."

A chorus of "me, toos" rang out. Next thing, Carrie and her entourage had piled out and were streaming into the bar.

"Coming?" Faye asked Treflee.

Treflee shook her head.

"No?" Faye looked quizzically at her.

"Alcohol makes the motion sickness worse."

Faye shrugged, looking sorry for Treflee. And she was off.

Ty looked at Treflee. "Come with me. I'll buy you a cola while we wait. That always helps calm your stomach."

Treflee followed him into the restaurant and sat at a stool at the counter, sipping her cola while Ty shot the breeze with the girl behind the counter, browsed the souvenir racks, and made a purchase he obviously didn't want her to see.

"Presents for you girls." He winked as he clutched his plain brown bag.

Twenty minutes later, Ty loaded a well-stocked cooler and an overflowing picnic hamper into the back of the van. He tossed his brown paper bag on the front seat and eyed the bar. "Go drag them out, girl."

"Me? Why do I have to be the bad guy?"

"Hey, I'm just the amiable tour guide, not the cop." He shrugged. "They can stay as long as they like as far as I'm concerned. I don't mind blind hairpin turns in the pitch-black of night. In fact, I kind of like them."

"Oh, fine." Treflee glared at him. She found them sitting

at the bar, swaying on their barstools, piña coladas sitting in front of each of them.

"Hey, let's hit the road. The road to Hana is treacherous in the dark," she said to them.

It took them several minutes to settle the bill and decide whether they wanted the souvenir pineapple mugs. Which looked suspiciously like the mug Hal had bought Treflee at that burger joint. Finally, pineapple mugs won. But empty pineapple mugs were apparently anathema.

Carrie insisted on stopping by the grocery to pick up liquor to refill them. "You need Drama . . . Drama . . . mine."

Carrie nodded sagely, as if she were the best cousin in all the world and not simply using Treflee as an excuse.

Oh, boy! Slurred, choppy speech and sway were not good.

Finally, another ten minutes later, the bridal party from hell reappeared carrying brown bags full of liquor and pineapple mugs decorated with tiny umbrellas.

Carrie waved a box of Dramamine at her. "Got it!"

"Open the van doors, Ty," Treflee whispered to him. "Before they escape. Watching over them is like herding cats." She sighed. "I suppose you're going to insist on checking their mugs for bugs?"

"No need. I'm sure they're clean." He winked at her again.

Great, I'm the only one he doesn't trust to bring home a clean pineapple mug!

Carrie insisted Treflee down a Dramamine before they got in the van.

Treflee humored her. "Satisfied?"

Carrie nodded and waved the girls into the van. Finally, the girls were all loaded up.

Grinning like an idiot, in a way that only made him more attractive and brought up her hackles of suspicion, Ty climbed into the van and opened the bag.

"Think fast!" He tossed a small box to each girl and watched their reaction times. Definitely impaired. Hopefully they'd sleep it off before they reached Hana.

"Heard you girls are on the lookout for Carrie's ex. Thought these would help. Bonus—they're great for scoping out the flesh on the beach. Very subtle."

Carrie broke out laughing as Ty handed a box to Treflee.

"Hawaiian rearview spy glasses? 'Check out the beach bodies and action behind you without drawing attention.'" Treflee arched a brow as she read the front of the box they came in. "You got these at the restaurant?"

He nodded. "Awesome, huh?"

Oh, the man is good. He had a killer sense of humor.

"Funny, I didn't see Bond's gadget maker, Q, lurking about anywhere?"

He laughed. "He wouldn't be much of a spy if you did, would he?"

She shook her head and leaned in to whisper, "Is that where you go for all your spy gadgets?"

He just grinned.

"'Secretly see what's going on behind you. For ages over five'" Treflee read aloud from the back of the box. "And look, they have UV filter lenses and flexible frames. Wow! High-tech."

"Yeah, and they say Maui on them, too. Notice that?"

"Yeah, I did. Great camouflage for the vacationing spy. Blend right in with the other tourists and no one's the wiser," she quipped.

"Exactly!" He smiled and looked directly at the girls. "All the secret agents on the island use them."

And then she couldn't help it. She burst out laughing as she pulled hers out of the box. "Pink? Very subtle."

"And girly," he added.

Yeah. He knew pink was her fave. Nice of him to remember.

She put her glasses on and gave them a try. Hmmm, worked like a charm. She could watch Laci scowling at her with crystal clarity.

"Okay, let's get this show on the road." Ty started the engine. "We don't want to be on the road in the dark."

No, she didn't want to be anywhere in the dark right now. Not after the vicious attack on the volcano. Funny how even though it had happened in daylight, dark still seemed scarier. Then there was the fact that being anywhere in the dark with Ty was dangerous business—to her heart.

They were off. One thing you could say about Ty—he drove smoothly. No sudden starts or stops, just fluid motion with the scenery humming by.

He should be smooth. He'd taken enough extreme driving school classes for half a dozen men. You didn't get to be a high-performance driver like Bond without some schooling. Plus he loved to drive. Which meant that when they were out, he always did the driving and she did the backseat driving. Hey, whatever worked.

In this case, Treflee appreciated his smooth skills on the twisting, turning, sometimes one-lane roads, other times on the sharp turns. And she got to admire the view, which consisted partly of his strong profile.

In the back, the girls opened their liquor and had a round of pineapple schnapps, getting louder and sillier as they drove on.

Ty played tour guide to perfection, pulling over for all scenic spots and tourist traps. They stopped at the painted bark eucalyptus trees—beautiful. And the girls had another drink. The Maui Grown Market. Clink, have another drink. The Waikamoi Ridge Trail, where they strolled through trees, bamboo, and ferns. The Garden of Eden Arboretum, where they spent a fascinating few hours strolling the amazing gardens. And Ty got so up close and personal with her, Treflee began thinking of the reason

God had made woman for man in the original Garden of Eden. Back before there were fig leaves! Was it really appropriate to be fantasizing about your naked nearly ex?

And of course, clink pineapple mugs! Have another drink or two at the van before departing.

While the girls were distracted by their pineapple mugs full of spirits, Treflee was totally distracted by Ty.

Somehow at each stop, wherever she turned, however she turned, Ty was there beside her, flirting, teasing, smiling. He stood too close, brushed against her too often, touched her arm or her shoulder, whispered in her ear when a simple comment from afar would do. How he could be so calm when she was looking behind every bamboo shoot for a guy to jump out with a lethal bike pump was beyond her.

Still, in a weird way, she was grateful. His casual attitude and demeanor were calming. And if he could flirt, so could she. She backed into him, smiled at him, stroked his shoulder as she "brushed a bug off." She cooed and flattered. It had been years since she'd flirted like this and it felt good.

After the arboretum, they jumped back in the van. The highway pulled closer to the coast and water. As they came upon Nuaailua Bay, the road hugged the rugged edge of the hills, winding and curving into two narrow no-passing lanes. A concrete brick barrier, not tall enough or substantial enough for Treflee's tastes, hugged the downhill side of the road. It looked to her like a person, or vehicle, with enough initiative could topple over it with no problem.

The view—deep blue and green water, gentle waves crashing against volcanic rock below, blue, blue horizon, and tropical vegetation—took Treflee's breath away. It was both bluer and greener than anything she'd ever seen before.

Though the road was often crowded, this time of day most of the traffic was heading the other way, back to Lahaina.

Treflee relaxed. Though it had been only this morning, the race down the volcano seemed like days ago. "Wow! The view takes your breath away," she said to Ty.

He smiled and nodded.

"I can see how a person could live here. Live here and never grow tired of this."

He turned and looked at her. "Can you?"

Wrong thing to say! "Sure. Why not?" Though she was lying and was pretty sure he knew it.

He shook his head and smiled.

Devious girl that she was, Treflee got a wicked thought. He'd been tantalizing and teasing her for the entire trip. It was time to fight back. Treflee had taken her secret agent rearview glasses off several stops back and changed them in favor of her polarizing sunglasses. Now she pulled them out of her purse and swapped them again. In the backseats, the others seemed occupied with the view. Excellent!

She and Ty used to play a driving game to pass the time. No "I spy" or alphabet game for them. Their game had always had a much more sensual edge. It went something like this—she tried to distract him and he tried not to let it affect his driving, not to let the distraction show at all.

She leaned over and whispered, "Want to play a game?" At the same time she grabbed his knee and squeezed.

"You sure? This is a dangerous road. Most fatalities in the state."

He was mocking her. He wasn't afraid. He was up for anything she threw at him.

"You think I'm afraid?"

He nodded toward the barrier. "Lots of curves ahead. Not much protection if things get out of hand. Big drop-off. Water and rocks below."

"Bring it on." She ran her fingers along the inside of his thigh as he slowed and then accelerated into the next corner. "We're on the uphill side."

"Bet hedger."

She laughed and lifted the edge of his shorts with her fingertips, sliding her hand beneath the shorts, inching upward on his taut, defined leg. She knew this territory well and liked the feel just as much as ever. Just how bold would she be with her cousin and crew in the seat behind her? Good thing she had her spy glasses.

She glanced at the group in her rearview glasses. What handy little devices these were. The girls were all drinking and gawking at the view.

"Oh, shit!" Ty said.

I have him! The thought gave her particular delight. So long without her had made him way too susceptible to her touch.

Just then, Treflee caught a glimpse in her glasses of a car barreling up behind them and realized what his "oh, shit" was really about. "What's that idiot doing? Is he drunk? Tap your brakes. Make sure he sees us."

Ty shot her a quick deadpan look. "Oh, sweetheart, he sees us. Think bike pumps. Leis."

The bright Hawaiian sun felt suddenly cold. Treflee's mouth went dry. She squeezed Ty's thigh.

Ty stepped on the accelerator.

The van, definitely not a high-precision driving instrument, hesitated as if it were thinking about maybe moseying along someday. Meanwhile, the other car, which obviously had more horsepower, gained on them. Mercifully, the van lurched forward just as the car behind them came up on their rear bumper, way too close for comfort.

Next to her, Ty locked his arms. She watched him tighten his grip on the wheel.

Ty thinks they're going to ram us!

In the backseats, the others were still blissfully unaware of the danger.

Treflee started to shake. If this had been a Bond movie, the predatory car would have had some lethal ramming device on the front of it. A whirring saw blade. A stiletto tire puncher. Or it may have been equipped with an antiballistic missile.

She hoped they didn't have any missiles, tacks, or machine guns. The most lethal thing she had on her was the nail file in her bag. Ty probably had a gun. But how was he going to draw it and shoot with any accuracy while negotiating this tangle of a road?

Carrie had a gun. Back at the plantation. Thank goodness, because at this point of inebriation, she was as likely to hit one of her bridesmaids or Ty as the bad guys.

Treflee scanned the other car, looking for a sawed-off shotgun or a semiautomatic hanging from a window as she dug her nails into Ty's leg.

He grabbed her hand and pulled it off. "You're about to draw blood before they do."

"Thanks for the reassurance." She clutched the edge of her seat with the same enthusiasm, totally white-knuckling it.

Ty floored it into the next curve.

One of the girls in the back yelled, "Go, Ty! We're smokin'!"

The others began chanting, "Go, Ty!," and raised their mugs to him.

Treflee was not amused. "You're going too fast! The speed limit's fifteen." Backseat driver and wife instincts were hard to break.

"You're worried about a ticket?" He checked his speedometer. "Now?"

"I'm worried about smashing into the side of a volcanic hill at a hundred miles an hour."

"Calm down. I'm only going sixty." He glanced in his rearview mirror.

Afraid she'd get carsick if she took her eyes off the road and turned around, she looked in her rearview glasses again. The maniac was still closing in on them. She closed her eyes and prayed.

The girls in the backseats finally caught on to the danger and began swearing.

"Is that Kane? I bet it's Kane!" Laci's voice pitched an octave higher in fear and excitement, becoming piercing and slurred.

"Call him, Carrie!" Faye yelled. "Tell him we'll pull over and talk things out before he kills us."

"I'm not talking to Kane. He can just go to hell."

"Either he is or we are." Carla, who evidently was used to emergencies, sounded calm. Good to know she was a happy drunk. "How good is your first-aid kit, Ty?"

"Oh, for heaven's sake!" Brandy yelled. "You're going to talk to the man!"

Treflee opened her eyes and stared in her glasses behind her, trying to calm down. "Does he have a gun?"

Carrie swiveled around to get a look. "Hey! That's not Kane."

"Gun?" Treflee repeated.

She watched Brandy squint and shake her head. "No gun. But the driver looks mean." She paused. "And Chinese. He has a really cool tattoo on his neck."

"Fuk Ching," Treflee whispered, but not quietly enough.

"What did you say?" Carrie called up. "Did you just use the F-word?" She broke into a gale of giggles.

Treflee frowned. The things drunks found amusing.

The car rammed them, jarring everyone inside and shaking Treflee's teeth. The picnic basket in the back tipped over and crashed against the back door.

Ty punched the steering wheel and cursed. When that

didn't work, he resorted to sweet-talking the van into sub-
mission.

"The bastard!" Carrie yelled out as if she'd just realized there was some danger. "He's trying to run us off the
road!"

"No one runs *us* off the road, do they, girls?" Brandy
sounded indignant. She flipped the driver of the car the
finger.

"No!" Treflee screamed at her. "You'll make him mad."

Ty shot her another one of his understated deadpan
looks. "Really?"

"Mad!" Carrie screamed. "I'll show you mad." She
opened the window and tossed her pineapple schnapps
onto the attacker's windshield.

His wipers went on and he rammed them again.

Carrie cursed and shook her fist at him. "This is war!
Battle stations!"

Battle stations?

"You don't have your gun, right?" Treflee called back
to her, fingers crossed.

"Left it at the plantation," Carrie yelled back. She and
the others were waving liquor bottles and pineapple mugs
or reaching into their purses. "Ty, how you doing up
there? Can you handle the driving? Need me to step in?
I'm good at high speeds."

Oh, boy! Treflee could just see Carrie stepping in. No
way Ty would be down with that. "He's the designated
driver, remember?"

"Yeah. Too bad I've had one too many." Carrie sounded
disappointed. "I really *am* great at precision driving." She
opened her window and tossed her pineapple mug out.
"Bombs away!"

It landed with a bang on the pursuer's hood and bounced
off into the road. The driver shook his fist at them and

pulled a gun from the front seat, taking aim at them as he drove with one hand.

"Duck!" Treflee screamed.

Carrie laughed and cursed. "Damn, I missed the windshield."

Ty was going too fast. He took the curve wide, straying into the oncoming lane.

The gunman's shot went wild and missed them.

Treflee took a deep breath, waiting for impact. It took her a second to realize they were still alive. Thank goodness no one was coming the other way.

Their pursuer nearly hit the barrier himself. He corrected just in time and tossed his gun down into the seat next to him. He pulled up on the inside, hillside lane, forcing Ty to drive into incoming traffic.

"He's going to try to ram us over the barrier." Ty's voice was calm, almost unconcerned.

Treflee glanced at the way-too-short barrier. "Can he do that?"

He shrugged. "We have a high center of gravity." Without breaking his concentration on the road, he smiled. "Don't worry. I can drive us out of this."

Male confidence and bravado!

In the backseat, Carrie and the girls had opened their windows.

"He's dropped his gun! We have him on the run!" Carrie laughed with glee like a commander on the battlefield who smelled victory.

The girls began tossing out an arsenal of items, keeping score as if they were playing a video game as stuff flew out the window. So much for litter laws.

Treflee braved a bout of carsickness and turned in her seat to face them. "Hey, be careful! That guy's a dangerous Chinese gang member!"

"He doesn't scare us," Brandy said.

The rest ignored her.

"You missed him!" Carrie yelled to Brandy. "Watch this use of subterfuge! I can hit him without looking." She donned her rearview spy glasses and palmed a plastic container of tiny breath mints from her purse. "He won't see this one coming."

The Fuk Ching rammed them again, warbling Carrie's voice. Somehow, Ty corrected and kept them on the road, speeding way too fast around the next corner.

Treflee felt green and sick, certain she was only holding on thanks to antinausea drugs. *Thank goodness for Dramamine!*

Carrie clutched the mints, taking aim.

An absurd picture crossed Treflee's mind. "Hey, sober up! Those won't do any damage."

Carrie laughed. "Are you kidding? At this speed these babies will be like bullets. Scare the hell out of that guy. Watch this!"

She tossed out the mints. The container broke into a zillion plastic shards. The tiny orange breath mints bounced around like hail against the car.

The driver swerved, coming dangerously close to colliding with the hill. He turned on the windshield wipers to brush the mints away just as Faye scored a direct hit with her pineapple mug. It sounded like an explosion as the guy's windshield cracked.

Treflee jumped.

Ty grinned. "Nice to have a few drunk cops on hand," he whispered to her.

"Good one!" Carla clapped and passed around a nearly empty bottle of Hawaiian-made wine. "What's next? What do you think this will do?"

Ty shook his head as he drove for the relative safety of

the inside, and their rightful, lane, cutting the attacker off at the corner.

Carrie and crowd launched another assault round—a flutter of drink umbrellas that had absolutely no effect except to cause another gale of laughter. A shopping bag that went wide, catching a breeze and missing the target. Finally a fluffy Big Auau beach towel did its thing, spreading across the windshield as if for a day on the sand,

"Bulls-eye!" Carrie yelled. "One hundred points for Laci!"

The girls cheered. "Hooray for Laci!"

The assailant lost control of the car. It slammed into the concrete barrier with a sickening screech as they rounded the next corner.

Even Treflee gave Laci silent kudos. She'd probably just saved their lives. Treflee glanced in the rearview mirror and shuddered even though the accident was out of view.

Ty turned to Treflee and whispered, "Don't worry about him. I'll call my guys to take care of it."

She glanced at the bridal girls, feeling a strong sense of camaraderie with them after their life-and-death fight together. Carrie and her friends were real troupers. But she was still a little worried. "Let's hope none of them think to call 911. They'll want to give their fellow cops a heads-up."

Ty picked up his phone from the storage bin next to the driver's seat and waved it at the girls in the back. "You girls just relax. I'll let 911 know there's been a little accident back there." He hit a speed-dial number she knew wasn't going to be the cops, and whispered to her, "Satisfied?"

Treflee's hands shook. "Go, just go. Get us out of here."

CHAPTER FIFTEEN

Ty pulled into a parking spot at Keanae Park and turned off the van.

"Should we be stopping?" Treflee hissed in his ear, glad he hadn't gotten them killed while he was driving and talking in code to "his guys" on his cell phone, probably giving them cleanup instructions. At least he hadn't been texting and driving. Everyone knew how dangerous *that* was.

"What if our friend back there somehow managed to walk away and called for reinforcements? What if he's dead and the cops want to question us and bring us in for vehicular homicide?"

"Do you see any cops? Any guns blazing?" Ty winked at her. "Give me some credit. You have to trust me, Tref. My guys have this under control. Don't worry."

"Are we there yet?" Brandy called out, laughing at her own joke and interrupting any further argument.

Ty seemed unfazed by their brush with death. He popped right back into tour guide mode. "Keanae Park. About halfway. Time for a snack."

He whispered to Treflee. "Maybe some food will sober the girls up." He pointed toward a concession stand across the parking lot. "Banana bread, anyone?"

If the huge BANANA BREAD sign over the stand was any indication, that was their only option.

Treflee clutched her stomach. She wasn't so certain she wanted them sober. Drunk seemed to be a blissfully ignorant and happy state. Maybe they were better off that way—fewer questions.

Ty gave her a sympathetic look and reached over and stroked her bare arm. Just like he used to do in the good old days.

She swallowed hard.

"It'll be all right, Tref. Trust me."

She stared at him a moment. "I hope you're right." She took a deep breath and scanned the area. "Are you sure it's safe?"

Ty glanced around, apparently unconcerned. "Oh, yeah. This park's a little less touristy than other stops, a bit less crowded, but we're fine."

"Meaning?"

"We have a handle on things. Let's go!"

Before she could protest further, Ty jumped out and opened the van doors.

Not certain she believed him, Treflee climbed out cautiously, relieved to find she could still stand on legs that felt as if she'd just done a thousand squats in a row. She took another deep breath. Something about the smell of the warm, tropical salt air revived her. That and the tantalizing smell of banana bread and coffee. Not to mention the realization they were still alive. For the moment.

"That was fun!" Faye put her hands on her back and arched into a stretch. "And no boring report to fill out afterward." She shook her head as if amused. "I'd heard the road to Hana was a bore. Go figure."

Carrie seemed to be coming down from her drunken high and back to reality. "Fun? That was more than just fun. Holy piña colada, Batman! That was a fine piece of high-performance driving back there." She looked at Ty with admiration and suspicion shining in her eyes. "Ever been to the police academy?"

Treflee froze.

Ty shrugged it off and shot Carrie a humble look that said she was crazy. "I've driven that road a hundred times." He grinned. "Sometimes too fast." He winked. "Surfers like extremes."

Carrie didn't seem totally convinced. She slid her spy glasses off, held her hand over her eyes, and squinted into the bright tropical sun. "What did that bastard want with you?"

Treflee's stomach flipped.

Standing full-on in the sunshine with Carrie's piercing look bearing down on him, Ty didn't even break a sweat. He laughed. "With me?"

"The Fuk Ching certainly aren't after us." Carrie crossed her arms.

So Carrie hadn't been too drunk to catch that. And she knew who the gang was. She was a cop, after all.

The other girls had formed a ring around them and were leaning in, listening with interest. Treflee felt sick, and not just because of the wild ride.

Ty shrugged. "I may owe them some protection money."

Carrie arched a brow. "That's generally their racket. What do you owe for?"

"A little business I have on the side." Ty ran his hand through his hair, suddenly looking nervous for the first time.

He was faking it and doing a darn convincing job.

He lowered his voice. "Look, don't tell Tita. She'd can my ass." He blew out a breath. "I need the cash and a place to lay low right now."

Carrie assessed him. "How deep are you in?"

The hand through his gorgeous thick hair again. Definitely trying to manufacture a nervous gesture.

"Nothing I can't dig out of in a few days. I got a few dudes who owe me. Soon as they pay up, I'm golden."

Carrie leveled her cop stare at him, slightly blurry eyed from drink, but still effective enough that it would have driven the truth out of Treflee. Then again, Ty wasn't a wimp like she was.

"Chill. Really. That dude was just toying with me. Giving me a warning. If he'd been serious, I'd be dead. The Fuk Ching know how to use guns." He grinned at Carrie with just a hint of nervous twitch.

The acting classes had obviously paid off.

Carrie tapped her fingers on her crossed arms. "These dudes of yours will pay?"

"Oh, yeah." He crossed his heart.

"Soon?"

"Definitely."

"You're not selling drugs?"

"No way."

"You should call the cops and tell them you've been threatened," Carrie said.

"Yeah? Why? What are they going to do? Charge in and yell, 'Book 'em, Dano'?" Ty bounced on the balls of his feet and fidgeted with his hands. He played the nervous surfer very convincingly.

"You don't like cops? Don't trust them?" Carrie persisted.

Ty grinned. "Pretty cop tourists are okay."

Carrie raised a brow.

Ty grew serious. "I'm saying—what are the cops going to do? Issue a restraining order? The Fuk Ching aren't going down because I complained, you know? Better to just pay them off and keep my mouth shut."

Carrie shook her head. Finally, she let out a sigh. "Not my problem. I never heard anything. You never told me anything. I'm on vacation." She paused and looked Ty in the eye. "From now on, I carry my gun." She waved to the girls. "Let's get some banana bread."

The group took their bread and iced coffee and headed to the lava rock beach. Treflee sat on a large boulder at the edge of the water, well apart from the others. She munched her sweet, macadamia-nut-studded bread and stared at the rhythmic waves washing in, listening to the pounding of the surf and feeling the mist off the incoming water. She took off her shoes and dangled her toes in the little pools of water near her. Palm trees swayed on shore in the sea breeze. It was a pleasant, tropically pastoral scene.

Ty pulled up a rock beside her. "You okay?"

"I'll live. I think. Thanks to Dramamine." To emphasize the point, she finished the last of her banana bread and brushed the crumbs off her hands and shorts.

He grinned. "And my expert, *smooth* driving."

She shook her head. "Your smooth moves almost drove us right over the edge of a volcano."

"Yeah, sorry about that. Give me another chance and I'll show you some moves that will definitely drive you over the edge."

Treflee sputtered on a sip of iced coffee and turned to stare at him. "Shut up, smooth mover!"

The man was incorrigible. He was teasing. Partly. She recognized a lusty sparkle in his eye when she saw it. Her toes tingled in response. She cleared her throat and took another sip of coffee, hoping he hadn't noticed her reaction to him. He claimed her neck flushed when she was getting aroused and her breasts got bigger. The last thing she needed was him staring at her breasts right now.

Oh, shoot! Guess where his gaze is focused?

She cleared her throat, ostensibly to get the coffee out of the wrong pipe. Really, she wanted to draw his gaze upward. "Nice thinking back at the banana bread shack. I thought our cover was done for."

His eyes danced. "Never project your deficiencies onto others. You never could lie worth shit."

"You, on the other hand . . ." She set her cup down beside her and crossed her arms over her breasts. Yes, they were budding and she couldn't even blame a cool breeze. Maybe the mist . . .

He laughed again. Too bad it reminded her of better times. Safe, homey times. Memories were like that, floating up unbidden when you didn't want them.

She arched a brow. "Of course, now we have another thread to add to our cover bible. Another story to keep straight. And you'll have Carrie playing with shadows and watching your every move."

He nodded. "Good. I need ex-bridezilla and her lady warriors to be alert and aware of danger. The more eyes on our side, the better."

He was staring at her neck. She fought the urge to uncross her arms and put a hand to her neck. Damn him! He knew how to rattle her.

He picked up a rock and skipped it into the water.

Treflee bit her lip, not wanting to say what was on her mind, but feeling she had to. "We can't keep putting the others in danger."

Ty slid onto her rock, put his arm around her, tucked her hair behind her ear, and whispered in her ear with his hot breath and sultriest voice, "Are you suggesting we run away together?"

She should have pushed him away, right off the rock onto his butt in the lava bed. But he had a hold on her. He'd either take her down with him or hold steady and make a fool out of her. For the moment, she relaxed into him, hoping to give him a false sense of security. And enjoying the smell of his aftershave and the coconut lotion on his skin. Coconut really was her weakness. She leaned her head on his shoulder.

He sat with his legs spread wide, feet planted in the lava rock, his thigh brushing hers as the waves inched toward them. It's funny how something as simple as the sight of a leg can be so familiar, so comforting, and so sexy. No one had legs like Ty—firm and strong, covered with dark, curly, coarse hair that was springy to the touch.

Two can play games. She ran her hands lightly over the hair on his leg and watched him shudder with a shiver of pleasure. He liked a light touch. She knew everything he liked and to what degree. She knew too well.

His lips brushed the top of her head, just as a wave crashed near them.

The gentle touch of his lips on her hair and the warm rush of his breath on her part sent a shiver of desire through her. This was a dangerous game, indeed.

"Run away together? Away from this life altogether? Just start a new cover life of our own?" She paused, stunned by the emotion that had leaked out with her words and the temptation she felt to do just that, run away. She cleared her throat to cover the raw feelings she hadn't expected. "I was thinking divorce court."

He took her chin and tilted her face up to his. "Divorce court is out." His voice cracked. "I love you, Tref."

She felt a big *but* coming. Before she could protest or make him define it, he leaned down and kissed her. Softly. Sweetly. Insistently.

She closed her eyes and opened her mouth to him, pulling him closer as a wave brushed her toes and another round of ocean mist cooled her, but not her ardor.

She welcomed his tongue into her mouth. She'd missed him. Oh, how she'd missed him. She stopped thinking at all. If she had been thinking, she wouldn't have wrapped her arms around him, slid her legs into his lap, and pressed against him, wanting to feel. *All of him.*

She wouldn't have made out with him like a teenager with too many hormones coursing through her. She wouldn't have gone on the offensive and groped him. Or stuck her tongue in his mouth and kissed him back so hard and passionately she might be bruising his lips.

A wave roared and crashed over her. Unfortunately, it was not a wave of desire, but a real ocean wave that drenched them and brought her sputtering back to her senses.

She pulled away, pushing her dripping hair out of her eyes. Leave it to Mother Nature to douse her ardor for her.

Next to her, Ty wiped the water out of his eyes. "Damn."

Exactly.

He coughed and squinted out to sea, pointing. "Are those your shoes?"

She turned to look. "Shoot!" She bounded out of his lap after them.

He caught her hand and pulled her back. "They're gone, babe." He was no longer staring after her shoes, but at her wet, white T-shirt, which had gone transparent, along with her white sports bra.

She stared down at herself. A thousand curses on white! Her breasts had budded in the cool water bath and now her nipples stood out pink and pert. And growing more erect by the minute as Ty stared at them. She covered them with her hands, which only encouraged his leer.

Ty's yellow T-shirt had gone nearly transparent, too, and was molded against his muscular form. Looking at him, even scowling at him, only made matters worse. For both of them. His wet shorts didn't leave much to the imagination, either.

Only he didn't seem embarrassed by it.

She looked at the stretch of rough lava rock between her and the van. And then back at Ty. *Oh, boy! Big trouble.*

He laughed. "What's up, tenderfoot?"

"You know very well what's up!"

He reached out to her. "Let me carry you."

She shook her head, trying to keep her eyes above waist level and her voice from going all breathy with lust. "No, thanks. It's . . . too far. Go to the van and bring me back the spare pair of sandals from my overnight bag."

He raised a brow. "Too far? You don't think I can carry a girl across a beach?" He crossed his arms. "I'm insulted."

"Come on, Ty. Don't tease me. Go get my shoes."

"I'm not your errand boy."

She pointed to the stretch of beach. "I can't walk across that."

He made a show of studying the beach. "I don't know about that. If people can walk across hot coals, you should be able to walk across a few sharp rocks. Power of positive thinking."

"Ty!"

He grinned and looked at his watch. "It's getting late. We'd better get going if we're going to make it to camp before dark. You don't want to be on the road to Hana after dark. Very treacherous. Especially for people prone to motion sickness and gang attacks." He turned to leave.

"Ty!" She sounded pitiful. "Don't leave me . . ."

He turned back to her wearing a wry, hopeful expression and a grin.

". . . here. Don't leave me here," she finished, smiling sweetly, helplessly.

"Well, well, look who's at my mercy now. It's the old 'keep them barefoot' trick." His eyes danced.

But not pregnant, she thought with regret and sadness.

"Please," she said.

He took several steps back and swung her up into his arms. "Keep up the cover. Act like you like it. And help out a bit, would you? It's a long way to the van."

She wanted to slug him. Instead, she put her arms around his neck and smiled up at him, molding herself to him like his wet shirt. At least this way her breasts were mostly covered, even if they did rub up against his chest in a most erotic way. "Better?"

"Much." He kissed her on the nose.

She hated it when he kissed her on the nose and he knew it.

But she refused to show it. Instead, she laughed and kept smiling, leaning up and brushing his lips with a light kiss.

"I hope the girls didn't throw all the beach towels out the window," she said, pretending to whisper sweet nothings in his ear.

He looked her in the eye. "I kind of hope they did."

"That wouldn't leave us much ammo for the next round." She was teasing, but with the reminder of danger, she became serious again. "Ty, when are you going to tell me exactly what's going on?"

"When I have no other choice."

CHAPTER SIXTEEN

They arrived at their private campsite a few miles outside Hana just before dark. Treflee hated roughing it in *any* form. She grumbled to herself about having to sleep in a bag on a hard patch of ground. She'd probably be kept awake all night by a lava rock beneath her back, the thought of her husband sleeping not far enough away, and the fear of being attacked in her sleep. Tent doors weren't much protection on that front. Nothing sounded better right now than the fluffy bed and stout, locked doors at Big Auau.

Had it really only been this morning that she'd seen the sun come up over Haleakala and an enemy spy had tried to murder her with a bike pump?

Now the dusky shadows were long, the colors vibrant. It was the kind of lighting that made even an avowed non-photographer reach for a camera.

They climbed out of the van and Ty opened the back. They each grabbed their own gear. Ty had repacked the picnic basket back at Keanae and salvaged most of their dinner. He tossed his bag over his shoulder, set the picnic hamper on top of the cooler, and picked them both up.

Carrie slammed the door shut for him. Ty locked it

with the remote and they were off through the jungle to their home away from home away from home.

Ty fell into step with Treflee. She really should have offered to help him carry something. But he was being paid to be their packhorse. She decided to let him earn his keep and keep her distance.

"I bet you've been looking forward to this," Ty said with a touch of taunt in his voice.

It galled her that he seemed to enjoy baiting her so much. He knew very well how much she "loved" camping. It was right up there with the way tourists felt about eating poi.

They trudged down a heavily vegetated path. Just when Treflee thought her bag was going to cut through her shoulder, they rounded a corner and came upon a campsite on the edge of both beach and jungle. The scene looked as if it had leaped from the pages of a Hawaiian style magazine— live like a star in total luxury.

Ty laughed. "Good man. Greg's been busy." He looked around camp and called out for Greg. "*Aloha!* Anybody home?"

Treflee gasped. A large, elegant white tent stood flanked by a smaller one on each side. Tall tiki torches rimmed the perimeter of the camp and stood ready to light the entrance to each tent. A banquet table, laid out with porcelain bird-of-paradise dishes, linen napkins, beautifully carved wooden serving bowls, and snowy white candles, stood in front of the large tent. A centerpiece of proteas dominated the middle of the table and a fresh plumeria lei and white-wrapped package with bougainvillea-pink ribbon lay beside each place setting.

The other girls came to a halt around Treflee. Carrie stood next to her.

Treflee looked at the main tent again. And then it struck her. This wasn't *Hawaiian Style* nice. This was *Hawaiian*

Bride beautiful. She turned to Carrie. "Is that a wedding tent?"

Carrie's eyes sparkled with a mixture of buck-up defiance and tears. "Couldn't get my money back. It was either use it or lose it. Same with the flowers and catering. Kiss my deposit good-bye or apply it to a smaller affair."

Carrie sounded so practical it was scary. What was next for her cousin who was in denial and trying to pretend everything was all right? Tear up and retool the wedding dress into a gown for the annual policeman's ball? Turn the veil into a pair of curtains or maybe use it as mosquito netting?

Treflee had to give her cousin credit, though. If the scene before her was any indication of what the wedding would have been like, it would have been beautiful. Who knew Carrie was so romantic and girly? She'd been wrong to imagine Carrie having a cop version of a redneck wedding.

Treflee wished she could protect her cousin from the heartache she was going through. Wished she could convince Carrie she didn't have to put on a brave face, that she could let go and have a good cry, or rail at the world if she wanted to. Whatever made her feel better. Whatever helped her heal. She was among friends, people who loved her. Treflee put her arm around Carrie and gave her a heartfelt hug.

Seeing her, the other girls crowded around and joined in a group hug. As they stood together hugging in that beautiful bridal scene, Treflee felt close to them, really close to them all, even the tiniest bit to Laci. After all, Laci didn't know Ty was her husband. For the first time, Treflee was part of their circle.

To Treflee's surprise, Carrie squeezed back.

They stood together until Carrie released her and wiped her eyes with the back of her hand. "Come on, girls." Carrie readjusted the bag over her shoulder, putting up the wall again. "Let's settle in."

The girls traipsed after her like the obedient bridal party they were. Treflee followed right along.

Ty caught Treflee's arm. "What do you think now?" His eyes sparkled.

He'd known about this all along.

"The jury's still out," she said. "Are the beds any good?"

"Good question." His voice was low and sultry. "We could find out."

Greg came in at a run from the beach, interrupting her retort. *"Aloha!"*

Ty waved to him. "There you are, man. Hey, awesome job with the table and flowers. You've got a knack. Ever thought of entering the floral business?"

"Don't get too cocky. You're in charge of entertainment." Greg relieved Ty of the cooler and hamper. Ty grabbed Treflee's bag and showed her to the girls' tent, lingering in the doorway as she took it in.

Inside six cots were outfitted with fluffy pillows and cotton blankets. An overturned crate with a camp lantern sat beside each. Out back, there was a Porta Potti and a sun shower hung from a tree. All in all, pretty elegant digs.

The only thing worrying Treflee were the canvas walls. Any old machete could whack through them in a swing or two.

The others had already claimed their cots. Ty set her bag down on the empty cot nearest the door.

Ty whispered in her ear, "My tent's just to the left."

"Good. Any attacker from the north will get you first."

He laughed. "Freshen up and dress for dinner, ladies." He disappeared before Treflee could ask any questions.

Treflee turned to her cousin. "Dress for dinner?"

Carrie shrugged. "I told you to bring a sundress."

Treflee addressed the other girls. "Anyone have an extra dress I can borrow?"

Ty dropped his gear off in his tent and caught up with Greg.

"Heard you had an adventure up on the mountain," Greg said to him. "Got some good stuff and had an incident during your ride down."

Ty nodded. Emmett spread the word quickly.

"Had a little fun on the Hana Highway, too," Ty said.

"Really?"

Ty filled him in.

When Ty finished, Greg let out a whistle. "So now you owe money to the Fuk Ching. Good to know. The last guy, the one on the Hana Highway, was he Fuk Ching?"

Ty frowned. "He had the tattoo and all the markings. He was out to take out Tref. RIOT has somehow gotten it into their heads that she's the master spy here."

Greg laughed and shook his head. "Yeah, I heard a rumor to that effect. RIOT must be desperate. It's risky and way too flashy to take out a tourist van full of women."

"Yeah, but they failed with the more subtle bike accident." Ty frowned in thought.

"Something bothering you?"

Ty sighed. "Yeah. Why an accident? Two to the head is more effective. It's not hard to evade detection. RIOT could smuggle their killer off the island and back to China before the body's even been discovered. Plenty of water around here to dump it."

Though as Ty knew, dumping didn't always work the way you'd planned. *Damn glass-bottomed boats!*

Greg nodded slowly.

"What do they want with Tref?" Ty mused. "What's their goal?"

"Revenge?" Greg said. "Intel?"

Ty didn't think it was either. He shook his head. "Accidents can go either way. It's hard to get intel from a dead body. If they want her out of the action, they kill her. If they want info, they grab her. What else is there?"

Greg took a minute answering. "Just because the accident itself doesn't kill her doesn't mean she won't end up dead." He paused. "There's another possibility—they don't care whether the accident kills her or not."

Ty felt like he'd been punched in the stomach. Of course that was it. Greg's theory explained why there'd been no gunplay. He'd been so blind. "They're trying to distract us?"

Greg corrected him. "Her."

Her. Ty let out an exasperated sigh. "Yeah, trying to distract her from a wedding and a live video feed. They don't know we know about that." Ty paused. "Which means they'll strike again and keep striking at Tref until she's dead or hospitalized, and they've got Pinpoint."

"They won't get Treflee or Pinpoint." Greg slapped Ty on the arm. "You and I will stop them."

Ty appreciated Greg's confidence. He wished he felt as sure. Worrying about Tref was messing with his self-assurance. "Any news on Hal?"

Greg shook his head. "Nothing new. He seems calm. Looks like he's just hanging out until Saturday."

Ty nodded. "I've sent everything to HQ. Let's hope Emmett has a handle on things. In the meantime, I'm not leaving Tref alone." Ty paused and grinned. "She'll be sleeping with me tonight."

Greg laughed. "Making progress on your other mission?"

"I will be."

Unfortunately, either the other girls hadn't brought an extra dress or didn't have one that fit her. Treflee was forced to wear her black beach cover-up to dinner. It was sundresslike, as in, if you used your imagination you could pretend it was a real little black dress, not simply something you throw on over a wet swimsuit. The wooden beaded ties gave it away. But this was Hawaii. Treflee told herself you could get away with almost anything here.

The others changed into their brightly printed cotton sundresses, looking fetchingly coordinated as they cascaded out of the tent and into the tropical evening paradise.

How in the world had she been out of the loop so often on this vacation? She felt a lot like she had at family dinners of old. She and Carrie used to discuss coordinating what to wear to holiday meals with the other girl cousins—jeans, pants, skirts, or dresses. Inevitably, they'd all agree on something. Treflee would show up wearing it and all the others would show up wearing something entirely different. Cousins seemed universally duplicitous where wardrobe was concerned. But this time, the other girls really had tried to help Treflee out.

The sun had set. Greg and Ty had lit the tiki torches and the candles on the table, which put out a delicate coconut scent. An iPod played sensual Hawaiian music over a pair of portable speakers. Ty stood behind a stocked tiki bar, playing bartender.

She needed to sharpen her powers of observation. She hadn't noticed the bar when they'd first arrived. Now there was no way she'd miss it. Not with her husband at it pouring deep ocean-blue drinks that looked as luscious, tempting, and mysterious as he did.

He wore a tasteful Hawaiian print cotton shirt and linen pants. The flickering torchlight highlighted his artificial blond streaks, the strong set of his jaw, and the planes of his bearded face. He looked handsome, suave, very spylike in a Bond sort of way. Bond could be blond or brunet these days. Ty was a combo.

His eyes met hers. Her pulse leaped. She had to be careful, very careful. She was on a mission herself. She was going to get whatever he palmed on the volcano this morning. No, she hadn't forgotten. And she hadn't changed her mind, either—she needed that divorce. For her own sense of peace.

She realized that if she was going to get that little key to her freedom, she was going to have to play very nice to Ty and get up close and personal with him. So close, she might very well get burned.

Most divorcing couples yelled and screamed at each other, traded insults, hid assets, slashed each other's tires, or devised ways to cheat the other one out of everything.

Just how many divorcing couples pretended to be falling in love with each other? Flirted? Gazed deeply into each other's eyes as if the mystery were still there and the spark just igniting? Brushed fingertips and shared kisses?

The problem with all this flirtation was that it didn't exactly breed contempt. In her case, it pushed her to dance a little too close to friendly fire.

And forced an uncomfortable realization—she was still in love with her husband. And she lusted after him with a passion.

It wasn't an admission she'd make to anyone else. And it wasn't going to stop her from pursuing her goal. Just because you loved someone didn't mean they were right for you. Or that you could live happily ever after with them. It didn't mean that you dealt with the loneliness or jealousy any better. Or the realization that their passions, the things that thrilled you about them, also kept you from them.

She would flirt with him. Sweet-talk him. Even sleep with him if that's what it took. But she wouldn't give him control of her heart and life again.

He looked up and caught her staring at him.

Good. She smiled at him, slowly, letting herself feel the joy that flirting with him brought.

Carrie came up beside her. "It's an open bar. Drinks are on me until the liquor runs out. Go for it." She gave Treflee a shove in the bar's direction.

As Treflee approached, Ty raised the bottle of blue curacao he was holding. "Blue Hawaii?"

Just one for courage. He'd find her affections more believable if he thought alcohol had loosened her inhibitions. She strolled over and leaned on the bar. "Depends on what's in it."

"You'll love it. Crème de coconut, light rum, vodka, this blue stuff, pineapple juice, and sweet-and-sour mix."

"You had me at crème de coconut," she said, eyeing an appetizer platter on the counter.

"Somehow I knew I did." He handed her a small plate and a napkin and pushed the appetizers toward her. "Pupu?"

"Pupu? These Hawaiians have a different name for everything. Some of them better than others."

He laughed. "Try the Maui onion dip and taro chips."

Delicious as the dip looked, onion breath was not going to further her cause. She pointed to another dish on the platter. "What's this?"

"Another excellent choice. Macadamia-nut hummus. Try it with the macadamia-oil pita chips."

"Garlicky?"

"Somewhat."

Hobson's choice. "What are you having?"

He picked up a pita chip and dipped it in the hummus, holding it out to her to take a bite. "Both. Eventually. Try it. You'll like it."

As long as he was eating it, too. She took a bite and made an appreciative noise. "Hand-feeding the patrons. This really is a full-service bar. I suppose now you'll expect a big tip?"

"I'd rather use one." His eyes sparkled with lust.

She felt an unwelcome jolt of excitement. "Just make my drink, will you?"

He made a show of mixing her drink. Then he stabbed a long pineapple spear with a pick and garnished her drink with it. "You like them long."

He was incorrigible.

"I like them sweet." She picked up her drink and walked off to join the others.

One drink and her head was buzzing. No doubt Ty had made it extra strong. Greg called them to dinner. Bird-of-paradise place cards designated their seats. Treflee found her place at the table. She'd been seated as far away from Laci as possible. Carrie sat at the head of the table, a bride holding court without her jilted groom. Treflee was seated next to Faye who was next to Carla. Laci and Brandy sat across from them.

Treflee shot a glance at Carrie and smiled, grateful to her cousin for her thoughtful seating assignments. Carrie put on her lei. Everyone else followed suit.

If pleasant smells led to pleasant thoughts, plumeria had definite aphrodisiac properties.

At least Treflee hoped that explained why Ty looked so delicious as he set a second Blue Hawaii in front of her. "Heavy on the crème de coconut. Just for you."

She smiled at him. "Well, aren't you sweet?"

He grinned. "I've heard you like sweet."

"Oh, I do."

"Wait until you see what's coming." He disappeared to play waiter.

A few minutes later, Ty and Greg rolled out a family-style

Hawaiian feast—char siu, chicken lu'au, hulu-huli chicken, chicken long rice, taro rolls, fresh fruit, and macaroni salad. A Hawaiian take on the usual rubber-chicken wedding dinner.

As the feasting and conversation wound down, Laci raised her glass to make a toast. "At a wedding reception, it's customary for the maid of honor to toast the bride and groom, gush about what a perfect couple they make, and wish them a happy life together.

"Since this is an *un*-wedding, a celebration of an escape from couplehood, I'd like to talk about my best friend, Carrie. She's perfect . . . all by herself." Laci's voice cracked as she smiled at Carrie.

"She's the best friend any girl could ever have. I'm so lucky she's mine. She has your back, you know. You can always talk to her and tell her anything. She deserves the same in a man. One day she'll find him."

She reached over and gave Carrie's hand a squeeze. "Until the right guy comes along, wishing you all the happiness there is in the single life." She raised her glass higher. "To Carrie!"

Treflee clinked glasses all around. Maybe it was the alcohol, but she got misty-eyed, too. Weddings did that to a girl, apparently even weddings that didn't happen.

Faye raised her glass. "Echoing Laci's feelings—Carrie's the best. Who else would cancel a wedding and take her friends on the honeymoon?"

The girls laughed.

Faye winked at Carrie. "You're going to do just fine, kid.

"To Carrie and the freedom of the single life! No sharing. No compromising on dish patterns. No toilet seats left up!"

"Here, here!" Laci clinked glasses with Faye.

Everyone clinked all around.

Carla was next. "Nursing's always on my mind, I guess. In that light, there's no cure like an old cure—a rebound guy!

"To nursing a broken heart! And mending it with a far better, ahem"—she winked and made a gesture indicating well hung—"man!"

The girls exploded in laughter. Everyone drank.

Brandy raised her toast. "Oh, to hell with men. Down with men! Up with freedom!"

Everyone except Treflee laughed and applauded. The toasting had just taken a dangerous turn that wasn't beneficial to her mission. The last thing she needed Ty thinking was that she was down on men, him in particular. As she glanced at him, she noticed he was looking a bit uncomfortable, too. She had to get the mission back on track and not lose that loving feeling she'd been cultivating with Ty all evening.

And yet, it was up to her to end this thing with a bang.

"Treflee?" Laci shot her a challenging top-that look.

Treflee smiled and raised her glass with too much vigor, sloshing the blue contents out onto the white tablecloth as she thought on her feet.

Ty was clearing dishes at the far end of the table. She had to send him a very clear come-hither message so she could get him naked and find that thing from the mountain.

She cleared her throat. "I may not be the closest person to Carrie, but I have bragging rights for knowing her longest. Our moms used to sleep us in the same crib." She smiled at her cousin.

"You all know what I'm going through with a certain man right now."

The girls murmured and nodded. Ty looked away, seemingly very busy stacking dishes.

"Which I think qualifies me to give some advice and say this—fate chooses your family. Sometimes convenience chooses your friends. But your heart chooses your husband."

Her voice broke with emotion, which startled even her. She cleared her throat and smiled through it. "You vow to love each other for life. Which is why, in the end, he's the only person who can really, truly hurt you."

Ty looked up from clearing dishes.

Which was when she noticed no one had raised their glasses and the group had gone silent.

She took a deep breath. "Don't close your heart off to love. Go for it. If it takes a rebound guy to get you back in the game, do it." She deliberately smiled at Ty.

The girls stared at her staring at him. Which was exactly what she had intended—to telegraph her intentions so she didn't lose her nerve. The girls knew she had a thing for him. They'd be downright disappointed if she didn't make a fool over herself with Ty soon. And here was the perfect opportunity.

Was that a little sigh she heard?

She smiled at her cousin. "You'll love again." She gave Ty a sidelong look. "To second chances at love!"

Ty stared back at her, studying her as if she were sending a coded message he wasn't certain he was deciphering correctly. Usually he didn't have any trouble picking up on her signals. Maybe the dim lighting was interfering with her transmission.

But a little mystery never hurt anyone, even a master spy, she thought with satisfaction.

"Bottoms up!" Still staring at Ty, she drained her glass while the other girls joined her.

Carrie cleared her throat. "I think it's time for cake. Ty?" She held her hand to the side of her mouth and made an aside to Treflee. "Calm yourself. This isn't the bachelorette party. He isn't going to be jumping out of it covered in frosting."

Carrie knew how much she loved icing. She'd lick it off a piece of cardboard.

Everyone but Laci laughed, but even she wore an expression of resignation. Treflee had bested her in the competition for Ty.

Ty nodded and disappeared to get the cake. Treflee thought he moved a little faster than normal as she made a show for the girls of ogling his backside. *Oh, isn't a buzz fun!*

Carrie clapped her hands. "Present time!"

Brandy picked up the box by her plate, held it to her ear, and shook it. "You didn't have to give us a bridesmaid gift, Carrie."

"Yeah?" Carrie smiled. "I won't look so magnanimous once you open them!"

Treflee ripped into her presents with the other girls. But unfortunately, she knew her cousin's tastes all too well—sparkly and flashy.

And she wasn't disappointed. Carrie gave them each a gaudy hot-pink rhinestone bracelet with a silver heart charm engraved with their name and Carrie's wedding date, and a matching pair of monogrammed taffeta wedding flip-flops.

Carrie picked up one of Laci's flip-flops and displayed it for the group like a shoe salesman with a tempting new offering. "You were supposed to kick off your heels after the wedding and relax in these babies while still styling. With the woven mats, they're really comfy."

"Oh, let me see!" Laci snatched it out of Carrie's hand and put it on.

Laci stood up and strutted once around the table, hand on hip, modeling the flip-flops and bracelet before taking her seat again.

Carrie laughed and applauded. "Fabulous! But for future

reference—never engrave or monogram any bridal gift until *after* the wedding."

"Better to never monogram anything. *Ever.*" Treflee hooked her bracelet on. It may have been on the showy side, but it sparkled prettily in the tiki light.

Carrie raised her glass. "To a monogram-free world!"

"Cheers!"

A few minutes later, Ty arrived carrying a luscious three-layer guava cake.

Carrie clapped again. "Let them eat cake! I get to cut." She grabbed a silver cake server.

Faye chimed in. "Cut me a sliver to put beneath my pillow."

"Beneath your pillow?" Carla gave her a gentle elbow. "Who are you planning on dreaming about?"

Faye slid her bracelet on and winked. "The one man I definitely should *not* marry!"

As the other girls laughed, Treflee couldn't help shooting a surreptitious look Ty's way. Would dreaming about him with a piece of called-off wedding cake beneath her pillow have stopped her from marrying him?

Laci grabbed a slice of cake and pushed back her chair. She eyed the bar. "I need a drink to wash this cake down with."

Brandy slid back, too, slipping on her taffeta flip-flops and slapping them against her feet with her toes. "And some music to try out these new dancing shoes."

Ty took his cue and headed for the bar.

The way the girls drank, he'd be busy for hours. While Ty was occupied, Treflee intended to seize the opportunity to search his tent. Not that she seriously believed he'd leave anything valuable lying around for her or anyone else to find. But she was desperate and bound by the code of suspicious and highly curious wives to take a look.

CHAPTER SEVENTEEN

Treflee paused at the opening to Ty's tent. The last time she'd searched his room, someone had tried to kill her with a lei. She looked down at the pink and white plumeria flowers looped around her neck. Unlike plastic, this real flower one was too delicate to do much damage.

While Greg unwittingly created a diversion as he banged, scraped, and loaded dishes into the caterer's bin, she slipped into Ty's tent.

Not surprisingly, it was a real bachelor-pad tent. A backpack and half a case of beer tossed in the corner, a full-sized inflatable air mattress in the middle of the space, a couple of towels and some toiletries and clothes lying around. All that was missing for the perfect ambience was a box of condoms.

She tested the air mattress with her foot. Not bad for an evening romp if it came to that. Pretty cushy, with a fair amount of bounce.

She looked through the towels, toiletries, and clothes. Nothing, as expected. She replaced them as she'd found them. Outside, Greg shattered a dish. She jumped.

Did real spies startle so easily? Did her terminally unperturbable husband, Ty? If she was going to keep this up much longer, she needed to develop unflappable nerves and eyes in the back of her head.

She grabbed the backpack and riffled through it quickly. Nothing, nothing, and more nothing! She did a little mental cursing. Foiled again! She put everything back more or less as she'd found it. Having a photographic memory would have been a big asset right about now.

Something rustled outside. She froze, heart pounding. Listening. Barely breathing for what seemed like an eternity.

Silence, pan clanking, and drunken laughter. No psychotic lei stranglers jumped in from the bushes. Finally, she peeked through the tent flap and made her exit.

She'd tried to avoid it, she really had, but fate had left her only one option—get Ty out of his clothes and search them. And him.

Out of the corner of his eye, Ty saw Treflee sneak off as he poured the girls another round. A few more and they'd pass out. It wouldn't surprise him if Treflee was off to search his tent. The woman had prying eyes and her curiosity was anything but idle. She was probably looking for more dirt on him and a way to get him to sign those damned papers. He knew better than to believe her suddenly flirtatious act. She was up to something. He intended to make sure it backfired on her.

He wondered if she really thought he'd leave anything lying around. She'd always been too optimistic for her own good. He'd even hidden the pearls he planned to give her tonight.

He smiled to himself. Just how far would she go to get what she thought she wanted? He knew what he wanted— her naked and in his arms. No divorce. Ever.

He had a plan to get her there. Just as soon as the eighty proof ran out.

* * *

Carrie caught Treflee's arm as she returned to the party. "Where have you been?"

Treflee pointed to the Porta Pottis behind the tents.

"You've been gone a long time." Carrie's speech was almost too precise, as if she were trying too hard not to slur.

Treflee shrugged, hoping Ty hadn't noticed her absence, too. She'd thought she'd been quick in his tent. Time flies when you're playing spy.

"I thought you'd chickened out," Carrie said.

"What?"

"That speech at dinner and the way you looked at him like he was a piece of huli-huli chicken. When are you going to make a move on our hot tour guide, Ty?"

"That blatant?" *Good, I've done my job.*

"Totally."

"He's playing bartender right now—"

"No problem. I'll release him!" Carrie made a grand gesture, as if she were a queen handing out pardons.

"Yeah, do that." Treflee's heart pounded. Ty naked — way too salacious a thought after a six-month abstinence stint.

"I will." Carrie nodded. "I will."

She grabbed Treflee's arm and dragged her to the bar. She snapped her fingers to get Ty's attention. "The girls have had enough. Shift's over."

She turned from him toward the girls and waved her arms. "Hey! Closing time. One last call if you want alcohol."

Brandy called out for her to grab what was left of the hard stuff and come join them.

Carrie slapped the bar. "Okay. You're done." She made a shooing motion. "Go."

She grabbed the remains of the last bottle of coconut rum and wandered off to share with the others.

Ty stepped away from the bar and watched Carrie walk off. "Your cousin's a world-class heavyweight drinker. Anyone else would have passed out by now."

Treflee nodded. "The ride back tomorrow should be fun. They're all going to have magnificent hangovers in the morning." She had a wicked thought. "How fun would it be if I hid their sunglasses?"

His eyes twinkled. "You'd have to hide their rearview spy glasses, too."

"Good point."

Ty leaned toward her and whispered in a low, sexy voice, "Any particular reason Carrie thought it was time to shut down the bar?"

Treflee tried to appear nonchalant. "She knows her limit."

"Does she?"

Treflee nodded.

Ty took her arm and whispered in her ear, "Rebound guy? Seriously?"

She stared up at him, trying to keep her heart from hammering out of control, and laughed for the others' benefit. "Why not? Ty the tour guide's hot and handy." She ran her gaze over him, letting her alcohol-induced flirty side take over. "I don't think my husband will mind."

He stared at her mouth, looking as if he wanted to kiss her. "No, I don't think he'll mind at all." He paused. "Why this change of heart?"

She stroked his cheek and whispered back, "Got to keep up the cover and make good on my toast. Ignore you and I ruin all that clever cover setup work."

The way he studied her made her knees go weak. Or maybe that was nerves and alcohol. Either way, it felt good. Since she was wearing the comfy taffeta wedding flip-flops, she was in no danger of toppling over. *Yet.*

He nodded toward the others. "We have an audience."

She stroked his arm. Nothing concealed up his sleeve. *Too bad.* She needed a more thorough and private search. "Yeah, we definitely don't want that."

"I know a place away from spying eyes." He put his arm around her. "Very secluded." His eyes had a devilish, sexy sparkle and his voice was low. "Someone's fantasy come true."

Such arrogance. Fantasy come true. Indeed?

He didn't give up. "Still like to skinny-dip?"

"I'm wearing a bathing suit beneath this cover-up."

He grinned. "No problem. I can fix that."

The night was balmy and calm, very pleasant. But it was Ty's heat beside Treflee that drove her wild. *Never drink and flirt.*

Ty shone his flashlight on the path ahead of them. He led, holding her hand with his thumb looped over hers, their elbows tucked together. In the deep darkness of the woods, with the fear of Chinese assassins lurking in the recesses of her mind, against all reason, Treflee wanted him with an intensity that thrilled. Him *and* that drop of his.

The forest smelled of damp night air, her tropical lei, and cologne. The combination drove her mad with lust. If she ever bought him cologne again, it was going to be something hideous and cheap, a benign drugstore variety scented like old man rather than primal need.

She stumbled over a root.

Ty caught her. Their eyes locked. Her breath caught. She'd been way too long without his touch.

He put a hot finger to her lips. "Sshhh. We don't want anyone following us."

No, we definitely don't want that.

She kissed his finger and smiled at him.

He grinned and pulled her onward.

The air grew moist and heavy with fine mist. The plants sparkled with dew in the beam of his flashlight.

She heard something very faint in the distance, a roar growing louder with each step they took. She stopped short, her heart racing, pulling Ty to a halt with her. "What's that?"

He stiffened, on high alert. "What's what? What did you hear?"

"That thrumming roar."

"Oh, that." Ty stared deep into her eyes. "Water. Falling."

Her eyes went wide as she searched his face. "You *weren't* joking?"

His grin deepened. His eyes reflected the moonlight and sparkled with lust as he squeezed her hand and stroked it provocatively with his thumb.

He wasn't joking. How many times have I told him I dream of making love with him beneath a waterfall? Someplace warm and tropical where naked is natural and comfortable. With soft sand beneath my toes and big fragrant flowers overhead perfuming the world? Somewhere I could let go and go primal.

"About what?" His tone was way too innocent to believe. "I never joke where fantasies are concerned." His words were low and sexy, definitely not teasing.

Part of her wanted to break away and run back to camp. You don't make love with your nearly ex-husband, act out your lifelong sexual fantasy beneath a waterfall, and come away unchanged. You also don't just get him naked, grab his clothes, and run for cover into a forest so lush you'll never find your way back. Especially not if your husband is an expert at tracking and extracting secrets.

Ty had just led her into a no-win scenario. And she'd bet he knew it.

"Coming?" He squeezed her hand, tensing as if he expected her to try to break away and run. "It's just ahead."

She looked back down the dark path they'd come. The odds were not in her favor. And she needed that drop of his.

Taking up the challenge, she squeezed his hand in return and ran the back of the fingers of her free hand along the line of his jaw, over the unfamiliar prickliness of his beard. "Can't wait."

"That makes two of us." Still holding the flashlight, he dropped her hand, took her head in his hands, and kissed her with a bruising passion, openmouthed, deeply, possessively.

His beard scrubbed her lips, reminding her of who and what he was. But right then, with his tongue hot in her mouth and her heart pounding in her ears, she couldn't remember why it mattered.

He released her suddenly and grabbed her hand.

Breathing hard, stunned by her reaction to him, and trying not to topple over, she stared at him, still feeling his kiss on her lips.

"When we get to the clearing, the water will drown out everything." He stared at her with the moonlight highlighting the fire in his eyes.

Hard as she stared back, she couldn't tell whether it was only lust she saw reflected there or something more. She was sure the mask was intentional. He only let her see what he wanted her to. Right now, as always, subterfuge served his purpose and kept her off balance.

"Drown out every whisper, every protest." His stare was mesmerizing. His tone contained a warning. "There'll be no going back. I won't stop. No one will hear you scream, babe."

The way he caressed the words made it clear he wasn't

planning on murdering her, unless killing her with passion counted. A ripple of desire coursed through her, making her wonder if she was spy enough to handle this mission.

"I won't catch a word even if you yell directly into my ear."

She took a deep breath, trying to shore up her nerves as she studied him. "And if an assassin jumps out of the bushes? How do I get your attention then?"

He bent and kissed her neck, grazing her skin with his teeth and his warm breath. "You'll figure it out."

She shivered with pleasure, certain he could feel the pulse leaping in her neck, giving away her fear and treacherous desire. "And when I do?"

"I'll protect you with my life." He was deadly serious.

She ran her fingers down his back, thinking about them naked together in a pool beneath a waterfall, him completely disarmed and unarmed. At her mercy. "With what? I'll be enjoying your big gun." She kissed his jaw.

He ran his fingers through her hair. "I'll figure something out. If someone takes a shot at us, dive. Three feet beneath the surface ought to do it."

She relaxed, enjoying the feeling of his fingers in her hair, and stared up into his eyes. "You don't think this is carrying the cover thing a little *too* far?"

"In the spy world, there's no such thing as too far." He kissed her again, deeply and fully.

When she couldn't stand the need building in her an instant longer she pulled away. "So, big boy, are you going to take me there?"

"I hope to hell so." He took her hand again and pushed through the bushes into a clearing so beautiful, just looking at it took her breath away. Her fantasies had done reality a grave injustice.

They hadn't included moonlight so strong it made the

water look like streams of silver, or the pounding thrum of water that left her senses taut and alive, or the cool mist that caressed her body.

Before she had a chance to catalog the other deficiencies of her imagination, Ty pulled her into a kiss. Not a little husbandly hello kiss like they'd fallen into just before the split. The full-on, full-in parting of the lips, thrusting of tongues, caressing of mouths that made her legs weak.

She cuddled into him.

All the better to feel for that thing he's hiding. Denial is such a convenient emotion.

She felt nothing but delicious, hard biceps, washboard abs, and strong shoulders. So tempting, she couldn't resist pressing her breasts against his chest and running her hands through his hair. Her aroused breasts were so sensitive. They'd certainly find anything that didn't belong. Unfortunately, everything she felt did belong. One very hard, very erect thing belonged very much inside her.

Ty switched off the flashlight and dropped it beside them. He trailed kisses over her shoulders as he pulled her cover-up down over her breasts, past her waist and hips, and completely off.

She stepped out of it and into him. Two could play at undressing. She unbuttoned his shirt. Kissed his chest. Sucked his nipples. Stuck her hands in his empty back pockets and cupped his firm cheeks.

Where have you hidden it, Ty?

He gave her no choice. She'd just have to look harder. She unfastened his shorts and pulled them off.

He untied the strings of her bikini top, pulled it loose and tossed it away. She was about to protest when his lips found her breasts and all rational thought left her.

She arched back and cupped his head against her. In the name of divorce, this was going *too* far.

He sucked and licked.

Or maybe not.

She kicked off her taffeta flip-flops.

He pulled off her bikini bottoms and slid his fingers between her legs.

She stepped out of her bottoms and pulled off his briefs. All she had to do now was probe his clothes with her bare toes. Tease him, get that device or drive or whatever it was.

But speaking of drives . . .

Ty knew he couldn't trust her. The mission to win her back was going too smoothly. She was up to something. But what the hell? She was tipsy, flirty, naked, and he wanted her.

He took her in his arms and lifted her off her feet, foiling any possible attempt at clothing theft. If she had any ideas about an exchange of his clothes for his signature on the dotted divorce paper line, he was going to thwart her efforts.

He kissed her as he lifted her off her feet and waded backward into the water. Deeper, deeper. On all counts.

When the water reached her toes, she wrapped her legs around his waist, splashing water up his legs and pressing into his kiss as she rocked against him.

He was hard and eager, on the very ragged edge, wanting to plunge in. Six months was way too long to be celibate, but he'd been trained in self-control. He had no intention of rushing things. No matter what happened later, she wasn't going to forget this fantasy, or him. Ever. He was going to make sure of that.

He waded deeper. Deeper. Until he was nearly waist deep. The water rippled against the curves of Tref's very fine ass. She pulled out of the kiss and stared into his eyes. He was an expert at reading emotions, but the dim light and his own desire messed with his mind. Other than lust, he wasn't certain what he saw. Maybe guilt. He hoped so. She never should have left him.

He nuzzled her ear. Another step and the cool water made her gasp. Or maybe that was his tongue in her ear.

She bit his shoulder until it hurt.

He took another step backward. The cool water hit them at waist level. Tref shuddered in his arms and sucked his neck. He tipped her head back into a kiss and fell backward into the pool, dragging her beneath the surface, still holding her in a kiss as they crouched.

She struggled against him, trying to break free and push to the surface. He knew what he was doing, knew her fear of the water. But he held her firm, kissing her deeply, sharing his breath with her. He wanted her to trust him implicitly. It seemed vitally important.

It was dark beneath the water, with only the smallest shaft of moonlight filtering through. Tref's hair floated around them, silky and soft as it brushed against him.

He caressed her gently. She stopped struggling, finally returning his kiss. She wrapped her legs around his waist and pressed into him. Satisfied, and running out of breath, he popped to a stand, pushing to the surface.

Water streamed down Tref's body, running in rivulets between her breasts, which shone pert and silhouetted in the moonlight. She threw her head back and arched up, face toward the moon as she squeezed him tight between her thighs, his very own mermaid.

She'd never looked more beautiful. He'd never wanted her more. He was ready. She was ready. He grabbed her around the waist and thrust into her. He had no intention of being gentle.

Treflee gasped as he plunged in. The water lapped at her bottom, heightening the sensation in a way she'd never imagined. The waterfall pounded and roared, drowning out everything but Ty and the tight, aching pleasure of him inside her.

He thrust again. She squeezed him between her thighs, inched up, and slid down onto him, riding him. Standing was nice, but couldn't match the wild, pounding frenzy she felt.

Ty must have felt it, too. Somehow, he managed to walk them into shallow water as she sucked his shoulder and dug her fingernails into his back. Without breaking contact, he toppled on top of her into the sand in inches of water.

He thrust into her without mercy as the lapping waves they created licked her bottom and sand ground into her back. Rough waves of pleasure just this side of pain coursed through her. Building, building, building.

She couldn't tell whether he meant to punish her or he'd simply lost control. As she had.

She pulled her mouth from his shoulder and stared into his eyes, looking for an answer. His eyes were dark. She lost herself in them, no longer caring what he meant. This was how souls joined.

She rocked and let the waves of passion roll over and over her. She leaned her forehead against his and rocked harder as the tension built.

She moaned.

He tensed and stiffened.

She arched and screamed in the ecstasy of climax as never before, letting the waves crash over her while the pounding thrum of the waterfall drowned out all else.

She didn't hear Ty grunt, couldn't hear him breathe. But she felt him. And that was more than enough.

As the crescendo subsided, she ran her hands through his hair, kissed his neck, and whispered, "I love you."

She swallowed hard and held his head against her neck. He'd never hear. He'd never know. She let the words tumble out again. "I love you, Ty. You. Always."

He squeezed her tight. His lips brushed her hair. His warm breath moved against her hair. He was saying something, but she couldn't tell what.

Eventually, he rolled off her.

She lay looking at the moon, holding hands with him until she felt a chill.

She sat up and scooted back out of the water onto the beach, feeling around in the sand for her clothes.

Ty reached over, grabbed her hand, and brushed her wet hair back off her shoulder. She recognized the look in his eyes. The man wanted more. So did she.

When it's been six months, it doesn't take long to lock and reload. He pushed her onto her back on their pile of clothes and entered her again.

As she arched against him, she grasped for something to hang on to in the soft sand. She grabbed onto his shorts beneath her and . . . there it was, the thing she'd been looking for all along.

CHAPTER EIGHTEEN

T*ref loves me. Mission two accomplished,* Ty thought as he and Tref strolled back to camp hand in hand. He was ridiculously happy. He'd never wanted that damn divorce.

He wore his rumpled, sandy, sex-stained clothes and wasn't the least bit embarrassed by his appearance. Let people look.

Greg was keeping watch as they entered the camp area. Ty gave him a nod. Greg gave him a quick thumbs-up. Tref didn't appear to catch it.

Ty's turn at watch would come at dawn. First he planned to get a few hours of much-deserved after-sex sleep. The sex had been so good, he'd sleep until noon if he wasn't careful.

Most of the time, he operated sleep deprived. Four or five on-edge, sometimes nightmare-filled, hours every twenty-four wasn't exactly what the doctor recommended for perfect health. It was something he'd never told Tref, but he slept better with her than he slept anywhere else. Particularly after lovemaking. Especially after it had been mind-blowing. He wouldn't tell her for two reasons—it made him vulnerable, and he didn't want her to think she was simply his sleeping pill.

There were other things he didn't tell her, either. Like how he'd heard every little moan and whimper she'd made at the waterfall. True, *she* couldn't hear a thing. Nor could anyone else. But he had his trusty white-noise-canceling spy ear, a minuscule earbud that fit unnoticeably into one ear. The ear, if she'd been paying attention, he hadn't let her nibble. Just thinking about her ecstatic scream made him hard again. It was almost as good as her confession of undying love.

They stopped up short in front of his tent. He pulled her into his arms and kissed her. "Spend the night with me?"

She stood on her toes and brushed his lips with a light kiss that fueled the joy welling up inside him. "Yes."

He kissed her again and held the tent door aside for her to pass through. "I have something for you."

He waited for her to enter the tent before he pulled the jewelry box that held the pearls out from where he'd hidden them. Holding her hand, he led her to the mattress and sat down beside her before he presented the box to her.

She took it hesitantly. "What's this?"

He grinned. He couldn't help it. "Something I picked up for you months ago. I missed you, Tref. You don't know how many times these last months I almost commented on the weather. I should have. I've never been a coward before. I'm sorry. For everything."

She reached over and stroked his arm.

"I'd like to work things out," he said, slowly. "Tref, I want you to know that what I do, I do for you and everyone I love. I want the world to be safe and beautiful for you."

Her gaze flitted between the box and him. Her eyes sparkled with tears. He saw her gulp. The last thing he needed was for her to start crying.

He put his arms around her, held her tight. "Go ahead. Open it." He felt like a kid at Christmas.

She opened the box slowly and gasped when she saw

the contents. She opened her mouth but no sound came out. He'd actually made her speechless.

He stroked her hair and kissed her cheek.

The pearls caught the moonlight filtering in and shone white and bright, miniature moons on a string.

She stroked them softly. "They're beautiful." Her voice broke.

"Princess-length pearls for my princess." He took the box from her hands. "Let me help you put them on." He clasped them around her neck. "Beautiful."

"I don't know what to say." She looked at him as if she were beseeching him to do something.

"Don't say anything. Just let me look at you wearing them." He pulled her bikini top off and stared at her naked breasts with the pearls above them. This was just what he'd imagined.

"Oh, Tref, I've missed you." He kissed her and guided her down onto the mattress.

Then he made love to his wife. Again.

As far as air mattresses went, this one was pretty comfy. Maybe it was because Ty was there beside her. She was still digesting his revelation—he'd missed her. Missed her for real, as in not faking it for some espionage-type purpose. And he'd bought her pearls, a whole string of them. And apologized. And wanted, sincerely, to work things out. And most importantly, this time she *believed* him.

Treflee rolled up on one elbow and studied him as she fingered the pearls around her neck. He slept on his back with one arm over his head. Relaxed in slumber, he looked handsome and younger, even with the goatee, more like the guy she'd married than the hardened spy he'd grown into.

She decided, as handsome as he was with the beard,

she liked him better clean shaven. He looked more like her Ty.

Her Ty.

Earlier Ty had pulled her close with one arm and fallen asleep. As any good wife knows, a satisfied man will fall asleep after sex. As soundly as Ty was sleeping, she'd made him a very happy camper.

She'd put her bikini back on. He slept with his rumpled shorts on, the very shorts that held a certain little device in a secret inside pocket. This in itself was a dead giveaway to the importance of those shorts or something in them. Wouldn't it have been more comfortable to sleep in his boxers? Or in the buff?

She tucked a strand of loose hair into the French braid she'd plaited her hair into. She stroked his bare chest lightly with her fingers, and ran her hand up his leg under the shorts. She kissed his cheek and ran her fingers through his hair. He loved it when she played with his hair. His breathing sped up.

She liked arousing him as he slept.

Her hand skimmed over the inside pocket of his shorts. She felt the tiny device inside and froze. *Welcome to temptation!*

She felt a trill of excitement. This Hawaiian adventure and all Ty's spy intrigue had somehow rubbed off on her. Could she do it? Could she lift it from his pocket as she'd planned before? Was she spy enough?

She had to see this top secret thing. This thing that would save the world. For once she wanted to hold her destiny in her hands and make her own decision from a position of power.

Still stroking Ty's hair, she slowly removed the device from his pocket. Ty sighed.

She kissed his forehead.

He stretched. She froze.

He rolled over onto his side. She let out a sigh of relief and pulled the data card out from beneath the cotton blanket. She stared at it in the dark. It was tiny, no bigger than her thumbnail.

Her cover-up lay rumpled next to the bed. She reached over, grabbed it, very cautiously rolled onto the floor, and stood up. Ty didn't stir.

She stared at the device in her hand again. She needed some fresh air and time to think and make up her mind. She slid on her cover-up and slipped out of the tent into the moonlight. The minuscule thing felt as heavy and radioactive as uranium in her hand.

Alone with her thoughts, she realized part of what had driven the wedge between her and Ty was her feeling of loneliness when he was gone. The idea that she thought about him all the time while she was out of his sight, out of his mind. That his work was more important than her, not something he did *for* her.

These last few days she'd gotten a peek at how scary the world was. She was more glad than ever there were people like Ty out there protecting everyone else. The world needed more of them. Which meant the people they loved, people like her, had to make sacrifices. They had to be understanding. And sometimes, they had to handle tragedies and difficult situations without their loved one right beside them. But that didn't mean they had to be alone in their grief. That they couldn't lean on each other.

She should have told Ty about the baby. Should have let him comfort her rather than been angry because he'd deserted her in her hour of need. She'd been keeping an awful secret. She'd have to tell him and hope he understood.

Holding the memory card, she felt like a traitor, a backstabber. Which told her all she wanted to know. Just this morning she'd thought this was what she wanted, that this thing would buy her freedom. But the waterfall, the pearls, Ty's apology . . .

She couldn't use this against him, not just because it was a despicable, traitorous thing to do, as she realized now, but because she didn't want to.

She turned the thing over in her hand and looked up and studied the moon. It was so clear she could see the man in it, laughing at her folly. Laughing because she'd thought her life would be better without Ty. Happiness bubbled up. She wanted to laugh with the moon.

She closed her hand around the little data card and squeezed. She had to put this back before Ty noticed it was missing. You didn't steal, or even borrow, secrets from a spy and expect to be forgiven. You became the enemy.

As she turned back toward the tent, a footstep crunched behind her. Her heart raced. "Kane?"

A hand shot out and clamped over her mouth. "Scream and you die, bitch. You have something we want."

As she kicked and reached to pry the hand loose with one hand, she tucked the device into her braid with the other.

"Keep struggling and I open fire on your friends there asleep in their tents." A gun gleamed in his hand, pointing directly at the big white wedding tent.

Ty woke with a start. Something was wrong. He lay still, surveying the surroundings. There was a cold spot next to him. He patted the bed. Tref?

All his senses sprang to high alert. He heard the unmistakable sounds of a nearly mute struggle going on just outside the tent.

He rolled to his feet and grabbed his gun. He felt for the SDXC card in his pocket—it was missing.

Tref! He felt as if he'd been kicked in the gut.

He moved silently to the tent opening and peeked through a crack. A hooded assailant held Tref at gunpoint.

"I wouldn't." Zulu Fong spoke softly and pressed a gun against the back of Ty's head. "Drop the gun."

Zulu had him dead to rights. Ty slowly released the gun.

"Turn around." Zulu pulled the pistol away from Ty's head. "Slowly."

Ty turned around and stared into the barrel of a gun aimed in his face.

Zulu stared at him with cold, calculating eyes. A second armed Fuk Ching lifted the back tent flap and slid in behind him.

Ty cursed beneath his breath. Once again Tref had distracted him from his duty.

Zulu's eyes sparkled as if he were enjoying himself. He kicked the gun to his associate. "My man *Bang*"—Zulu emphasized the name for effect—"has your girlfriend outside with a gun to her head, too."

"Yeah, I saw," Ty said.

Zulu grinned. "She has something we want. Maybe you know where she stashed it?"

"I don't know what you're talking about, dude."

Zulu hit Ty with a left hook to the side of the face. Ty's head snapped around so hard it felt like his brain had come loose in his skull. For a second Ty saw stars. When the astronomy show cleared, he tasted blood running from the side of his mouth. He took a deep breath and wiped at it with his bare shoulder.

"Did that spark any memories? Maybe now you know what I mean? I want the software she picked up on Haleakala. If you don't hand it over, I'll have to strip-search the girl. If you play nice, I'll let you watch."

"I don't know what you're talking about. Neither does Tref. Let her go."

Zulu was a martial arts expert and quick. He kicked Ty in the stomach before Ty had a chance to react.

Ty doubled over and fought for breath, trying not to get sick.

Zulu stuck the gun back against his temple. "Protecting the girl. Very noble. Or very stupid." He turned and hissed to the other guy, "Search the tent."

A Chinese thug marched Ty out of the tent. Treflee gasped into the hand covering her mouth, feeling a thick slice of guilt. Ty's lip ran slick with blood that looked horror-flick black in the dark. He clutched his stomach and shot her a quick look of disgust and anger laced with betrayal. A welt rose on his cheek and around her heart.

Though she'd heard his stories of being beaten and escaping the bad, real-life members of *evil*, she'd never seen him bloodied in person before. The sight scared and sickened her. She'd brought this on him by being stupid. *So stupid.*

She pleaded silently with him for understanding.

He was man enough to shoot back a look that told her to buck up and play spy tough. Never surrender.

There has to be a way to get out of this mess. There has to be!

She'd violated stupid-expendable-horror-movie-victim rule number one—never go outside alone. Especially in the dead of night, unarmed. Especially if there are crazed killers who attacked you earlier in the day. She didn't dare make a whimper or others would die.

The two Chinese thugs dragged them silently down a path toward the ocean away from camp and finally into a damp, dark cave at water's edge. They shoved them in and dumped them on the black sand beach, shining flashlights in their eyes to keep them disoriented. In another situation and mood, this hidden cove and silky black sand would have been a second fantasy in the making.

Outside, the waves lapped and crashed, making a calming white noise that could lull a baby to sleep. In the dampness of this perfect killing cave, it muffled all voices and obliterated any calls for help to the outside world.

Treflee had been studying Ty, trying to imitate his bravado and discover if he had a weapon on him. Maybe a switchblade in his shoe, or a phone programmed to call Spy-1-1 when he stamped three times. Was it too much to hope he had a plan? He always had a plan. At any second NCS agents could arrive with rocket guns blazing. Wouldn't they?

"You have something we want. Give it to us and we'll let you go," the one called Zulu said.

Let us go? Right. She'd seen enough spy flicks to know the bad guy never kept his promise. Half a second after she gave him whatever it was he wanted, they were fish bait and he pressed a button that destroyed the world. She'd never give up her new hair accessory.

"I don't know what you're talking about." She held out her empty hands, trying not to tremble. "I have nothing on me."

"Don't play games with me, spy."

Without thinking, Treflee turned to Ty. He wore his glazed surfer-dude look and shrugged as if dumb on the subject. It took her a second to realize Zulu was speaking to her. What an idiot she was! She'd almost just given Ty away. She was not only a bad wife, but a bad American, too.

"Spy?" Recovering quickly, she knitted her brow and did her best to look mystified, and even a little "woohoo, this guy's a nutcase."

"You've been watching way too many episodes of *Chuck,* dude. Spies are not around every corner trying to steal the intercept. Do I look like I'm wearing a trench coat to you?"

Zulu laughed. "Spy girls wear bikinis in the movies all the time."

Damn that Bond! Zulu was right.

"I like bikinis better," the evil assistant said.

"Me, too," Ty chimed in.

Treflee glared at him. "Shut up!"

Ty shrugged. "Dude, it's Hawaii."

The assistant trailed his flashlight beam up and down her suggestively, doing a Tinker Bell dance on her breasts. Can a beam of light have a leer? This one did.

Treflee fought the urge to scoot out of the spotlight and into the darkness where she'd probably get shot for trying to escape. Instead, she shooed the light away with a brush of her hand.

"Hey! Why would any real spy choose the stupid cover I'm living? Half the time I don't even like my cousin Carrie. I can't stand her friends. And then I have to pick Carrie up and console her for bailing on her groom days before the wedding. Like it wasn't her choice." She crossed her arms, striking a "refute that" pose.

Zulu shrugged. "We all have shitty relatives. Why not bring them along and hope they get shot?" He laughed an evil laugh. "For a small fee, I can take them out for you."

He was serious.

Treflee gulped. She'd thought she was protecting Carrie and her friends by pretending she didn't care about them. "I don't have any cash on me. You should have caught me when I had my pocketbook."

Zulu laughed long and loud, but his gun stayed aimed at her heart. "I like you. You look hot in a bikini. Too bad we didn't meet under different circumstances. I could use some eye candy for my left arm."

Now that sent a chill through her. Murderers thought she was hot. *Ouch.*

"If you're so innocent, why did this 'cousin' of yours just happen to book the plantation next to Mrs. Ho?"

Treflee fought the urge to turn to Ty for help. Instead, she tossed her hand, waving off Zulu's accusation as ridiculous.

"Oh, very damning evidence, big guy. *Lots* of people stay at Big Auau. Are you going to accuse every one of them, too? Break into their campsites and wave your guns around?"

"No one else is staying there and snooping around at this very important time." Zulu shone the light directly in her eyes.

She held a hand up to shield them. "Yeah? Well, that's coincidence for you. You have to book these places a year in advance. You think the CIA has the foresight to plan a year ahead? Anyway, what does Mrs. Ho have to do with anything?"

She resisted the urge to say, "Have to do with the price of tea in China." Maybe a comedic racial reference wasn't the best way to go, here.

Even without her shot at levity, Zulu put his fierce face back on. "You were sneaking around Mrs. Ho's property. Why?"

She shrugged, remembering to stick to her cover story and wondering if Zulu knew about the lei strangler. "Taking an innocent stroll to admire the view is called sneaking now? I've never been near her place except that one time when I ran into her clothesline. The woman's a menace. I think she likes hurting tourists who choose Big Auau over her place."

Treflee was still trying to picture the wedding-minded Mrs. Ho, with her purported booby-trapped clotheslines, as a master spy. Next to her, Ty didn't look all that surprised. Or maybe he was just playing things cool.

Zulu shook gently as he laughed. "Oh, very good. You lie like a trouper. Too bad for you that I know the truth. I know who strangled you. And he's been punished."

She instinctively clutched her neck and felt the pearls, which made her feel even worse. "Hey, wait a minute!" Anger blindsided her. She dropped her hand and forgot the old adage about engaging brain before putting mouth in motion. "That was your guy with the lei?"

Zulu towered over her. He sighed with exasperation. If he hadn't been holding a gun and had an armed accomplice, she would have kicked him in the shins.

"Are you crazy? You nearly killed me!"

"Yet you didn't call the cops."

"Right! Who wants to spend their vacation talking to cops?"

"Innocent girlies who've just startled an intruder."

Next to her, Ty didn't make any kind of movement or expression to indicate whether he thought she was performing up to NCS standards or not. And he didn't come out slashing with switchblade shoes, either. He dabbed at his fat lip, which only made her feel horrible.

"Spies trying to plant a bug on Ty to spy on us, those kind of people avoid the cops." Zulu dropped the light from her eyes and shone it on Ty. "You should have picked someone smarter to be your innocent dupe."

Oh, boy! Ty did not like being called a dumb dupe. It took a wife to sense his anger and read how badly he wanted to punch Zulu. Or shoot him. On the surface Ty appeared calm enough for government work, but she knew he was seething.

"Plant a bug on someone who hangs with us. Very smart plan and very dumb, too." Zulu shook his head. "We don't play around. You should know that. We've already killed one of your agents." He shrugged. "And then we had to kill one of our own men. Shen Lin got jumpy, scared. He was a liability."

What is he talking about? What agent?

"But, on the positive side, his death put everything back in balance. You should have left us alone. What is another unsolved murder of a Chinese immigrant to you?"

She didn't answer.

"Now that dragon lady wants something you have." He appeared to be trying to suppress a shudder. "I promised to get it for her."

"I don't know what you're talking about. You lost me at taking out one of my supposed agents."

"Cut the dumb-blonde act." Zulu was losing patience. "I saw you myself escaping from Woo Ming's after we took out Shen Lin.

"We even cleared out and gave your cleanup crew plenty of space to get rid of the body. Right before the early-bird dinner special. Fewer questions that way. Less police involvement. Good for all of us, except Cook. He was angry because you interrupted his preparations for the dinner rush.

"It wasn't our fault your guys bungled the disposal. We could have told you the currents are unpredictable too close to shore. They should have gone deeper."

Yeah, that was obvious. Can you be incredibly relieved, happy, terrified, and sickened at the same time? Apparently you can, because that's how Treflee felt at that moment.

Ty hadn't killed the waiter! She could've kissed him. Gently, in consideration for his fat lip.

She wished Ty could give her some clue as to what she was supposed to say now. "That's very decent of you" didn't seem fitting somehow. In her nightmares, she still saw the fish eating Shen Lin's face.

She couldn't very well tell the truth—that in both cases, she was spying on her husband, not them, and evidently not being too subtle about it. If she did, she'd give Ty away. She'd just have to bungle her way through pretending to be a top NCS agent. With any luck, they'd get cocky thinking she was a sterling example of NCS incompetency and relax their guard so the real spies could do their job.

She shrugged and said the first thing that popped into her mind. "It's hard to get good help these days."

Zulu laughed and nodded as if he agreed completely. "So true. Now, hand it over."

She stared him in the eye, trying to appear brave and flippant like heroines in movies. "You'll have to be more specific."

"I want the device your agent passed to you at Haleakala."

"Agent? Haleakala? You're imagining things again. If I were an agent, why would I go all the way to the top of a volcano to get a device? I'm sure I could think up better drop sites."

"Maybe because AMOS is up there and that's where your guy works?"

AMOS again.

Just then, Zulu got a text and pulled out his cell phone. He read it and frowned. "Cong didn't find it in the tent. Search her, Bang."

Bang dropped his flashlight, grabbed Treflee, and yanked her cover-up down before she could even scream. She clawed at him and struggled, trying to grab the gun from the arm that held her and create a diversion for Ty.

Taking her cue, Ty rolled to his feet and rammed into

Zulu. The two men went down with an *oomph* into the darkness as Zulu's flashlight went flying and splashed into the water near the mouth of the cave. It floated and bounced along in the water, pushed by the waves, and casting eerie shadows as it caught flashes of action.

Splashed in the water? There was no water a few minutes ago. Oh, my gosh! The tide is coming in.

Bang grabbed her around the waist and lifted her off her feet. He stuck his hands between her breasts, felt beneath her bikini top, and squeezed her nipples. She kicked and clawed and tried to pull his disgusting hands off her as he rolled her nipple between his fingers. Bang released her breasts and stuck his hand down her bikini bottom. She gagged and screamed for Ty.

The grind of fist hitting flesh, followed by a grunt, echoed off the cave walls. Please let that be Ty who'd thrown the punch, not taken it. If she'd been better trained, heck, trained at all, maybe she'd have known how to break free from Bang and his probing, disgusting fingers.

Finally, he pulled his hand free. "She doesn't have it!" Bang yelled to Zulu. He put his gun against her head.

Little did he know how close he was to the device he wanted. Blow off her head and he blew up the software in her hair.

"Give it up, Ty. I have a gun on your girlfriend's head. Step out where I can see you before I kill her."

Someone pulled the flashlight from the water. The next thing she knew, the beam shone in her eyes.

"I'm right here," Ty said.

Zulu loomed behind him, a dark shadow slowly rising to his feet.

"Trying to blind me won't work," Bang said without a trace of concern. "I don't need to see to kill point-blank."

They all knew that if Ty had come up with the gun, he'd be using it.

"You okay, Zu?" Bang called.

"I'm fine." Zulu breathed heavily. "Never mind her, shoot him!"

"No!" Treflee screamed. "No! I'll tell you where it is. Please, please don't kill him." She was too afraid even to cry.

Zulu came up behind Ty, grabbed the light, and kicked him in the back, sending him face-first into the sand. "Where is it?"

Treflee wished she possessed a spy's mind-set and more than the limited self-defense training Ty had given her during their marriage. She'd opened her mouth with no real plan except to save Ty.

Where could she send Cong, Bang, and Zulu where they wouldn't hurt an innocent bystander? Someplace far away from camp and the others.

Zulu stared at her. "I'm waiting."

"Let him go first."

Zulu scanned the cave floor with a beam of light and retrieved his gun, which he aimed at Ty. "No."

"Then no deal."

"We outgun you."

"Fine, shoot me." Treflee shrugged. "That'll just guarantee you won't get what you want." *Especially if they shoot me in the head.*

"Why would I shoot you? I have a hostage," Zulu said. "How would you like to watch him die? Does a nice, slow bleed-out appeal to you? I know where to shoot him to make that happen."

Treflee's mouth went dry. She tried to think like Ty. "It wouldn't be the best show I've ever seen. I'm not a fan of bleeding out."

Zulu laughed. "You think he'll moan and cry?"

I think he'll go down like a hero and it will break my heart.

"Let's take Ty's death off the table. Before I tell you where that thing is, I need some reassurance you won't simply kill us after I do."

Zulu's diabolical laughter filled the cavern, echoing and blending with the ocean surf. His tone tinged with amusement, he uttered a string of curses. "Shit! I expected more out of a master spy." He laughed again. "Why would I kill you?"

Until he has what he wants, Treflee added silently. He'd kill her for sure then.

She was in the proverbial no-win situation. Either she resisted and Zulu killed Ty before her eyes or she told him what he wanted to hear and then he killed them both. Any way she turned it, they came up dead. It was just a matter of now or later. Later, however, held the possibility of escape or miraculous rescue. Plus it might allow her to make a few amends with Ty. Better to die with a clear conscience.

"Here's the deal," Zulu said. "You lead me to the device while Bang here guards Ty. When I have the device, I'll order Bang to let him go."

Treflee shook her head. "No. No way. For all I know, Bang will kill him the minute I walk out of here."

Bang's arms trembled from exertion, but he still held her midair with an iron grip.

A wave rolled in. It splashed at Zulu's ankles and lapped at Ty on the ground, coming up just short of where Bang held her farther into the cave. The tide was coming in quickly.

"Let's be honest about things," Treflee said. "There's no way you're going to let me live once you have that device."

Zulu didn't jump in to dispute her.

"But you can't kill me until you do. I'm not going to tell you a thing until I have a deal that will give me a fighting chance at surviving." She tried to stare where she thought his eyes would be, which wasn't easy with him shining the light in hers.

"Here's my proposal—I tell you where the data card is. You leave us in this cave with a hope of getting away before we drown in the incoming tide.

"No mess, no fuss for you. If we don't make it out, we simply wash out to sea. You have what you want. We're all good."

Zulu studied her. "And if you're sending me on a wild-goose chase?"

She shrugged. "I'm not. But if I was, you'll just have to hurry. Work fast enough and you'll still have time to come back and try again before I drown."

Zulu considered a moment, then shrugged. "What the hell. Bang!"

Zulu nodded toward a volcanic outcropping that rose out of the cave floor. "Cuff them together around that."

Zulu stared at Ty with a merciless look. "Face to rock so they can't sit." He tossed Bang a pair of cuffs.

Bang pulled another from his pocket as Zulu held a gun to Ty. Bang worked quickly, handcuffing her right hand to Ty's left and his right to her left as they hugged opposite sides of the rough rock.

"This is what you call giving us a chance?" Treflee said as Bang walked away.

"Put the key on the top of the rock," Zulu instructed Bang. "I call this a very fair chance. Volcanic rock has plenty of foot- and handholds. Easier to climb than your basic climbing wall.

"Climb up, get the key, free yourselves, and you're golden." He laughed again. "Now, where is it?"

She gave detailed instructions about hiding it in one of the catering bins she'd seen Greg load into the van. Her only hope was the van was parked far enough away from the campsite that they wouldn't hurt anyone else searching for it. And that it gave Ty and her enough time to get free.

"You better be telling the truth." Zulu waved his gun at them. "Bang!"

Treflee jumped before she realized Zulu was talking to his assistant.

Zulu laughed and nodded toward the cave entrance.

They'd tied Treflee to the side of the rock deeper in the cave. Ty was cuffed with his back to the opening. Treflee leaned her head around the rock, watching them go, taking the last of the light with them.

"Hey! How about leaving us a flashlight?" Treflee called after them.

Zulu laughed again. "Afraid of the dark? No one said I was that fair."

Damn it! They'd duped her. How were she and Ty going to find footholds and the key in the dark?

She scowled after the jerks, watching their beam of light reflect on the waves pounding deeper into the cave. Watching the two Fuk Ching wade out into the incoming surf. Zulu and Bang reached the cave entrance in knee-deep water. Their light shone on open ocean.

She took a deep breath, trying to collect her wits just as Zulu spun his beam of light around into her eyes. He raised his gun arm and squeezed the trigger.

CHAPTER NINETEEN

Treflee screamed, watching as Zulu's arm bucked with the kick. Simultaneously, Ty crumpled, pulling Treflee into a face plant with the rough rock, dragging her shoulder and arm down as the stretching fingers of the waves lapped at their feet. Treflee listened for the ricochet of gunfire. The surf drowned it out. She had no way of knowing how many shots Zulu got off or even if he continued to fire.

"Ty!" She pulled her head away from the rock, scraping her bare stomach and legs against the rough pumice stone as she tried to rearrange and pull up his dead weight. Her arm was scratched and bleeding. Her cheek throbbed. "Ty! Don't die on me, don't you dare die on me."

Zulu and Bang disappeared. Everything went pitch-black. The only sound over the surf, barely discernible as human, was Ty's ragged breathing.

At least he's alive.

"Ty! Ty! Talk to me." She grabbed his hand and squeezed for reassurance. With her other hand, she felt wildly for a pulse.

Finally, he squeezed back. "Don't tell me you didn't expect that."

"What? Why would I? No one expects a Chinese execution." Treflee was so relieved by the sound of his voice she sagged against the rock and held his hand in a death grip.

"You knew they weren't going to just let us walk out of here." Ty's voice was weak, but ironic.

No, I hadn't expected them to shoot Ty. She'd been so stupidly naïve, so smug thinking she'd done everything right. She held back a sob.

"Hey, don't beat yourself up. You did great. Better than the average civilian. Zulu didn't leave you much of a choice."

Treflee lifted her head. Ty sounded sincere.

"At least you bought us a chance. Emmett will be proud. Probably give you a medal," he said.

She didn't want a medal. She wanted to get out of here. *Alive.*

"They promised to give us a fair chance," she muttered, trying to suck up some courage. "Where are you hurt?"

Bleeding out. Zulu's words came back to her. She shuddered, trying not to panic, realizing how much she couldn't stand to lose Ty.

"My left calf. No place vital. Just a flesh wound."

Just a flesh wound. She pictured him gritting his teeth against the pain.

"Did the bullet pass through?"

"Maybe."

"Are you bleeding?"

"Yeah."

"Badly?"

"I have my right shin pressed up against it. It's sticky with blood, but I've got good pressure on it now." He squeezed her hand.

She poked her head around the rock, trying to get a

look at him, but the dark was so deep she couldn't even see the rock in front of her face.

"Where's the SD card you stole from me?" Ty sounded as if speaking took effort, but his tone was casual, normal, almost reassuring. His mother was the only other person who knew him well enough to detect the edge of hurt and anger in it.

Treflee didn't bother with denial. What was the point? "In my hair, safely tucked into my braid."

"Good thinking."

A wave rolled in, soaking Treflee's taffeta flip-flops, splashing and stinging the scrapes on her legs like a brush with nettles. Ty stiffened and squeezed her hand. Hard. She pictured him wincing.

"Salt water," he said tightly. "We're going to have to get moving. You know what they say about pouring salt in a wound."

He was talking about more than his bullet wound. His tone was clear—he was talking about her.

"I was going to put it back. Ty, you have to believe me," she pleaded, fighting back tears of fear and frustration. "I wanted to see this thing that's going to save the world. I wanted to know for sure I was making the right choice by giving us a second chance. I was just turning to come back in when Bang jumped me."

"Yeah, bang! That's how it felt to me, too."

The wave rolled out. Ty relaxed the grip on her hand. She kept squeezing. His voice and touch were the only things keeping her sane in the black void. If she let go, she'd lose everything.

"Orders be damned, when we get out of here, I'm giving you that divorce. Who am I to fight the tide?"

"Orders?" She was confused. "What orders?"

Ty laughed weakly and humorlessly. "Emmett's. Not to divorce. To win you back."

Treflee felt as if she'd just taken that shot, but to her heart. "Orders? That's what that was at the waterfall? Orders?"

He didn't answer.

"Ty!"

"Whatever you want to believe, baby."

No, she didn't believe it. Yes, she believed the imperious Emmett would order Ty not to divorce. The man had gall. An ex-spouse was a dangerous loose end. She just hadn't really thought about it before. But no, she didn't believe the waterfall was about orders. Or the pearls. She couldn't believe it or she'd lose it right here and lie down to drown.

Ty was angry. Trying to hurt her. Not that she blamed him. She'd think about it later.

"Can you stand up straight?" she asked him.

He inhaled deeply. "Yeah."

"And still keep pressure against the wound?"

"I'll have to."

Somehow, with a lot of hand-holding and maneuvering, they managed to return to the starting point, which took the pressure off her shoulder. From the relative slack in the cuffs between them, Treflee assumed Ty was leaning heavily on the rock.

"Zulu was right. This *is* porous rock. There should be plenty of footholds," Ty said. "We just have to find them."

His hand felt clammy in hers.

"How are you going to climb with one leg pressed against the other?"

"I'll use my arms. I have plenty of upper-body strength. The legs will just be for balance. What kind of shoes are you wearing?"

She tried to lighten the mood with a little humor. "Is that a dirty question? What kind of shoes are you wearing?"

"Slightly soaked athletic shoes with good treads." Ordinarily, he would have laughed and flirted back, but instead he remained serious. "Either one of us slips, the other goes down, too. Look how I brought you down when Zu shot me. Shoes?"

"Taffeta wedding flip-flops, size seven, hot pink, rubber bottoms, woven mat insole."

"Kick them off. You'll do better barefoot using your toes to grip."

"If I have any toes left when we're done. Pumice stones are great for pedicures, but they're coarse and razor-blade sharp. This rock will eat my feet up." Her arms, chest, legs, and stomach had already been scraped and rubbed raw in places.

"You seriously think you can climb in flip-flops?"

"Why not? I dance in six-inch heels."

He sighed so loudly, she heard it over the surf.

She distracted him. "You've been in this kind of situation before?" She both wanted to know and didn't.

"Tighter."

She found that bit of intelligence only slightly reassuring. "Handcuffed to whom?"

"No one you need to know about."

Fair enough.

"We're going to have go by feel," he said. "This rock formation is only about ten feet tall. Reach up and see if you can feel a grip a couple of feet up."

They worked in silence, reaching, grasping, patting down a piece of rock that would just as soon cut them to ribbons as hoist them to freedom. They played ring-around-the-rosy, circling the rock. By the time they found a suitable first jump-up point, the waves were to Treflee's calves and stung every open scrape and cut. The water no longer receded completely, but merely ebbed and flowed, flowing higher each time.

"On the count of three," Ty said.

And then they were up, hanging on by sheer will and fear. She felt the tremble in Ty's arms as they hung just feet off the ground on the rock face.

"You okay?" she asked him.

"A little light-headed." He sucked in a deep breath. "Give me a minute."

She clenched his hand. For him to admit even the slightest weakness was really something. It scared her. She needed the reassurance of his touch. "I've got you." She squeezed his hand so tightly, she nearly lost feeling in her fingers.

She thought he grunted, or maybe it was a lame attempt at a laugh. He didn't believe she'd be able to hold him up. Neither did she, but she was trying to be supportive and encouraging. "Just don't faint on me. I'm not good with the Florence Nightingale thing." She didn't mean to sound irritated. It just came through when she was worried.

"Wouldn't dream of it."

"Talk to me." She had to keep him focused and conscious. "Or I'll go mad. The authorities have it all wrong. Chinese water torture is not a slow steady drip on the forehead, but the constant roar of the surf as an incoming tide threatens to drown you." She searched for her next grip as she spoke, struggling with her flip-flops to keep from slipping back into the water.

Another wave lapped against the rock, splashing them with stinging salt spray. Treflee's heart raced. Of all the ways she'd ever imagined dying, drowning in a Hawaiian cave hadn't even crossed her mind. It was suddenly her least favorite choice. Right below shark attack.

"So this thing in my hair, I hope it's waterproof? It's certainly not the prettiest hair accessory I've ever had."

"Oh, yeah. And hardened. And definitely the most expensive thing you've ever worn in your hair. But let's try not to put it to the test. Just keep it above water anyway, shall we?"

"That's the plan. Good to know it has some redeeming qualities."

"Tref, my fingers are tingling. Ease up on them a bit?"

She relaxed her hold. Slightly.

"I've found another grip we can use." He guided her hand to it, pressing her fingers into the crevice.

The teamwork and the gentle touch of his hand reminded her of better times. A lump welled in her throat.

"On my count," he said. "One . . . two . . . three."

As she grabbed the handhold and pushed with her feet, her taffeta flip-flops slipped on the wet rock.

Ty caught her wrist and arrested her fall.

"Darn flip-flops." Heart pounding above the surf, she kicked them into the water.

"Did you just lose your shoes?"

"Oh, shut up," she said. That was no way to behave after he'd just saved her. "Sorry. You were right."

"Nice to hear you admit it. Let's try again."

And they were up another level. She hung on by her toes. She had no idea how Ty hung on with his one good leg. The rock was tapering off. There was play in their arms. They had to hug the rock, rather than stretch around it.

"This thing feels like Everest," she said. "Any idea how much farther to the top?"

"Four feet or so, I'd guess."

"Four feet!" She clunked her head against the rock.

"Hey, don't give up. We just have to climb high enough to reach up and throw one pair of arms over. Then we can grab the key, unlock ourselves, and get out of here. The next handhold should get us there."

She had a moment of panic. "Do you even remember where the opening is?" With all the moving around the rock, she'd lost her bearings.

"Yeah, don't you?"

He knows I don't. "Don't be snide. You must be feeling better."

"It'll be sunrise soon. The light will guide us to the opening. If that fails, there's always the pull of the tide."

"Sunrise! But that's high tide." She went cold. "We'll never make it. We'll drown before then."

He started laughing. Really laughing. "Is that why you've been plowing along so quickly?"

"What?"

"This isn't the Bay of Fundy."

"No, this isn't fundy at all," she said, holding on to her irritation and trying not to slip off the rock.

"Tref, this is Hawaii. Unlike Fundy in Maine, Hawaiian tide surges are so small, you barely notice whether the tide's in or out. We're talking two-foot tides max."

"Then we're in no danger?"

"You mean other than I might bleed out and Zulu, Bang, and Cong will be discovering any minute now that you've duped them and will be back to torture the truth out of you?"

Bleed out. There were those words again.

"If Carrie and company haven't scared them off or apprehended them already."

"What?" he said.

"Why do you think I sent them to the van? Carrie and the girls are on the lookout for Kane. If they see three goons prowling around, they'll get them."

"They don't have their guns," he said.

"They'll think of something." She paused.

"Good point," he said. "I guess there's no hurry, then." Could he sound any more cynical?

"Except that I don't want to be chained to a bloodless dead man."

"Yeah, and being chained to this live one all these years has been so much fun."

Her heart sank. He hadn't forgiven her. All this happy chatter had made her hopeful. Guess she shouldn't tell him she wasn't as confident as she sounded about Carrie and the girls.

They hoisted themselves up.

"If we stretch, I think we can reach the top and search for the key," he said.

"Are we reaching with your right or mine?"

"You mean who gets the key?"

They were both right-handed. Whoever wielded the key ruled and did the unlocking.

Treflee gave him this one. "You have more handcuff experience."

"My right, then."

Ty found the key first. Treflee felt his hand clamp around it.

"Got it!" His voice rang with the thrill of victory. "Now all we have to do is swing one set of arms over the rock and maintain our balance while I unlock us."

"In the dark," she said, "don't forget that part."

Just then, as if to make a liar out of her, a glimmer of pearlescent predawn light lit up the cave opening.

She'd never seen a more beautiful predawn in her life, even if her view of it was limited. "Okay, I was wrong. Let there be light!"

Ty sounded considerably less delighted. "I was joking about having all the time in the world."

"Yeah, I got that."

"We just lost the cover of darkness." Ty pulled himself up on the rock. "As we toss our arms over, clamp on tightly with your legs."

"Don't worry about me," she said. "I have leg clamping

down to a science." She'd fastened them around him enough times for him to know that.

He got her meaning, looked away, unmoved by her lame attempt at flirtation, and got on with business. By the time they got their arms over their minivolcano, enough light shone in to make the keyholes in the cuffs visible.

Clinging to the rocks like birds on a perch, they played a game of Operation with the key. Aim, jab, miss, buzz, sorry, play again!

"Aim off today?" Treflee said. Goading Ty frequently spurred him to victory.

"My aim's fine. You're moving." He stuffed the key into the lock in Treflee's cuff.

He stilled, his hand poised on the key.

She rattled the cuffs, shooting him an impatient look. "To the victor go the spoils."

He stared at her, unblinking. "Tell me one thing first. When did you stop loving me?"

Treflee stared at him, stunned by his direct-hit question and the pain in his eyes. "I never stopped loving you."

He studied her, looking as if he wished he had a dose of truth serum on him. He didn't trust anyone to tell the truth. Not even her. Maybe especially her. She blamed Langley. They'd taught him distrust. Though she had to admit she hadn't helped things. She never should have taken that stupid device that was tucked in her braid.

"So what is this divorce business, then? You can't live with me?" He sounded resigned.

Or without you, she wanted to say, but didn't.

"The last time I was gone something changed," he said softly. "What was it? Another guy?"

"No!"

He sighed. "Then what did I do?"

"Nothing."

He stared at her so hard, she felt dizzy, as if she were losing her grip on everything.

"That's the problem, isn't it?" The resignation and pain in his voice played at her heart. "I was supposed to do something, but I didn't. What was it, Tref?"

She swallowed hard. He deserved to know. But she couldn't look him in the eye. She stared at the waves below her instead. "I got pregnant and lost our baby. You weren't there."

"Baby?" His shock sounded genuine. "We hadn't decided to have kids. You got pregnant without telling me?"

"It was an accident." She pleaded with him.

"How could you keep something like that from me? I'm your husband. I had a right to know, Tref." He spat the words out.

"I wanted to." She caught his wrist. "I wanted to tell you in person. Not in a text or a phone call. But you didn't come back in time. I miscarried and then there was no point. I had this great, big hole in my life where the baby should have been. And you refused to consider having another one."

"I needed time to think. A baby's a huge liability. For any spy." He glared at her with hurt in his eyes. "Think kidnapping and blackmail." He shook her hand off. "How could I help you? I had no idea what you were going through. How could I?"

She shrugged. She had no answer for him. She should have told him.

He shook his head. "To hell with it, Tref." He sounded hurt and angry again. "To freedom." He turned the key.

Her cuff opened. Her hand fell free of his. She clutched the rock, trying to keep her balance now that they were no longer attached on one side.

"There's one more thing I should tell you," Ty said.

"Zulu isn't going to let us simply walk out of this cave. He's got a guard posted at the entrance. That guard will either pick us off or follow us, hoping we'll lead him to the device. Then he'll kill us. So don't get any ideas about swimming out of here until we make a plan."

He thrust the key at her. "Take it and turn me loose."

Great! Danger, danger, hurt, and more danger!

Her hand shook as she lunged the key toward the keyhole on the second pair of cuffs, emotion blinding her.

The whir of a boat motor startled her.

Ty looked over his shoulder, moving just at the wrong time.

The key fell into the churning two-foot-deep waters below.

CHAPTER TWENTY

A man sat silhouetted in a speedboat at the mouth of the cave. He had a gun trained on them.

"Jump!" Treflee screamed. She propelled herself off the outcropping into the swirling, shallow waters below, taking Ty down with her.

They plunged into the waves stomachs first. The stinging slap of water stole her breath. An instant later, the sandy bottom banged out what little air she had left. Dragging Ty's arm with her, she popped to a sit on her knees, gasping for air in the salt spray and praying the gunman had bad aim. There wasn't three feet of water to dive into and avoid taking a bullet.

Next to her, Ty came up sputtering and wiping the hair out of his eyes. "Damn it, Tref! Learn to recognize the cavalry." He clenched his teeth and fists. "This salt water stings like hell!"

He lifted his arm and waved to the guy in the boat. "Greg! Over here."

Greg? She studied the man. No longer under the influence of gun-induced panic, she easily recognized him and felt silly. This was why she wasn't the spy.

Greg waved back. "Hey, nice belly flop. Very impressive splash. I give it a nine. Next time try it in deeper water." He looked like he was laughing. "I can't come in any farther. I'll run adrift. I'll wait for you here. Are you hurt? Can you make it out? Should I throw you a life ring?"

Ty glanced at Treflee.

"I'm good," she said.

He yelled back to Greg. "Yeah, we can make it." He turned to Treflee and stared at her braid. "How wet's my SDXC card? Still got it?"

That's all he can think of, his stupid card? Treflee had begun to have pangs of guilt over opening old wounds and one very new one that had started bleeding again into the water. But now she was just angry.

She glared at him as she touched her braid. "It's still there."

She pointed toward his leg in the water. "You're creating a blood slick. Do something about that leg before you start attracting sharks."

He shot her a stony look and pushed himself up, pulling her to a stand with him.

They walked to the boat, his arm slung over her shoulder as he leaned on her, both wincing like two people wading through glass. At the boat, she handed Ty up first. He scowled at her chivalry.

"What's this?" Greg pulled them in and shook their cuffed arms. "Resorted to the old 'cuffing yourself together' form of marriage counseling, have you?"

Ty collapsed onto a cushioned bench seat, tumbling Treflee next to him. "Took you long enough to get here. Got any fresh water?"

Greg handed him a water bottle. "I had a little matter of a concussion to deal with."

Ty rinsed his wound with the water, sighing with relief. "Good thing you have a hard head. I was worried Zulu had killed you."

"I'm touched by your concern, man. That Zulu is one silent, slippery bastard." Greg shook his head. "What happened to you?"

Treflee brushed the hair out of her eyes with her free hand and took a deep breath. *Safe at last.* "Zulu shot him in the leg. We need to get him to the hospital. He's been threatening to bleed out on me all night."

"What a romantic dude," Greg said.

Ty held their cuffed hands toward him. "Get us out of these."

"Don't tell me you want your freedom from the old ball and chain already?" Greg reached into his shoe and pulled out a universal handcuff key.

Treflee turned an accusing look on Ty. "What happened to *your* shoe key?"

"Left it in my high-tops."

Greg laughed. "Liar. He hasn't earned his shoe key yet." He unlocked them.

She was finally free. Treflee rubbed her wrist and stood up, allowing Ty to stretch his leg across the seat. "How did you find us?"

"Tracking device." Greg pulled out a first-aid kit and opened it. "Let's take a look at that leg."

"Tracking device? Where?" It wasn't in her teeny, weeny bikini. Treflee looked at Ty. "In your pants?" It was the only place she could think of.

"No, that would be a homing device," Greg said with a twinkle in his eye.

Ty shot him a dirty look. "The thing in your hair."

Ty turned on his stomach so Greg could see the wound better. "Did I mention it also self-destructs when commanded? I'd be careful if I were you."

Her hand flew to her hair. She pulled the device out and handed it to Greg as if holding out a bomb. Let Emmett and the rest of the NCS gang keep tabs on Greg for a while.

The men cracked up, but she didn't know whether it was because they were kidding or because they found her reaction amusing.

Greg pocketed the device and took a quick peek at Ty's leg. "This is nothing. Just a flesh wound."

"What is it with you guys and 'just flesh wounds'?" Treflee watched Greg wipe Ty's bullet hole with antiseptic. "Am I the only one who's worried?"

The two guys stared at her as if she'd just won the world worry wart title.

"Yeah," Ty finally said, gritting his teeth as Greg knelt beside him and wrapped a bandage around his calf.

"We'll get him looked at." Greg spoke sympathetically. He winked at her. Out from beneath his plain-sidekick cover, he was an attractive and confident guy. "But in my nonmedical, unprofessional opinion, he'll live." He pulled several spare life jackets out of a storage bin and lifted Ty's leg up onto them. "Let's get this elevated."

Treflee took a calming breath. They were in a boat. The sun was shining. They were going to be okay, except—

"Shouldn't we be motoring out of gunfire range before the big Zu gets back? Or one of his stakeout goons takes a potshot at us?"

"We took out the stakeout goon. Zu won't be coming back. Carrie and the girls apprehended him and turned him over to the 'cops.' The cops were really our guys. Don't worry. We won't let Zu and his crew get away," Greg said.

Treflee shot Ty a smug look. He ignored it.

"They heard a noise at the van and thought Kane had found them. The rest was a melee of killer estrogen. Or so Zu and his boys said when I came to and rescued them.

"Gotta give the ladies credit. Those girls are vicious. They had Zu and his men bound and subdued with a patchwork of hot-pink rhinestone bracelets, tent ropes, stakes, taffeta flip-flops, leis, and coconut-rum bottles."

Ty looked like he was having a hard time picturing that particular scene. "Only the bottles? Hope they didn't waste the rest of the good stuff I left in the bar. I could use a stiff shot."

Treflee got the visual immediately. "I told you Carrie can take care of herself. I hope Carrie wrapped a lei around Zulu's neck and gave it a great big wrench for me. *Aloha, mahalo* Zulu!"

"Vicious," Greg said.

"She's not a forgiving woman," Ty said.

Zing! Another direct hit.

Treflee crossed her arms. "Why should I feel the love for people who try to kill me?"

Ty gave her his hard-assed angry-husband glare. "What about for people who've saved you repeatedly, Tref? Feel any loyalty or love for them?"

Treflee averted her eyes and bit back a tart response. She'd hurt him enough already.

Greg cleared his throat and rose to a stand beside Treflee. "Back to the real enemy here. We have another problem. Hal has disappeared."

"Hal's disappeared?" Ty looked about ready to explode. He swore beneath his breath and this time the object of his wrath didn't have anything to do with pain. "I thought we had an eye on him."

Greg arched a brow. "We did. He isn't a great analyst for nothing. He works for us. He knows our methods. And MSS's. And RIOT's. Makes it tricky to outwit and outplay him."

"Aha! I guessed Hal was from Langley. I knew he was the bad guy." She pointed an accusing finger at Ty. "I can't believe you made me have lunch with him."

"Bygones," he said.

Treflee's gaze bounced between the boys. They looked unimpressed with her deductions. "Just what is he up to?"

"Selling one of our top secret projects to RIOT byte by byte," Ty said. "That's all you need to know."

Treflee turned to Greg for help. "Oh, come on!"

Ty shook his head. "Just because he's been playing nice guy this mission, don't look at him like he's a soft touch. He's a hardened spy like me, Tref. The less you know, the less RIOT can torture out of you." He sounded exasperated.

It was worth a try, Treflee thought. Most of the American public didn't even know RIOT existed. Treflee'd only heard rumors by accident, aided by a bit of spousal spying. She knew only one thing about them really—they were bad, bad, *bad* dangerous. They'd torture a kitten if it suited their needs. "And my great, new hair accessory?"

"The key to destroying what Hal's already sold RIOT and stopping them dead." Without missing a beat, Ty turned to Greg. "Anything in particular spook him?"

Greg shrugged as he jumped into the driver's seat and primed the engine. He patted the seat next to him, indicating Treflee should have a seat. "Could have been when RIOT burgled his condo."

Ty swore louder. "Subtle."

"Yeah, they were." Greg shrugged. "Did a decent job of not leaving any trace or evidence behind. But Hal hasn't worked for Langley for nothing. He noticed he'd had an intruder. And he knows both RIOT and the Chinese. They're cheap. Why pay for something when they can steal it?"

Ty squinted into the sun. He looked pale and in pain. "They get anything?"

Treflee took pity on him. She rummaged around a cooler on the floor in front of her seat and found a can of cheap beer. "Stiffest stuff we have." She popped the top and handed it back to him.

"No," Greg said. "But word is Hal also got wind of the attempts on Treflee."

"Hal takes a girl out to lunch and suddenly someone wants her dead? Nice tip-off, guys." Ty let out an exasperated sigh and shook his head. "Terrorists."

"Yeah, but Hal's hot for your wife." Greg grinned at Treflee. "He's itching to make that big sale and play hero. He wouldn't mind having Treflee on his sleeve when he plays billionaire bad boy with the money he's looking to bring in. Seems he wants his own Bond girl, or should I say, villain's girl?

"It appears he's the one person in this mess who's convinced Treflee's *not* a spy. He's too cocky to believe he'd be taken in by a spy of our own. Prides himself on knowing Langley's MO. He *is* one of our top geopolitical analysts, after all." Greg did a fair imitation of Hal. "Fortunately, Treflee's not in our playbook. He thinks he can trust her."

"Wait a minute!" Treflee turned back over her shoulder to stare at Ty. "Just who all thinks I'm a spy?"

"Everyone but Hal. Haven't you been listening?" Ty took a sip of beer and leaned his head back against the seat. "So Hal thinks RIOT thinks he handed the device off to Tref? That she's his accomplice?"

"That's the assumption we're working on. He's itching to ride in and play white knight." Greg turned the key and the engine roared to life.

Ty cursed some more, mumbling about everyone giving Treflee more credit than she deserved.

Greg backed the boat out of the mouth of the cave. "Hal's too greedy to stay hidden for long. Eventually, he's going to pop up and get that software to Mrs. Ho. His future financial happiness depends on it."

"Mrs. Ho!" *Just how many times can they shock the*

spit out of me? Treflee took a deep breath and leaned her head back against her seat, willing herself to stay calm. "Don't tell me she's—"

"RIOT. Yep," Greg said.

"The wedding couples?" Treflee said.

"Innocent pawns," Ty said.

"Oh, boy." She whipped around in her seat to confront her husband. "And you're encouraging me to go on another date with Hal the traitor? And take you to the wedding at Sugar Love, right into the heart of the evil RIOT bitch's lair! She's going to ruin poor Abi's wedding." And take a lot of lives. Treflee paused mid-tirade.

This wasn't going to be over until someone stopped Hal and Mrs. Ho. And that someone was going to be her. She was pissed now. And when she was angry, she lost all sense of reason and was both unreasonable and unstoppable. She'd had enough. She was going to end this. Anyway, what more danger could she possibly get into?

"I bet Hal would come out for a wedding at Sugar Love on double happiness day. Especially if I invited him as my date." She smiled at Ty. "Sorry, but we'll have to break our date. You don't mind, do you?"

"Brilliant!" Greg said. "Hal won't turn down the opportunity to get the payoff and save the girl. He thinks he's too smart to be caught."

Treflee nodded, feeling a rush of thrill-seeking adrenaline. "You two will be there waiting for him. We'll be like the Three Musketeers."

"Or the Three Stooges. No!" Ty shook his head. "The deal's off. No date with Hal. I already told you I'd sign the damn divorce papers."

She put her arm around the back of her seat and stared at Ty, bracing for a fight. "This has nothing to do with you and the 'damn divorce papers.'"

She pointed at him. "You need me." She turned away

from the look in his eyes to Greg, hoping to get him on her side.

Ty ignored her visual plea to Greg. "It's too dangerous, especially now that Hal's spooked."

She whipped around to look at him again. "You do this kind of crazy, dangerous stuff all the time." She made thin, angry eyes back at him. "It's my turn to do something more dangerous than risking a paper cut."

"Since when have you wanted to wade right into danger, Miss Risk Avoidance?" Ty shook his head at her folly. "No way. We know how to handle it. We're highly trained espionage professionals." Ty looked like he wanted to toss his beer can at her, or at the very least, shake it up and give her a good spray.

Greg remained calm and unperturbed by their latest round of marital squabbling. His cell phone played the theme from *Get Smart*.

"A text from HQ," Greg said.

Naturally.

He read the text silently before turning the phone around and handing it over his seat for Ty to read. "Emmett says to send her in. Hal's already accepted her invitation via an untraccable text. He's shielded his cell phone so we can't get a location on him."

Treflee shot Ty a smug smile, only slightly uncomfortable to know that Emmett had been listening in.

Greg shifted the boat into gear. They jolted forward in full throttle, the noise of surf and engine drowning out any further objections from her husband.

The doc Greg took Ty to see wasn't your normal hospital emergency room variety, but a top secret NCS field trauma specialist.

"The very best," Greg said. "With all the leading-edge medical breakthroughs at his disposal."

The doctor and his staff met them at sea in an unmarked white medical boat with a fully equipped surgery. Two medical corpsmen helped Ty onboard and carted him into the surgery. Another checked out Greg and pronounced him fit for duty. No lingering ill effects from being smashed on the head.

A few minutes later a corpsman returned with a set of clothes for Treflee. He escorted her to the head to change. She returned to the deck to find Greg making a phone call. He pointed to the phone and mouthed, *"Your cousin Carrie."*

"Yeah, they'll be fine," Greg said to Carrie. "They were coming back from a dip in the waterfall when they startled Zulu.

"Uh-huh, sure. Yeah, they have clothes." Greg winked at Treflee in her spanking new shorts, top, and canvas deck shoes. "Yep, Ty took one to the back of the leg. I agree. Zu's a coward to shoot someone in the back. Yeah, good thing he's a bad shot. Sure, they looked happy." Greg shrugged as he grinned at Treflee. "No, just a flesh wound. Yeah, yeah, you're right, a flesh wound's nothing."

Treflee rolled her eyes. Carrie *would* agree with the boys.

"Take the van and meet us back at the ranch. We'll catch a puddle-jumper back to Kahalui and rent something there. Sorry we're not around to pack up for you. Yeah, you, too. Glad you're not disappointed in your stay. Yeah, crime everywhere. What can you do? Drive safely. That's a dangerous stretch of road." He signed off, laughing.

Treflee plunked down across from him, the wind blowing in her face.

Greg leaned forward and squeezed her hand. "Ty's going to be fine."

She nodded and looked him in the eye. "Fill me in on the mission. How are we going to stop Hal?"

* * *

An hour later, the doctor pronounced Ty fit for duty. Two hours later, they arrived in Kahalui and stopped at Mc-Donald's for a fried Spam breakfast.

Treflee wrinkled her nose at it. "I hate Hawaiian food."

Ty's appetite seemed undimmed by his recent trauma. He ate his Spam with relish. "Shut up and eat your rice."

"Whatever the doc did to you certainly restored your sunny nature," she shot back. "I suppose he used some experimental new fast-acting healing agent? Cloned skin? Synthetic blood? You're not going to turn into a monster now, are you?"

He lifted a brow. "You mean any more than I already am?"

Greg shook his head at the two of them. "Play nice, kiddies, and eat up. We have work to do. We have just one day to turn Treflee into one of us, a highly trained espionage professional."

Ty frowned at Greg and turned to study Treflee. "Look at her! Bruises around her neck, scratches all over, bags under her eyes." He looked away suddenly and shook his head. "She's not going to entice Hal looking like that."

Although accurate, Ty's insult stung. Treflee lifted her chin. "Thanks so much for your vote of confidence. You're no prize right now yourself, limping boy."

Ty ignored her. "We don't have time to fly Malene in from the mainland."

Greg nodded his agreement.

"Malene?" Treflee cut in. "Who's she?"

"The best cover life artist NCS has," Ty said. "We'll have to go with our local girl. Kiki isn't going to be happy. She's got her work cut out for her making Tref pretty."

"Hey!" she said. "Slow down here. Cover life artist?"

Ty sighed and shook his head in that patronizing way he had when he was trying to annoy her. He lowered his voice. "You don't think we pick out our disguises and wardrobes ourselves, do you? Do our own styling, set up our own cover homes? We have stylists and designers for that."

"Like in the movies?" She was thinking Ty was so dead for living this glamorous life behind her back.

"Yeah, and they're damn good at what they do," Ty said.

She cocked a brow. "Malene's responsible for the goatee and dyed hair?"

"Yeah," Ty said.

Malene knows her stuff.

"I'll give Kiki a buzz." Greg aimed his phone at Treflee. "She'll need a snapshot to work with and plenty of time to shop."

Before Treflee could protest, Greg had snapped her photo and texted it off to the mysterious Kiki.

A four-foot-tall carved wooden tiki stood on the veranda of Big Auau to the right of the front door. Even though the doc had done a great job of patching him up, Ty favored the leg as he moved gingerly around the tiki, giving it wide berth.

"This is new." Tref paused to inspect it.

Great, my wife chooses now to become observant.

"What a cute little potbellied guy!" She reached out to touch it.

"I wouldn't if I were you," Ty said, doing his best to sound ominous.

She froze. "Why not?"

He could play head games and spook her all day long. She deserved it. "That's a fertility tiki."

She turned to stare him in the eye. Then she very deliberately reached down and stroked the tiki's tummy, baiting him. "Nice to meet you, little guy."

Ty got a mental image of the previous night at the waterfall, wondering if Tref was still on her birth control. He'd been too caught up in the moment to even think about using a condom. If there was anything to that fertility tiki, he was going to be owing Tref child support.

He grabbed her arm and whispered very softly in her ear, "It's probably bugged. Act normally. Don't say anything we don't want the enemy to hear."

Behind him, Greg sniggered.

Ty turned on him.

Greg had a hand in his pocket.

"Call the exterminator," Ty said.

"On it already." Greg whipped out his cell phone.

Treflee shook Ty's arm off and bounced into the plantation house.

Ty paused just outside the door, spy sense on high alert, filled with a sense of dread and foreboding.

Behind him, Greg slapped him on the back. "No use delaying the inevitable, dude."

Greg was right. Ty reluctantly stepped inside. A vibrantly colored life-sized oil portrait of the beautiful, seductive Haumea hung over the entryway end table.

Tref was staring at her. "She's lovely, isn't she?"

"She's the goddess of fertility. I'm sensing a theme here." He couldn't help sighing as he took in the painting and the present-packed table below her. Tita used it as a gift table for weddings. It was large enough to hold gifts from over a hundred wedding guests. The way it was loaded with goods, it looked as if a wedding were already in full swing. "Behold the fallout from a full-scale gift war."

Greg whistled. "Quite a haul. Wonder how much reciprocating set Tita back?"

Three monkeypod bowls carved in different shapes filled with different tropical and Chinese candies lined the table, along with two baskets of fresh fruit, a huge spray of protea, four tiki masks, and a large assortment of goods he was cut short of cataloging as Tita lumbered in.

"*Haole!* Greg! You're back safely." Tita pulled Ty into a hug.

"*Aloha, wahine.*" He hugged her back. He released her so she could hug Greg and Tref.

"The girls told me what happened. Bad spirits in those men." Tita clicked her tongue. "You saw the doctor? Let me see the leg."

He modeled his bandage for her.

Tita studied it closely. "Not a bad job. I'll make you some herbal tea and sweeten it with sugar cane. Nothing heals like a little sugar cane." She nodded and studied him some more. "Do I need to perform *hooponopono,* the healing ritual, on you?"

"I thought that was the *kahuna*'s job, *wahine,*" Ty teased her.

She laughed. "I *am* the big *kahuna, haole.*"

"And I'm fine. Modern medicine should be good enough this time." Ty spread his arm toward the table. "Is everything in balance now? Has harmony been restored? In other words, have you given up on this gift war?" He shook his head and gave her a quick one-armed hug and release.

Tita stiffened, looking suddenly apprehensive as her gaze bounced between Tref, Greg, and him.

"Almost. Just one more obligation and I call it quits." Tita clasped her hands in front of her and looked at them optimistically.

"Uh-oh," Greg said. "I know that look."

"What have you done, Tita?" Ty said.

Tita giggled nervously. "Mrs. Ho has invited us all to the big Chinese multiwedding on Saturday. She says it's a very big deal for her, a big promotional thing with much potential for new business from China. She insists we all come as her honored guests."

Ty got a sinking feeling in the pit of his stomach. Beside him, Tref started to tremble. No doubt she'd just gotten the same feeling, and maybe her phobia of Chinese people was resurfacing.

Tita smiled at her and reached out to pat her arm. "You've been through so much, poor thing. Have a piece of candy. Sugar is good for the nerves." She grabbed a monkeypod bowl from the table and held it out to Tref.

Tref grabbed a piece of wrapped corn hard candy.

"I wouldn't eat that one if I were you," Ty told her. He shouldn't have used that ominous tone on her again, as if the candy were poison. Cry wolf one too many times. "You won't like the taste."

She relaxed and shrugged. "What do you mean? I love candy corn. One of my faves."

She was angry at him. So she did what she always did when she wanted to get back at him. She ignored his warning with a defiant look. *Her loss.*

She unwrapped the candy and popped it in her mouth. Almost immediately, she spat it back out into the wrapper and made a face. "It tastes like buttered corn."

He shook his head at her and shrugged, resisting the urge to say *"I told you so."*

Treflee glanced at Tita and blushed, as if she just remembered Tita was standing there. "I'll save this for later." She shot Ty a look with almost enough spite to kill.

What have I done to deserve that?

Ty addressed Tita. "What do you mean by Mrs. Ho wants 'us all' at the wedding? That can't include the hired hands."

Tita grinned at him. "Sorry, *haole*. I've already RSVPed for you and Greg, and all of my guests, including Treflee."

"Carrie agreed to go?" Treflee looked pained on her cousin's behalf. "Saturday was supposed to be *her* wedding day. I thought the plan was to tour the pineapple plantation and get bombed on piña coladas afterward."

"Change of plans." Tita nonchalantly set the monkey-pod bowl back on the table. "I gave Carrie a discount on her stay and told her about the open bar and the free *jiu,* Chinese cocktails. Mrs. Ho is never stingy with the *jiu.*"

"Oh, boy," Treflee whispered with a degree of enthusiasm close to dread.

Ty exchanged a look with Greg. Why did Mrs. Ho want everyone at the wedding? To keep an eye on them? Or to take them out?

Stir a drunken, depressed should-have-been-a-bride lady cop and four of her friends into the mix and the odds of the operation going smoothly just dropped by half.

CHAPTER TWENTY-ONE

Treflee lay in her fluffy Big Auau bed with the covers pulled up to her nose, the windows and doors locked, and the fan on high, purely for its noise. If a Chinese assassin was hell-bent on breaking in and slitting her throat in the middle of the night, she didn't want to hear it. Better for him not to interrupt her rest and simply kill her as she slept. After all, dying in your sleep was the way everyone wanted to go.

What a hellacious twenty-four hours she'd had. Too stoked, too scared, and too torn up about Ty to sleep, she lay there with thoughts of her upcoming mission dancing through her head.

This was the spying life Ty loved. Even with her life-long love for the quiet life, she was forced to admit the adrenaline rush of spying had its appeal. So did being a part of something bigger than herself. And getting revenge on the bad guys. Definitely getting revenge on the bad guys.

So many brushes with death and seeing Ty shot and thinking he might die had irrevocably changed her, and reinforced her determination to win him back. At any cost.

She glanced toward the door. Speaking of Ty, he'd

sworn to protect her. Why wasn't he slipping through her locked door like the spook he was?

She tightened her grip on the sheet at her nose, feeling miserable and empty. She'd been trying to kick him to the curb for the better part of a year and now that she'd succeeded she was desolate.

It's just that . . . she loved him, thrill-seeking adventurer and all. She simply *had* to win him back. Before he slipped back into the espionage ether again, lost forever. Even if she had to beg Emmett for help.

Emmett! Oh, boy. He really couldn't afford to turn her loose into the civilian world now, not with all she knew.

The head of National Clandestine Services could surely do *something*. Emmett didn't want this divorce to happen any more than she did. He surely had tricks up his sleeve, mind-altering techniques, maybe, to reprogram Ty's psyche to forget how she'd hurt him and learn to love her again.

The door rattled gently. She wouldn't have even noticed if she hadn't been staring at it. Ty slid in silently and closed and locked it behind him.

"You're back," she whispered.

"Yeah, honey, I'm home," he whispered back as he shed his shirt and dropped it on the floor by his side of the bed.

She hadn't even startled him.

"What? No divorce papers on my pillow? I'm disappointed." He slid under the covers as close to the edge of the bed and as far away from her as possible.

Treflee rolled over on her elbow to face him. "I didn't think you were going to show up."

"I don't break promises. I don't abandon missions." He punched his pillow and turned away from her.

He's abandoning his mission to stay married to me. And suddenly wanting to break that little promise about "until death do us part."

She stared at his back, wondering how to engage him. He never slept next to her without wanting her. She couldn't stand the heartbreak of his apathy. Before they married, they vowed never to go to bed angry at each other. She'd broken that vow a hundred times this past year. It stopped here.

She touched his shoulder. "Does the device still work?"

He stiffened beneath her touch. "Yeah."

"Good. So we're still on with the swap." Refusing to back off, she reached out and cupped Ty's cheek, wishing she could take away his hurt, itching to caress him.

He froze.

"I think I understand now about your job, the pressures, the reasons you can't always be with me."

He didn't reply, but she sensed he was listening.

She bit her lip and took a deep breath. "I didn't betray you." Loyalty was king with Ty. There were so few people a spy could trust. "I didn't steal the device. You have to believe me. Okay, I borrowed it.

"But I was going to put it back. I swear. I hate Zulu! I hate him because he grabbed me before I could put the data card back. Because that made you doubt me." She sighed. "I wish you'd never known."

Ty moved her hand off his cheek. "Give it a rest, Tref."

She swallowed hard. "I should have told you about the baby." Though she'd intended to sound calm, her voice broke. "You don't know how sorry I am. The pregnancy was an accident. The miscarriage was an accident. This whole thing seems like a horrible nightmare. Can't we just start over?"

"Go to sleep." He sounded tired and hurt. "We have a couple of big days ahead of us."

She wasn't giving up. Tomorrow was another day. And she didn't plan on either dying or giving up on her marriage.

* * *

Friday passed in a blur of briefing, planning, quick lessons in firearms and self-defense, and being styled and beautified by the talented Kiki. Ty took Treflee to town for the training, telling Carrie and the others Treflee and he had follow-up doctor's visits. No one questioned them even though they were gone from sunup to sundown.

Friday night, Ty sneaked into Treflee's room and bed well past midnight, waiting, she was sure, until he thought she was asleep. He should know her better than that. How could she sleep the night before her first big mission? And a wedding mission at that.

Heck, maybe she'd even catch the bouquet. She was eligible. Sort of. And as there were twelve bouquets to be caught, the odds were definitely in her favor. Unless Laci knocked her out of the way and claimed more than her share. Or she was discovered and dead, or being tortured by then.

Ty slipped into bed so smoothly, he barely bounced the mattress. He hovered so far from her at the edge of the bed, she was convinced Kiki must have outfitted him with Velcro briefs. How else was he staying on the edge?

For her part, she was barely hanging on to her nerves.

But being a spy *had* taught her one thing—if you want to succeed, you need to take risks. Put yourself out there. She rolled next to him, pressed up against his bare back with her breasts, and ran her hand over his shoulder, down his side to his waist—

He shoved her hand away before she got far enough south to find a hard package. "No sex before a mission."

"Sex?" Even though she knew he was still hurt and angry at her, his rejection stung. She had to channel her inner spy girl to keep her hurt from showing and lashing back. "Just cuddling up for sleep."

"Uh-huh."

"Anyway, no sex is not how James Bond plays it," she whispered in his ear. "A little tumble puts James on his game, eases the stress."

Ty stiffened, but not in the right and enticing places.

"Bond's a fictional spy." He punched his pillow and stared at the wall.

Treflee fell onto her back and stared at the ceiling. *That went well. What is it going to take to win him back? Whatever it is, flirting with Hal tomorrow is not going to help my case.*

The plan was simple—Treflee would stick to Hal like day-old poi. She would transmit and record every move he made with her trusty hot red organza hibiscus-flower hair-clip video camera studded with sequins and Swarovski crystals. Kiki had picked it out, probably from the most recent issue of *Vogue for Spies*. Though she might have bedazzled it herself. The hibiscus cam perfectly matched Treflee's plunging red halter dress and coordinated with the color of her fingernails and toenails. And it was equipped with a tracking device, too. Yeah, a deluxe model.

Ty had a hand in picking the dress from three options Kiki presented during cover fashion selection. The dress was just a dress, no extra features, but Ty called it killer. Treflee called it a bra fitter's nightmare—no back to the waist, very little front. Kiki shrugged as if it were no problem and gave Treflee plastic cups to tape to her breasts.

The cups worried Treflee. They weren't the kind of lingerie that turned Ty on. And yes, she planned to ditch the dress later and entice Ty into some hot after-mission makeup sex. She just hoped she didn't have to take him prisoner to do it.

When Treflee modeled the dress for Ty, he eyed her like

a designer looking for flaws, not a possessive husband. "Lots of cleavage. Plenty of skin. Good. Epic. Hal's eyes should be on you, not us. Should keep him distracted."

Treflee should have been flattered. She would have been if Ty had been his usual self and had had that sexy leer in his eyes, that "I'll grab you later and we'll make passionate love" vibe about him rather than the cold calculation of a mission planner. She felt like a whore, probably because he'd dressed her like one. Revenge would only be sweet when she won Ty back and let the dress work its magic on him.

She wore a pair of black Havaianas, also studded with Swarovski crystals between her toes. Later Treflee could kick them off if she liked or dance until dawn. She just hoped Kiki had incorporated a handcuff key in them or an inflate-a-coat. Never knew when you'd need either of those.

Treflee would dance all right—once Hal and Mrs. Ho were behind bars and Ty was hers again.

And against Kiki's fashion advice, she wore the pearls Ty had given her. Kiki had wanted her to wear a drop necklace instead.

While Treflee distracted Hal, Ty and Greg would be stealthily following up with everyone Hal came in contact with, looking to see if he'd made a drop. Using their magical spy skills and light pickpocketing fingers to swap the real SDXC card for the counterfeit one.

Easy, Ty had said.

Oh, sure. Easy if nothing went wrong. Easy if the evil Mrs. Ho didn't get wind of the plan and off them at the buffet table or while they were enjoying a *jiu* at the open bar. Easy if Treflee's video equipment worked like it was supposed to. But since when did video equipment ever do what it was supposed to? Some piece of equipment always screwed up. And hair clips? Don't get her started.

She hadn't had a hair clip stay properly in place since first grade.

But her objections fell on deaf ears. Clips falling out of hair weren't things spies worried about. She'd just have to cope. In the meantime, she obsessed about little things as she played with the charm bracelet Ty had given her, liking its jingle, jingle, jingle. About stupid things like why the bracelet hadn't been in exactly the same spot under the mattress where she'd hidden it.

Ty came up to her as she stood on the Big Auau veranda waiting for her date for the wedding. She preferred her husband and wanted him again as petulantly as Scarlett wanted Rhett back.

Treflee fiddled with a gift she held for Abi and Feng, hoping they didn't already have a monkeypod butter dish and koa wood butter knife. Then again, why would they? The guy in Lahaina had assured her they were unique.

Next to her, she felt Ty's heat. She either won him back now, or he'd find some way to sign those papers before disappearing into spookdom for good.

The thought of reading about his happy nuptials to a femme fatale colleague in the latest NCS family newsletter totally depressed her. She wanted him, pure and simple. She just wasn't sure how to get him back. He'd never been cold to her like this before.

If she could prove she was up to the spying life, that she understood now that sometimes he couldn't help being absent, then maybe.

Ty pointed at the bracelet. "Where'd that come from?"

"You, baby. I take it everywhere with me." She smiled sweetly.

He cursed beneath his breath, mumbling something about wives on missions.

"You shouldn't be wearing it." He didn't sound particularly touched that she kept it with her at all times.

She jangled the bracelet for his benefit. "With all these charms for luck, why not?"

"Didn't know you were superstitious."

"Maybe I'm not. Maybe I just like having you near."

He sighed and shook his head as if to say, oh what the hell. "Just don't go waving my picture around."

"On a date with another guy? Wouldn't dream of it," she said with complete honesty. "It's not good form."

Ty shook his head again and stared off toward the horizon. "Should be a great sunset for the wedding tonight."

He looked handsome, but solemn, in profile. He wore flat panel slacks, a pale yellow tropical-print Tommy Bahama camp shirt, and crossover sandals. Perfect Hawaiian beach wedding apparel, compliments of Kiki's keen eye for style.

Good grief! If Kiki dressed him every day, Treflee would never be able to keep her hands off him.

He held a pair of TV sunglasses, all the better for viewing her and Hal with. When he put them on he could watch TV in the corners of the lenses.

"Nervous?" he asked her.

"Yes."

"Don't worry, I have your back."

"Good. It's exceptionally exposed tonight, thanks to you. Retribution?"

His expression remained masked. "Good policy. Make him hot, Tref."

Not exactly the kind of thing you like to hear from your husband.

She touched his arm and took a chance. "Ty, there's no need to rush this divorce. Let's sit on things. Try to work things out for the sake of your career. Emmett will be furious if we don't. I know too much now. And you don't want a failed mission on your record, do you?"

He didn't reply so she kept talking. "I'm happy to go on

as before. Emmett could find us a good marriage counselor, someone we could really talk to, someone from Langley maybe. Don't say anything now. Just think about it while you're off on your next mission."

He stared at her. "I've never kept any secrets from you that I didn't have to, nothing, ever, about our personal life. I've always had your back, Tref. The question is—do you have mine?"

She blinked back tears, but she wasn't going to beg. He hated begging.

At the sound of a car approaching, Ty stepped back and cleared his throat. He nodded toward it. "There's your date. Knock him dead." He slid the sunglasses on.

She swallowed hard and tried to lift the mood. "Can you see me now?" She tilted her head so the flower cam took in her cleavage and the flowing skirt of her dress.

"In perfect hi def."

"And how do my bumps and bruises look?"

"Your bumps look . . . perky. Use them to your advantage." Still no hint of flirt in his voice or manner, all business. "Kiki did wonders with that body makeup. No bruises in sight, even in hi def."

He looked directly at her, but she couldn't see his eyes through the sunglasses. "Be sure to keep him on your right, in view of the camera, Tref."

Ty waved to Hal and bounced off the veranda to join Carrie, Greg, and the girls. They waited for him on the edge of the lawn on the path through the sugarcane fields between the plantations. Treflee wished she could bounce off and join them, too. If she didn't have to save the world, she would have.

As expected, Carrie looked subdued. That was natural enough for a woman in her position. The others laughed and joked as if they were going to a luau with plenty of beer. They waved at Treflee as they headed off.

As Treflee waved back, she whispered a silent prayer that nothing would go wrong. Everything about this mission from her hair clip to Carrie was an opportunity for failure.

Hal parked and stepped out of his red Porsche Boxster. He grabbed a wrapped gift and a plastic corsage box from his passenger seat.

His eyes lit up when he saw her. "*Aloha, mahalo.* Aren't I the luckiest guy at the wedding tonight?"

Those twelve Chinese grooms were certain to disagree. They were guaranteed to get lucky tonight. She kept that thought to herself, though. Instead, she smiled and tried to steady her racing pulse as she walked down the veranda stairs to meet him. "You look pretty terrific yourself."

Pretending he was Ty, she let her gaze wander down him appreciatively. He wore casual slacks, a brown batik camp shirt with a front pocket, and nubuck sneakers. He looked good enough to make flirting easy, but not as delectable as Ty.

He hugged her, running his hands down her bare back in a way that indicated his interest. "So glad you texted. I didn't think I'd get to see you again." His voice was husky with lust.

He definitely has the idea I'm hot for him. Just what did Emmett tell him? She had a horrible vision of some text sex.

Maybe some suggestive texts would work on Ty. It's just too bad the wrong guy wants me.

She smiled back at Hal. "So glad you came."

Hal held out the corsage box to her. It contained a large white hibiscus flower. "For your hair. I figured you'd be bored with leis by now."

Yeah, especially since they could be used as weapons.

"How sweet of you." Treflee set the gift she carried on the bottom step and took the box. She stared at it. What did she do now? Her first spy mission snafu, trouble in paradise. "It's lovely. Simply gorgeous."

He noticed the organza flower pinned over her right ear, and already slipping. "Ah, don't fake it, Treflee. It was a good thought, but I'm too late. You already have one."

"It's a great thought. I'd rather have a fresh one." She pulled the organza flower out of her hair as inspiration struck. "Here. Wear this for me?" She tucked the organza flower into the front pocket of his shirt. "There. A boutonniere. Now we're wedding ready."

Ty balled his fists as he watched his wife's ringless fingers tuck the hibiscus cam into Hal's shirt with loving care in hi def.

Damn it, Tref. He cursed beneath his breath. *Stick with the plan.*

Though he grudgingly gave her points for thinking on her feet, now there was no way to track her if something should happen. Not to mention the minute she pinned that flower on Hal, all Ty got in his glasses was a view of her very pert, sumptuous breasts. Boob cam. Damn. He squirmed as he rose to the occasion.

He hung out on the lawn in the Sugar Love reception area, pretending nonchalance, senses on high alert. Staff was setting up for the meal following the ceremony. Already bored with making small talk with the other guests before being seated, he eavesdropped on the Chinese couples, watching Abi for a cue.

Emmett had provided him with a map of the labyrinth of volcano tubes below Sugar Love. Abi was supposed to have disabled the security systems and left a trail of breadcrumbs so he could make it to the video lab once he'd made the switch.

A wedding photographer was taking posed shots of the bridal couples on the lawn with inordinate care. Ty wondered if there was something in the setup of the shots that conveyed a code as well. Maybe the placement of the couple's hands or the way they faced?

Speaking of placement, in the corner of his sunglasses, Tref's breasts bounced as she walked with Hal into the reception area. Bounce, bounce, jiggle, jiggle. He was going to have wet dreams for a week.

Out of the corner of his eye, he watched as Tref set a package on the gift table.

"For Abi and Feng," Ty heard her tell Hal. "Abi invited me, but I really don't know the other couples at all. Who's your gift for?"

"Abi and Feng, of course," Hal said. "Your friends are my friends."

Ty rolled his eyes as he tried not to stare at Tref's cleavage in hi def in the corner of his glasses while she cooed at Hal, "Aren't you the sweetest guy? And look how pretty that lavender paper is with that silver ribbon. You wrap that yourself?"

Ty had to give Tref credit. She was doing her job nearly as well as a pro, giving him a description in case he hadn't gotten a clear view. Ninety-five percent certain this was the drop, Ty moved within range to scoop up the package. This was almost too easy. Ty felt a ripple of unease. Things going too smoothly right away were a bad omen.

"Store wrap," Hal said. "I'm only good at unwrapping things."

Ty recognized the tone; in guy speak it meant Hal'd love to unwrap Tref later.

Ty took a deep calming breath as Tref took Hal's arm and mercifully Hal turned toward the tables set up for the reception following the group wedding. Ty got a good view of flower-filled tables and the ocean beyond as Tref and Hal continued toward the beach.

As Tref paused by a table and held up a package of

Chinese double happiness cigarettes, Ty moved next to the gift table.

"Cigarettes? Does anyone still smoke anymore?" Tref was saying, trying to keep Hal distracted as Ty lingered near the gifts.

"The Chinese do," Hal told her, taking the pack and pocketing them next to the clipped-on boob cam, temporarily jostling Ty's view. "For later."

Right, buddy. No after-sex smoke for you. Touch my wife and you're dead.

Possession is nine tenths of the law, and Tref was still Ty's. Yeah, he was jealous. Surprisingly so, given how betrayed he felt by her.

Good thing Hal was too far away to take a swing at. Ty would have taken off half his jaw. Instead, he was forced to hear Hal make innuendos about double happiness and watch as he pointed out the double happiness candy strewn across the table. "Sweet like you, babe."

Fortunately, right about then Ty got a break in traffic near the table. With no one watching, Ty grabbed Hal's gift and headed for the powder room for an early Christmas.

CHAPTER TWENTY-TWO

Minutes later, Ty deftly unwrapped the gift, found Hal's SDXC card, made the switch, and reapplied the tape. During that time, Hal put his arm around Tref's bare back and whispered how hot she made him and how much he was looking forward to taking her back to his place and showing her the view.

Ty felt his blood pressure rise along with his anger as he watched Hal on the boob cam "accidentally" brush Tref's breasts with the tips of his callused, thieving fingers.

Wives on missions are a damn distraction, Ty thought as he put the gift back on the gift table.

He texted Greg. *"Switch made."* That's when he remembered Greg was also wearing a pair of TV sunglasses with a feed of the boob cam.

Damn distraction, he repeated to himself.

"Brides' or grooms' side?" An usher with a strong Chinese accent and trouble pronouncing his *r*s asked Treflee and Hal.

"Abi's, brides'," Treflee answered without hesitation as she tried to stifle a shudder. This was an awful time for her phobia of Chinese people to return. It wasn't that she feared nice Chinese people like Abi, but the usher gave her the creeps. She wondered if he were Fuk Ching and half expected him to slit her throat as revenge for her part in bringing down Zulu, Bang, and Cong.

Hal had his arm around her waist. As if sensing her fear, he pulled her closer.

Pretend Hal's Ty, she told herself. *Just pretend he's Ty.*

The usher led them along a bumpy piece of red carpet spread over the uneven sand to an empty row of folding chairs facing the ocean. Carrie and her bridesmaids were already seated in the row in front of it. Faye turned around, made a funny face, and gave Treflee a sympathetic look. Fortunately, Hal didn't seem to notice.

None of the girls could understand how Treflee could take Hal to the wedding when it was clear she was head over heels for Ty. Treflee had tried to explain that she'd promised Hal another date before she and Ty had hooked up. Going to a wedding with him seemed like the safest, most benign kind of date.

If only they knew!

Hal waited for Treflee to go into the row of seats first. She would have preferred the aisle, but saw no way to make that happen.

"Beautiful view," she whispered to Hal. The sun sat just above the water, ready to make its grand exit within the next half hour.

Hal seemed relaxed and almost ecstatic as he stared down at her cleavage. "Fabulous."

Treflee wondered how much firepower he had on him. Would the tiny tranquilizer dart she carried be enough to subdue him? She wished she'd had more training so Ty would have trusted her with a real gun.

Ty lingered near the gift table, waiting for one of Mrs. Ho's minions to grab the package. Greg was at the beach keeping an eye on Hal and Tref and hopefully keeping Carrie and the girls in line.

A Hawaiian guitar and drum ensemble began playing prelude music. The Chinese couples, hand in hand and laughing, grooms in traditional Western wedding tuxedos, brides in white wedding dresses and bare feet, paraded past him, followed by a dutiful videographer. Seeing them so happy and innocent of the trials of married life brought back Ty's own wedding day. If he could go back and do it all again—

One of Mrs. Ho's Chinese waiters walked by and scooped up Hal's gift with barely a glance at it. Ty waited a second and followed him into Sugar Love like a shadow, through the entry and past the bustling kitchen. The waiter paused at what looked like another pantry door. When no one was looking, he slipped inside. Ty waited a second and followed suit. Turned out he didn't need Abi's bread-crumbs.

Stairs led down to a series of underground volcanic caverns. Fortunately, the noise from the bustle above masked the sounds of his pursuit. He followed the waiter deep into the bowels of Mrs. Ho's evil headquarters without the waiter seeming the least bit suspicious. Never drop your guard. It's bad policy. And lethal.

Ty waited until the waiter scanned his print into a secure thumbprint-accessible-only door and started through.

Now or never.

Ty pulled a tiny tranquilizer dart from his pocket and jabbed it in the guy's neck. The dart was fast-acting. The waiter fell onto the floor unconscious, still holding the package.

Where in the world is Ty?

Treflee tried to glance around for him without being too obvious. Greg lurked at the back of the crowd. But Ty was nowhere to be seen. A row in front of her, Carrie held a tissue and had already dabbed it to her eyes when she thought no one was looking.

Treflee frowned.

Hal touched her arm. "What's wrong?"

She pointed toward Carrie. "My cousin. This was supposed to be her wedding day."

Hal nodded sympathetically. "Poor girl."

Thank goodness for the cover of Carrie's pain. Kind of. Treflee may have had her differences with her tough cousin, but she'd love to see her happy. Really happy. It appeared that all those worries over Kane showing up were pointless. He obviously didn't care about Carrie enough to follow her to the islands like he'd promised. What had he been doing? Teasing her? The bastard.

"Wong, is that you?" A guy Ty recognized as the wedding photographer's assistant sat with his back to the door, working on an expensive desktop PC.

Ty grunted.

The guy kept working with his back to Ty. "Just in time. The boss is getting antsy. He's on my ass wanting to know what he got for his money. I'll be able to get that software embedded in the wedding feed before they get to the vows. Wong?"

The assistant twirled around in his chair, right into the barrel of Ty's gun. Ty held the package out to him. "Looking for this?"

Ty dropped it in his lap. "Plug it in. Get it streaming. Then I'm going to need that encryption software, stego genius."

A Chinese minister walked to the front of the row of grooms and crowd, which consisted mostly of the gang from Big Auau and some Chinese travel agents. "Welcome most honored guests to this ceremony of great happiness and joy . . ."

Still no Ty.

The minister finished his welcome. A Hawaiian guitarist began playing the opening strains of "Ke Kali Nei Au," the Hawaiian Wedding Song. The minister lifted his arms, indicating the crowd should stand. The brides began the walk up the red carpet aisle.

Abi looked glowingly happy and beautiful as she walked up the aisle toward Feng. She smiled at Treflee and nodded ever so slightly as she walked past her. Treflee smiled back, trying not to cry. Weddings were meant for tears, but this one in particular got to Treflee. She and Ty had been that beamingly happy once.

The couples took their places in front of the official.

The ceremony began in Chinese without waiting for Ty to show up.

The underground room was shielded as tightly as a top-secret U.S. government facility and carefully concealed, a real marvel of engineering below the old historic plantation house. And even with the electronic whirs and buzzes, exceedingly creepy.

With the waiter bound and gagged and stuffed into the corner with the photographer's assistant, Ty made a copy of the encryption software that embedded the analysis model code into the video stream of the happy couples. He'd just sent the file off to Langley when he heard the click of the door opening behind him.

An older Chinese man, a father of one of the grooms, got up and gave a speech, shouting in such a loud, military-drill-sergeant voice he probably interrupted sunset weddings all along the beach.

Looking bored, Hal pulled his cell phone from his pants pocket and checked something on the Internet. By the time he slid his phone back in his pocket, he was grinning as if he owned the world.

Just confirmed his payoff, no doubt.

Treflee had to stifle the urge to crane around and look for Ty. Instead she focused on Abi. Where was that man? Her nerves were completely and utterly frayed. Not knowing what was going on was the worst kind of torture. She forced herself not to panic.

Hal grabbed her hand and squeezed, probably resisting doing a victory punch.

The father finished his speech and took his seat again. The Chinese official took his place in front of the line of couples and said something to them in Chinese. In unison, the grooms bowed toward their brides, looking like dippy birds as their heads bobbed low toward the sand.

"The deeper the bow, the deeper the groom's love for the bride," Hal, who seemed to know a bit about Chinese weddings, whispered to Treflee.

"How romantic," Treflee whispered back, noticing how low Feng bowed to Abi, so low he practically kissed her tiny feet. She was very lucky.

Where is Ty? Treflee had a vision of Mrs. Ho standing over him with a bloody knife. Speaking of Mrs. Ho, where was she?

"I wonder where Mrs. Ho is," she said aloud for Ty's benefit, hoping to warn him, wherever he was, that Mrs. Ho wasn't at the wedding. "You'd think the wedding planner would be out here."

"She's probably overseeing the preparations for the reception." Hal sounded too smug. He knew very well that she was probably checking her purchase.

* * *

Mrs. Ho burst into the control room and trained her semi-automatic on Ty. "*You!* You're the spy?" She looked dumb-founded.

Ah, the element of surprise. Unfortunately, the wrong kind. At least my cover was good. And Tref, in her ineptitude, was a second too late with the "Mrs. Ho's not at the wedding" warning.

"Who is the girl, then?"

"What girl?"

"Don't play dumb with me!" She waved the gun at him. "Tleflee, the one with Hal."

Ty shrugged. "A guest of yours, I imagine. Like me. I thought I saw her at the wedding." He nodded toward the semiautomatic. "Is that any way to treat a guest who's wandered slightly off track?"

Mrs. Ho ignored his jibe and called out to someone behind her. One of the wedding ushers entered the room. She spoke to him in Chinese. Fortunately, Ty understood her.

"We've been compromised. Tie him up. Call the helicopter. Then release those two and activate the self-destruct sequence." She stared at Ty with eyes glittering with hate and returned to English. "I could shoot you now, but why waste good bullets? You'll be in a million pieces soon enough."

Ty shook his head, trying to buy time and think of a way out of this mess. The odds were definitely against him. "Blowing me up is really going to throw things out of harmony now, isn't it? How will you ever put them back in balance?"

He rolled to his feet and charged her.

The Chinese wedding official raised his arms, smiled, and said in English, "I now pronounce you men and—"

Treflee frowned. She was sure she heard the pounding

of footsteps coming from behind her from Sugar Love. *Ty?* She turned to look.

"Stop! Stop this ceremony!"

"Oh, boy," Treflee whispered when she saw who it was. Every head turned now.

Kane came running down the aisle, ambling like the great big defensive-tackle kind of guy he was. "Carrie! Carrie!"

He looked around wildly, trying to find her and seeming confused by the one hundred percent Chinese wedding parties up front. Not a white girl in sight up there at the figurative altar. Just a bunch of terrified-looking Chinese brides whose wedding day was rapidly deteriorating into a spectacle.

Someone had given Kane bad intel.

He scanned the crowd. "Don't do this to me. Don't marry someone else. I love you, baby! I never cheated. I swear." He waved a piece of paper he held. "I have the lie detector test to prove it. It's right here. Right here, baby. Done by your favorite examiner. Twice.

"You know, *you know,* baby, these things are nearly one hundred percent accurate. If you won't believe me, believe it."

In front of her, the girls were all encouraging Carrie to talk to Kane. Carrie slumped down and dabbed her eyes with the tissue. Since she was smiling, they must have been tears of joy she was wiping away.

Carrie is going to ruin poor Abi's dream wedding if she doesn't respond to Kane soon.

Treflee gave her cousin a nudge in the shoulder and leaned forward to whisper, "Come on. Give the guy a break. How long are you going to make him beg? Do something. The Chinese brides up there look like they're going to faint."

"You have to believe me," Kane yelled. "This is our day, damn it!"

An usher half his size stepped in to block Kane from making it to the altar. He slammed into Kane with the full force of his puny half-pint size. As his shoulder hit Kane in the chest, the ground shook with the force of a volcano erupting, knocking Kane to his knees and sending the usher flying. The roar of an explosion rocked the air. Behind them, Sugar Love plantation house exploded into a ball of flame, spewing debris and bits of wedding feast two hundred yards onto the beach.

Treflee stared in horror as the implications of what had happened hit her. Last time she'd seen Ty he'd been standing right next to Sugar Love. She kicked back her chair and stood. "No. No. No! Ty! Ty!"

She'd blown her cover. But it didn't matter. Her ears rang so loudly she couldn't even hear herself. The explosion and crackle of flames had rendered them all temporarily deaf.

The brides' shoulders shook, crying silently. The grooms held them in their arms. Abi broke away from Feng and ran toward the plantation.

Beside Treflee, Hal shoved back out of his chair and started to bolt.

No! No way was he getting away. Rage took over. Treflee threw herself into him, tackling him and thumping him onto his back on the red carpet. She jumped on him, knocking his breath from him, straddling his hips with her flowing skirt spreading around them.

"Not exactly the way you planned to have me straddling you, is it?" She pulled off a flip-flop, wishing it were a lethal high-heeled stiletto, and began beating him about the head, screaming for Ty. He'd been inside Sugar Love. She was sure of it.

Oh, damn you, Ty! Where are you? Just don't be dead or dying.

Next to her, Kane held Carrie in a passionate kiss. With the flames in the background, they looked like a movie poster for an action adventure flick.

Faye, Brandy, Carla, and Laci formed a protective barrier around Hal and cheered Treflee on.

Treflee bounced on Hal and pummeled him with her ineffective flapping jeweled flip-flop as he struggled to get his breath back and flailed, trying to grab her arms.

She leaned in and yelled into the hibiscus cam in Hal's pocket, "Ty! Ty, I love you, baby. I have Hal pinned on the beach. Get the software, take down those bastards in there, and come out here and help me!"

Next to her, Kane broke away from kissing Carrie. From the corner of her eye, Treflee saw him studying her. He leaned down and yelled at her in a booming voice she felt more than heard above the surf and the ringing in her ears. "Need help?"

She shook her head no. "Thanks. I got him." No way was she giving up the pleasure of subduing Hal. Not until her rage was spent, anyway.

Kane shrugged and slipped off his sturdy leather dress slip-on shoe. He grabbed her arm and shoved it into her hand.

She hefted it. It had a manly-sized clunky heel. Excellent! A pulverizing size thirteen was so much more effective than a size seven thong. She knew she hadn't been wrong about Kane. He had keen police sense, recognizing the bad guy right away. She liked him more than ever. Carrie could do far worse.

As if hearing Treflee's thoughts, Carrie snuggled into Kane's arms and rested her head against his chest. Kane squeezed Carrie tight, watching Tref with that look in his eye that said he was ready to step in and subdue at a moment's notice.

As Treflee raised Kane's shoe, she caught the silhouette

of Mrs. Ho running into the sunset from the plantation. At the same time, a helicopter appeared on the horizon over the ocean. The sun sat on top of the water, creating a sunset as brilliant as a Haleakala sunrise.

The bitch is escaping!

"Don't let her get away!" Treflee screamed. She tugged on Kane's pant leg, pointing toward Mrs. Ho and pantomiming a cop taking down a criminal.

Carrie caught her drift first. She grabbed Kane's arm and motioned to the other girls. They took off after Mrs. Ho and the two goons who appeared from the foliage following their leader.

Wait! Is that Abi chasing Mrs. Ho, too?

As Treflee lifted the shoe to clobber Hal again, a strong hand caught her wrist.

She looked up, startled and ready to take down anyone who'd come to help Hal. Her breath caught. "Ty!"

Ty grinned and shook his head. "I leave you alone for a minute and find you riding another guy."

At least that's what she thought he said as she read his lips. It was the kind of thing he would say, anyway.

He pulled the shoe out of her hand and tossed it away. "You know you could have subdued him with your sedative dart?"

In the heat of the moment, she'd forgotten all about that.

Greg appeared beside him. Both men glistened with sweat tracked with soot. Treflee wiped a hand across her eyes. She was a smudge pot of mascara. Always wear waterproof to weddings and explosions.

Ty pulled her to her feet and into his arms. Greg cuffed Hal and removed the hibiscus cam.

Treflee braced her hands against Ty's chest. "What are you doing here?" She pointed toward the approaching helicopter and Mrs. Ho's sunset silhouette. "Mrs. Ho's getting away! After her!"

He remained fixed in place. She wasn't sure he could hear her. She pointed more wildly.

Ty shook his head no and pointed between Treflee and himself before crushing her to his chest.

"Damn you, you scared me to death," she said into his shirt as she cuddled against him and hung on to him for dear life.

"Nice to see you, too." Ty pressed her against him and kissed the top of her head as she listened to the reassuringly calm, steady beat of his heart. His breath moved against her hair. He was saying something. She hoped it was, "I love you, Tref." She believed it was.

Back at the plantation, Tita greeted them with cold glasses of guava juice and directed them to paramedics to be checked over. Carla was in her element as head nurse.

Having brought in Mrs. Ho's two accomplices and demonstrated his fidelity and undying love for Carrie, Kane was the hero of the day. And Carrie, having decided she would marry him after all, was the happy, radiant, and slightly sooty bride-to-be.

After being poked and prodded and pronounced fit and able to hear again, Treflee found Ty on the lanai, staring out at the ocean.

"You let Mrs. Ho go. You came for me first," she said, tentatively, trying not to choke up.

"Yeah," he said, and turned to face her.

"Does this mean I'm forgiven?" She could barely get the words out.

He smiled at her in the light streaming out from Big Auau. "What do you think?"

She threw herself into his arms. "I love you." She wrapped her arms around him and pressed her head against his chest.

He responded by wrapping his arms around her. "Wow,

I save you from a strangler, rescue you from drowning, scare off a vicious bike-wielding assassin, give you pearls, and take one to the leg for you, and still you want a divorce. I let a dangerous RIOT agent escape and you're all over me. I'll never understand women." He sighed. "Does this mean the divorce is off?"

She squeezed him. "Let's set the record straight. I wanted to call the divorce off after the pearls."

"Give a woman jewelry and she'll follow you anywhere!" He laughed. "You did a hell of a job as a spy. Ever thought about a career with the Agency?"

She laughed. "Never. Living with a spy is excitement enough for me. You were in Sugar Love, right? How did you escape?" She stared up at him as if he'd disappear again at any minute.

"Underground volcanic tunnel after I rushed Mrs. Ho."

"And you just left her there and hurried to me?" She couldn't keep the joy out of her voice.

"Yeah, you were pleading for help, remember?" He tipped her chin up, ready for a kiss. "Besides, Abi, Greg, and Kane had things under control."

"Abi?"

"MSS."

"Of course. Kane?"

"Conveniently there."

She smiled and met his lips.

Carrie came out onto the lanai, and cleared her throat. "Get a room, you two. I have an important announcement. Wedding here tomorrow. You're both invited. Attendance mandatory." She was beaming ear to ear as she grabbed Tref's arm and yanked her away from Ty. "Can I speak to you a minute? In private."

Tref looked helplessly at Ty and reluctantly let go as Carrie dragged her into the empty dining room. Carrie nodded back toward the lanai and Ty. "Back with your husband?"

"What?"

"Don't play dumb with me. I'm a cop. I know how to sniff out the truth." She put her hand on her hip. "Beach bum and tour guide Ty is your husband, Ty, no?"

Carrie had her.

"Wait a minute," Tref said. "Did you happen to rifle through my room and look inside a certain locket on a particular charm bracelet hidden under a mattress?"

Carrie grinned. "You should find a different hiding place for your treasures. You've been hiding stuff under your mattress since we were kids."

"Shoot." Treflee caught Carrie's arm. "Look, you can't tell anyone back home about Ty being here or let the other girls know who he really is. The work Ty does—"

Carrie stopped her short. "Yeah, I figured something like that. Top secret work. Probably for the feds." She punched Treflee lovingly in the arm. "My quiet little cuz is married to a secret agent!" She laughed and shook her head in wonderment. "Your secret's safe with me. No one would believe me anyway. And the other girls? If they've figured it out, you can count on them to keep mum, too." Carrie paused and gave Treflee the cop stare. "Still going through with the divorce?"

Treflee smiled. She couldn't help it. "What is this, the Hawaiian inquisition?"

"The way you two look at each other hasn't been lost on me." Carrie winked at her.

"Divorce a secret agent? Heck, no. Someone would probably have to kill me." Treflee laughed. "I'm not going to divorce him. Nor he me." She grabbed Carrie's arm.

"But let me tell our moms, will you? I've been in their doghouse over Ty too long. I could use a few brownie points." Treflee shook her head as a thought occurred to her. "Speaking of your mom—as happy as she's going to be about you and Kane, she's going to kill you for getting married without her. She was hell-bent on seeing Hawaii. And Mom will be right behind her." Treflee became serious. "You really *are* going to marry Kane? Do you love him?"

"Yes, and hell, yes. And Mom will forgive me when I explain how romantic Kane was when he charged in to stop the Chinese wedding with that crazy lie detector test to prove his innocence, and how he refused to wait another day to marry me. She's a sucker for a love story with a strong hero and a happy ending."

Treflee nodded. Yeah, she could see her aunt reacting like that. A romantic streak ran through the family. "Good. No doubts?"

"None."

Treflee pulled Carrie into a hug, feeling a deep affection for her. "Be happy."

Carrie hugged her back. "You, too. Now let's get back to our guys."

Greg stopped Treflee before she walked back onto the lanai. "We caught Mrs. Ho. Her chopper landed on a ship that was very fortunately *just* inside American waters." He winked and handed Treflee a familiar blue legal file. "A gift from Emmett."

Treflee's eyes went wide. She recognized these. "*You* were the man in the hat at the lawyer's office? Emmett ordered the theft?"

Greg grinned. "Forgive Ty, Treflee. The spying life is hell on marriages. I ought to know. My wife kicked me out, too."

Treflee stared at the divorce papers. It took a minute to find her voice. "I will. I have."

She looked Greg in the eye. "I hope things work out for

you, too. I really do." She paused. "Maybe Emmett can get your wife involved in a mission? It worked wonders for us."

Greg shook his head. "Not likely, thank goodness. My estranged wife can't lie to save her life. Or mine."

Treflee blinked back tears. She gave Greg a heartfelt hug. He seemed embarrassed by the show of affection. When she released him, he gave her a lopsided grin and walked away. "Take care, Treflee."

She found Ty still sitting on the front steps. She tossed the legal file on the step beside him.

He arched a brow. "Where did these come from?"

"Emmett," she said without hesitating as she plunked down beside him. Well, it was true. Sort of.

He thumped the papers and faced her. "I never wanted this."

"I know." She paused. "I *was* going to return that device. I'd made up my mind I didn't want the divorce, either."

As he nodded, his eyes danced with desire. "I know."

She reached around him and grabbed the file.

"What are you doing?"

"Making a grand gesture." She struggled, trying to tear the file in half.

"Allow me." He took the papers from her and ripped the stack in half with ease.

"Wow!" She squeezed his bicep and leered at him. "They teach you how to do that in spy school, big boy?"

"YouTube." He made a neat stack of the papers.

"Hooray for YouTube." She ran her fingers lightly down his sooty arm.

"Oh, you dirty girl." He pulled her into his arms and kissed her. "You still look damn good in that dress. What do you say to getting clean together?"

"Only if we can get dirty after."

"I say we keep it dirty during." He ran his hands over her bare back.

Shivers of delight ran through her. He was good with his hands. This was just a tiny sample of his talents.

"Deal."

"Love you, Tref." He stared into her eyes. "About the baby—I would have been there if I'd known."

"Yeah, I know. Mea culpa. I promise not to keep something like that from you again."

"You forgive me?" His eyes pleaded with her.

She swallowed hard and nodded. "I think I understand about your work now." She looked up at him with her best sultry, flirty look. "How do you feel about babies these days?"

He shrugged. "We could give one a try. But we'll have to pray it doesn't inherit the sticky-fingers gene from its mother."

"Or the thrill-seeking gene from its father." She kissed his cheek. "Glad you're receptive to the idea." She whispered in his ear, "Because I went off birth control when you left. The good time we had at the waterfall? I'm thinking that was day fourteen."

"No." His expression was priceless.

"Maybe." She kissed his neck. "We'll see in a few weeks. Tonight, we'll just have fun."

STINGER

Emmett Nelson leaned back in his high-tech desk chair with his hands behind his head and reflected on a mission well done. He'd just gotten word from the Pentagon that RIOT had hit dead air and made quite a splash in clear blue shipless ocean with an expensive new top secret Chinese missile.

Gave the navy a good look at its firepower and what it could do. They recovered a few good bits and pieces, too. Good intel for the Pentagon boys.

The terrorist chatter was saying the U.S.'s Pinpoint Project software was faulty. A scam. Trying to save face, are you, RIOT?

Emmett laughed to himself, pleased as he scanned his happily cluttered office. Organized chaos all around him—stacks of papers, his top-secret historic spy gizmos collection, books—mostly thrillers and an esoteric mix of nonfiction topics—superhero action figures. Not an empty surface in sight. Exactly the office one would expect of a creative mind.

His computer pinged. He had a new e-mail. From Ty.

A picture of the happily reunited couple. Emmett ran a quick stego-detect on the picture. It revealed a message, "Mission happily accomplished."

That's my boy!

Emmett had known from the beginning Treflee was just the "agent" he needed to thwart Hal. No way Hal could have predicted her.

Emmett's grin deepened. He hadn't earned his reputation as the Puppeteer for nothing.

And what a damn good matchmaker he was, too. Ah, really, it was nothing. A little knowledge of the human psyche was all it took. He'd even forgive Ty his insubordination and Treflee the names she'd called him.

He picked up a pen and twirled it. The spying life was damn hard on a marriage. Emmett should know.

He turned his attention to the next firestorm brewing on the radar—a situation in Seattle that involved Russian RIOT operatives and the estranged wife of Agent Drew Fields, alias Greg the Hawaiian beach bum.

Funny thing—Emmett had just the man for the job.

Read on for an excerpt from Gina Robinson's next book

DIAMONDS AREN'T FOREVER

Coming soon from St. Martin's Paperbacks

D rew Fields pulled to the curb and parked in front of his former home. He hated the bland, midsized sedan the Agency insisted he drive as part of his mind-numbingly dull, assigned cover life. A marketing manager for a microbrewery? Really? At least there'd be free beer. He hoped.

That was the Central Intelligence Agency for you. The government sanitized everything. Even his official title—National Clandestine Services core collector. He was a spy, a secret agent. What kid wanted to grow up to be a core collector? Sounded more like nuclear reactor work.

Which, come to think of it, pretty nearly described his mission to reconcile with his estranged wife. If Staci ever found out what he was up to, she'd explode. In epic proportions. And there would be fallout. Plenty of it.

He shut off the ignition. Next time he was going to insist on an Aston Martin DB5. A sexy car made up for a lot of crap.

He took a deep breath. How was he going to convince Staci he still yearned for her tragically? Especially after he'd agreed to the divorce without a fight. And why now?

They had an anniversary coming up a week from Friday. Maybe he could play off that?

In all modesty, he was something of a phenom when it

came to lying, a natural talent. His inborn gift had gotten him out of more than a few scrapes when he was a kid, and even more as an adult. But there were limits to his ability. He wasn't James Bond.

Drew had tried to convince his boss, NCS Chief and head spook Emmett Nelson, to send some other guy in to infiltrate Staci's life. But Emmett held firm—Staci's emotions were too raw. She wasn't likely to start dating and open up to someone else so soon. It had to be him.

Stalling, and hoping to be clobbered by a stunning blow of inspiration, Drew studied the two-story house he still owned half of, looking for security lapses. Staci kept the bushes in front of the windows well trimmed and away from the house, and the sidewalk, driveway, and front entry clear of any hiding places.

She'd resisted her natural botanical urge to plant flowers and trees over every square inch of property and columns of junipers on each side of the door. Open spaces made for less stealth and more safety.

Before their marriage went sour, he'd picked this gated neighborhood for Staci because of its low crime rate and excellent security measures. A spy's family was never one-hundred-percent safe.

The Redmond Chief of Police lived here, a senator made her home away from the nation's capital here, and at least two state legislators, and several high-profile entrepreneurs lived in the higher end, pricier part of the development.

Drew hated what he was about to do to Staci. The sooner he completed this mission and found an assignment overseas, disappearing deep undercover, the better. In the meantime, his Farsi was getting rusty.

He never should have married Staci in the first place. What had possessed him to think a girl who couldn't lie to save her life would make a good wife for a spy like him?

She had a tell as obvious as Alaska. The woman couldn't even keep from giving herself away when she played Clue.

Worse, she had no interest in learning. Lying went against her highly tuned scruples. In her worldview, it was wrong. Period.

Ironically, that's what he'd loved about her—she was the one person he could believe, the one honest thing in his life. A little slice of black and white shining through an otherwise gray gloom. When she said she loved him, he knew she absolutely did. With all her heart. When she said she wanted a divorce, she broke his.

And now here he was, at her insistence, stopping by the old homestead to pick up a box of odds and ends from their former life. A box Emmett had planted to give him an excuse to see her.

Drew glanced at his watch. Ten thirty. Right on time. He got out of the car, wondering exactly how he was going to convince Staci to give him another chance. Somehow he'd handle it. He always did. His best inspiration and lies tended to be organic, springing from the moment. But this was his toughest assignment ever.

He still couldn't believe he was undercover as himself, dressed in Staci's favorite shirt, wearing his good guy, boy-next-door persona on his sleeve. He'd rather be back in Hawaii, living as a tour guide as he had last fall, the invisible sidekick rather than the main man, the hero. He'd spent the last month back in Hawaii, a minor follow-on assignment to last year's big operation. He hoped Staci didn't notice his tan. But how could she miss it? In May, most Seattle-ites, and that included the residents of Redmond, were still a pasty shade of pale. She'd give him hell over it.

He slammed the car door shut to give her fair warning he'd arrived. The weather was pleasant—clear skies, temperatures in the low sixties. He left his jacket in the car. As he approached the door, he half-expected her to

throw his stuff at him. He resisted the urge to shield himself with his arm. The woman had laser-beam aim. Instead, she made him ring the doorbell.

"Coming!"

Her voice didn't sound like hell's fury, but he didn't drop
his guard. He never dropped his guard. He wondered if
she'd decided they were going to be one of *those* couples,
the ones who seemed so cordial you wondered why they
ever got divorced in the first place or how they even got up
the gumption to file.

She opened the door partway and stood before him, just
slightly breathless.

The sight of her gave him an unexpected jolt of desire.
Old habits die hard, he told himself. This was just an au-
tomatic reaction to a beautiful woman with snapping
brown eyes and slightly parted, highly kissable lips. Lips
he was used to possessing. He dubbed it the JBR, the
James Bond Response. Bond couldn't resist any woman
under forty. A hazard of the spy's life.

The smell of freshly baked cookies drifted out from the
house, diverting his thoughts. Chocolate chip. He hoped
his stomach didn't growl. He hadn't had a home-baked
cookie in a good six months.

Staci's hands were empty. He'd expected her to thrust a
box in his arms and shove him on his way.

Evidently, whatever had possessed him to fix up had
also gotten hold of her. She looked like great sex on a rainy
day. Her dark-brown hair was recently highlighted with
streaks of auburn and flat-ironed shiny and straight. She
wore skinny jeans, black pumps with three-inch heels, and
a tight, low-cut, ruffled magenta blouse, belted with a wide
black belt just below her eye-catching breasts. The belt
made her waist look about two inches wide, her hips curvy,
and her breasts double-D.

The heels might have been her idea of a power trip. She'd

never liked being so much shorter than he was. Maybe she was hoping the heels would make them see eye to eye. Personally, he was having a hard time seeing anything above her breasts. He forced himself.

"Drew." She smiled and opened the door wide to let him in.

Right away his defenses went up. He couldn't act too eager and happy to see her. She'd never buy that. "Where's my stuff?"

"On the kitchen table."

To his surprise, she remained pleasant despite his gruffness. What was up with her?

"It's heavy. You'll have to get it yourself." She stood aside to let him in.

He surveyed her outfit again. "Going out?"

She stared straight into his eyes, still smiling. "No. Why?"

He looked her up and down. "No reason."

Just that she usually wore jeans, T-shirts, and Converse tennis shoes around the house. No way she'd dressed up for him, had she? Maybe there was hope for this mission yet.

Staci kept her smile plastered on, thinking positive thoughts and going to her happy place so the smile would reach her eyes. She couldn't believe she'd missed this last box of Drew's junk. His stuff seemed to be multiplying like the hairs that appeared when she cleaned the tub. But she was determined to be civil now that their marriage was almost over. It was just unfortunate the divorce would be final so close to their anniversary. Drew probably didn't even remember it.

He walked past her so closely he brushed against her pushed-up-and-out biofit breasts. She got a whiff of his delectable cologne. Her breath caught. Involuntary reaction on her part. Intentional foul on his, she was sure.

He wore the navy-blue shirt she so loved on him, the one that made his eyes look even bluer than normal. It hugged and showed off his broad shoulders and every biceply muscle he owned. The man looked hot enough to eat. And tan for this time of year. His sandy-blond hair was light and sun-bleached. Should a woman be so physically attracted to her husband mere weeks before their divorce became final? Shouldn't her hurt feelings take him down a peg or two on the attractiveness meter?

Maybe not. She reminded herself Drew was exactly like his boss Emmett. He could throw on the invisibility cloak or devastate you with charm and good looks. All without the aid of makeup or stage paint.

Just why Drew was putting on this persona confounded her. Last time she'd seen him, at her lawyer's office, he'd been impassive and quiet, a study in calmly ignoring her.

She'd wounded his pride. She knew that. Andrew Collin Fields never failed at anything. Losing her was a slap at his James Bond spy machismo.

She took a deep breath, subtly. Already, she had doubts about the outfit she'd chosen to wear. Judging from the way Drew gawked at her, it screamed "woman on the make" instead of her intended "look what you gave up."

Weighed down by hurt feelings, she wanted to spark jealousy and regret that he'd chosen his career over her. In the name of her pride, she was also determined to be pleasant. But she didn't want him getting any other ideas, something crazy like she was regretting her decision to divorce. Life apart was safer. *For both of them.*

"You look tan," she said to make conversation. "Been on a mission someplace sunny?"

He hesitated, looking as if he didn't want to answer. "I was back in Hawaii this past month. Following up." He had the good grace to appear sheepish and almost apologetic.

He'd been promising to take her to Hawaii for a second honeymoon for years. Well, up until this latest unpleasant divorce business. Soon she'd be free to take herself. When she found another job and got a little cash ahead. She forced herself to smile. "Tough life."

He cleared his throat. "In the kitchen? Something smells good in there."

She nodded, surprised he was being so pleasant. "After you."

She followed him in, nearly colliding with his backside as he abruptly stopped just inside the kitchen door.

"Whoa! Give me a little warning before you brake," she snapped, without thinking. He hated it when she used that irritated tone on him.

Fortunately, he didn't seem to notice. He was too busy scanning the racks of cooling cookies that lined the counters and the island.

"Why, Scarlett, you've been baking!" He pointed to the racks as if counting. "There must be ten dozen cookies, at least." He turned and stared into her eyes.

Her heart did an involuntary little flip. "Baking calms me. You know that."

Oops! She'd slipped up again. Now he'd think she was nervous about seeing him. Which, of course, she was.

"What are you going to do with all these cookies?" His gaze flicked to her midsection.

"Eat them all myself," she said, deadpan. No, she wasn't going to eat herself into oblivion and a spot at Weight Watchers over him, if that's what he thought. He could just dash any fantasies about her being an old, fat broad he was lucky to have ditched. She stared back at him, trying to keep her lips from twitching at the thought of disappointing him.

He must have seen her trying hard not to laugh. He broke into a smile himself. "Seriously, who are they for?"

"Little Jessica next door. Her class is having a bake sale. Her mom's out of town and her dad can't bake. I offered to help her out." She shrugged as if to say "no big deal."

"Uh-huh."

In front of her, he was almost salivating. Oh, yeah, he loved her baking. One more thing he should have thought of before putting NCS, the spying arm of the CIA, before her.

She took pity on him anyway. Though she'd purposefully made the cookies so the house would smell of tempting vanilla and chocolate, in the end, no one could call her a hard woman. "How about taking a few off my hands? I think I overdid it."

She headed to the pantry for a plastic Baggie without waiting for an answer. "Your box is on the table if you want to take a look. Are you staying with your parents for the rest of your furlough? I imagine your mom won't be happy about fitting another box into the garage—"

An explosion cut her off mid-sentence as she reached for the pantry door. Behind her, she heard the tinkling rain of shattering glass. Something whizzed past her head, buzzing like a bee about to sting. She reached instinctively to swat it away.

"Get down!" Drew tackled her from behind with all the finesse of a quarterback sack.

Her breath left her body with an unflattering *oomph* as her ribs hit unyielding ash. Her cheek smacked the cold floor and throbbed on impact. Wood flooring wasn't exactly cuddly and soft like her microfleece sheets.

Neither was Drew as he covered her with his hard body. Her heart pounded wildly in her ears over the hum of a lawnmower somewhere outside. She couldn't catch her breath.

Another gunshot sliced through the door above her.

Much as she wanted to blame her difficulty breathing on the wide, tight belt she wore, it accounted for only a small part of her problem. Fear and the weight of the man on top of her, and her physical attraction to that particular one hundred and eighty pounds of maleness, accounted for the rest. She needed a nice, safe boyfriend. One with no enemies.

As the nerve-wracking silence stretched out, Drew remained in place longer than strictly necessary.

"Off!" she finally managed to mutter, fighting off panic and unable to stand the intimacy of their position another minute.

He rolled off, next to her. "You okay?" His voice rang with tender concern, making it even harder for her to catch her breath.

Somehow she managed and inhaled deeply. Her cheek began to throb again, along with her ribs, wrists, and elbows. She'd be bruised, but she'd live. "I'm fine. Thanks for making me a part of this." She was trying to be brave and make light, but inside, she was trembling.

"You're welcome."

She started to push up on all fours, feeling as wobbly as a partially filled water balloon.

Drew shoved her back down, none too gently. "Stay down."

She glanced up at the pantry and the newly splintered bullet holes at head height. Not the conversation piece she dreamed of for her kitchen. Too Bonnie and Clyde for her taste.

Still stunned, she looked at Drew. "Two to the head. Someone wants you dead, execution style." She used her "what else is new" tone because it was better than screaming like a panicked maniac. "You owe me a new door and a new window."

Drew peered back at her and shook his head, obviously thinking she was deranged. He pointed up at the holes. "Me? You're crazy. *I* wasn't standing next to the pantry."

She went cold and her spit dried up. *He's right.* The men he played with wouldn't make a dumb mistake like that.

Drew pulled his cell phone from his pocket. She couldn't believe it—he was actually dialing for help. In the spy world, that was practically like asking for directions. Taboo even in the spur-of-the-moment danger situation.

"Who are you calling? Spook central or the cops?" she asked.

"Neither." He showed her the screen of his phone.

She watched, feeling her anger rise, as a security feed of her house, inside and out, and the surrounding area scrolled past.

"The bastard's good at hiding," Drew said, studying the screen again. "He'll have left a clue. He can't have gone far. We'll get him."

She felt her indignation rising. "You promised me you'd never look at the security camera feeds again. I changed the security code."

He shrugged. "As if that could keep me out."

"Hey!" She smacked him in the shoulder, hard. "You promised."

"I lied." He didn't wince or look one bit sorry. "I was supposed to leave you to the mercy of my enemies?"

She glared at him, wishing eyes really could shoot daggers. "You'd better not have been viewing the feed from my bedroom camera."

He grinned.

"Damn it. Exes don't have peep-show privileges." Her voice had gone hard and icy, veering off from her make-him-sorry plan.

Drew pushed to a squat, carefully avoiding glass splinters. "Stay put while I investigate."

Not being the brave, charge-into-danger type, she wasn't going to argue. "It's dangerous weather out there. Take a weapon with you."

He flashed her a glimpse of his handgun.

She should have known. "And what am I supposed to do for protection?"

He handed her a razor-sharp butcher knife from the block on the counter.

"You're taking your life in your own hands." She stared at the knife in her hand, then up at him. "What if I turn out to be a backstabber?"

He looked her right in the eye and laughed. "Cutting up raw chicken gives you the willies." He lowered his voice into the sultry range. "Tell me you could really stick a knife into the hot flesh of a man who's given you so much pleasure over the years?"

Stupid, smartass, nearly ex-husbands.

She swallowed hard, hoping he hadn't noticed her reaction to his words. She lifted her chin. "Don't tempt me. Just because I prefer ready-roasted fryers doesn't mean I don't know how to use a knife."

He smiled and shook his head.

"If that's what you really believe," she said, "you're leaving me with a weapon that's about as useful as if it were made of rubber."

"You'll get over it if it's your life or his." Then he laughed and sneaked out with all the stealth and confidence of a commando on the prowl.

"Y'all come back now, you hear?" she called after him.